Before Us

JEWEL E. ANN

BEFORE US

JEWEL E. ANN

To Cleida, the strongest and most inspiring woman I have ever known

"I have never met a person whose greatest need was anything other than real, unconditional love. You can find it in a simple act of kindness toward someone who needs help. There is no mistaking love. It is the common fiber of life, the flame that heats our soul, energizes our spirit and supplies passion to our lives."

—Elisabeth Kübler-Ross

Chapter One

AT LEAST I didn't soil my pants this time. Or did I?

The hovering faces above me come into focus. Words gain clarity like someone unmuted this embarrassing scene.

"I'm fine," I declare after my fingertips graze the crotch of my leggings to ensure they're dry.

A short-haired brunette frowns an inch from my face. "EMS is sending an ambulance. I'm a nurse. You had a seizure."

My head rolls to the side, eyes surveying my surroundings. I'm in the bank lobby—cold tile at my back. Fanfuckingtastic. "Uh ... no." I scramble to my feet.

"Don't try to get up," the nurse says.

"I have epilepsy. Nothing to see. I'm good. Totally good. Cancel the ambulance." I hold out my hands, giving everyone the signal to stop.

Stop messing with me.

Stop worrying about me.

Go on with your day.

Too late. I hear the sirens approaching.

All eyes in the lobby are on me.

A nervous laugh sputters from my chest. "Just a little seizure." I run my fingers through my hair. "Probably missed a pill. I'm good."

The bank tellers give me wary expressions and sympathetic smiles before encouraging the next people in line to step forward.

I glance at my watch, wincing from the pounding in my head. I'm going to be late for my job interview. And I *can't* be late. I need this job.

A young girl with braided pigtails hands me my bag.

I smile and whisper, "Thank you," before her mom pulls her toward the exit just as the EMTs push through the doors.

Before I can disappear into a corner—or a black hole—the nurse, who so kindly called for the ambulance, decides to rat me out when the EMTs search the lobby for the person in need of medical attention.

"She had a seizure," the nurse says to them while pointing at me.

"I'm sorry you were called. I'm good. Just leaving."

"You can't drive," the nurse says.

I'm not in a hospital. You're not my nurse. Thanks for your help, lady, but move along.

"Um ..." I search my pockets and then my purse for my phone. "Yep. I know that. I'll call someone."

Holding up my phone, I force a grin and turn in a circle like I'm threatening to detonate a bomb.

I have less than fifteen minutes to make it to my interview on time.

But I've seen that look before, the one the tall guy in uniform is giving me. He's not okay with me walking away.

Here we go ...

———

AFTER THE EMT checks me out in a non-sexual way, I shoot a quick text to Zach Hays, letting him know I'll be late for the interview. Then I wait in my car—my temporary housing—pretending I'm waiting for someone to get me until the emergency vehicles leave the bank.

I have a college degree and live out of my car. There should be a program for that. And free therapy.

I waste no time changing my clothes, showing no regard for anyone who might see my half-naked body.

"You're going to be legendary," I say to the woman in the rearview mirror. "An artist of..." I frown, as does the reflection in the mirror "...of some sort. But today..." I apply gloss to my lips "...you're going to get this job. Clean toilets like DaVinci painted the Mona Lisa and be grateful for it like..." I twist my glossed lips "...Gandhi."

Damn ... my head hurts.

After a short drive to my interview, I slick back a

few flyaways of limp blond hair and climb out of my temporary housing, making my way to the house at the end of the cul-de-sac. It's not a million-dollar home or anything like that, but it's nice and the only one that doesn't look like all the rest in the cookie-cutter neighborhood with its low-profile roof of asymmetrical lines.

Windows wrap around the sprawling single-story, giving it a glasshouse appearance. I don't clean windows, so I hope that's not going to be a dealbreaker.

This should be a slam dunk if they're not upset over my tardiness. The Mumfords, an older couple *and* my best clients, referred me to the Hayses. I was told Mrs. Hays is sick, and Mr. Hays needs help cleaning so he can spend time with her. These new clients could be my ticket to stationary housing. Next step? A job that involves a camera and lots of traveling. Benefits like health insurance to pay for my medication and unexpected trips to the hospital would be nice too.

Giving my cuffed-sleeve blouse a quick adjustment to hide its wrinkles, I tug it down to meet the high waist of my capris.

Shoulders back.

Chin up.

Confident smile.

I ring the doorbell and gaze through the glass front door.

A few beads of sweat work their way to the surface of my armpits. I tell myself it's the heat, but it's only spring here in Atlanta. It's probably my concussion.

BEFORE US

Epilepsy can be a bitch—so can a life without health insurance.

A tall man, maybe in his thirties, struts toward the door, wearing a kind, boyish smile, faded gray sweat-pants, and a black tee. Their son or son-in-law, I assume. Before opening the door, he scratches the back of his head and yawns like he just woke up. His dark hair is only slightly longer than the five o'clock shadow covering half his face.

"Good morning. You must be Emersyn?" He breaks my name into its three punctuated syllables. It's a little amusing.

"Yes. Emersyn Clarke." I return a half-smile with a slight squint, trying to read him.

He offers an easy nod and steps aside. "Please, come in."

"Thanks." I slide my feet out of my Birkenstock knockoffs. "Are you the son? Son-in-law?" Stray hairs brush my face, so I tuck them behind my ear on one side.

Eyes narrowed, he purses his lips into a tiny grin and slants his head to the side as if I'm not speaking English. Maybe I slurred my words. *Is* my brain okay?

"Or ..." I wrinkle my nose. "A family friend? None of the above? I'll just shut up now, and you can get Zach. I texted him that I was running late, so I hope he's still here."

He gives me a hesitant laugh as confusion deepens along his brow. "Um ... I'm Zach."

My eyes widen as my lips part, but I have no words yet.

"I got your name from the Mumfords," he says.

Ever so slowly, I nod. The Mumfords, a sweet couple in their seventies, said they gave my name to "friends" of theirs. And for some reason, my head painted a picture of another old couple because elderly people only have elderly friends. Right?

Wrong.

"I ..." I clear my throat. "I made an assumption." My face sours into a cringe. "An incorrect assumption. This is a ... little embarrassing. I thought you were ..."

"Old?"

With a nervous laugh, I nod. "My bad." I rub my temples for a few seconds.

"You feeling okay? If not, we can do this another day."

"No." I drop my hands and force a smile. "I'm fine. There was an incident at my bank. Someone had a medical emergency. By the time the ambulance arrived, and things settled down, I knew I wasn't going to make it here on time. And I hate running late. So I'm fighting a little headache from the stress." Half-truth. I should get partial credit for not completely lying.

"Not like an armed robbery or anything, I hope."

"What?" I squint. "Oh. No. Just uh ... a customer passed out. They're fine. I assume." Does he sense how flustered I am? My mouth moves. Words spill from my lips; however, I'm not sure they're the right ones.

I need this job.

I need some sleep.

I need my brain to cooperate for once. Just this once.

"Well, the Mumfords rave about you, so I'm glad you made it."

"They're good people."

"Just old," Zach says with a slight grin, once again, eliciting a nervous laugh from me.

"Older than me. And uh ... clearly you too."

"I'll have you pop into the powder room and wash your hands. Then you can meet my wife. After that, I'll show you around."

Oh great ... a germaphobe. It's not what I need right now. Germaphobe equals pain in the ass. I follow him around the corner to the powder room. I've worked for a few others like him. It's not my preferred working environment, but I can play the OCD part when I'm desperate for money ... which happens to be right now.

After I do a surgical scrub with the door open so he can witness my attention to detail, he leads me into a sunroom. And ...

Oh my god ...

It's the Amazon. I'm not exaggerating. I've been in homes with a fair number of plants, but this is next level. In the middle, there's a woman settled into a basic gray, oversized recliner. A vibrantly colored patchwork quilt covers her elevated legs. She applies lip balm and adjusts the floral scarf around her head as we approach.

"Welcome to the jungle," Zach says. "This is my wife, Suzanne. Babe, this is Emersyn Clarke." Zach squeezes her foot, and she playfully bats his hand away with a tiny kick.

My gaze flits between Zach's warm smile and Suzanne's impish grin.

"Nice to meet you, Emersyn. I'd shake your hand, but it will cause Zach to panic. He's afraid I might get sick and die." She laughs. "Newsflash. I'm already sick and dying."

Okay ...

It's not that I don't have a good sense of humor. After all, I'm homeless with a neurological disorder and a pile of past-due student loans and medical bills, and I haven't slit my wrists. However, I don't know if it's appropriate to laugh at Suzanne's joke.

She's laughing.

Zach grins and shakes his head.

I'm ninety-nine percent certain she has no hair beneath that scarf on her head because she's also missing her eyebrows. So they're laughing at what I assume is cancer, and I play along and laugh a little— my perfected nervous laugh.

Hehehe ... yeah. I'm back in the uncomfortable zone. Cancer humor might be an acquired taste.

"Sorry. Bad joke in front of a stranger," Zach apologizes.

"No. I ... I'm sure it's important not to take things too seriously when you're dealing with something out of your control," I say, but what do I know? Maybe they do have control over it. Perhaps they've done *all* the experimental treatments, or they're choosing to let her die at home with dignity in the middle of eighty billion plants. I really don't know. And if I didn't need the money, I'd hightail it out of here. I'd rather not be scrubbing the toilet while a woman dies in the same house. What would be the protocol? Keep cleaning? Slither out? Call an ambulance? Do you call ambulances for dead people?

Twenty-three-year-olds like myself don't have enough life experience to deal with a stranger's death. We barely know how to deal with the loss of our favorite characters on whatever show we're bingeing during any given week. Well, I haven't binged anything in a while. Homeless people don't have Netflix.

"Smart girl." Suzanne winks at me. "I beat this once, and now it's back with a vengeance. My boobs are gone, but the cancer is back. Go figure."

Yeah, I'm way out of my comfort zone, and yet my next words are, "I have epilepsy, so ..." It's out of my mouth, a dog off its leash and two blocks out of reach in a blink.

So? Where am I going with this? So what? Why tell them that? Is epilepsy the new cancer? My illness shouldn't kill me if I take my medication and follow precautions, which I don't do that well, but that's on me. It's not like Suzanne can pop a pill, avoid taking baths alone, and surround herself with shatterproof glass, and her cancer will stay in check.

"Oh, sorry. Have you dealt with it your whole life?"

Suzanne actually acts interested, like I didn't just imply I know what she's going through because I've had a few seizures.

"I was diagnosed a year ago. It's no big deal. Really. Except for the time I had a grand mal seizure and lost control of my bowels. And ... I forgot to switch my emergency contact. The hospital called my ex-boyfriend, who was still listed as my emergency contact. Oh ... he was also married with a child. Imagine getting called to the hospital for your ex-girl-friend ... who had a seizure while in bed with another random guy she met on a dating app. The early twenties are brutal ... even for an optimist."

Silence.

Too much silence.

I overshared. A lot.

There's never a rewind button when you need one.

Zach and Suzanne share a look—something between a grin and a grimace.

Why did I think my best way out of the cancer topic was to talk about epilepsy, swiping right to hook up, and wetting the bed?

Zach clears his throat. "Are you on medication for it?" Of course, he wants to know if he will have to deal with me seizing while he's taking care of his sick wife.

Pinching the bridge of my nose, I stare at my feet. "I am," I whisper past the suffocating embarrassment. "And I'm uh ... sorry." I glance up, nose crinkled. "That was more than you needed to know. I'm good. It's a mild form of epilepsy, and I'm basically cured if I take my meds."

IF I take my meds. IF I can afford them.

And what's a "mild form" of epilepsy? They're not calling me out, so I stick with it.

Suzanne's grin works its way to her eyes. "If you can't find a little humor in tragedy, life will kick your ass."

I return a stiff nod.

"In the meantime, let's talk about your outfit. It's adorable." Suzanne eyes my shirt and capris. "Girl after my own heart. Anthropologie?"

Glancing down, I run my hand over the bottom of the wrinkled top. "Uh ... maybe." I smile. "I'm not the original owner." I bite my tongue for a second. "That sounds weird like I stole it. I didn't steal it. I ..." They don't need to know I buy my clothes "gently used" because my bank account balance doesn't support my expensive taste. I think the bedwetting confession is enough for today.

"I love Anthropologie," Suzanne says as if I didn't just verbally vomit my way through a shitty explanation as to where I buy my clothes. "I bet that's where they're originally from. I haven't been there in forever. Zach isn't much of a shopper."

Zach tries to give her an exasperated expression, but it won't stick to his face. He can't look at her for more than two seconds without his blinding adoration stealing his features and settling into his golden-brown eyes. It should be every woman's goal in her romantic life to never settle for a man who looks at her with anything but *that* level of adoration.

I'm pretty sure Random Hookup Guy was not gazing at me like that the night I seized in his bed and wet myself. And I know this because he texted me the next day requesting I buy him a new mattress. Apparently, the urine seeped into the padding.

"Baby, I love doing anything with you," Zach says.

That's it. Right there. Life goals. I need to find a guy that says, *"Baby, I love doing anything with you."*

"Follow me ..." Zach nods in the opposite direction, keeping his attention on Suzanne for a few more seconds.

That adoring, *lingering* gaze also gets added to my wish list.

"Nice meeting you." I give Suzanne a smile that I hope erases my ridiculous epilepsy comparison to cancer and my cringe-worthy oversharing of bedwetting.

"You too, Emersyn. I hope this works out."

"Em." I give her a tiny shrug. "My friends call me Em."

"Em ..." Suzanne nods several times. "Em it is. And my friends call me Suzie."

"Bye, Suzie," I say over my shoulder while following Zach.

He turns on the light to a bedroom. "We're just looking for basic cleaning."

Nothing about him or this house seems *basic*.

"Thorough dusting. Thorough sweeping. Thorough mopping. Thorough—"

I chuckle. "Save some oxygen. I'll assume all duties are to be done thoroughly unless otherwise stated."

Zach gives me a sheepish grin that shows just a hint of his white teeth. "Fair enough."

He turns on the lights in the main bathroom, and I step inside, taking mental notes of what needs to be cleaned. Large tile shower. Soaker tub. Two sinks. Vanity with backlit mirror.

Next to the vanity, there's a huge jar filled with flat rocks. Each rock has writing on it.

"She's always called me her rock," Zach says, drawing my attention away from the jar and back to him. He leans his shoulder against the doorway. "After she was diagnosed, I started collecting rocks. Every morning, I wake up early and write something I love about her on the rock." He shrugs. Extra color floods his cheeks, and he glances away for a second. "Every day, I give her a rock, so she knows there are an infinite number of things I love about her, and all of those little things are what gives *me* strength."

"That's ..." I'm not sure of the right word.

"Pathetic?" He chuckles.

"No. I was going to say romantic, but that's not the right word either."

"Cheesy?"

I laugh, inching my head side to side a few times. "Definitely not that. Endearing, and it's ... yeah. Endearing."

Zach's lips twist for a second. He's contemplative, which makes him a little mysterious. He says a lot with his eyes, but I don't know him well enough to translate his expressions into words. "I'm sticking with cheesy."

I can't hide my grin.

"Anyway ... where were we? Oh yeah ..." He heads out of the bathroom and down the hallway. "We have three bedrooms, two full bathrooms, and a half bath. Living room, office, and kitchen. I don't expect you to do laundry, prepare meals, or wash dishes. I do all of that. And I'll clean the jungle."

"And *what* a jungle it is." I follow him through the kitchen to the opposite side of the house and the two other bedrooms.

Zach laughs. "It's her favorite room. Better air quality. I'm not going to lie; she talks to her plants. One of those infinite number of things I love about her."

No one has ever said they love an infinite number of things about me. Either Suzanne is the greatest woman ever, or I'm not that great—definitely not *infinitely* great.

Or ... and this might be the correct answer ... Zach is not like most other men.

"I'm not mocking it," I say. "It's a wonderful room." I mentally add a houseful of plants to my list of future goals, along with finding a man who cooks, cleans, washes the dishes, does the laundry, *and* loves an infinite number of things about me. How did my mom manage to find every man who was the opposite of Zach Hays?

"These bedrooms don't get used, but they still need a thoro—" Zach catches himself and smirks. "They still need a *good* dusting and vacuuming every week. We'll provide all the supplies since we want certain products used in our house. If there's anything extra you want or need, just let me know." After turning off the bedroom lights, he heads back to the kitchen. "Any questions?"

"Do Tuesdays work?"

He fills a glass with water from a stainless-steel dispenser on the counter. "Every week?"

I nod, tucking my fingers into my back pockets.

"What time will you start?" he asks.

"It's up to you, but I'd rather not start later than nine."

Zach twists his lips. "Nine-thirty?"

With a soft laugh, I lift a shoulder. "Sure. Nine-thirty will work. Do you have any other questions for *me*? More references? My social security number so you can run a background check on me? Fingerprints? How much I charge for my services?"

"No." Amusement flickers in his eyes. "The Mumfords are the only reference and recommendation I need because they are very particular and diligent. And old."

I roll my eyes.

"I'm sure you had to pass at least one lie detector test to work for them."

"They are *older*. And thorough," I say, nodding several times. "And I know you're a fan of thorough."

"Indeed." He focuses on the glass of water in his

hand for a few seconds. Since he's not drinking it or offering it to me, I assume it's for Suzanne.

"Well, thanks. I look forward to working for you. I can ... uh ... let myself out and see you Tuesday at nine-thirty."

"Thank you, Emersyn."

"Em."

"Emersyn." He presses his lips into a firm line like he's biting his tongue.

Okay, he prefers Emersyn. I bolt out of the house before he has a chance to see my grin.

Chapter Two

"HEY, BABE!" Brady strolls with a client toward the free weights.

My eyebrows peak in a subtle acknowledgment as I take a swig of water. There are a few perks to dating a guy who manages a gym, like free membership. This means I have access to the locker rooms—specifically the showers.

Not everyone can have a guy give them a rock each day with something they love about you written on it. And not every girl gets to have a bounce house for her birthday party either, but that's stuff for a therapist to deal with when I can afford one.

Brady doesn't let me spend the night after we have sex. If I ask to shower, he'll get suspicious. If I flat-out tell him I'm homeless at the moment, he'll dump me. Brady constantly brags about my creativity, hard work ethic, strength, and independence. I like who he thinks I am, and I realize that's messed up since it's a little misleading at the moment. His vision of me is a goal, and I could use a goal to work toward. Photographer. Travel blogger. Homeowner. A moderately put-together human being.

My dream of finding an unconditionally loving man to marry seems to wane a little more each day. I want everything my mother never had—love, emotional security, and a partner in life.

After working out for an hour to justify my shower, I head toward the women's locker room with a good ninety minutes to spare before I need to be at the Hayses' house. That extra half-hour Zach requested might be a blessing.

"You'll have to run home to shower, babe," Brady says from behind me.

I turn and release my hair from its ponytail. "Why?"

He leans down and kisses me while sliding his hand over my ass, giving it a firm squeeze. "Because they just put a new layer of sealant on the grout, and it can't get wet for twenty-four hours."

"Well, that's inconvenient. I have to get to work, and going home is a little out of my way."

"You clean houses, Em. I'm not sure why you need to shower until you're done with work anyway."

I hold out my hand. "Give me the key to your place and let me go shower there." He lives two blocks from the gym.

Brady smirks, scratching his jaw. He's a massive man, a total gym rat with a closely shaven head and a few tattoos on his biceps and chest. He's sexy and protective. Some days he's even a little generous, so I can overlook the parts of him that aren't the Zach Hays Gold Standard.

Brady clucks his tongue several times while shaking his head. "I have a rule: no one in my shower unless I'm in it too."

I guess this isn't a generous day. That stinks ... and so do I.

"Fine. Let's go to your place and shower together." I cross my arms over my chest and push up my cleavage.

He takes instant notice. "I'm working, babe."

"You're the boss. You can run a quick errand."

"Can't," he says while his gaze remains glued to my chest.

"Sure? Because I'm feeling very generous." My tongue makes a slow swipe along my bottom lip.

"How generous?"

I remind myself that he *is* my boyfriend, and I *do* love our sex life, so offering sex in exchange for a shower is not the worst sacrifice. I'm just pissed off that he won't hand over his key and let me grab a quick shower at his place without getting something in return.

Glancing at my watch, I frown. "Anything you want. Yes or no, Brady?"

"Meet you in five."

Men. So predictable.

I beat him to his place, but by the time I step off the

19

elevator, he's pushing through the stairway door after sprinting up the three flights.

"That's just lazy, babe." He rolls his eyes before unlocking his door.

I return the eye roll, stepping into his meticulously clean apartment. The funny thing about me? I clean homes, but the rest of my life is chaos. Even when I had a place to live, it was a disaster. How can one be good at cleaning houses yet live amongst such clutter? It requires a unique talent.

"I don't have much—" *Time* ... I think as his mouth crashes into mine before he gets the door closed behind us. We turn into a tornado of limbs and discarded clothes as we stumble our way to the bathroom.

"Brady ..." I reach toward the shower, trying to turn it on. I do, in fact, have a limited amount of time. And despite his belief that my job is dirty and, therefore I can arrive at my clients' homes sweaty and smelly, that's not my level of professionalism.

He pulls away from me and smirks. "You said *anything I want.*"

"As long as it's quick. I have to work."

His head bobs side to side. "It can be quick, but I'm not sure you'll want it to be quick."

———

THINGS DON'T GO as I imagine, but he does cup my face and says, "I love you," for the first time. A curious moment to profess his love to me.

I bite my tongue because the ego's favorite meal is dignity. After Brady gets his *anything* promise fulfilled, my ego sinks its teeth into a big piece of my dignity. Strong people don't always make the right decisions; they excel at moving on from the bad ones. I know I should be honest with him, but I can't. Not yet.

It's not that I don't want him feeling sorry for me. That's not why I don't tell him about my homeless status. It's because I know he *won't* feel sorry for me. He'll feel sorry for himself. Brady's much too cool to have a homeless girlfriend.

I should leave him, and I should salvage what's left of my dignity. But ... I need a shower. And I need that gym membership because this won't be the last shower I need while I sort through my financial situation. So as much as I want to tell Brady that I'm living out of my car ...

Because I lost my trailer.

Because I have a shit-ton of medical bills.

And because I have epilepsy.

I just don't.

I don't trust him to care that much.

I don't trust him to do the right thing.

I don't trust his kind of love.

After taking it up the backside (literally), I'm rewarded with a quick shower and no conditioner. Brady waits at the door, sipping a sports drink—his proverbial cigarette. He wears smug better than most men. It's not his fault I'm a hot mess who *did* promise anything for a shower.

"Can I buy you dinner tomorrow night?"

I think that's the least he can do after I just bartered the integrity of my anal sphincter for a shower.

Forcing a smile, I draw in a confident breath. "Dinner sounds nice. Your place?"

Sex.

Shower.

Maybe I'll get to spend the night too ... since he loves me now.

"I could do dinner tonight if you want." I head toward the stairs, knowing there's no way he'll take the elevator with me.

"I'm going out with some friends. Don't you have friends to hang out with?"

No. I don't have friends.

I left my friends behind when I cut ties with my mom and moved to Atlanta. And my friends from college have moved away to use their degrees. Mine resides somewhere in the back of my car, the most expensive piece of paper I have ever purchased. Brady would know this if he spent time asking me about myself. I know *everything* about him. I could fill out his family tree and recite his resumé. If he ever introduces me to his friends, I'll know them by name on sight because I've asked Brady so many questions over our three months together.

Three. Months.

Really ... we should know each other.

"Of course, I have friends." I jog stiffly down the stairs. "I've told you all about them a million times."

"I know, babe. Just kidding."

Yeah, he loves me *so* much.

Before we part ways in the parking lot, he pulls me into his arms and kisses me while one of his hands slides to my ass and squeezes it. He smiles, releasing my lips, and I know what he's thinking.

It's not happening again. Ever.

"Message me the time and place for dinner tomorrow." I peel his hand from my ass and plaster on a fake smile.

"Sure thing, babe."

———

I ARRIVE at nine forty-five instead of nine-thirty.

"Late on your first day?" Zach eyes me sternly as I step into the entry and remove my shoes.

"I'm really sorry. It won't happen again." I cringe. "The showers at my gym were not available for use this morning, so I had to shower at my boyfriend's apartment, which was a pain in the ass, and it put me a little behind." If he only knew just how much truth I'm giving him in that one sentence.

"I was kidding. It's fine. Maybe just call or send me a message if it happens again so we don't worry about you."

God ... I hope it never happens again. And *worry*? It

takes a minute to find the right words because he's caught me off guard. I've never had anyone worry about me.

"Absolutely." I swallow past the tiny lump in my throat. "And, again, I'm very sorry. So ..." I blow out a long breath. "Do you have a preference as to where I start?"

"We'll be in the jungle, so start wherever. All the supplies are in the kitchen, including the hose and heads to the central vac."

"Cool. Thanks. I'll get to work then."

"Great, Emersyn." He again accentuates my name. *Mmm-er-syn.*

I chuckle, fixing my ratty, damp ponytail. "You really can call me Em."

"I could." Zach has the most wickedly playful smile, but it's also kind. He has no idea how much I need some genuine kindness right now.

"How's Suzie today?"

"Tired. She had her last chemo treatment yesterday. It was a rough night, but she's a little better this morning."

I'm so young, and my lack of response proves it. There is no easy way to talk about cancer with someone who is going through it themselves or living through the suffering of a loved one. All the idiomatic phrases that would fit something like a bad cold or the flu don't work with cancer.

Hope she gets better soon.

Have you given her chicken noodle soup?

She's got this!

This, too, shall pass.

It is what it is.

"I don't know what to say," I respond in a soft voice and shy shrug. That's my truth, and I hope it doesn't sound insensitive.

He shakes his head. "There's really nothing to say. It is what it is."

Okay, so he can say it without it sounding horrible, but I still won't utter those words around him or Suzie.

"Anyway, I'll let you get to work. I'd hate for you to do a perfunctory job because I made you run later than you're already running." He grins, so I know he's kidding, sorta kidding.

Perfunctory. I grin. "Yes, sir, Mr. Hays." Then I salute him and make my way to the kitchen.

———

AFTER I *THOROUGHLY* CLEAN ALL THE bedrooms, bathrooms, and office, I finish in the kitchen.

"You *are* still here and looking cute as a button in your high-rise jeans and ruffled blouse. Too nice to be cleaning my house."

I glance over my shoulder, pausing my pink-gloved hands that have been scrubbing the sink.

Suzanne climbs onto one of the stools at the kitchen island.

"Hi. Well, I wear leggings and tees to work out. If I

25

don't wear these clothes to work, I'll spend every day in activewear, and that would be depressing."

My mom wore old, shitty, unmatched clothes. She preferred drugs to cute jumpsuits or matching socks for that matter. So many of my choices in life are a mix of conscious and subconscious fuck-you's to her.

"I feel ya," Suzie says. "Sometimes I shower, do my makeup, and throw on something cute just to feel ... alive. Feminine. Desirable. Lounge pants and oversized hoodies can get a little depressing."

I nod slowly. "Um ... where's Zach? Are you okay? Do you need anything?"

She tips her chin to the right. "That cabinet with the glass doors and the china?"

I point to it.

"Yes. The second drawer beneath it has placemats and cloth napkins. Under those is a box of Cap'n Crunch. Could you get it for me?"

After processing her request, I peel off my gloves and *thoroughly* wash my hands. Then I retrieve the hidden box of cereal and set it on the island in front of her.

"Thank you, Em." She shakes a small amount onto the white and gray granite.

"Do you want a bowl? Milk? A spoon?"

"Nope. I'm good. Want some?" She slides five or six pieces of cereal across the counter.

"Uh ... I'm ..."

"Come on, don't make a dying woman sneak cereal

alone." She flashes me an irresistible grin while tossing a few pieces into her mouth.

I mirror her expression and pop a few into mine. "Where *is* Zach, and why are we sneaking cereal?"

"Zach ran to the store and the pharmacy. Despite how he coddles me, insisting I take it easy all day, I'm functional. He has work tomorrow. My sister, Michelle, takes me to my appointments and keeps an eye on me when he's gone."

"What does Zach do?" I shove my hands back into the pink latex gloves.

"He's a pilot. Most days, he can return home. So it's only a handful of times each month that he's gone overnight. Seniority has been a godsend."

A pilot. I can only picture him in sweats and a tee, not a captain's uniform.

"And you? What do you do?" I bite my lips together. "Sorry. Of course, you're ..."

Sick?

Dying?

She pours more cereal onto the counter. "I was a flight attendant, and that's how I met Zach. We had known each other for years before we ended up together. When we met ... I was with someone else."

My eyebrows inch up my forehead. I think this might be a good story.

Popping more cereal into her mouth, she smirks. "It's not as forbidden as it sounds. Zach is five years younger than me. I didn't give him a second look when we met because I was over the moon for my first love ... Tara. My first soul mate."

She lets me blink slowly for several seconds before smirking. "Love is fluid for me. Ya know?"

I nod. Maybe I don't know it precisely as Suzie knows it, but I understand love comes in many forms. Sadly, I've felt very little love in my life, not even a mother's love.

Suzie's smile wanes. "Tara died of an aneurysm. Just ... poof ..." Her gaze stays affixed to the cereal. "We had breakfast together. Oatmeal. Berries. Coffee. I kissed her goodbye and headed to the airport. When I landed in Boston that afternoon, I got a call from her boss. An hour after returning from lunch, she ..." Tears glisten in her eyes. "Well ... it was fast." Suzie clears her throat. "And that's how we all deserve to go. My biggest fear isn't dying; it's suffering. It's comforting to believe that Tara didn't suffer."

"I'm sorry," I whisper. I should be working, scrubbing, and *thoroughly* doing my job, but I can't move. Suzanne mesmerizes me, and it's hard to explain. I feel like she thrives on optimism while still keeping reality in focus. But I'm not sure anyone dies quickly from cancer like an aneurysm bursting. And that makes me sad for her.

"Everyone said a year plus one day. That's how long I needed to grieve Tara before I'd be ready to move on—whatever that really meant. I took a week off work, and I did nothing but look through every photo we'd ever taken together. Some days I didn't get out of bed; I just stared at photos. An unbearable empty, *hollow* feeling in my chest. Then I slept so I could dream of us. She never dies in my dreams." When Suzie glances up at me, I don't blink. I can't. "When my time off ended, I packed up all the pictures and put them in a box. All the recent photos on my computer went into a folder on my hard drive. I donated her things, put on my big girl pants, and went back to work. It was a step forward. Sure, I looked back. I still look back. But I took a step. I moved on. A year plus a day, my ass. I don't think love is expressed through wasted time. What a waste of time to sulk for that long. Sorry … I know I sound insensitive. Everyone's needs are different. But it pissed me off that everyone else thought they knew what was best for me. Ya know?"

I nod slowly. It's the only thing I seem to be able to do.

"When I die," she continues, "I want Zach to give himself a week. Hell, I'd like him to walk away from my grave the day of the funeral and just get on with life, but that's probably too much to ask. A week is good. After that, I want him to walk out the front door in his uniform, get on a plane, and never look back."

"You don't think the chemo is working?"

"At this point, it's like trying to drive across the country on one tank of gas. I'll go a while, but I won't make it the whole way. Even Zach knows it's *when* and not if."

"Are you scared?" I whisper.

JEWEL E. ANN

"No." Her face relaxes, and it calms me—but only a bit.

I don't know why I'm afraid for her; I just am. It's probably because I've thought about my own mortality since the epilepsy diagnosis. Nobody knows how many tanks of gas they have to make it to wherever their final destination is in life.

"Tara is waiting for me. And as crazy as it sounds, my believing that is comforting to Zach too."

"He's not jealous? It doesn't make him feel like Tara was the love of your life and he's second place?"

Closing the box of cereal, Suzanne winks at me. "I know you're young, but I'm going to give you a spoiler alert to life. Soulmates are not S O L E mates. Without one, we are not alone. Many souls feed our own. Humans are interchangeable puzzle pieces; we fit into more than one space. I fit with Tara. And I fit with Zach. I've never had children. Still, I imagine it's how a mother can love all her children equally, even if differently. I don't love Zach more or less than I loved Tara. I love him differently."

"Well, he's lovable. He told me about the stones in that jar, and that's ..." I shake my head.

Emotion fills her eyes. "I know."

"But you ..." I grin, trying to keep her from crying. "You're artsy."

"What? No. I'm not." She laughs, wiping the corners of her eyes.

"Yes. You are." I turn and start scrubbing the sink again. "I'm not sure what I'm doing most days, but I know who I am. I am an artist—an artist who loves photography. That's my true passion, so I feel like I recognize fellow artists. Maybe you don't design clothes, sculpt, paint, or take photographs like me, but you see emotions. And emotions are invisible. Artists take the intangible things in life and give them form—give them life. You just made the idea of soulmates tangible for me with your words." I laugh a little. "It's a huge weight off my conscience to know that I'm not looking for *the* soulmate, just *a* soulmate."

Suzie nods a few times. "But don't rush it," she says. "We women tend to fall in love with love. Don't settle. Even when Zach got up the courage to pursue me after Tara died, I made him work for it. Even after he had full custody of my heart, I made him continue to work for it."

After rinsing out the sink, I turn and peel off my gloves again. "The way he looks at you..." I shake my head "...well, I can't imagine how amazing that must feel."

A sad smile pulls at her dry lips. "Mmm ... indescribable. That's just Zach. He gives a hundred and ten percent to everything he does. His job. His friendships. His marriage."

I twist my lips. "I'm glad I can give him more time to be with you."

"Well ..." She rolls her eyes. "A dirty house isn't keeping him from me. You're feeding his need for control and order, so in a way, he's using you as an extension of himself. Zach can't save me, so he will make sure he can do everything else. A clean house will not grant me one more day than what I'm probably predestined to live."

"Can I ask ..." I pause a second.

"Ask me anything."

Trapping my lower lip between my teeth, I nod slowly. "How much time do you have?"

She shrugs. "You can ask, but I can't answer that."

"They didn't give you any idea?"

"No. They did. I should have been dead six months ago."

Chapter Three

Zach

"How's Suzanne?" Matt asks as I exit the plane. He and Suzanne used to work together.

I slide my bag over my shoulder. "She finished her last round of chemo."

"That's good, right?"

"Yeah. It's good." I don't tell him it's the last trick in the bag. I don't tell him it didn't get all the cancer. I don't tell him hope has turned into acceptance. I don't tell anyone these things because I can't say them aloud.

"Well, tell her hi for me and that I miss her overly cheerful self."

My mouth finds a small smile as I nod. It's true. Suzanne has always been glitter and confetti. Knowing her is a gift. Loving her is life. Saying goodbye will gut me.

On the way home, I pick up a bouquet of fuchsia

tulips—her favorite. When I walk into the house, I hear the TV from our bedroom. After removing my shoes, I wash my hands in the kitchen, put the tulips in her favorite recycled glass vase, and carry it to the bedroom.

She's there.

She's alive.

That's all I need for this to be a great day.

"Captain Hays." My wife grins from her side of the bed that's raised to a forty-five-degree angle.

My gaze attaches to hers while she shuts off the TV as if she can click the button before I notice that she's watching a reality TV show. She's not wearing anything on her head—a peach with a bit of hair attempting to sprout back to life.

She's too thin.

She's too frail.

She's too sick.

But she's always perfect in my eyes. Every time I see her, I have to take a minute to catch my breath and tell my heart to chill because it's impossible *not* to fall in love with her every single time I see her.

"Trashy TV, Mrs. Hays?"

"Are those for *me*?" She ignores my TV comment and acts surprised that I brought her tulips.

I always ... *always* bring home tulips.

"They might be for you. I haven't decided yet." I set them on the nightstand and sit on the edge of the bed.

"Give me those lips." She wets hers, but I'm already leaning in to take them. The way she ghosts her finger-

34

tips along my jaw as I kiss her never fails to make my skin tingle all over.

"How were your flights?" she asks, pulling back just enough to put a breath between us.

I used to answer that question with something like *"Long and lonely without you,"* but my fear and impending grief would only steal her happiness. And we have so little time left I don't let myself look forward. I don't let myself feel anything outside of this moment. "Smooth sailing. And Matt said to tell you hi."

She draws in a long breath and releases it with a smile. "Mmm ... that's good stuff. Are you going to grab your guitar and play me a song?"

"I'm going to crawl in bed with you." I pull back the covers.

We lie next to each other, spooned like one person instead of two. She's warm, and her chest rises and falls in time with mine.

"Zach?"

"Hmm?" My lips press to her head.

"You know how you always say I'm too generous?"

"Uh-huh."

"When I die ..." She says it so matter-of-factly it sucks all the oxygen from the room. "Will you do something extraordinary for someone else? Someone who needs it? Will you do it and think of me?"

I don't want to talk about this.

"Because I don't want you to ever question life or

your purpose in it after I'm gone. So go big. Change a life. Make it your purpose."

"And how will I know what that is?"

She shrugs, hugging my arms to her waist. I feel the sharp bones covered in loose skin, magnifying how much of her I've already lost. "You'll know. It will be a feeling. Or you'll see a sign."

I grin despite the pain in my chest, despite the way it feels like she's melting away in my arms—sand in an hourglass. In a blink, I will be hollow, empty, and out of time. "You and your signs."

"Signs are everywhere. And it's not that people don't see them; they just don't want to acknowledge them. I said yes to our first date because that day we were leaving the rainy terminal, you held your jacket over my head to keep me dry. When I was a young girl, my mom told me to never settle for a man who is anything less than a complete gentleman."

With a laugh, I kiss her head again. "I was just trying to get into your pants."

She laughs so hard it brings tears to my eyes. If I can't hear her laugh, then I might as well be deaf.

If I can't hold her, then why do I need arms?

The thought of life without her cripples me in ways I can't even articulate. And that's why she knows I will question life and my entire existence when she's gone.

"I found you," she whispers as if she can hear my thoughts. "When Tara died, I found you. And nobody could have told me that *before* she died. The idea of sharing my heart with another in that way was unimaginable. But ... I found you. I've told you so many times, we have more than one soulmate."

Nope. I don't buy her soulmate theory. I'm not finding anyone else. But like so many other things, I don't tell her that. It gives her a sense of peace to feel that I might find love again. And I will offer her anything—say anything—to ease her mind and grant her a feeling of peace. "Signs everywhere. Change a life. Go big. And find love again. Got it," I say.

If she turns around, she'll see all the tears streaming down my face. I hope she stays still and doesn't feel my heart in my throat, barely beating and completely suffocating me with grief.

————

On Tuesday, Suzanne insists on a shower, makeup, and a silk scarf.

"Why the need to do all this for the girl who cleans our house?" I bend down and kiss her neck as she eyes me in her vanity mirror.

She caps her lip gloss and takes one more look at her reflection as I pull on a T-shirt and ruffle my wet hair.

"Her name is Emersyn, not *the girl*, and I like chatting with her. Did you know she has a textile design degree, but her love is photography?"

"Yes, I read her résumé. However, I wasn't aware that she has a love of photography. I'm not surprised that someone with a fine arts degree is cleaning houses. I bet cleaning houses pays better." I wink at her reflection.

Suzanne gives me her best stink eye, but she knows I'm right. "Anyway ... I don't like to scare her by looking like death warmed over, and I see the worry in her eyes when I'm not looking so great. She's young. She needs to focus on life—being stylishly dressed with great hair and endless possibilities."

"There's more to life than hair and clothes. And you don't care what your sister thinks."

"Michelle shaved my head, and before that, she held my patchy hair back when I vomited on the days you were working. I think it's a bit late to save her from my worst side. Besides, she can't quit being my sister. If I scare Em, she might quit and find a job where death doesn't loom all around her."

The doorbell rings, prompting Suzanne to stand slowly. Each day renders her a little weaker.

"I'll get it," I say.

"I'll come with you."

I roll my eyes but offer her my arm just the same. She blows me a kiss and loops her arm around mine. Suzanne waves to Emersyn through the glass door when we turn the corner.

"Look at her gingham romper! She's just the cutest."

Again, I roll my eyes, even though I can't help but grin at my wife's excitement. I imagine she was a lot like Emersyn at twenty-three.

"Good morning. Have you had breakfast?" Suzanne asks the second I open the door for Emersyn.

"Um ..." Emersyn narrows her eyes into tiny slits of blue. "Yeah, sort of. Why?" She steps inside and removes her sandals, curling her toes painted in flaking pink polish. Without hesitation, she heads straight to the bathroom to wash her hands like she's diligently done for the past month, leaving behind a scent I can't distinguish. Amaretto and maybe cherries, like a pastry.

"Zach is making eggs Benedict. Would you like some as well?" My wife follows Emersyn to the half bath.

"I should get started cleaning." Emersyn dries her hands and turns toward the door and my eager wife, who has befriended our maid in a very unexpected way.

"You don't need to vacuum the spare bedrooms." Suzanne flicks her wrist as if the notion of our maid cleaning what we pay her to clean is absurd.

Emersyn's gaze jumps to mine as I hover behind Suzanne. She curls her blond hair behind her ears, a few strands falling back into her face as she digs something from her pocket.

Lipstick. Maybe lip gloss. As soon as she uncaps it, I recognize the scent—cherry and amaretto.

I didn't know I was making eggs Benedict this morning, but I will. I'll make her anything.

Do anything.

Go anywhere.

Be anyone.

I love her beyond words. So I clear my throat and smile. "Emersyn, you should have eggs Benedict with us, and if you don't have time to vacuum the bedrooms, so be it."

I'll do it later because it's going to get done one way or another. I thought we hired a maid to clean and allow me more time to spend with Suzanne on my days off. Apparently not. If she wants to have breakfast with the girl in *cute* clothes ... if that makes her smile, then that's my purpose this morning.

"Sounds yummy. Thanks. I'll start on the bathrooms."

When breakfast is ready, I head to the jungle to get Suzanne, but her chair holds nothing but a half-folded quilt. I search the patio before heading back inside, lured by the sound of giggling. Suzanne's perched on her padded vanity stool with Emersyn on the floor at her feet. She's braiding Emersyn's stick straight hair.

Has Emersyn cleaned *anything* yet? Lifted a finger to earn so much as a nickel of pay? I'm conflicted at the moment. This hiring-a-maid thing has taken a direction I didn't see coming.

"Em has the best hair. Don't you think, Zach? Of course, everyone has better hair than I have at the moment."

I fear my wife looks at Emersyn and sees everything she used to be and will never be again.

The smile falls from Emersyn's face when she sees me. Her lips curl inward like she can eat it before I see it. I'll likely be cleaning our bathroom later too. Probably the whole house.

"Breakfast is ready." The best I can do is offer Emersyn a toothy grin, the kind where my tongue bleeds from biting it so hard. But I'd rather die than say something that wipes that beautiful grin from my wife's face. And Emersyn seems to be the reason for it, so ... what's a guy to do?

"Hold this, Zach." Suzanne nods to the end of the braid in her hand. "I need to grab a hair tie from my drawer if I still have any. I might have given up on ever needing them." She laughs softly like it's no big deal, again making subtle references to her dance with death that inches closer each day.

I take the end of the braid as Emersyn continues to bite her lips together, her whole body stiff like she's holding her breath. Caught by the boss ... not working. Will she charge me for cleaning the whole house? I shouldn't make her squirm, but I find it slightly satisfying. A reprieve from the heavy stuff.

"Thanks, sweets." Suzanne takes the braid from me and wraps the tie around it. "Did you know that Em's boyfriend manages the fitness club we used to belong to? I remember him. Brady? All the tattoos? Do you remember, Zach?"

I nod several times. "Yeah, I remember him, but no, I didn't know he's her boyfriend. Probably because I let her do her job instead of playing twenty questions with her." My smile escalates to capacity, hiding my sarcasm. Or maybe it's jealousy. Am I jealous that

Emersyn is the one that's brought Suzanne to life today? I might be on the verge of growing out my hair if Suzanne finds such joy in braiding.

Emersyn springs to her feet and helps Suzanne up before I get the chance to do it.

"Stop being such a spoilsport, Zach. Life is too short to worry about a bit of dust or a few water stains on the shower door." Suzanne playfully narrows her eyes at me.

I love this woman so much. That's why I keep smiling despite my thoughts. *Sorry. My bad. I just assumed that's why we hired her.* Again, I was so very wrong.

While the two women get cozy in the nook by the window overlooking rows of garden beds, I serve them eggs Benedict and fresh-squeezed orange juice. Emersyn tracks my every move. I'm not sure if I make her nervous or if she's never seen a guy make eggs Benedict. Suzanne winks at me when I hand her a cup full of vitamins, her pain meds, and a tall glass of filtered water to go with them.

As if she can read Emersyn's mind, she pats the empty seat between them, beckoning me to sit. "Zach has always been a good cook, but he took it to the next level when I was diagnosed with cancer the first time."

"It's good. *Really* good," Emersyn mumbles over a mouthful of food.

My wife smiles and takes my hand, bringing it to her lips for a soft kiss. "He is the best. I'm a lucky and *loved* woman."

Matching her smile, I swallow more emotion brought about by her tiny verbal reminders that things are coming to an end for us.

"Who has the green thumb?" Emersyn nods out the window to the rows of raised flowerbeds and vegetable gardens.

"Suzanne. The jungle is all her. The garden. Everything that has life ... it's her."

While addressing Emersyn's question, I don't miss Suzanne flinching at my words. We're good at tiptoeing around reality while leaking our emotions into benign comments. She is truly the person in this house that gives it and everything else life. I don't know what I will look like without her. Will I even see my own reflection in the mirror? Or will I feel so hollowed out that I'm nothing but a ghost of the man I am now? An empty jar with tiny cracks and a lost lid. Useless.

"Zach is a good student. There is nothing he won't do or try to do. He's spent hours reading botany books so he can take care of my plants on my bad days. He watched YouTube videos to learn how to give me a perfect pedicure. When I was first diagnosed with cancer, I swear he was on his way to earning a medical degree so he could have intelligent conversations with the doctors about my treatment."

I know it's not her intention, but I hate when she makes me sound like a saint. I'm far from it, just an ordinary man who loves his wife. It's what my dad has always been to my mom.

"So ... you and Brady ... is it serious?" Suzanne

makes a quick change of subject. I love her for that. "Is marriage in your future?"

I'm not into girl talk, but my wife is addicted to love stories, romance, and gossip. When she and her sister, Michelle, discuss their favorite reality TV shows, that's my cue to get out of the house.

"I hope not." Emersyn stares at her plate while relinquishing a nervous laugh.

"Oh, Em ... don't tell me you're wasting time with a guy who isn't worthy of you."

I can't shovel my breakfast down fast enough and get out of here.

"Not every guy is a Zachary." Emersyn's lips pull into a sheepish grin as her eyes turn to me for all of two seconds.

Great. She, too, thinks I'm better than I am when I'm just good at hiding my flaws. My biggest one is loving too hard and losing a sense of control and a grip on reality. I want my love to be some magical solution to everything, but it's not.

"True." Suzanne rubs her foot against my calf. "All the more reason to weed out the ones who are not up to par. I don't know Brady that well, but he's always seemed nice."

"Brady is nice," Emersyn says, but there's little enthusiasm behind her words. "And honestly, it might be me. I might not be worthy of him. He's focused on where he's at right now and where he wants to go in the future. He's chasing his dreams, and I'm still just dreaming without direction. And I'm fine with that. It just makes us feel incompatible most of the time. However, I do like him, and whatever we have seems to work for now. So why walk away if neither one of us has anything better at the moment? We're ... *useful* to each other right now." Emersyn drops her gaze to her plate again as she moves her food around with her fork, lips twisted as if she's figuring something out.

"Useful." Suzanne laughs. "Fair enough. Just promise me you'll never settle when it comes to love."

Emersyn nods slowly, but she doesn't look at us.

"Maybe you'll find a younger man like I did."

I smirk, standing with my empty plate.

Emersyn grins, her gaze ping-ponging between us. "Maybe. Thank you so much for breakfast. It was too generous ... really." She carries her dishes to the sink and rinses them off. "I better get to work."

I take Emersyn's dishes and load them into the dishwasher. "You're welcome."

She leans down as I'm bent over the open door. "Don't worry. I'm going to vacuum everything ... *thoroughly.*"

Amusement hijacks my twisted lips, and I lift my gaze to meet hers. Something changes between us, and I can't find the right words because this shift throws me off-kilter. She can read my mind like my wife can. Great. Two women reading my mind. Busting my balls. I'm doomed.

As soon as she disappears down the hallway, I saunter toward Suzanne, her full glass of orange juice, and nearly untouched eggs Benedict. "How are you going to take your pills without food in your stomach?" I say softly as I pull my chair closer to hers.

"She's beautiful. Isn't she?"

"What?" *Did I really hear her correctly?*

"Em. She's beautiful ... and refreshing." Suzanne's knee playfully nudges mine.

"Should I be worried? Are you going to leave me for the maid?"

My wife giggles and shakes her head. "No, but maybe *you* should leave *me* for the maid. Her breasts are delightfully perky."

"Fuck you," I whisper with a manufactured smile. I'm not mad, but that hurt. She knows I don't care about perky tits, and she knows I love her with every fiber of my soul.

"I wish you would. I wish you would fuck me, and if not me ... maybe someone like Em."

"Jesus, Suz ..." I run my hands through my hair. "Where the hell is this coming from? Just..." my hands drop to her lap "...take your pills."

"Maybe I don't need the pills."

I frown, scooping up a bite of food and holding it at her mouth. "Maybe you do."

She pleads with desperate eyes as I maintain my challenging expression for several seconds. With a sigh, she succumbs to my request by opening her mouth barely enough to fit the food into it. Chewing in slow motion, her beautiful face sours into a painful grimace. She's not hungry, and it's all she can do to swallow it, no matter how much she used to love my eggs Benedict. Days have passed since she's taken more than one or two bites of her meals. And if I force her to down the pills with so little food, she'll throw them up.

"Babe ... if you don't eat ..." I say the words slowly, just above a whisper.

"I'm tired." She rests her hand on my cheek and tilts her head to the side, giving me that loving smile that I can't refuse. She can get me to do anything with this one look.

"Want me to take a nap with you?"

She nods. "Yeah, that would be perfect."

I have a million things to do around the house: furnace filter to change, leaks to fix, a garage to clean, and grass to mow. But all those things will be here later. *They* are not going anywhere.

The only thing these hands and arms need to do right now are hold my wife.

Chapter Four

Emersyn

WHEN I'M NOT CLEANING houses, browsing thrift stores, peering through the lens of my camera, or working to build my following on social media, I search online for … something. Anything to get me out of this rut. It's not that cleaning houses doesn't pay well; it's just not my dream. Every day I lose a little more focus of that dream.

Tossing my phone into my gently used Hammitt handbag, I release a long, exasperated breath and climb out of my temporary housing on wheels. When I knock on the glass door, Zach appears within seconds. After last week's awkward breakfast, his welcoming smile is exactly what I need this morning. It took forever to clean their house that day. Zach may have hired me as their maid, but I think Suzie would rather I be her Tuesday friend. And if I could get paid to be her friend in good conscience, it would be a great job.

"Good morning," Zach says. "I'm leaving in a few minutes. I wasn't supposed to work today, but things changed. I'll be back late this evening, and Suzie's sister will be here by three." He talks without taking a breath while I step inside and remove my shoes. "I'm not asking you to watch her. She doesn't think she needs anyone, but if you wouldn't mind checking on her a few times—"

"Zach." I cut off his rambling, feeling every ounce of anxiety radiating from his body. "I've got this." Surprising myself with a high level of fake confidence, I add a big, reassuring smile to sell it. In reality, I'm not sure I have anything. Hanging out with Suzie while Zach is here, or at least within twenty miles running errands, is a more trivial responsibility than what he's asking me now. Even if he's trying to downplay it, I know he's panicking.

"You sure?" His face scrunches as his teeth plant firmly into his lower lip.

"This is my only house to clean on Tuesdays. So if it takes me longer or if you'd like me to stay until her sister gets here, it's no problem."

"Would you stay?" he replies so quickly my head spins.

"Yes." I chuckle. "I'll stay."

"You're the best." He shrugs a shoulder. "Okay, Suzanne's the best. But you're close. If it wouldn't be completely unprofessional, and if I had more time, I'd hug you or braid your hair." Zach winks, and it makes me giggle and shake my head.

He pivots and heads toward the bedroom. "Don't worry. I'll pay you more."

As I sort through the cleaning supplies he has on the kitchen island, he peeks his head around the corner. "Gotta go. You're awesome. If someone hasn't told you that today, then now you know."

"Hey, you don't need to pay me to be with Suzie. It's my pleasure because I like her … a lot." I follow him toward the back door.

Zach turns just before reaching for the handle. After a few seconds of silence, I wonder if he's lost his ability to speak. Finally, he gives me a sad smile and nods. "I like her too … a lot."

My eyes instantly burn with emotion. He's breaking my heart. Zach is a lost puppy, even though his owner is still alive.

"Um …" He clears his throat and shakes his head. "She's in the jungle reading a book. Again, thank you for … everything. Really. You're …"

I give him a slight grin. "The second best. Got it. Have a safe flight."

The tension along his face softens, and his grimace turns into a genuine smile. "Thanks. All emergency numbers are on my desk."

I nod.

AFTER I CLEAN the bedrooms and bathrooms, I check in on Suzie.

"Hey!" She catches me peeking my head around the corner.

"Hi. Do you ... need anything?" I inspect the jungle as I mosey toward her recliner.

"I need you to stop cleaning things that aren't even dirty." She nods at a striped ottoman. "Have a seat. It's where Zach sits to rub my feet, but you don't need to do that. I just want you to tell me everything." She sounds a little stronger today, and that's probably why Zach was in a better mood.

Playful.

Full of gratitude.

And overflowing with compliments.

He thinks I'm the one doing him a favor. He's so wrong. Neither he nor Suzie know how much they feed my soul with something. Friendship? Compassion? Just something that feels like nothing I've ever had before now.

"Everything, huh?" I laugh while taking a seat.

"Everything. Start at birth and work your way up to cleaning my house." Suzie adjusts the scarf around her head before folding her bony hands on her lap. Her skin has a slightly mottled appearance.

"Are you sure I can't read you a book instead? There are so many good stories out there, but mine isn't one of them."

With a slow headshake, she clears her throat. "I don't want a fairy tale. I want something real." She points to herself. "I'm all about real at this point in my life."

On an easy nod, I take a deep breath. Where to begin? I give her the CliffsNotes.

My mom and her addictions. Her favorite pastime involved sleeping with men—mean men.

No clue who my dad is or was.

No siblings.

Suzie gives me her complete attention, and I can't remember the last time someone cared this much to listen to me. I find myself glancing away to compose myself. Is this what it feels like to have someone really care?

"I pretty much raised myself. No time for sports or anything like that. I had to find odd jobs to make enough money to eat when my mom blew through her paycheck buying drugs and alcohol. And her paychecks weren't reliable anyway because she never kept a job for longer than a few months."

Suzie frowns, but I continue. "When I graduated, my mom tried to convince me to go to the University of Georgia—close to home. I laughed in her face, stole her car because I felt like she owed me *some-thing,* and drove to Atlanta. Let's see ..." I twist my lips and stare out the window for a few seconds. "College. Student loan debt. An epilepsy diagnosis. A job at Walmart. It's such an amazing story, huh?" I release a nervous laugh because I've needed to say these things. Something just beneath the surface of my pride needed to really hear those words. I've spent so much time wondering how the hell I got here. Feeling lost.

"One of the other employees at Walmart told me she cleaned houses on the side. So I used my first few paychecks to buy cleaning supplies with my discount. And I started going door to door, looking for jobs. Never landed one that way. I met an older woman while walking out to my car after work. Margie Mumford." I grin. "She dropped her wallet a few feet behind her, but she didn't notice. I picked it up and returned it to her. Then fate stepped in and opened a door for me. She mentioned being distracted because she had a party coming up, and her maid went into labor. That was my first job, and her referral to friends led to me having enough houses to clean that I could quit my Walmart job. And here I am."

Suzie nods slowly. Does she pity me? God, I hope not. I'm good; I don't need her pity. It would ruin the excitement I get when I know it's Tuesday, and I get to hang out with my two favorite people.

"Well ..." She blows out a long breath. "That was awfully generic. I'm giving that story three stars. Maybe three and a half."

"What?" I laugh. "Story? You didn't want a story. You asked for a recount of my life."

"And I still know very little about you. How did your mother's vices impact you? Who are you because of her choices? Why art? Why photography? Have you ever been in love? Do you have dreams? When you're not cleaning houses or dating hot fitness trainers, what do you do? What kind of music speaks to your soul? What food makes you moan with pleasure? When was the last time a single moment gave you butterflies or sent chills along your spine? If you answer those questions, then I'll know *you*."

"I need to clean your house." I offer another nervous laugh, a little off-kilter from her emotional probing. How does one answer the question *What makes you ... you?*

"No. You don't need to clean anything."

Pulling my feet onto the ottoman and crossing them, I close my eyes for a few seconds. I've never taken the time to think about myself beyond the circumstances that have led me to this point. "Saul. He was one of my mom's boyfriends. I think the only good one." Opening one eye, I frown. "He didn't last long. He was too good for her. He was an artist who bought me paints and clay, pencils and sketch paper. Saul let me use his camera. One Saturday afternoon, we drove to the beach when my mom was a little hungover. She stayed in the car most of the time. Saul and I played in the sand. We built castles with moats and pretended I was the princess and he was the knight trying to save me. And he did. Saul unearthed my love for art—creating and capturing the essence of humanity in its many forms. He showed me beauty through creation, and he was my first love ... not in a weird or inappropriate way, just ... he gave me a glimpse of what love looked like. And I haven't seen it since him. I haven't felt butterflies, but just hearing my mom's voice gives me chills along my spine. Because of her, I am driven not to be her. Oh ... and I like R&B music. The sexier, the better."

Suzie grins.

I continue. "I dream of a family, which is funny because I don't know what that looks like. But I see mothers and daughters shopping or eating at a quaint café at one o'clock in the afternoon on a Thursday, and I imagine what it would be like if that were my life.

"And I don't think about food often because I haven't had many chances to enjoy it beyond the simplicity of calories to fuel my body. When I'm not cleaning houses, I'm snapping photos or shopping for great designer finds at thrift stores."

"Girl ... you're speaking my language," Suzie says in a huge grin.

Her words encourage me to continue. "I love reading biographies because it's fun to be someone else for a few pages. Crazy, huh?"

"Mmm ..." Suzie hums. "Not crazy. I know exactly what you mean. Right now, I'm you."

"Oh no. Choose someone better than me." I chuckle.

"No. I want to be you. A dreamer with a tiny tether to reality. An appreciation for life ... never taking any of it for granted. And oh ... the possibilities. You can be anything. Do anything. Go anywhere. You have those butterflies to feel for the first time. Em! You. Have. Butterflies. To. Feel! God! I wish I could go back and feel them again. It's not that I still don't feel them with

Zach, but they're never as strong as the first time. You have a million firsts left in your life. I have a handful of lasts. Don't waste a single minute being anything but courageous."

Courageous ...

Am I courageous for living out of my car?

Am I courageous for having no clue what it's like to have a healthy, *honest* relationship with a man?

I think she's mistaking courage for hidden fear.

"Say it." Suzie claps her hands several times.

"Say what?"

"I am courageous!" Suzie raises her hands above her head, fingers stiff, grin to her ears.

"I am courageous," I say.

"No! What was that? Try it again, like you mean it. Better yet, actually mean it."

"I am courageous!" I add some power to my words.

"Again. Don't forget the arms."

I giggle. "I AM COURAGEOUS!" I jump up, land on my feet, and shoot my arms toward the ceiling.

"Attagirl! That is your soul, girlfriend. Do you hear me? That is your *soul*. The hair, your body, the epilepsy ... that's your genetic vehicle for this life. Use it for pleasure, and use it to do good. But never let it define you."

I plop down onto the ottoman, and before I know it, I'm wiping a few stray tears.

"Oh, hey ..." She slowly leans forward and reaches for my leg.

I shake my head and smile past the emotion. "Sorry. I just ... I think I've needed a therapist or a ..."

"A friend?"

I nod and sniffle.

"Well, you have one right here. Okay?" She finds my hand and squeezes it.

I blow out a breath and smile, eyeing her frail body while feeling her inner strength. "You're not letting the cancer define you?"

She shakes her head. "I have too much living to do. It might not be in this lifetime, but that's okay. I'll grab a cancer-free vehicle and take it for a new journey in my next life. I don't believe we ever end; we simply move on."

I don't know what to believe. But if thinking like Suzie means life is full of pleasure and adventure without fearing death, she just converted me to a new religion.

Chapter Five

BY MID-SUMMER, Suzie becomes more than my friend. She's my mother, my sister, and my mentor. If—when—she dies, it will hurt more than it would if my biological mom died. I still clean her house on Tuesdays, but I also hang out with her in the evenings when Zach has a late flight home. One might think our age gap would leave us with little to talk about, but it's quite the opposite.

Suzie loves watching me edit photos. And I enjoy snapping a few candid shots of her when she least expects it. She gives me an eye roll, and I peek around my camera and give her a wink.

She's always interested in talking about my mom and her sordid past. I think it's her way of giving me therapy, which I can't afford. I enjoy her mentoring me on gardening and caring for her jungle. At the same time, she shares all the places around the world she visited during her career as a flight attendant. And we both love reality TV, celebrity gossip, and all things fashion.

There are good days and bad days—days I think she's miraculously beating the cancer and days that feel like the end is near. So many times, I've come close to confessing my housing situation. I've casually mentioned student loan debt and *a few* medical bills— but I've never told her they're piled a mile high. I don't want her pity. I'll figure out my own shit ... eventually. For now, I just want to be her friend.

"Thank you," she says.

I glance down at her from the ladder, dusting the lights above the island while she eats her Cap'n Crunch. That's how I know today is a good day. Cap'n is always a good day. "It's my job. You pay me, and no thanks required." I wink.

"I'm not talking about that. I'm talking about us. You're the only friend I have who doesn't give me the pity look. You don't bombard me with questions about new treatments. You don't tell me I should be on a juice cleanse and meditate every day. When we're together, it's easy to forget I have cancer."

My attention returns to the lights because she's trying to make me cry, which would look like pity. She's set the bar high. I'll have to really watch what I say, how I look at her, and definitely not suggest too much nutritious food. I'll drop off a pint of her favorite ice cream if Zach is working tomorrow.

"Sometimes I forget that you hired me to clean your house, especially since Zach has been so grateful.

When I first started working for you, I felt like he was unsure about our friendship. Like maybe he resented it? But now I feel like he's truly grateful that we've bonded. I've never had a boss say thank you as much as he does."

I finish wiping the last light and toss the dusting rag over my shoulder. Grabbing the cereal box, I help myself to some breakfast contraband—sans washing my hands. We know I'm not going to kill her with a bit of dust and dirt.

Suzie smiles, adjusting her red beanie. It's ninety-five degrees outside, but she's chosen a winter hat to cover her head that still hasn't seen much hair growth. She's cold all the time, but I don't say much. There's not much to say when it comes to her physical state.

It is what it is.

"Zach is ..." She smiles, and it's love. Unconditional love. And it's a little heartbreaking because I don't think their story ends with a happily ever after. "Listen, Em ... don't clean houses forever ... unless it's really what you want. But I think you're going to be a wildly famous photographer someday, so don't spend all the interim cleaning houses. It's a big world. Travel. Make memories. Make mistakes. Make love. Blow an entire paycheck on a handbag or the most impractical shoes. I saved my money. I should have bought the shoes. Be better than me, Em."

Suzie is everything good in my life. What will happen when she's not here? Will all the holes she's filled in my life feel hollow again? I pop a few pieces of cereal into my mouth and smirk. "I can't imagine there's anyone better than you, but I like how you think. Even if some of the lovemaking is a mistake."

Suzie shrugs. "Two birds. One stone."

I shake my head. "Where were you when I needed this advice? When my mom was too busy being a truly horrible person?"

"Well, I don't want you to think of me as a mom ... that makes me feel old. Big sister?"

Too late. Suzie's *everything*.

"Big sister it is." I slip behind her and wrap my arms around her narrow shoulders, giving her a gentle hug while kissing her cheek. "Do you think we were friends in another life? I feel like everything is easy with you, like I could tell you anything."

Like I could tell you I'm living out of my car.

But I don't, even though I feel everything in my life is more manageable when I share it with her. Suzie has a way of reducing mountain-sized problems into boulders ... minor bumps in the road.

"I do," she says. "I think we were ... something. But it's just going to be you again. Okay? Don't let yourself stay in a rut. Think of the mistakes I made, all the things I wish I would have done differently. Then you do it better. When you're questioning your purpose or can't see which direction you're headed, pack up your crap and change the scenery. I regret the times I spent trying to repaint the same canvas." Suzie sighs. "But for now, be done." She turns as I release her. "No more cleaning today."

"But I'm *not* done." With a firm smile, I try to hold my ground. I know she's getting ready to suggest something that will prevent me from doing my real job, something that will make it hard to accept my paycheck when Zach hands it to me with a sincere thank you. How many bosses thank their employees every week? One.

Just one.

Zach Hays.

When he thanks me, it feels like he's thanking me for so much more than dusting and running the vacuum.

"This afternoon, there's nothing to clean and cancer doesn't exist."

My eyes narrow just enough to make me feel responsible for a few seconds. "Well ... I definitely like the part where you don't have cancer, but Zach coming home to a half-clean house doesn't sound as appealing."

"Screw Zach."

I giggle. "As appealing as *that* sounds ..."

Suzie's eyes widen, and her jaw relaxes into an undecipherable expression.

"Joking ... I'm completely joking. Please tell me you know I'm joking."

Closing her mouth, she covers it with her hand as she snorts a laugh.

Thank god. She knows I'm joking.

"I'm sure Zach could use a good screw about now. It's been a long time."

My cheeks flush. We haven't talked about sex—well, her sex life—which is surprising because we talk about everything else.

"He still thinks he could break me. I'm fragile, but not *that* fragile. And I can't think of a better way to go than dying from sex."

A giggle sneaks past my lips even though this topic feels a little inappropriate and morbid.

On another dreamy sigh, she continues, "It's hard to explain how losing my breasts crushed me, not because clothes would never fit right again. Not because I worried about people noticing. No ... it was knowing that a part of me, which brought Zach so much pleasure, was gone—like cancer stole a piece of our intimacy. *Not* that he's ever looked at me with anything but complete love and desire. It's different than other cancers that leave internal scars but stay hidden in places we can't see. Nope. We can't be intimate and *not* see—not feel—it in the most physical way.

"I worried so much about him. I worried he would miss my breasts and feel wrong about ever admitting it. Then one day, I was looking in our bathroom mirror after a shower, and I said, 'I miss my breasts.' He glanced up while buttoning his jeans, and he replied, 'I do too, but not as much as I'd miss you.' And oh my god ... I nearly died. I didn't expect him to admit it. But the fact that he did—that he was honest with me—then followed it up with that last part ..." She shakes her head again, tears in her eyes.

"I fell in love with him harder than I did the first time."

Suzie swallows hard several times, fighting to keep the emotions from having their way.

"Well ..." I twist my lips, nose wrinkled. "That's just the cheesiest thing I've ever heard a man say."

It was epic. And we both know it.

Suzie groans and rolls her eyes. "I know, right? Like, come on. Who says that? Try to be a little more original, Zach. Total cheeseball." Her smile says *thank you for lightening the mood.* Her smile reminds me that we agreed I would not be a maid this afternoon and she would not have cancer.

"Movie. Sugary coffee drinks ..." I tap my chin with my finger.

"Mani-pedi?"

I nod slowly. "I like how you think."

"My car or yours?"

Gulp ...

"My car is loaded with cleaning supplies. It's a mess, and I'd have to clean it out just to fit you in it. So maybe we should take your car, or I'm totally cool with paying for an Uber."

Suzie stands and shuffles her feet slowly toward her bedroom. "We can take my car."

Thank god ...

———

After an unforgettable afternoon with my new BFF, I work out at the gym, shower, and meet Brady at his apartment for a surprise. Our relationship has been a little rocky over the past few weeks, and I blame Zach and Suzie for showing me what my life is missing ... a life.

Okay, I might blame myself more. I should just be honest with everyone about my living condition and financial situation and see who stands by me. I already know the answer. Brady will leave me, and Suzie will attempt to adopt me like an abandoned puppy. All I really need is a shower. Maybe I can start cleaning my clients' bathrooms with the door locked and grab a shower.

Brady's not the best for my self-esteem. The sex is good, and the conversations we have are okay. Still, I can't help feeling like I'm doing it all for the gym membership, aka locker room privileges. Does that make me a horrible person? Or just a survivor?

"There's my girl." Brady pulls me into his arms the second he opens the door to his apartment. He palms my ass as he kisses me, and I hope he's not wondering when I will lube up again and let him in the back door.

"So, what's the surprise?" I wriggle out of his hold and set my handbag on his sofa. "You said you have a surprise for me." I give him a curious expression while praying that it's not a new sex position. I envision him with a bag of sex toys like butt plugs, nipple clamps— and a gag for my mouth so he doesn't have to listen to me question every move he makes.

"Do you remember our first date? What you said you wanted?"

No. And I can't believe he remembers.

"Um ..." I pinch my bottom lip between my fingers. "I'm sure I said many things on our first date—like how I want to travel the world and work on my photography portfolio. Do you know someone looking for a photographer?"

"No, Em. I'm talking about something else."

I nod slowly. "Okay ..."

He grins like a young boy. I don't get to see this side of Brady very often, and it's moderately endearing. So I feel lucky to be the recipient of this level of happiness. Still, I have no clue what surprise he has in store for me.

"Stay here and close your eyes."

As I close my eyes, a zing of excitement rushes through my veins. I do like surprises.

"Okay. Keep 'em closed and hold out your hands."

Holding my hands out, I shiver, a little giddy. Then something warm and furry touches my skin, and my eyes fly open.

"Surprise!" Brady smirks like he's the god of gifts.

"You got a cat?" I hug the white and black patched kitten to my chest, nuzzling my nose in her hair.

"Well," he chuckles, "I got a cat for you."

"For me?" I no longer feel as smitten with the kitten because I fear what he means.

"On our first date, you said you liked cats and wanted to adopt one someday."

I did say that. Now, let's break it down. *I* wanted to do the adopting. And *someday* is not today, when my current residence is my car. Unless you're married or living together, you don't buy someone a living, breathing creature. That's a huge fucking responsibility.

"I ... I can't believe you got me a cat."

"I feel bad about how things have been between us lately. I've been working nonstop, and I've kinda been a dick about you staying the night."

I stare at him with a slow nod and an equally slow raise of my eyebrows. "You're going to let me stay over? Is this *our* cat?"

"God, no! I'm actually a little allergic to cats ... all pets, really. I just thought you'd feel less lonely at your own place if you had a cat. I mean ... that's why you said you wanted one, right?"

"I'm ..."

Say it! I try so hard to get the nerve to tell him the truth as the kitten sniffs my chin, tickling me with her whiskers. *Her* ... I'm not sure if it's a her.

"Speechless?" Brady looks so proud of himself. In his own special way, I'm sure this is a huge gesture and show of love.

"So speechless." I reposition the cat only to see that it's a boy. He got me a tomcat? Figures. I wanted a female cat, but it's really not my biggest problem. It's mid-summer in Atlanta. Hot as fuck. I live out of my car. I don't know if I can train my cat to do its business outside like one can train a dog. A litter box in my car is a bit too much. And what the hell am I supposed to do with him during the day when I'm working? Leaving him in my car is not an option.

"Why don't you look as happy as I thought you'd be?"

I shrug while offering a nervous laugh. "Sorry. It's quite something that you remembered that little nugget of information from our first date, and I'm probably just in shock. That's all."

Brady frowns. "I expected high-pitched squealing, hugs, kisses, maybe other kinds of gratitude." He waggles his eyebrows.

Really? Does he really expect sexual favors for a cat? I should buy him a gift certificate for a new tattoo and expect him to let me move in with him. How would he like that?

"Well, now I have a cat. What am I supposed to do with her..." I wrinkle my nose "...*him* while expressing other forms of gratitude?"

Brady's mouth opens to speak, but I cut him off.

"I think it's best if I get this little guy home, and we hang out another night."

Never. I'm breaking up with him right now; he just doesn't know it yet. Screw it. I'll use body wipes until I figure out an alternative plan. I can't risk him buying me a sofa or something else for a place I don't have. Later, I will send him a lengthy message after I give my explanation more thought. It will go something like this:

Dear Brady,

Thanks for the cat and the gym membership. I will always remember you as my first anal partner. I think we have different needs at the moment. Best of luck with your quest to own your own gym. It's been fun. ~Em

P.S. I've been living out of my car for nearly three months, and I have epilepsy.

I'm just spitballing. I might tweak a few parts of it, hence the need to give it some more thought. I'm living a lie, waiting to get caught, and I can't go on any longer. What if I have a seizure? What if he gets some harebrained idea and decides to come to my house, a trailer where someone else lives now?

It's all too much work for *just* a shower.

"I can put the cat back in the box, and it won't take that long." He reaches for the cat.

My jaw unhinges. "You've kept him in a box? Are you serious? What is wrong with you?" I won't elaborate by telling him the way to a woman's sexual soul is not with the words: It won't take that long.

With an eye roll, Brady parks a hand on his hip. "There are holes in the box. I'm not an idiot, Em."

"I just can't. I'm too excited." My words hold *no* excitement, so I nuzzle my nose into the cat's neck and bring out the baby talk. "You don't want to go into a box, do you? No. Not my little guy. We need to get home and name you." Shooting Brady an apologetic smile, I sigh. "Sorry. Rain check?"

Brady's nose twitches, and he sniffles. "Yeah, it might be a good idea. My allergies are already acting up."

This really highlights the seriousness of our relationship and how it's on a one-way track to nowhere. What if this cat lives ten years, give or take? Are we really planning on staying together but living separately for that long? Or would I have to get rid of the very cat he gave me if we moved in together or got married?

"Thanks again." I step forward to kiss him, but he backs away, eyes turning red. I try to keep from laughing at the insane irony of the whole situation.

"Later." He returns a stiff smile. Is it possible that he, too, is questioning his decision?

Chapter Six

Two of my four clients are not home during the time I clean their houses. Guess who's guaranteed two showers a week? Guess who needs more than two showers a week during the hellish heat of summer?

Since I sent Brady the breakup text two weeks ago, things have been a little chaotic, and not just in the personal hygiene department. Turns out, Harry Pawter —yes, I named my cat Harry Pawter—doesn't like being led around by his collar and leash, like a dog, to go to the bathroom. He's super fucking finicky and insists on a litter box, probably because they got him used to one at the shelter.

Sans any other great ideas, I've been hiding him in basements (and sneaking his litter box into houses) while I work. Then I have to pussyfoot him back out when I'm done at each house. Nighttimes are tricky, depending on where I park for the evening, which is usually at one of the big box stores that allow overnight parking.

After a few rough nights with Harry Pawter and a couple of pee accidents on my clothes, I come across a fortunate discovery. Suzie and Zach's garden shed is in the shade, and it's relatively cool. Problem solved. Around ten at night, I sneak Harry Pawter to the shed with his litter pan, food, water, and a blanket. Since I've been helping Suzie lately with her gardening, I'm the only one who goes into the shed.

Until today ...

While Suzie takes her morning nap (she's been quite exhausted lately), I clean the guest bathroom and myself. For the past two days, I've been as ripe as a brown banana. Someday, when I'm living in a modern penthouse with a well-lit corner for doing custom photo shoots and one of those showers with a slew of shower heads, I will look back on this time in my life and remember how I learned to appreciate the simple things ... like body soap and running water.

"Emersyn, what do you know about the cat in the —" Zach opens the bathroom door that I didn't lock because Suzanne is sleeping, and he's supposed to be in the sky working.

I should have locked it. I'm an idiot!

"Shit!" I contort my arms to cover my naked bits on full display through the glass shower door.

"What are you ..." He turns and takes a step out of the bathroom. "Doing? Why are you cleaning the shower naked?" His voice hits a pitch higher than I've ever heard come out of his mouth.

I speed rinse the shampoo from my hair and shut off the water. Grabbing my own towel, I quickly wrap it around my body. "Why are you home?" I say from behind the partially ajar door.

"Canceled flight. Where are your clothes? And what do you know about the cat that was in the shed?"

"Was?" I poke my head around the door, water dripping from my hair.

"*Was* as in it ran out the second I opened the door. What's going on, Emersyn?" Zach keeps his back to me.

"What do you mean he ran out? Where did he go?" With total disregard for my single-towel attire, I bolt past him toward the back door. "Harry Pawter? HARRY PAWTER! Come to Mommy!" I race to the shed, but it's empty. Then I tighten my towel and inspect the beds of vegetables and flowers. My heart hammers.

Yes. I'm about to get fired.

Yes. The neighbors can see me half naked.

Yes. My feet are covered in dirt and grass clippings.

No. I didn't think I cared this much about my *male* cat until he ran away.

"HARRY PAWTER!" I skitter toward the side of the house.

"Emersyn!" Zach chases me. "Stop!"

I whip around. "Which way did he go?"

Zach pinches the bridge of his nose, head down like he's still attempting to be a gentleman. If he were the true gentleman Suzanne paints him to be, he'd help me find Harry Pawter. Instead, he blows a quick breath out of his nose and smirks. Fucking smirks. It's slightly hidden beneath his tucked chin, but it's there. And goddammit ... this isn't funny!

"He ran up the tree by the shed," Zach says, peeking up at me.

"Call 9-1-1." I march past him.

"I don't think that's the best use of emergency resources." He tails me as I stomp my way toward the tree, eyes squinted against the sun, searching for Harry. "It's not an actual emergency."

"Says the guy who doesn't have his cat stuck in a tree."

"I don't have a cat."

My head swivels to shoot him the stink eye for a few seconds before resuming my search for Harry Pawter. "There he is!" I start to point my finger, but my towel decides to slip a few inches, and I barely catch it before it reaches the point of no return. "Listen ..."

Zach's eyebrows form two curious peaks. "Listening ..."

I don't appreciate the amusement on his face. "I'm going to hose off my feet and get dressed. Then, I'm going to get your ladder from the garage. I just need you to keep an eye on him until I get back."

Pressing his lips together, he returns a slow nod. He's a little more intimidating in his uniform and tie. "Then we'll talk about the events that have taken place in the past fifteen minutes?"

I deflate and push a harsh breath out my nose as I brush past him toward the house and the water spigot. "Yeah, yeah ... we'll talk about it."

By the time I get dressed, Zach already has the ladder leaned against the tree trunk, and he's at the top grabbing Harry Pawter by the scruff of his neck and pulling him off the branch.

MEOW!

"Harry Pawter doesn't like being scruffed."

Zach retreats several steps, dropping Harry Pawter into my waiting arms. "I don't like coming home to a cat in my shed. So Harry Pawter has bigger concerns than his aversion to scruffing."

I kiss Harry's head, and he instantly starts to purr as Zach reaches the ground.

"*Your* cat?" he asks as if there's any question by this point.

I nod, nose still nuzzled into Harry's hair.

"And ... why was he in my shed?" Zach questions while lowering the ladder.

"Because ..."

Can I quit (like I basically quit Brady) and send Zach a similar text?

Dear Zach and Suzie,

Thank you for the job. I've really enjoyed working for you and forming such a close friendship. I'll think of you often and pray for a miraculous recovery. ~Em

P.S. I've been living out of my car for three months. Don't feel bad for me, it's only going to make me stronger one day. I. Am. Courageous!

"Because?" With an unblinking gaze, Zach steadies the ladder in his hands and waits for my response.

The thing is ... I'm not ready to quit Zach and Suzie. I'm also not ready to have them take pity on me. It's embarrassing. I don't know how I got here; I just know that it sucks.

"Because I haven't had him very long, and he doesn't do well at home by himself. So I put him in the shed where I can check in on him every hour or so."

Lies are nothing more than wishful versions of the truth. I think optimists, like myself, probably tell the most lies. The truth is usually less than appealing and far from optimistic.

Zach inspects me, *my* reaction to my own lie. My chin juts out and up, shoulders back.

"And you were cleaning the shower without any clothes on because?"

"Don't be an asshole." It's out. I just said that to *my boss.*

Zach chuckles. "I'm sorry ... how is asking a logical question suddenly *being an asshole*?"

I don't enjoy lying to Zach or anyone for that matter. People who lie, cheat, and steal don't always do it because they're bad people. Sometimes they do it because they're desperate. And if he's never truly been this desperate, then it's easy for him to judge those of us who are just trying to survive.

So I lie.

"Maybe something personal happened to me. Maybe I wet my pants or started my period and things

76

got ... messy." *Where the hell am I going with this?* "Must you call me out on it? Do you really *need* to know why?"

Zach's eyebrows lift while his lips part, as they should because I could have suggested I spilled coffee on myself or some cleaning solution that made my skin itch. Who jumps straight to wetting herself or a heavy menstrual cycle?

I roll my eyes to make sure he knows I'm kidding about the gross part. "The showers at my gym were unavailable *again*, so I didn't have time to run home and shower without being late. I chose to be on time ... to be here when Suzie woke up and forgo my shower until she took her morning nap. And I *was* cleaning the shower too, not just myself. For the record, I'm dropping my membership to that gym since their shower availability is so unpredictable. There. Are you happy now?"

The unfortunate thing about lying is that it just gets easier and easier to do. I should write fiction—I have so many made up versions of life in my head.

Hopes.

Fears.

Dreams.

It's disturbing how easily people can shape the world in their heads and give it a false reality with empty words. It's even more disturbing how I can treat my employer like he's the one at fault here.

When Zach doesn't respond, I force myself to look him in the eye. And I swear ... I really swear he sees right through me. Every single hope, dream, fear, and lie. In this moment, something shifts. I don't know what, but something. And that something tells me I'll reflect back on this moment in the future.

He's not my husband.

Not my lover.

I'm not even sure he's my friend.

He's a trespasser into my ... well, I don't know yet.

"Okay."

My eyes narrow. "Okay? Okay what?"

"Okay. I understand now. The shower. The cat. Its name is a little weird, but it's your cat not mine."

"That's it? Just ... okay? I'm not fired?"

"No, Emersyn." He chuckles, heading back into the house. "I'm not the *asshole* you think I am. Just lock the bathroom door if you ever clean in your birthday suit again, and I'll make sure to open the shed door slowly next time."

It's not pity—at least I don't think anyway. He doesn't know about my living situation or my massive piles of debt. It can't be pity. Well, it *could* be pity. I must have looked quite pitiful running outside with nothing but a towel wrapped around me, screaming, "HARRY PAWTER!"

Zach disappears, probably snuggling in bed with Suzie, so I finish my cleaning duties in record time and sneak out before I have to face him again.

Chapter Seven

Zach

ON SATURDAY, Michelle comes over to stay with Suzanne while I take a much-needed run. As I round the corner at the park, I see a familiar car with its windows partially rolled down. It's Emersyn. She's asleep with the seat reclined, head tilted to the side, and a string of drool down the side of her face.

"Emersyn?"

Her body twitches like she's having trouble waking from a dream. Did she have a seizure?

"Emersyn?"

Again, she stirs but doesn't open her eyes.

"Emersyn!"

She jumps.

I wipe my sweaty forehead and rest my other hand on my hip.

"Zach?" she asks, squinting her eyes.

"What are you doing?"

She sits up, raising the back of the driver's seat. "Napping. What are you doing?"

"I'm jogging."

She nods several times, eyes still squinted like she's fighting a headache.

I inspect her car, in particular the back seat and the hatchback space loaded with a shit-ton of stuff. Not just cleaning supplies.

Clothes.

Towels.

Boxes.

Harry Pawter.

A bag of cat food.

A black bra hanging over the headrest of the back seat.

Shoes.

Fast food bags wadded on the seats and floor along with a littering of empty water bottles.

Just ... everything.

"So ... it's a little hot to be napping in your car. Why aren't you home?" I tear my gaze from the piles of *stuff* and eye her through my own slitted eyes.

"Just an accident. I wasn't planning on napping. We were enjoying the shade and breeze, then boom!"

There is *no* breeze.

"I drifted off to sleep." She shrugs.

"It's not safe. It's hot as fuck. Really, your cat can't be comfortable either."

"Where's Suzie?"

"Home with her sister. You should go home too."

"Good plan." She starts her car. "Nice seeing you. Hope Suzie's doing okay?"

Again, I inspect the back of her car.

She clears her throat, bringing my attention back to her. "I'm glad to see you're jogging. Suzie wants you to take care of yourself."

I return an absentminded nod, not really registering what she's saying because ... this car is utterly disgusting.

"Well, tell Suzie I'll stop by tomorrow and pull weeds in the garden."

"You're living out of your car."

"I've been busy. I need to clean it out. Obviously." She rolls her eyes. "But I'm not living out of my car." She snorts a laugh, but I don't miss the uneasiness in her eyes.

The fear.

The growing redness in her face.

As I stare at her, her gaze shifts to the windshield, to the people on the trail and the kids at the splash pad.

"Emersyn," I say slowly, feeling confused. Is she homeless? How can that be? She has a job. A college degree. A boyfriend.

"Zachary," she says without looking at me.

"Where do you live?"

"Why? You coming for a visit?"

A few seconds of silence and tension settles between us.

"Don't mind if I do."

Before she can mutter the slightest protest, I round the car and plant my ass in the seat next to her.

There's a stench in the car, but I try to keep from wrinkling my nose.

Dirty laundry.

Cat piss.

Partially eaten food.

How long has this been marinating? All summer?

Emersyn starts the car and drives out of the parking lot.

First left.

Second right.

Another right.

Two lefts.

She drives me all around the city until there's no other choice ... then she steers the car back to my house. I remain quiet the whole time. I know she has nowhere to go. This tour of Atlanta has been to bide her time.

She puts the car in *Park* in my driveway.

"How long?" I ask.

Emersyn swallows hard as tears redden her eyes. "Not that long," she whispers like she can barely hold it together.

"How long is not that long?"

She bats away her tears the second they escape. "Since spring."

"Jesus ..." I pinch the bridge of my nose and shake my head. "How? Why? I don't get it." I'm angry. Not at her. Well, kinda at her *and* the absurdity of this. Also ... I ... I just want to know how the fuck this is possible.

She averts her gaze out her window to the yard overgrown with weeds and in desperate need of mowing. I chose to use my hour of time away from Suzie to jog instead of mow the lawn. Is Emersyn thinking it's rich of me to question her life when I'm clearly not the best role model?

"Don't you have family? Friends? You had a boyfriend when you started working for us. How is it that you were living out of your car and not with your boyfriend?"

Silence seems to be her answer of choice.

I grunt a laugh, shaking my head. "Your boyfriend ... you never told him. Did you?"

More silence.

"Was he just too much of a dick? Or were you too proud?"

She chews on the inside of her cheek, gaze affixed to the steering wheel.

"You can't pay rent with the money you make cleaning houses?"

"No," she murmurs. "I can pay rent ... *or* I can buy medication for my epilepsy, pay my student loans, and have a basic cellular plan."

"Yet ... you got a cat."

"I didn't get a cat! My *dick* boyfriend got me a cat."

I stiffen, anger building as I drum my fingers on my knees. "Because he didn't know you were living out of your car?"

"Your yard looks like shit. I should mow it for you."

She *is* judging me. "Fuck the yard. My wife is dying, and her new BFF is living out of a car ... with a goddamn cat."

"I'm temporarily living out of my car. But I *have* a car. And I have a job. My life is not ideal right now, but I'm young. I'm talented. I'm hardworking. So I will get through this just fine. Living out of one's car *temporarily* is not the worst thing ever." She exudes a surprising amount of confidence given the fact that she's singing her positivity song in a stinky, trashed car, after lying to us for months.

"You're her."

"Who?" she asks.

"Suzanne. You're an eternal optimist even when you know you have no cards left to play. But I think she's an optimist for me more than herself. You're the real deal."

"Even if you fire me for living out of my car, the Mumfords won't fire me. I still have three other clients, and I have a few other people who wanted to hire me when my schedule was full. I can check with them. So I'd hardly say I don't have any cards left to play."

I don't know if I should grin because she's so tough, a side to her I didn't know existed, or if I should be offended that she thinks so little of me. "I'd never fire you for being homeless."

"Dude ... I have a car."

"I'm not going to split hairs with you." I massage

my temples. "Let's take your stuff inside." I open the door.

"What? No. Why?"

Ducking my head back into the car, I lift my eyebrows. Is she serious? "To give you a safer place to sleep until you get things figured out."

"I don't want your pity or your charity. And I definitely don't want you to tell Suzie."

"I bet you want a shower. I bet your cat wants out of the heat." I close the door then slowly open her hatchback.

Fucking hell ... who lives like this?

Things spill onto the ground. Emersyn hops out and hustles to get her belongings picked up, including a pair of panties barely hanging on to the bumper.

"Just ..." She cringes and tries to bat away my hands as I reach for her things. "Let me do it. I don't need to bring everything inside just to shower and give Harry Pawter a break from the heat."

"Suzanne will insist you stay."

She snatches the bra from the top of my shoe at lightning speed. "That's why we're not going to tell her."

"I can't keep this from her."

Her frantic hands pluck a sandal and tube of lipstick from the driveway before she snaps her spine straight again. "Listen, Zach, you have a pass. At least from me. I get the need you must have to somehow do right by Suzie's every wish, but she nor you need a live-in right now. And you know this. She's still here with us, so you need to focus on her. You need time alone with her. So stop acting like you're honoring a dying request. A final letter. A forced promise in a weak moment. Or maybe just good old-fashioned guilt. I know she'll want you to take me in like a stray dog. I don't want it. No." She shakes her head. "Just no."

"Why have you always given me this vibe that you're a little unsure about me?"

"Unsure?" She cants her head to the side.

I shrug. "I don't want to say I think you don't like me, but it's a similar feeling. You get a little stiff whenever I walk into the same room as you and Suzanne— like I'm spoiling some party or that I, for whatever reason, make you nervous."

I don't get an answer from her. I get her crossing her arms over her chest and her hip pushed out to the side as she scowls at me.

What did *I* do?

Emersyn

ZACH WILL FOREVER PUT my nerves on high alert.

First: I have an innocent crush on him. It's his fault for being the perfect husband.

Second: I have an innocent crush on him. It's his fault for looking sexy *all* the time.

Third: I have an innocent crush on him. It's Suzie's fault for telling me about their sex life. Since she's dying, she gets a pass, and I'm forced to now blame that on him too.

All crushing aside, I don't know how to read Zach. I don't know how to read men at all. If I psychoanalyzed myself, everything would boil down to daddy issues.

Acting as confident as I can (which isn't much since he knows my secret and the disgusting odor from that secret is wafting out of the back of my car), I take a deep breath and blow it out my nose. "I've been a little lost. And since Suzie befriended me, I've felt a little found. You hired me to clean your house, and I fear I don't do that as well as I should do it. I think you're happy that I can sometimes be with Suzie when you're not here, but when you are here ... I feel like an intruder because ..."

Zach cocks his head to the side. "Because?"

Nibbling at my lower lip, I shrug. "Because there's this intense intimacy between the two of you. The second you walk into the same room as Suzie and me, I instantly feel like I've overstayed my welcome."

He frowns. "My wife is dying. That's not ..." Zach's head inches side to side.

"It's *intimate*. It's personal and private. I don't think I *really* know what that's like, but I do know that when you walk into the room and she looks at you ... the earth turns a little slower on its axis. All these unspoken words seem to hang heavily in the air. I can barely breathe when I'm in the same room with the two of you."

Zach blinks several times before his throat bobs

with a hard swallow. "Maybe *you're* the oxygen in the room. Maybe it is a little hard to breathe around us. All I know is whatever you two discuss makes her smile, even on the days I know she's in pain. And that comforts me in ways I can't express. So don't ever feel like you're intruding."

Surrendering as my last ounce of pride evaporates, I shove a few things into a plastic bag and hand it to him. Then I retrieve Harry Pawter, his litter box, and the partial bag of litter—some of which has spilled onto the floor of my car. "It's not about the cancer." I head toward the house. "We rarely talk about the cancer. I think I make her feel normal. Normal makes her smile." I stop and wait for him to open the door because my hands are full. "I think her other friends reek of grief and pity. Even when they don't mention the cancer, I bet she can see it all over their faces."

He pushes down the door lever. "How do *you* look at her?"

Tightening my hold on a squirmy Harry Pawter, I shrug. "Probably in disbelief that she treats me as an equal. Not as hired help. Not as a young, stupid woman who hasn't had the same life experience."

Zach maintains a blank expression like my answer needs some time to sink into his brain and make sense. Suzie doesn't want anyone's pity for her cancer just like I don't want anyone's pity for my homelessness. I don't know ... maybe she *will* understand. Maybe I should have told her my whole situation before now. I don't know what it's like to have someone trustworthy in my life, so my default mode is to distrust everyone.

I clear my throat. "I'm going to fill his litter box and jump in the shower. Then I'll tell Suzie. *I'll* tell her. And if she doesn't suggest I stay here, you don't say one word. Okay?"

Zach relinquishes a tiny nod before pushing the door open.

After a long and much-needed shower, I dry my hair and slip on a sundress. Turning the corner to make my way to the kitchen, a pile of things inside the guest bedroom catches my attention.

It's my stuff. Everything from my car is neatly piled at the end of the bed.

Zach told her. I'm going to kill him.

He did exactly what I asked him not to do. I head down the hallway, hoping I find him before seeing Suzie, but I spot him outside. Opening the door and softly closing it behind me, I stomp my bare feet to the driveway where he's using a Shop-Vac to clean out the inside of my car.

"What are you doing? And why did you tell her? I asked you to let me tell her!" I flip the switch on the vacuum to shut it off.

Zach tosses a glance over his shoulder, confusion on his face until he sees me. "Why did you shut it off?" He backs out from the rear of my car.

"Why did you tell her?"

"I didn't. She's sleeping."

"Then why did you haul all my stuff inside? And why are you cleaning out my car?"

"Christ ..." He tosses the hose aside and sits on the bumper, scrubbing his hands over his face. "Because I know my wife. And instead of waiting for her to wake up and tell me to do exactly what I'm doing right now, I figured I'd get a jump start on it," he mumbles behind his hands before dropping them to his side. "What are you afraid of? Someone helping you? Have you not heard the proverb 'Pride goeth before a fall?'"

After a few seconds of silence between us, I slowly shake my head. "This is so..." I whisper "...humiliating."

"Hey, look at me."

I force my gaze upward.

"Having epilepsy is not your fault. The shitty healthcare system—or lack thereof—in this country is not your fault. Okay?"

I know it's not my fault, but it's still my problem. And things that feel like problems start to feel like mistakes and faults.

"Go let Michelle know you'll stay inside and wait for Suzie to wake up. She's in the laundry room mending a button on Suzie's pants."

I nod while slowly turning, feeling unavoidably weak. Taking two steps, I glance over my shoulder just as he reaches for the switch to turn on the Shop-Vac. "Zach?"

He lifts his head. "Yeah?"

"You're a good man."

After a few beats, he gives me a tiny smile.

So handsome.

So unexpectedly kind.

So ... broken.

If one's soul can leave its body before death, I'm certain Zach's soul is slowly slipping away, chasing Suzie's fading existence in this world. I can't imagine what that kind of love would feel like.

Chapter Eight

MICHELLE FINISHES her sewing project and leaves just as Zach fills a bucket with soapy water to wash my car. Round two of embarrassment.

I curl up on the paisley blue and white chair in the corner of the bedroom and watch Suzie sleep. She's so peaceful. What visions fill her dreams? Does she dream of things in this life? A past life? Maybe she dreams of leaving her sick, frail body and reuniting with her previous love.

"Are you going to watch me sleep all day?"

I grin as Suzie's eyes flutter open. "Only if you're going to sleep all day."

She eases onto her side, facing me. "Why the sad face, Em?" Her voice is different. Not as strong. It's a reminder that she's dying.

And here I am, adding something to her life that she doesn't need. Tears burn my eyes, but I will them away while I pull in a slow, deep breath. "Zach caught me at the park."

Suzie's eyes narrow, making the carved lines around them deepen even more than her lack of proper nutrition has already done. "Caught you? Were you falling?"

On a tiny grunt, my head inches side to side several times. "He caught me napping in my car."

Suzie blinks a few times. "Okay ..."

Averting my gaze to the side, I blow out a shaky breath before returning my attention to her. "My epilepsy has landed me in the hospital several times. No insurance. And ... I had to choose between rent and medication. And student loan debt is on top of that as well. So I've been temporarily living out of my car. But before you decide how to react to this, just know it's not the first time I've lived out of my car. And the fact is I have a car and a job. So I'm not as homeless or ... *desperate* as it might seem. I'm actually quite fine. This is temporary. Nothing lasts forever. Right? I mean ..." My nerves have hijacked my thoughts and sent jumbled words spilling from my lips. "It doesn't make me less courageous. If anything, it's made me more courageous and resilient. So ..." I bite my lips together to stop the incessant rambling.

Something changes in Suzie's expression. I can't decipher it. Easing to sitting, with her back against the padded headboard, she folds her bony, wrinkled hands on her lap. "Okay."

I wait for more.

She doesn't say more.

One word. That's it.

"Okay," I whisper.

"Did Zach offer you one of our guest rooms?"

I nod slowly. "He ... well ... he thought you'd insist I stay, but I'm fine. I don't need to—"

With another wistful smile, she nods once. "Then you'll stay as long as you need to stay."

"That's just it. I don't need to stay."

She shrugs, her body slumped, her smile weak. "Then don't. But make the decision that's best for you and Harry. Don't let your ego make the decision. Don't let pride rob you of the chance to have a bed, a shower, air-conditioning, and more time with your feeble friend before she dies. I would've been too proud. Don't be me. Be better. Live better. Embrace humility because it will make you stronger than the most stubborn pride."

"Suzie ..." Now the emotions come. I won't cry for me, but I'm not strong enough to hide my feelings about the inevitability of losing her. In one blink, a half dozen tears escape all at once, and I brush them away just as quickly.

"It's fate."

I shake my head. There's no fate in cancer. No fate in dying young. It's tragic. She doesn't want to hear that from me because I'm her escape until it's physically impossible for her to escape the end. If mind over matter gives her a few more breaths, maybe several extra days or weeks toward the end, then swallowing—

choking—on my real emotions and suffering this chronic heartache is worth it.

"Fate's a *courageous* word." I sniffle and wipe my eyes one more time while making my way to the bed and crawling up next to her.

She takes my hand, interlacing our fingers and resting her other hand over them. "Zach is going to struggle with this."

This. She's referring to her death.

This or that. No big deal. It's just a life. We probably have many lives. No need to pretend that anything is truly the end of the world.

Internally, I laugh at my thought process. Suzie has imparted her way of thinking upon me. It will come in handy in the coming weeks and months—probably for the rest of my life. We are bonded by optimism, and I don't believe this life is the end of our friendship because it never felt like the beginning. Our souls have met before.

"Many people will struggle with *this*." I chuckle to ward off any more watery emotions.

"Maybe. But Zach will try to fade into a dismal level of nothingness. I just feel it. So I need you not to let that happen."

Another painful laugh. "And how will I do that?"

"I don't know. You'll figure it out. You're smart."

"You did catch the part where my intelligence didn't manage to keep me from living out of my car, right?"

"Just tell me you'll stay here until life takes you in a

new and exciting direction. Promise me you'll stay until you find something truly better."

"That's a lot of pressure. What if I don't find anything better?"

"Then Zach will never be lonely, and that's a perfectly acceptable outcome as well."

I stiffen.

"Don't." She rests her head on my shoulder while giving my hand a little squeeze. "I see the way you look at him, and the way he looks at you."

"Suzie ..." My head shakes and my voice does too. "I don't—"

"You do. You look at him like I looked at him even when I was with Tara. It wasn't love, of course. It was joy—an honor to be friends with such a kind man. Sometimes we start to fall in love with people before our hearts recognize what's happening."

I'm not in love with Zach. My heart is too fond of Suzie, my friend, the sister I never had. Suzie has hit the point where her mind isn't working right.

"Well ... I ... I can tell you Zach doesn't look at me like anything more than the woman who should be cleaning his house instead of watching reality TV with his wife."

"He doesn't see it now. And for the record, he adores you. I think he sees a younger version of me in you. Your spirit. Your kindness."

"Suzie ..." I'm not sure I've ever felt this uncomfortable. This is a terrible conversation.

"Shh ..." She lifts her head from my shoulder. "I'm

not saying anything will come from it. I'm just saying it's okay if something does happen."

Nothing will happen.

Zach will always be Suzie's husband to me. Friends don't fall in love with friends' husbands. I'm fairly certain that's written in stone somewhere.

"Now ..." She releases my hand and presses hers together at her chest like something exciting is about to happen. "Aside from my new best friend moving in with me, tell me something that will ... I don't know ... make me laugh."

I've got nothing.

Except ...

I have a slightly morbid sense of humor, of which I'm certain is a direct result of her bad influence on me.

"Please don't tell your husband that you want the maid to fall in love with him after you're buried six feet under."

Suzie's jaw drops and her eyes widen as her hand flies to her mouth. A second later, she snorts a laugh that breaks completely free in the next breath.

I giggle.

Then we fall inward, collapsing into each other in a fit of laughter like two young girls talking about a mutual crush on a boy in school.

"I won't." She laughs. "It will be our little secret."

"What's your little secret?"

We jump, swallowing our last giggles and holding our breaths as Zach steps into the bedroom.

"If we tell you, it won't be a secret," Suzie says.

I climb off the bed without making eye contact with Zach because I can't. Not yet. Not when Suzie thinks I look at him a certain way.

"I'm ..." I nod toward the door and squeeze past Zach. "I'm going to give you some privacy. Thanks for ... everything. Really."

"It's our pleasure," Suzie says.

I'm not sure taking in a homeless person is a *pleasure*, but it's kind of her—of them—to be so generous.

After organizing my things in the spare bedroom, I sneak out to the kitchen, not expecting to find Zach at the stove cooking something in a big pot.

"Hey."

He turns and smiles. "Hey. I'm making pasta for Suzie. She thinks plain pasta sounds good. Do you like pasta?"

"Oh ..." I shake my head. "You don't need to cook for me. Really, the room is enough. I might pick up a few groceries, but nothing that will take up much space in the fridge. I promise."

"So ... is that a yes or no to liking pasta? If she eats more than three bites, I'll be shocked. That leaves a pound of pasta minus three bites and a full jar of sauce. I work for the next three days which means it will get tossed into the trash. So ... yes or no to liking pasta?"

"Who doesn't like pasta?"

Zach grins. "Grab the jar of sauce from the pantry."

And that's it ... that's all it takes for me to fit into their life.

Chapter Nine

Over the next few weeks, I clean my other clients' homes, mow Zach and Suzie's lawn, take a million photos, *bribe* Suzie to eat, and do whatever I can to free up every possible minute of Zach's time at home so he can spend it with Suzie.

Again, she cycles through good days and bad days. A lot of bad days. I haven't seen a good day in quite a while. It's wearing on Zach.

His anxiety.

His demeanor.

His entire existence seems to fade along with her.

I don't know what to do. Maybe there's nothing I can do.

There's a heavy cloud of suffering in the house that's felt by everyone.

When I arrive home on a Wednesday, just after four o'clock, I'm a little surprised to see Zach's car instead of Michelle's. He told me this morning that he would be home late, his last day working because he can't be away from Suzie right now, not when she's deteriorating so quickly. The house is silent. Too silent. It's more of a chill in the air than a lack of sound that slows my steps.

Meow.

Harry Pawter runs toward me. I pick him up and kiss his head. "Hey, buddy," I whisper. "Is everything okay?" After I set him back on the floor, I tiptoe down the hallway. Suzie's sitting on the edge of her bed in a light blue nightgown, pale feet dangling, hands gripping the side, head bowed. It's the first time I've seen her sitting up in days.

"Hi."

Her head lifts slowly.

"What's wrong?" I pad my way to her and kneel on the floor, resting my hands over hers as she stares at me with teary, red eyes.

"I can't eat," she says in a raspy voice.

"What do you mean? You're not hungry?"

"Nothing will stay down."

She must be less than a hundred pounds.

Protruding bones.

Scaly skin.

Cracked lips.

Her sunken eyes have lost every ounce of shine. Suzie has *lifeless* eyes.

"Okay ... well, have you tried a smoothie?"

"Em ..."

"Maybe some fresh squeezed juice?"

"Em ..."

"Or—"

"Emersyn."

I stop and bow my head, staring at her tiny legs hidden beneath her threadbare nightgown. "Where's Zach?" I whisper.

"He left. He's upset. Michelle wants him to call hospice," she whispers.

I nod. "What can I do for you?"

She leans to the side, a painful moan escaping her chest as she grimaces. I help her lie down then cover her with a blanket.

"Find him."

I nod again. "What do you want me to say to him?"

Closing her eyes, she tries to wet the dry craters covering her lips. "You'll figure it out. You'll ..." her voice begins to fade as she drifts off to sleep. "You'll ... figure ... *him* out."

Beside the bed, there's a tub of lip balm and a cup of swabs. I apply a little balm to her lips then kiss her cheek. I check every room for Zach. Then I check the garage. His bike is here, and his car is in the driveway. He wouldn't go far. I know that much about him. Even if he's upset, he wouldn't leave her for long. That's just not Zach.

Stepping out the patio door, I close it behind me and listen.

Nothing.

"Zach?"

Nothing.

I start to make my way to the side of the house.

"I'm here."

Turning, I spot him sitting just around the corner of the garden shed. Knees pulled to his chest. Hands threaded in his hair, gripping it tightly.

As if any quick movement could scare him away, I tread lightly to the shed. Resting my back against the warm wood siding, I slide down and plant my butt next to him, pulling in my knees just like him. For many minutes, I simply exist beside him.

Waiting.

Searching.

Patiently welcoming any wise words into my mind.

I've got nothing.

"I'm scared out of my mind..." he pauses and swallows "...that I won't be here when she dies."

I nod slowly. Words are too inadequate. I now know why he's home instead of working.

"I'm scared out of my mind ... that I *will* be here when she dies."

My heart is suffocating from his words squeezing it so tightly.

"So ... the selfish asshole part of me just doesn't want to be here. What if I just go first and wait for her?"

Oh, Zach ...

I want to tell him that he would never have had any sort of life with her had she adopted the same mentality after Tara died. But I don't. Zach isn't asking for a pep talk. He's asking for someone to listen to all the thoughts that are going through his head—the raw, honest part of his heart that needs to be set free so he *can* live, so he can be here with Suzie when she leaves this world. Like the ebb and flow of the ocean, the inhale and exhale of breath, life depends on the coexistence of holding on ... and letting go. It's how we navigate this life, mere children struggling to cross the monkey bars without falling.

Sometimes we need a hand to hold.

Sometimes we need someone to hear us.

And sometimes we need a few minutes sitting behind a shed to catch our breath. A tiny timeout from reality. A few moments to reconcile our greatest fears.

"Zach?"

Blowing a long breath out his nose, he turns his head toward me. I can see it in his eyes, that pain bracing for me to say something too emotional, too encouraging, too something.

"The mower is not cutting well. I think you need to sharpen the blades."

I wait.

And wait a little more.

Until ...

A smile steals every inch of his lips, and his eyes redden with tears I know he'll never shed in front of me. On a slow nod, he whispers, "Thanks." A few more nods. "Thanks for telling me."

"Sure." I grin and stand, holding out my hand to him.

Of course, he doesn't need my hand to stand up,

but he takes it anyway. I lean back with all my weight as I pull him up to his feet. We dust off our backsides and risk a glance at each other at the exact same moment. And now that our gazes are locked, I can't look away and neither can Zach.

Not because we're in love.

Not because of any sort of attraction.

No.

It's a silent exchange of respect. I think he's possibly the most wonderful husband to have ever walked the face of the earth. And if I'm reading him correctly, he thinks I'm the worst maid to have ever walked the face of the earth ... but I've done something far greater than keep his house dust-free. And for that, I feel his unspoken gratitude. As I smile, I think he feels my gratitude as well.

"Zach?"

He stops just before reaching the back door.

"She's in pain," I say.

Swallowing hard, he nods slowly and disappears into the house.

Chapter Ten

FOREWARNINGS ARE GREAT. For example, those bumps on roads outside of town to forewarn drivers of an upcoming stop sign. Clouds growing dark before the onset of a storm. And hospice nurses arriving at houses to make sick people as comfortable as possible ... and to forewarn family of what to expect.

Zach calls hospice, which makes it feel like it's only a matter of time until the inevitable. It also feels like forever. It's been a week. A week of moments that have felt like the end. A week of moments that have felt like she's rebounding. Doing better, not worse. How many times can family say a final goodbye? The uncertainty has everyone on edge.

She's on morphine, and that seems to help, but it also robs her of these last chances for coherent moments. It's hard to watch Zach struggle with his desire to keep her out of pain and his desperate need to connect with his wife, not the drugged-up version of her.

Alert but in pain?

Or ...

Sleepy and disoriented?

I'm not sure Zach would have ever called hospice without a nudge. Denial blurs good judgment almost as much as whisky.

For the most part, I keep to myself, holing up in my bedroom with Harry Pawter. As close as I am to Suzie, I'm not her family. So I let them come and go, each time saying that final goodbye, just in case. I've replaced the tissue box in the hall bathroom three times, and I've gone through a whole box myself in the past three days.

As I scroll through my photos, there's a knock at my door. "Come in."

"Can you help me find something in the garage?" Zach asks, a little uneasy. Not frantic, but definitely anxious.

"Sure." I set my camera aside and follow him to the garage.

The boxes that used to be neatly stacked along the wall in the third stall are now scattered everywhere, ripped open and littered with things hanging half out of them.

"What ... are we looking for?" I swallow the lump in my throat and blink away my tears as I open a box that he hasn't torn into yet. The air is thick with tension as waves of restlessness flow from Zach.

"I'm not sure. It's a box that has some stuff from her childhood. Something blue. That's all she said." A nervous voice that could cut through the side of a mountain delivers his words on a rush of harsh, labored breaths.

My heart plummets into my stomach, sending an instant sensation of nausea into my throat—all hot and acidic.

"What about this?" I ask while peering into a box that has some old photo albums, a teddy bear, and a few dolls.

"That's it."

I step aside as he fishes through the contents.

My glass that's always at least half full feels a little on the empty side at the moment. I realize it's not just Suzie. It's Brady. It's Harry Pawter. Mountains of debt and the lies that have come from it. It's being estranged from my mom. It's my lack of friends. It's knowing that my one true friend is dying. It's having slept in a car for months and sometimes fearing for my safety. It's questioning my life and my future.

It's the man standing before me. So tired. And maybe he's thirty-three, but he looks at least fifty right now. A little gray in his hair and peppered in his five o'clock shadow. Permanent worry lines on his forehead. Bags under his eyes. But it's the look in his eyes that says the most.

Lost.

Zach looks irrevocably lost.

So, yeah ... I start crying silent tears that I brush away as quickly as they fall from my burning eyes.

"What do you think she wants out of here?"

He retrieves something that's snagged his attention, pulling out a dangly thing with feathers and beads.

"What is it?" I ask.

He holds it up between us as a sad smile graces his face. "It's a dreamcatcher. Before her mom died, she gave it to Suzanne to protect her from evil spirits and bad dreams. Suzanne was ten. Her mom said it would help Suzanne remember her life ... not her death." His gaze meets mine. "Thank you, Emersyn."

Without blinking, I look at the ceiling and bite my lips together to keep from losing it *again.* "Mmm-hmm."

"She's awake if you want to see her."

See her? He means *say goodbye.*

I hate goodbyes. I'm bad at them. I'm good at looking for any excuse to right wrongs and fix stuff. I'm an artist, a creator. I make things. I mend things. I find the upside to every situation.

Cancer doesn't have an upside.

Death can't be mended.

I can't upload her to Photoshop and erase the cancer.

There is nothing *good* about her dying. So why would I ever say goodbye?

My pain and anger recite ridiculous reasons for what I do and don't want as Zach waits for my answer.

"Okay," I whisper. I've adopted his foolish heart. It's

impossible to love Suzie and not want her here forever. So I don't let myself believe I'm going to say a final goodbye.

Zach opens the door and leads me to their bedroom, but a few feet before the doorway, I stop and press my hand to my chest. This feels too final, and I'm not ready for a final anything.

I can't.

I can't do this.

There's a constricting sensation in my throat, and my chest aches to the point of actual pain. I can't breathe or stop shaking.

Zach turns back toward me.

I don't move an inch. Not a breath. Not a blink. The tiniest of threads holds me together. If I move One. Single. Inch ... I won't just cry. I will sob like the day I left home, a death of its own kind.

Instead of taking the last two steps to the bedroom doorway, Zach retreats until I'm in his arms, his hand on the back of my head pressing my face into his body to stifle my sobs as he walks me backward as quickly as possible to the spare bedroom—my bedroom—on the opposite side of the house, closing the door behind us.

And ...

I cry for all the stupid reasons rolled together in one big breakdown that he doesn't deserve to see, let alone feel burdened with the need to comfort *me*.

Me! He's comforting me when his wife is dying. It's official. I hate myself right now.

I allow myself ten seconds in his embrace, and not

a second more, before I push away and wipe my face. "I'm sorry. Oh god ... I'm so sorry."

"Why are you sorry?" His eyebrows knit together.

My hand covers my mouth as I grapple with my emotions and suffocate from the lump clogging my throat.

"You don't have to be strong for her," he says.

Strong? Is he crazy? I'm not merely lacking strength. I'm an earthquake of emotions—shaking and crumbling from the inside out.

"There's no shame in walking away with the good memories."

I sniffle, shaking my head. "I hate you, Zachary Hays. Killing me with kindness. And ..." I sniffle. "She's not going anywhere. Okay?"

He blinks several times, veiling his emotions. Then he nods because that's what people do when children are on the verge of a breakdown. And right now, I feel like a child with no control of my emotions.

I want Suzie to live, and if she doesn't, I might throw a tantrum.

"I have to get this to her." Pivoting, Zach heads back toward Suzie.

Running my hands through my hair, I close my eyes and shake my head. Suzie would never run away. She'd put on her big girl pants and leave nothing unsaid because that's what courageous people do. Our friendship has only been measured in months, but it feels like years. True friendships form in a single moment and last a lifetime. It sucks that one spring and summer is the lifetime of our friendship.

"You can do this," I whisper. Then I wipe my face again and stop in the bathroom to blow my nose, frowning at my swollen eyes. Praying for two to three minutes of emotional stability, I pad my way to the bedroom and peek around the corner just as Zach sits on the edge of the bed next to Suzie.

He glances over his shoulder and offers me a sad smile, standing again to give me the space next to her. "Look who's here? And she found your dreamcatcher." Zach rests the dreamcatcher on the flat top to their padded headboard just above her.

Her head slowly tips back to see it. "It's for you, silly," she says in a weak, pained voice. "P-put it on your side."

Dagger to my heart ...

Of course it's for him. It's so he only dreams of her life, not her death.

Her comment obviously catches Zach off guard because he swallows hard and clears his throat as I approach the bed.

"Here," he says, extracting a dose of morphine from the bottle on her nightstand and syringing it into her mouth—which means she doesn't have long before she's disoriented and groggy again. He shuffles around to the other side to move the dreamcatcher as Suzie pats the edge of the mattress. I take a seat.

"Thank you," she whispers. She's speaking with the

most clarity I've heard from her in the past week. Again, she's giving us hope. False hope.

I nod, allowing hope back into my heart as my jaw remains locked to keep from losing it.

If Zach looks fifty, Suzie looks eighty right now. There's nothing flattering about one's organs shutting down. There's nothing flattering about starvation and dehydration. Yet, I, like Zach, see the beautiful woman beneath the thin, wrinkled skin that's awfully gray and mottled tonight.

"The answer is yes," she says in a raspy tone.

I narrow my eyes. "What answer?"

She feels for my hand, and I give it to her. Pulling our hands to her chest, she rests them there, a frail smile pulling at her dry lips. "You know. We talked about it. Wh-when the question pops into your head someday..." she blinks heavily "...you'll know the answer is yes."

The only thing worse than a ghost haunting me is living with the answer to an unknown question. We talked about many things. I can't think right now. Something tells me a million questions will pop into my busy mind in the future. Is she saying the answer to everything is yes?

"Okay." I nod. That's what you do for people on their deathbed. You agree to absolutely anything without question.

Take care of my ten cats.

Don't get a tattoo.

Follow your dreams.

Yes. Yes. Yes. Of course. Anything to grant a dying wish.

She's not dying!

My heart and my head battle with so many emotions.

"And keep an eye on Zach."

I glance up at Zach as he takes way more time than should be required to lay that dreamcatcher on the headboard. Those jaw muscles of his pulse as he flexes them. It's his turn to fight *all* the emotions that a forever goodbye creates. I'm twenty-three, so I can only imagine, but what I do imagine is the definition of unimaginable.

What does he think of her request for me to keep an eye on him? I'm sure he's thinking, *"Just what I need, the maid keeping an eye on me."*

To appease all parties involved, I return a simple nod before leaning down to hug her. Is this it? Is this the last time I'll see her alive? How will I know when she's dead? Will Zach come tell me? Will I hear him crying? Will an ambulance come to get her body? Maybe a text is sufficient, so I'll know when it's okay to come out of my room. It's not like I can ask him now, right here in front of her.

"Yo. Mind shooting me a text when she passes?"

Grief and fear do weird things to a person. I can't believe this shit is going through my mind. I don't even say the word *yo*.

I should feel grateful that I'm only losing it on the

inside. Outwardly, I've managed to present the resemblance of an emotionally stable human being.

It's time. Goodbye is not the word I want to say. I said it to my mom, knowing I might never see her again. But I can't say it to Suzie. And it's silly if I'm going to see her in the morning anyway.

"Okay," Suzie whispers. "You say o-okay when you d-don't know what else to say. It's ... i-it's acceptance."

I squeeze her hand, not wanting to accept her impending death.

She returns a weak squeeze. "You don't ... have ... to l-like it. I accept my fate ... b-but I don't like it."

Zach clears his throat, sitting on the opposite side of the bed with his back to us. Is he hiding his emotions too?

I slowly stand and just as slowly release her hand. Tears fill my eyes again, so I know it's time to leave. "Okay."

"Okay," she repeats.

I turn and blink, setting free a new round of silent tears as I exit their bedroom, holding my breath until my chest burns.

Beyond the pain and unfairness of it all, I find something to hold on to—I was very lucky to have been in Suzie's life, even if it was for a short amount of time. I will never forget her, and I will always miss our friendship.

Chapter Eleven

Zach

"We n-need to say ... all ... the things th-that need to be s-said," Suzie whispers a few minutes after Emersyn leaves.

I grip the side of the bed until my hands go numb and my head feels too heavy to lift. "We have time." My denial is childish, but this crippling helplessness makes me *feel* like a child. Where are my mother's arms when I need them? Can I hide under the bed until this nightmare ends?

For the past few days, during her short coherent moments between morphine doses, she's asked me to say all the things that need to be said. If I don't say them, then she won't die. That's my new level of reasoning because it's worked thus far. I don't say it. She lives.

She's in pain ...

"Zach ..."

"Don't say it." My voice cracks like my heart—like my soul.

"Just ... h-hold me."

The anger inside builds until I can't find a breath, until my ears ring, until I can barely see through the tears blurring the life that's slipping away from me.

I'm. So. Fucking. Angry.

And I don't know who or what is to blame. Suzanne is a better person than I am—times infinity. The morning of the day Tara died, I'm sure she said all the right things, did all the right things. Suzanne never leaves things unsaid because she knows every second matters. She's practiced in losing part of her heart while holding on to her dignity and doing the right thing. That's not me.

I don't want to hold her until she stops breathing.

I don't want to give her permission to die.

I don't want to tell her that I'll be okay.

No.

I want to beat my fists into the wall until they bleed.

I want to yell and give the whole goddamn world the middle finger—the biggest fuck-you ever.

I want to kiss her until she's no longer just herself, until we are one, and I can fight this for her.

Breathe for her.

Beat for her.

Live for her.

"B-be mad."

Her words lift my head, and I turn it a fraction as if to confirm I heard her correctly.

"Be mad, Zach." It's a whisper, barely even a breath, but I hear her. I understand her.

Tiny muscles in my face twitch as I clench my jaw and fight the burning in my eyes.

Be mad, Zach.

Grabbing the lamp on my nightstand, I hurl it across the room. "FUUUCK!" It shatters. My chest heaves with heavy breaths. My heart rages. Next, I punch the wall a half dozen times, "IT'S. SO. GODDAMN. UNFAIR!" until it's cracked and stained with my blood.

Suzanne blinks and a single tear trails down her cheek as her lips quiver.

My face scrunches while a sob chokes me. Pointing toward the door, I shake my head. "It's not *okay*. It might be okay for her." I jab my finger signifying Emersyn. "But it's not okay for me. It will never be okay. So don't ask me to say okay. Don't ask me to say goodbye. Don't ask me t-to ..." I grimace from the pain in my chest as I press my palms to the side of my head.

"I l-love you too," she says, closing her eyes and shaking with emotion. "A-and I ... I'm s-scared."

I freeze. Shocked by her confession. Stunned.

She can't even begin to understand how much I've needed to hear this. Her strength has made me feel so weak. Her acceptance has made me feel ungrateful.

My wife is dying, and it's awful. I *need* it to be awful.

That is the only thing that is *okay* with me. I can only accept the truth.

It's unimaginable.

It's cruel.

It's wrong.

It's harrowing.

It's tragic.

Her death holds no purpose.

I will never be okay with it. There might not be a light at the end of this tunnel. And I can't imagine there will come a day that my heart won't feel severed, a day it won't bleed, a day that I will accept this.

In the next breath, I'm at her side, pulling her into my arms as I kiss her head.

With a single light on us, I slide into bed next to her and hold her so tightly I fear I might break her frail body. I know I can't keep death from prying her from my hold, but it doesn't stop me from trying.

I breathe in the floral scent of the lotion I've applied to her skin for weeks and the faint vanilla from the lip balm.

Several hours later, she shifts in my arms, moaning a bit. I feel her pain. I hate her pain so much.

"Do you need more for the pain?" I whisper, kissing her forehead.

She doesn't open her eyes, she just mumbles something.

"What, babe?" I lift onto one elbow and adjust the pillow under her head. "Better?"

"The rabbit ... don't go." Another painful moan.

I narrow my eyes at her mumbling. "Are you having a dream? Are you awake?" I kiss her forehead over and over again, unsure of what to do for her—unsure of what to do with the fear clawing at my chest.

She stills and I still with her.

No. No. No ...

Then her lips part and she draws in a breath—a sharp but shallow breath like she's been holding it.

I exhale too, feeling relieved. "Don't scare me like that." I kiss the corner of her mouth, lingering for seconds.

Again, she moans. It's been this way for too long. In and out. Dancing with death. What a terrible dance it is.

She's suffering ...

This isn't love. I'm holding on too tightly, and it's killing her *slowly*. This isn't ... love.

So I say it. I say what I think one is supposed to say if they truly love someone. "It's okay, baby." I swallow hard as more tears fill my burning eyes. "You can go," I whisper in her ear. "You ... can ... go ..."

Another moan. I hate it. HATE. IT!

If God wants her so badly, then why doesn't he just take her?

For another hour I hold her, listening to her shallow breaths, one foot in this life and one in the next. She gurgles a bit. Fucking death rattle.

I sit up and stare at the bottle of sublingual morphine on her nightstand. It's been hours. She needs more. I don't want her in pain. No more pain.

No.

More.

Pain.

I fill the syringe.

My shaky hand moves the syringe to her lips, the tip of it disappearing between the crease, and I slowly press the plunger.

I start to set the syringe on the nightstand, but I stop. Suzanne taught me patience, but she also taught me mercy. Refilling the syringe, more tears blur my vision.

I love her. I love her this much. I am her rock. These same words loop in my head as I give more ... and more ... as I give her mercy.

I lie next to my wife for the last time, and that time vanishes as I listen to her heart beat until ... it doesn't.

One.

Two.

Three.

Four.

I feel nothing.

"Baby?" I press my hand to her cheek.

She doesn't move.

A silent panic snakes up my spine, wrapping itself into a noose around my neck. I rest my ear on her chest.

And I wait.

I wait for a beat.

I wait for a breath.

Five.

Six.

Seven.

Eight.

I wait.

I did this. I did it for her. I *was* her rock, even in death. "I love you," I whisper. "I love you *this* much."

This rock is broken.

Chapter Twelve

THE SUN SHINES, but I don't feel it. As I sit in the jungle with Suzanne's quilt over me, my family and hers mill around the house, whispering and sniffling. I'm sure they're in pain too, but I can't feel anything past my own gutted chest. An hour after they took her body away from me, I sent out a group text to everyone. I just sent one message to everyone in my contacts. I bet there are some people in there, like my hair stylist and a few of our favorite restaurants, who won't know how to respond to: she died.

There's not much for me to do. Suzanne planned everything before she died, including the music that will be played at her funeral. She asked her sister to read her favorite E.E. Cummings poem, and her friend, April, will sing something entirely too inspirational for death. I only have one job—be the grieving husband.

Done.

If I could make money grieving Suzanne, I'd be a

very rich man. For a guy with many talents (or so my family and friends have always said), I think grieving is my new profession. I pride myself on being the best at whatever I set out to do. Watch out, world, I'm going to be a fucking pro at this.

No need to eat.

No need to shower.

No need to speak.

No need to move.

If I stop breathing … so be it.

At the moment, I kinda hate my life and all life in general. Suzanne would be disappointed at my lack of strength and perseverance. Fuck it. I'll persevere in my next life. In the meantime, some dead chick named Tara is reuniting with my wife. She's probably already forgotten about me.

The ironic part? Nobody is taking the time to even acknowledge me. I haven't been asked to do anything. No questions about plans. Just a wide perimeter of space. Ten bucks says Suzanne left this part in her post-death instructions as well.

Leave Zach alone. He's a pathetic pussy who will try to crawl into a ball and die. Give him a few days, then shove him into the shower and put him in that gray suit that looks so handsome on him. He wears black for work, and I don't want him to look like he's grieving. It's not a funeral. It's a celebration of life.

Okay, newsflash … if you want people to celebrate your life, you have to live. You have to *have* a life. Dying earns you a funeral, blubbering over your casket, and organ music.

The day passes. People come and go. Plates of untouched food on the TV tray next to me get replaced every few hours with fresh food. Then I'm blanketed in silence, and the lights go off. It's dark outside. I have no idea what time it is, so I close my eyes and go to sleep. Maybe Suzie will be back in the morning. Maybe Tara's gained a little too much weight in the afterlife or she's straight, or she's found some hot dead chick, and Suzie will decide to come back and fight a little harder to live. Yeah, I'm banking on that.

That I'd be *okay* with.

As EXPECTED, by the third day—the day of the funeral —my dad and brother haul my ass out of the chair and put me in the shower.

"Fuck!" My back arches when the cold water hits me, taking my breath away.

"Good ..." My dad snickers. "You feel that. Guess that means my oldest son is still alive. I was starting to wonder if you'd make it."

My teeth chatter.

"Soap up." Aaron forces a bar of soap into my hand before squeezing a shit-ton of shampoo onto my head.

I stand in place and shiver, letting the bar of soap fall from my hand with a *thunk* at my feet.

"I'm not crawling between your legs to pick that up.

So bend down, pick it up, and wash your dirty ass." Aaron gives my face a few firm slaps.

My gaze slides to his.

He frowns and deflates with a sigh. "I don't have a good pep talk for you at the moment because I loved her too. We all did. But she wanted you there today. And it's my job to get you there in some sort of presentable form. So unless you want Mom coming in here to wash your naked, grown ass, get to scrubbing."

I stare at the soap on the floor of the shower for several seconds as the water warms up. Then I bend down and pick up the dented bar of soap. My body slowly goes into autopilot. I just want this day to end, but it feels like everything is on hold, waiting for me to do my part. And grieving husbands go to their wives' funerals. I suppose that is my part. So I shower.

I shave.

I dress.

I get into the car waiting out front for me.

I sit in the front row staring at her casket.

People talk. People sing. The poem is read.

At some point, I hear laughter, but I'm not sure what's said to draw such a reaction. It could be one of a million stories about Suzanne. She had a way of bringing joy and laughter to everyone she encountered. I could use a little right now, but she took it all with her.

After the final prayer, we're ushered out behind the casket. I don't have to greet anyone, hence the reason Suzanne didn't request a visitation. She knew I wouldn't like that. Always thinking of me, first and foremost.

The burial ends in a blink. My mom releases my hand and whispers something in my ear. I think it's, "Take your time," but honestly, my senses are still numb, and I'm cognitively sluggish.

A few minutes later, there's a gentle tug on the arm of my suit jacket, and I turn. "Hey." Emersyn blots her eyes with a tissue in one hand while holding out a bouquet of fuchsia tulips with her other hand.

I stare at them for a few seconds. "Did she tell you to bring these?"

Emersyn shakes her head. "No." Exhaling a nervous laugh, she shrugs. "I think she probably assumed you'd bring them. But ... I'm sure you've had other things on your mind. So I grabbed a bouquet on my way ... just in case."

Taking the bouquet, I meet her red-eyed gaze. Her blond hair whips in her face as the wind picks up. It's supposed to storm later today. I'm not sure how I know that. I think I heard my dad say it on our way to the cemetery. It's amazing I registered it. "Thank you," I murmur.

"You're welcome." She averts her gaze and twists her fingers together in front of her. "Well, I'll give you some privacy. If you need anything, you know where to find me ... for now. I'll be out soon. It's high on my list." She nervously moves her mouth so fast, I can't catch all her words or their meaning. God, I hope she's not telling me anything important. I can't do important today.

When she finishes her spiel that I believe ends with her tidying up the house and mowing the lawn, I nod once.

She inspects me with a world of pain in her eyes for several seconds before pivoting and tiptoeing in her heels out of the grass to the stone path. The last time I heard Suzanne laugh to the point of snorting, she was beached out on our bed with Emersyn, watching *Bridesmaids* on the TV. It was such an unexpected friendship.

"This is it, my love." I rest my hand on the shiny wood casket while laying the tulips next to the large spray of flowers in the middle. "I pulled it together enough to be here." Tears sting my eyes while I swallow past the mass of grief in my throat. After holding it together throughout the entire funeral and burial service, the reality of the very last goodbye hits me so hard in the chest I can't find a breath.

My feet remain rooted to the ground for so long I can't feel my toes. Blinking over and over, I wait to wake from this nightmare. I wait for God to say, "Oops, wrong person. Suzanne is too young and too good to take so early. My bad. Go home, she'll be waiting for you in the garden. She's picking vegetables for dinner tonight."

Thunder sounds in the distance.

I don't move.

The wind picks up.

I don't move.

Sideways rain slaps my face despite the tent over my head.

I don't move.

I know someone, most likely my family, is somewhere watching me. They're giving me space and time. They know we can't reschedule this moment to another time or day, so if it rains ... it rains. I won't melt. I will dry. I will live.

I'll live without her.

Chapter Thirteen

Emersyn

I'LL NEVER FORGET the clatter of the lamp crashing against the wall or the *thump thump thump* of Zach's fist making a hole in it.

I'll never forget his blank stare and lifeless voice on the day of the funeral.

But more than any other moment in my life ... I'll never forget what I saw him do.

I shouldn't have been there, but after all the commotion, the yelling, the banging, and the tornado of anger, I needed to know if he was okay. Standing in the shadows of the hallway just outside of their bedroom, with barely a sliver of visibility, I watched. Crying my own silent tears, my hand cupped to my mouth to prevent a single peep from escaping, I witnessed Zach saying goodbye—his face twisted in agony, every time she moaned, stabbing a knife into my heart.

Time vanished. Had it been minutes? Hours? I had no clue. Grief paralyzed me. A numbing pain settled into my extremities until the only thing I felt was the burdensome thudding of my heart.

Zach slowly sat up.

I managed a heavy blink and a tiny step backward.

His shaky hands filled the syringe with morphine. The expected, the norm, the routine ... it turned into something else. It took a moment to register what I was witnessing. My mind screamed, *"What are you doing?"*

My heart answered that question. It knew. It understood.

I had to leave. I had to escape to my room before he saw me. I wasn't supposed to be there. Whatever name there was for what he did, it wasn't mine to bear witness. Holding my breath, my shock, and my strangled sobs, I tiptoed my bare feet back to my room. I left Zach with the final goodbye and her last breath because it belonged to him ... and him alone.

"You have my number. Call if he doesn't eat or get out of bed by at least noon. Okay?" his brother Aaron says to me as he opens the front door to follow his parents to their cars congested in the driveway.

I shake my head for a second, bringing my thoughts back to the present. "Uh ... yeah."

Today, his family is officially leaving him by himself. I'm not sure if they've been on suicide watch for this past week since her funeral, but someone, besides me, has been here the whole time. Day and night.

As for me, I've stayed in my room and out of the way since the night she died. I think their families have forgotten I'm here, except when I've slithered out of my room to tidy the kitchen or clean out the fridge and freezer to accommodate all the food.

"Emersyn?"

My gaze shoots to Aaron's, and I force a smile. "Yes. I've got this. No problem," I say with questionable confidence as I pretend I've got this.

After a moment's pause, Aaron nods. "Thanks. Talk soon."

The door shuts behind him, and the house is silent for the first time in a week. I pad my way to his bedroom—their bedroom—to check on him. Zach is curled on his side—jeans, no shirt, hugging a pillow. I think it's Suzie's pillow. He's holding her.

It's a few minutes before seven. I'm not sure if he had dinner, but I'm not going to ask. I won't say a word to him tonight. I'll deal with him tomorrow. After taking a few steps, I turn and go to the plant room. Snatching Suzie's quilt from her chair, I take it to the bedroom and drape it over Zach before closing his door to keep Harry Pawter from bothering him.

I have to be the one in the house who takes care of myself so that Zach can be the one who's broken and lost. That means I will eat, work, shower, and be everything he cannot be yet.

The next morning, I water her garden and the plants in her jungle.

Her ... are these things still hers? When one dies, can things still belong to them? Does Zach wonder if *she* still belongs to him? Or has she found Tara? That thought must hurt.

At 12:01 p.m., I knock gently on his bedroom door.

No answer.

I ease it open. Zach is in the exact same position as he was last night.

"Zach?"

No answer.

I don't know what to do. Aaron seems to trust me. Why? That's a mystery. Suzie trusted me too, as if she thought I'd have this magical Zach intuition after she died.

I don't.

Part of me wants to pack my bags, grab Harry, and leave. Never looking back. Does Zach even care if I clean the house now? Probably not.

Does he want me here? Probably not.

Does he need me? I don't know. I try to put myself in his shoes and imagine what I would want or need. But when I do this, I imagine him wanting everyone to leave him alone and let him decide what happens next. Let him decide if he wants to go on or if he wants to chase her into the next life by leaving this one now.

While I think on it, I take a seat in that paisley chair a few feet from the bed. There's just enough light prying through the blinds to let me see his face. Pulling my knees to my chest, I wait.

Nearly an hour later, he opens his eyes. It's so slow and hesitant; I imagine the sound of a door creaking open against the will of its stiff hinges.

"Hi," I whisper.

After a few blinks, he returns a gravelly, "Hi."

"I'm supposed to get you out of bed and feed you. But I'm okay with you not eating until dinner. I just ..." I swallow. "I just can't let you ..."

Die?

Can I say that? No.

"I can't let you check out. Sorry."

With painfully stiff movements, he pushes his body to a sitting position. His bare feet dangle off the edge of the bed. "I have to take a piss."

"Of course." I stand. "I'll let you do that by yourself."

He leans forward, resting his hands on his knees before lumbering to standing. "That would be great." There's no detection of life in his voice, but he's standing on his own. That's something. I'll take that small victory today.

I close the bedroom door behind me and retrieve a bowl of pasta salad from the fridge, giving it a quick sniff.

So much food ...

As I spoon some into a bowl, Zach appears a few feet behind me. "Oh ... hi. Um ... I'm having pasta salad. Do you want some?"

In his right hand is a wadded-up shirt. After giving me a blank stare for a few seconds, he nods and wrestles with his shirt, threading his arms and head through the holes. Then he takes a seat at the table. As I spoon salad into a bowl for him, he stares at the empty chair beside him where Suzie always sat.

Where she will never sit again.

We eat in silence. Zach goes back to bed until the next day. We repeat the same routine for several days, only it's not pasta salad the next day. It's a chicken and rice dish.

Taco casserole.

Lasagna.

We will never run out of food.

Aaron and his mom text me to check in every day. I fudge the report, saying he's doing pretty well. Eating. Getting out of bed. I just don't mention that he only gets out of bed for an hour and he's only eating one meal.

With each passing day, he stays out of bed a little longer. He showers. His family visits. And I get back to my normal routine. But we don't talk. Zach doesn't say much to anyone. He's perfected the tiny fake smile and easy nod that makes everyone think he's hearing them. And I'm sure he does hear us, but I know he's not listening.

Zach is with Suzanne—straddling this life and the next one—figuring out where he belongs, where he can find happiness. I see it. The eyes don't lie. They can't, not like faking a smile, not like nodding or murmuring the occasional, "Mmm-hmm." Is he missing her? Is that what consumes him the most? Or is he thinking about what he did? *That* consumes me the most.

Chapter Fourteen

Zach

"Oh ..." Emersyn jumps as she turns away from the toaster. "You're working?" She eyes me in my uniform. Face shaven. Hair combed.

I'm playing the part.

"Yeah." I sidestep her and reach for the pot of coffee she made.

Emersyn's done everything.

Cooked.

Cleaned.

Mowed.

Laundry.

"That's good. I think." She clears her throat and sits at the table.

I sip my coffee and lean against the counter, giving a shrug. "It's work."

"It's a..." she bites her lower lip, maybe weighing

her words for a beat "...logical choice. Since you have a job."

"Sure." I stare past her, out the window, for several seconds. "I retired the grieving husband. I cut the anchor. It doesn't matter how unfair I think life is; I can't change my reality. It's just me and time. It's moving forward without me. And I'm ... stuck in the middle, suffocating. I feel like I've been dragged for miles." I close my eyes. "Everything hurts, but I'm still alive. Everything hurts, but she's still gone."

Her gaze remains affixed to her toast like a safe zone.

"I go to the grocery store ... because I'm tired of family and friends leaving food on my doorstep. And ..."

She risks a glance up at me before I continue, "... the other day, somewhere between the bread aisle and the refrigerated section, I realized I'd put ten things into my cart without thinking about her." My eyes close for a brief second. "And I felt terrible. I felt like a parent who left a child behind because they were too distracted. How did I let myself get distracted by things so insignificant like tomato sauce and peanut butter?"

"I'm not staying with you," she blurts out so quickly, it takes me a second to register her words. Emersyn's nose crinkles while she brings her toast to her mouth, taking rabbit-sized nibbles. Eyes wide.

I haven't missed the way her gaze tracks me, the way she stiffens in my presence. Is she tiptoeing around something?

"You've helped," I say, trying to relieve her palpable anxiety. "Just being here and not being like my family … not looking at me like my family looks at me … it's helped. Thank you."

Emersyn blinks several times and fumbles her words before managing a clipped, "You're welcome." She clears her throat. "What I mean is … it's been my pleasure. Well, pleasure isn't the right word … I'm just saying, it is I who should thank you for letting me continue to stay here since Suzie …" She bows her head and pinches the bridge of her nose.

"She died," I say, just before sipping my coffee. Who knew two words could gut me all over again?

"What time is your flight?" Emersyn manages to glance up at me again.

"Eleven."

She nods.

"Where are you going?"

"Orlando. Dallas. Back to Atlanta."

"Will you be home for dinner? Uh …" She shakes her head. "That sounds so …"

"No," I say.

"Me neither. I'm going to meet up with some … one." Her gaze averts to the window.

"A date? That's good." I dump the rest of my coffee into the sink and put the mug into the dishwasher.

"A date," she repeats my words like she's deciphering what that is.

"Enjoy your date." I head toward the door to the garage.

"Have a safe flight."

"Thanks." The door closes behind me, and I pause, taking a deep breath. "I'm going, babe," I whisper before my feet take reluctant steps to my car. "I'm ... going."

———

OVER THE NEXT MONTH, I take all the flights I can get. I feel closer to Suzanne when I'm flying. And when I'm home, I feel nothing but a big void because she no longer resides in all the places I've been used to seeing her.

The jungle.

Our bed.

The garden.

The fucking empty vanity stool in the bathroom.

It's weird having Emersyn here. It's not like it was with Suzanne. It's not like it's ever been with any roommate I've had before. We don't see each other that much. We both work a lot. When I'm home, I jog and visit my parents. Emersyn spends her free time taking photos or staying holed up in her room editing them. Occasionally, she burrows into the corner of the sofa, like she doesn't want to take a full cushion, and works on her computer. Suzanne used to love watching her tweak the images in Photoshop. She said it was soothing, the epitome of satisfying.

Sometimes we cross paths in the kitchen. If I'm around, I'll make us dinner, but Emersyn wolfs it down and escapes to her bedroom with Harry Pawter. Tonight, I want her to stay.

"Want to open a bottle of wine with me?" I ask as she stands to take her plate to the dishwasher.

She pauses, eyes wide like she needs to verify that I'm talking to her. "What do you mean?"

Chuckling, I shrug. "I mean, do you want to have some wine? With me? Tonight? But if you have a date or something else to do, that's fine. Just thought I'd ask."

"O-kay." She's been giving me the deer-in-the-headlight look a lot. I think she's tiptoeing around me, afraid that I'm nothing but a broken man taking in the stray.

I clear my plate and retrieve a bottle of wine and two glasses. Emersyn plunks down at the table again.

"We can sit in the living room."

"O-kay."

Her apprehension makes me laugh again. It feels good to smile without putting forth a lot of effort. With each passing day, I start to see all the things Suzanne saw in Emersyn. She's kind and polite. And her big blue eyes light up when she sees me—the way they did when she looked at Suzanne. Maybe it's her youth too. I find myself staring at her with contentment when she does tuck herself into the corner of the sofa (like now), scrolling through her photos and social media apps—occasionally glancing over at me with a tiny grin. Suzanne was right. It's soothing. She's soothing.

By the time I pour two glasses and peek into the

living room, Harry Pawter's at her feet in a similar balled up position, not taking up more than one of the three cushions on the sofa.

"Thanks." She gives me a nervous smile when I hand her the glass before taking a seat at the opposite end of the sofa.

"So ..." Things are awkward. They weren't this awkward when Suzanne was alive. "How's work?"

She shrugs. "Good." After taking a sip of her wine, she gives me a tight smile. "How's your job going?"

"Good." I internally kick myself for echoing her reply. I'm a grown-ass man who should know how to carry on a conversation beyond one-word replies. "It's been a good distraction. I love to fly. Always have. And it's been a while since I've worked for longer periods like I've been doing lately."

"Go anywhere fun?"

"Two days ago, I was in Shanghai."

"Your first time?"

"No." I grin. "Have you done any international traveling?"

"Absolutely. Mexico for spring break my second year of college." Her soft laughter fills the room as if the wine is already relaxing her.

That sound. It's not Suzanne, and I know it. I'm well aware that Emersyn is not Suzanne, but my wife was quite taken by this young woman. And ... well, I guess I feel like I want to *feel* something too.

Can she make me smile?

Can she make me laugh?

141

Can she help me escape my reality—even if only for a little while?

"Mexico is good." I bring my wineglass to my lips to hide my grin, the grin I've made myself believe can't be real. When Suzanne died, I knew nothing that felt good would ever be real. And while I can't help but think I'll regret this later—that I won't be able to escape the guilt for stealing a breath of happiness—I let it in for a moment or two. I allow a smile to claim my face, instantly feeling the endorphins numb some of the pain.

Emersyn's wry grin tells me there's a lot more to her Mexico trip story. She makes me miss my early twenties, when I spent my time flying around the globe without a care in the world.

Before Suzanne.

Before cancer.

Before death.

"It's my dream to one day travel the world with my camera." Her eyes light up like the rest of her face. It feels good. Warm and bright.

Again, I see a little more of the Emersyn that drew Suzanne to her.

After another sip of wine, she rubs her lips together and hums. "It's funny ... many people think that spending so much time taking pictures means you're missing the bigger picture—like you're only seeing life through a tiny lens." She shrugs, swirling her wine. "I think that's fifty percent true. But there's another side. Life moves so quickly, we often miss some of the subtle moments that hold so much emotion. Tiny expressions that last no longer than a breath—the sun just seconds before disappearing behind the clouds. These micro moments deserve to be remembered and savored. That's why I love taking photos of everything. I feel like I capture far more than I miss."

Harry Pawter makes his own catwalk to me and stretches out across my lap.

Emersyn's eyes widen as her jaw unhinges. "Harry Pawter? What is this about? Are you a traitor?"

I stroke his back and smile like I've won some contest. "If you must know, we hang out a lot when I'm here and you're at work. Just us guys."

Her expression softens, and her gaze slides from him to me. "I have a stupid fine arts degree that I may never use. A stupid amount of student loan debt. And it makes me feel ..."

"Stupid?"

She grins and nods. "Yeah."

"Then why did you get that degree?"

She shrugs a shoulder. "Self-worth. My mom used to complain that she couldn't find a good-paying job because she didn't have a college degree. And I haven't been certain about a lot in my life, but one thing I've never wavered on is my determination to not be like her. So here I am ... broke and homeless. That plan went to shit. Right?"

"Shit happens."

She snorts and quickly takes a drink of wine to

hide the rest of her amusement. A few breaths later, her smile vanishes and she stares at her wine glass. "Zach, do you remember when you told me about your trip to the store after Suzie died? You didn't think about her for a little while and it felt bad? You wondered how you let yourself get distracted by things so insignificant like tomato sauce and peanut butter? And I didn't answer you. I didn't know *how* to answer that kind of question."

I return a slow nod.

"Do you still feel that guilt?" she asks.

"I ... I don't know." It's true. I still don't know how to navigate the future without clinging to the past *and* without forgetting every little thing that made me love her. I have a whole jar of those reminders in my bathroom. "Why do you ask?"

"Because I'm here. And I've been here longer than I ever planned on staying. I not only feel indebted to you for your generosity ... I feel indebted to Suzie for being my friend. And I know she'd want me to make sure you're good. Ya know? Make sure you're not crippled by her death. I mean, I see you go to work and make meals. I just hope you don't feel bad if you think of peanut butter and tomato sauce without thinking about her at the same time."

I release the hint of a laugh despite the pain that's still alive in my chest. "Is that a litmus test for my mental health? Peanut butter and tomato sauce thoughts without her?"

"Well..." she lifts a shoulder "...yeah, I suppose it is."

"It's hard. The guilt is still there, just not as demanding. I don't know what's okay. What's normal and healthy? How many times a day is it okay to think of her? Is it okay to look at pictures of her? Is it time to go through her side of the closet? And what do I keep? What do I give away? She's ... everywhere yet nowhere. Is she thinking of me? Does she see me? Hear my thoughts? Feel my pain? Or has she moved on? Has she reunited with her Tara?"

"How does that feel?"

I squint at her. "How does what feel?"

She picks at some of the cat hair on my sofa. "How does it feel to think that she sees you? That she can hear your thoughts or feel your pain? Is that what you want? Does it make you feel less lonely? Does it ease some of the pain? Because I think I would hate it." Her nose wrinkles. "No offense. I'm just saying ... I would hate feeling like everything I thought, did, or felt could be scrutinized by someone who is no longer here to share it with me. I'm sure in moments that are good, you'll naturally wish she were here to see and experience the moment. But what happens when you trip? We all trip. We all make mistakes and have thoughts that we wouldn't want anyone to know we're thinking."

"It ..." My response feels instant, but the second I open my mouth the truth behind her words sinks in, and I question everything. "I don't know. Her voice is still in my head."

"What's she saying?"

"Do it."

"Do what?" She chuckles and tucks her blond hair behind her ears.

"I don't know."

But I do. I know.

She's waiting on me to make a difference in someone else's life. It's like she won't truly rest until I do. Maybe I won't stop hearing her voice until I do. Am I ready to stop hearing her voice? It's only been two months.

Only? Already?

I have no idea where time fits into this equation anymore. Have I been too slow to move on? Too quick? *Was* it terrible of me to think about peanut butter and tomato sauce and not her?

"You should call Michelle and ask her to help you clean out Suzanne's closet. She might want some of her clothes. And her family and yours would probably love to see that you're taking that step."

"I can't do that."

"Oh ... sorry. Too soon? I get it."

I shake my head. "If I ask Michelle, she will weep the whole time."

Emersyn drains the rest of her wine and sighs while standing. "Well, you clearly need to *do something*. If you don't want her voice haunting you for the rest of your life, I suggest you figure it out."

My lips twist as I think about her words.

"Thank you for dinner and the wine. It's been—"

"Will you do it?" I ask.

She taps her empty wineglass against her chin. "Do what?"

"Put all her things in boxes."

"You should go through them."

I shake my head. "I'm keeping her quilt and the dreamcatcher. That's it."

"Are you sure?"

"Does that make me a pathetic dick in your eyes?"

She laughs and stumbles back a few steps. "Are you really worried about being a pathetic dick in my eyes?"

I frown. "Well, I am now that you basically dodged that question."

Emersyn leans down and presses her fingers to the inside of my wrist.

"What are you doing?"

"Checking for a pulse. Good news. You have one, therefore you are the strongest man I know because you lost your wife and kept going. That's a superhero kind of power, Zach. You might be my new idol." She smirks and saunters to the kitchen. "Don't be surprised if I get a little crush on my superhero roommate."

It's funny. It's cute. It's ... confusing as hell.

Chapter Fifteen

TWO DAYS LATER, I finish my last route and head home for a three-day weekend. On my way, I purchase fuchsia tulips and take them to Suzanne's grave. I miss her, but I don't miss seeing her in pain, and that's what I focus on when I visit her. Today, I give her my blessing to be with Tara. I want her to be loved —always.

After a "See you later, my love," I grab some groceries and drive home to my roommate and Harry Pawter.

"Hello?" I say, toeing off my shoes and shutting the front door. To my right are three rows of boxes with labels.

Sweaters.

Shoes.

Dresses.

I can't help my smile. Emersyn went through Suzanne's closet for me. For a few seconds a little guilt comes over me. Maybe I should have forced myself to do it. Maybe I should have invited Michelle over to help and just endured her weepiness. Truthfully, I didn't want her to make me cry again. I'm past that. I've learned to feel the pain without letting it crush me, but I know she would bring it out of me again.

"Emersyn?"

Harry Pawter meows and traipses around the corner, making red paw prints on the wood floor.

Blood. So much blood.

"Emersyn!" I gulp my next breath and trudge through my fear, driven around the corner to the kitchen on a nauseating wave of panic. The bloody paw prints lead me to the other side of the island. "Jesus ..." For a nanosecond, I pause, unsure of what to do first. "Emersyn ..." I hunch next to her bloodied body as I reach for my phone.

"9-1-1. What is your emergency?"

"I need an ambulance for a young woman. She's fallen into the open dishwasher racks, and there's broken glass and blood everywhere. She has epilepsy. I think she may have had a seizure."

Emersyn tries to move her hand, but there's a thick shard of glass lodged into her forearm. She's bleeding all over—her arms, her face, her neck.

"A-Zach ..." Emersyn starts to cry, her breaths erratic as if what happened just registered.

"It's okay. Just try to hold still."

I confirm my address and attempt to answer a series of questions for the operator. As much as I want to help her, I'm afraid to move her, especially with glass wedged into her neck so close to her carotid artery. That familiar helplessness I felt with Suzanne comes rushing back like a hundred-pound weight crushing my chest.

Aside from keeping Harry Pawter out of the way, there's nothing I can do when the paramedics arrive.

"Is she your wife?"

Tearing my gaze away from the congestion of men and women around Emersyn, I focus on the woman asking me that question. "No," I whisper. "My wife died."

She doesn't need to know that. I'm not sure why I said it.

This question gets asked again and again.

By another medic.

And once we get to the hospital, I'm asked the same question by several nurses there.

"Does she have family we can contact?"

I shake my head, trying to see past the second nurse questioning me as they take Emersyn through two big metal doors. A cold draft replaces her presence for a few seconds until the doors close again.

I fucking hate the cold, the bitter antiseptic smell, the suffocating lifelessness of hospitals.

"She doesn't have any family or emergency contacts?" I'm asked again.

Another slow headshake. My brain can barely see through the thick fog. "She lives with me. She's a ... friend. I suppose I'm her emergency contact."

When they determine I'm completely useless, I take a seat in the waiting room.

Four hours later, I'm allowed to see her because she's asking for me. Suzanne's voice still whispers in my ear, telling me to *do it.*

Do what? I think, feeling angry because I know she wants me to do something grand in my life, but I'm kind of preoccupied with her ex-BFF having been slaughtered by our dishes. I'm doing the best I can for Emersyn.

"Hey ..." Emersyn's voice drifts across the room before I can bring myself to inch closer. The bandages look like a half-ass attempt at a mummy, a patchwork of hidden tragedy.

"Hi."

"I'll replace the dishes. The nurse told me. She said I fell into your dishwasher when I had a seizure. It's ... kind of fuzzy right now. I don't remember it happening, but I remember some things from after it happened."

I drag my heavy feet toward her bed. "I'm not worried about the dishes."

"What about Harry Pawter?"

"I called my brother. He's getting him checked out."

She swallows slowly, and her tired eyes gloss over with unshed tears.

"He's going to be fine." I rest my hand on her bandaged arm like it could break if I press too hard.

"It's not ..." She sniffles.

"It's not what?"

"Nothing." She draws in a shaky breath, trying to chase away the emotion.

Before I can say anything, a nurse comes into the room, a little too happy for my taste given the situation. Suzanne always had the overly cheery nurses as well.

"Hi, Emersyn. I'm going to draw some blood, then you'll go for an MRI."

"No," Emersyn blurts out so quickly it wipes Happy Nurse's smile right off her face. "Just ... it's expensive. And I don't need it. You know I have epilepsy. What do you expect to find?"

The nurse glances at me, and Emersyn follows her gaze to me as well.

"Oh, I can step outside for few minutes," I say.

The nurse returns her attention to Emersyn, waiting for her to give the final say as to whether I should stay or go.

"I'll go." I offer my own synthetic smile and nod toward the exit. "I might grab something to drink. I'll be right back."

Emersyn won't look at me, and I don't wait for her to say anything.

After grabbing a sports drink from the cafeteria, I make my way back to her room, slowing my steps as I approach the desk where Happy Nurse talks to another nurse.

"She doesn't have insurance. She hasn't seen her doctor in six months, and she wants to check out today."

The other nurse frowns. "The system is broken."

"Yeah, but she needs to have her medications adjusted."

"But if she can't afford it ..."

"I'm going to have someone see if she qualifies for any sort of assistance."

They glance in my direction as I pass the desk. I keep my head down as if I wasn't eavesdropping. Then I stop because ... Suzanne won't keep quiet today.

Do it.

Chapter Sixteen

Emersyn

WHAT IS the saying about squeezing blood from a turnip? That's me at the moment. I never envisioned my life taking up residence in the crapper of life, not that anyone does. I made a conscious effort to do things better than my mom. Be a better person. Make better decisions. And even now, I'm not sure what I did wrong. Living with intention can't outweigh sheer luck —or lack thereof.

"I heard you're checking out tonight," Zach says as he saunters into the room, wearing a reserved smile and clutching a red sports drink.

"I'm fine. And I think they're fine with it too, since I don't have an insurance company paying for the inflated fees and unnecessary tests. And let me tell you ... as a repeat offender of seizures, I know just how criminal the price of everything is in the hospital.

Seventy-five dollars for a warm blanket. No joke. Insurance or not, people should be upset and revolt."

Zach digests my words with his eyes narrowed a fraction and lips rolled together. "I'm concerned about you."

"Because I sound like a conspiracy theorist?"

"No." He chuckles. "I talked with the nurse. She said you shouldn't drive again until you've gone six months without having a seizure. Have you thought about that?"

My gaze angles toward the window. "I just need a different medication or dose or something."

"Then let's have your doctor decide what you need."

"Cha-ching." I laugh at his expensive idea. They just spent the afternoon removing glass from my body. I can only imagine how much that bill will be.

"I'll pay for it," he says.

"No. It's not your problem. We're not talking about a fifty-dollar loan. There's a reason why people need insurance—because without it, you can't afford to be sick. But ... stupid me. I had to be a fucking epileptic."

Zach shakes his head, quickly stifling his amusement. "Sorry. I'm not laughing at your situation. I just..." he fists his hand at his mouth "...haven't heard you swear like that before."

"Gee, *Zachary* ... so glad I could entertain you today."

"Listen ..." He clears his throat. "This isn't sustainable. We need to figure something out for you."

"We? It's kind of you to take me into your home like the stray that I am, but my health and financial issues aren't your burdens to bear."

"I understand. Still ... *we* can discuss it without me feeling burdened by you ... which I do not."

"Liar." I narrow my eyes and he rolls his.

Then ... we get the hell out of here.

———

ZACH'S EAGERNESS TO discuss my situation seems to fade before we ever get home. He's quiet, distracted, and not the bossy guy from the hospital. Has reality sunk in? Is he tired of taking care of women who need constant care?

I refuse to be his burden. I'll move back into my car before I let that happen. Suzie wanted me to make sure he moved forward. I'm hardly helping him move forward.

"Harry Pawter." I grimace as he pokes his coned head around the corner, bandages wrapped around two of his paws, making us twins.

Aaron appears just behind him, the lone, runty towhead in the dark-haired, brown-eyed Hays family. "The vet said to change the bandages daily. There's an ointment on the kitchen counter. And he has to wear the cone as long as he refuses to leave the bandages alone." He stuffs his hands into his back pockets.

"Thanks. What do I owe you?" I ask.

"Nothing. I've got it," Zach relinquishes his first

four words since leaving the hospital. He guides me to the sofa and helps me ease my ass onto it.

"Aaron, what do I owe you?" I repeat.

Aaron's eyes widen, darting back and forth, signaling his disinterest in getting involved in my little financial squabble with Zach. "Welp. Feel better."

"Traitor," I grumble.

Aaron chuckles and pats Zach on the shoulder. "You're a good man. Let me know if you need anything else."

Good man. Yes, Zach is a good man. That might be an understatement.

"You are too. Thanks." Zach gives a weak smile to his brother as he brushes past him.

When Aaron's footsteps fade behind the closed front door, leaving us in silence, I try to stand.

"What are you doing?" Zach steps toward me, reaching for my arm.

"I'm going to the bedroom."

"Oh." He helps me get to my feet. "Good idea. You should rest."

"Yeah," I reply on a long sigh.

When I'm nestled in bed with Harry Cone Head Pawter, I close my eyes—anything to shield my guilty conscience from the toxic stress lining Zach's face.

The pain. It's pure angst.

I did this. And I feel terrible.

As I listen to the descent of his steps, I speak. It's just too much to keep inside. "I'm moving out."

Silence.

More silence.

I blink open my eyes, unsure if he heard me.

He stands in the doorway with his back to me, unmoving, head bowed. "Why?"

"Look at me, Zach. I'm a walking disaster. And while I have the best intentions for digging myself out of this hole, it's not going to happen overnight. In the meantime, I'm pulling you into it. That was never my intention. I should never have stayed here in the first place."

He slowly turns. "Where are you going?"

"Don't worry about it."

"That's code for you have no fucking clue."

Whoa!

I'm not the only one dropping the f-bombs today. Why is he angry? He should be relieved.

"That's code for you lost your wife, and I'm not your problem. That's code for I've made it this far, I'll figure something out. That's code for you're off the hook. Smile. God! Please smile because I hate the look you've had on your face since we left the hospital. Doom and gloom. Panic. It's actually palpable at this very moment."

His head eases side to side. "It's not what you think."

"Bullshit! You took me in because you knew Suzie wouldn't have had it any other way. And that look ... right there..." I jerk my chin in his direction... "that look says it all. It says you're in over your head, and you can't figure out how you're going to get the walking disaster out of your house ... out of your life ... so you can truly move forward and figure out what's next for you."

Zach rests his forearms on the door frame, a twisted expression marring his handsome face. He's not mine. I'm not supposed to feel any attraction toward him. I was supposed to look out for him. Bravo. I've done an amazingly awful job at it. Suzie befriended the wrong person. I have no clue what I'm doing.

I'm broken—physically and emotionally.

"For your information, the look on my face is one of angst. I'm trying to figure out how to suggest something—ask you something—without you losing your shit and flying off the handle into one of your ego-driven tangents about how you don't need anything or anyone."

"I don't fly off the handle." I do. I'm stubborn to a fault, but I will never admit that to him or anyone else *because* of said stubbornness. "Just say what you need to say or ask or ... whatever."

"I have to preface it with a few things."

With my less injured hand, I scoot my body up a bit so I'm resting against the headboard. "Preface away."

"Okay. But please don't interrupt me because what I'm about to say will sound a little harsh at first."

I swallow hard and prepare for his version of harsh.

He continues, "I don't know if I'll ever find love again, and I'm okay with Suzanne being the last woman I love. So what I'm going to say is not about love. It's about gratitude and trying to repay you for everything you did for Suzanne ... and for me."

My eyes narrow. "Zach ... you paid me—"

"I'm not talking about cleaning the house." He shakes his head a half dozen times. "She needed a friend, a true friend. A friend I couldn't be because I was too busy suffocating her with my love. You gave her the kind of love she needed. The unselfish kind." He deflates a fraction, gaze pointed to the floor. "And you were ... you *are* my friend too. You were just..." he lifts his gaze again "...everything we had no idea we needed."

This is ridiculous. I'm living in his house, and he's thanking *me*?

"Before Suzanne died, she asked me to do something. She wanted me to make a difference in someone's life. And I've been hearing her voice in my head, telling me to do it. So this is it. I want to do this for you, and I want to do this for her. I *know* this would make her happy. And even in death, her happiness matters to me. I think peace is what we find after we die. Happiness is how we experience love while we're alive. She has peace. I need to seek happiness."

I have no idea where he's going with this. But if I die right now in the wake of Zach's words, I think I'd be good. Leaving this house won't be easy because he's felt like happiness, the kind I didn't seek. The kind that just found me.

"I can do something for you. I *want* to do this for

you. And someday I know you'll pay it forward, and that will make me even happier."

"What?"

He pulls in a long breath and lets it out as he drops his arms from the door frame. "I want to marry you."

Record scratch. Brakes screeching. Thunk of a mic dropping.

He doesn't let it sit unexplained in the air for long, but it feels like an eternity because the thoughts in my mind travel at the speed of light. And by the time he continues, I've already had a million thoughts and emotions paint a picture in my head.

"It will be temporary. No one will have to know. It will just be until you find a job with benefits or find someone else you want to marry for love. I have really good health insurance that would be yours. And you want to travel. Well ... I can get you incredibly cheap tickets. You can visit every wonder of the world and take pictures until your heart's content."

After at least a hundred unanswered breaths, I whisper, "A fake marriage."

"A legal marriage," he corrects me.

"Suz—"

"She died," he says. "But she would have wanted this for you."

I'm too shocked to appease him with the ego-driven tangent he expects. Did Suzie tell him what she told me? Did she tell him about the looks she thought we were giving each other, even though I don't recall any looks from either one of us? But he prefaced everything with "what I'm going to say is not about love."

"You don't have to decide now. Just ... think about it."

Answer? I can barely breathe or even blink, but I manage to scrounge a single nod.

"Okay. Sleep. I'll check on you before I go to bed. You might feel hungry by then." Zach closes the door behind him.

I used to envy Suzie, even with her terminal cancer. She married the most attentive man in the world. Loving and generous with every action. And I used to sleep in my car, in a Walmart parking lot, dreaming about what it would feel like to be married to a Zachary Hays or a clone of him. My dreams involved this clone coming home from work, loosening his tie, and smiling at me with a bouquet of flowers in his hand, the way he used to greet Suzie.

They were just dreams—innocent, unrealistic dreams. I never really imagined I could be *his* wife, yet that's the offer on the table. But he won't come home with flowers in his hand and look at me like I'm the brightest constellation in his sky. He'll come home and treat me like his roommate. He'll wonder how my search for a job with benefits is going. He'll wonder if I've met a nice man to marry so he can release me and feel satisfied with his good deeds.

Me? I'll spend every day wondering how I married the man of my dreams, though it will feel like the worst nightmare.

Chapter Seventeen

Not to brag, but over the next couple of days, I do a spectacular job of ignoring the ten-thousand-pound elephant in the room holding an invisible diamond ring. It's invisible, of course, because the elephant is invisible and the proposal is fake, but the marriage would be ... *legal*.

I'll be twenty-four next month. Marriage was in my ten-year plan. Babies in my fifteen-year plan. Fake marriages rank about as high as anal sex. To be fair to Zach, he lubed it quite well. He's made sure I know it will not involve love. No one will know. And it will only last until I find a job with health insurance *or* another husband. A real one—hopefully with health insurance as well.

"I work tomorrow. Do you want me to see if my mom or Aaron can stay with you?" Zach asks, squatted in front of me as he swaps out the bandages on my arms, neck, and face. The stitches come out in a few days. He'll do Harry Pawter's paws next. Poor thing is sick of his cone.

"Yes. I think you should find *the maid* a babysitter."

He pauses his hands and glances up at me. "Is that sarcasm?"

"When did you know you wanted to be a pilot? And no, I don't need a babysitter." Banter and subject diversion have become our official language.

Zach holds my gaze, and warmth snakes up my neck, settling into my cheeks. Those brown eyes ... they always seem to hold a secret. Even if I haven't been consciously pining for him, it's hard not to feel something beyond friendship toward someone who proposes to you.

"I'll have someone check in on you. And I knew I wanted to be a pilot when my grandpa bought me a remote-controlled airplane. I was ten. When did you know you wanted to be a photographer?"

I laugh at the simplicity of his question. "I fell in love with photography when the only decent guy my mom dated introduced me to it. Sometimes I wonder if all the photos I take are just pieces to a puzzle that will lead me to my destiny. However ... I have found a possible temporary job with a wedding photographer. I'm thinking about it. No benefits. But it's experience that might lead to something more. And it would just be weekends, so I could still keep my clients."

"Working with another photographer sounds like a good opportunity." He places the last new bandage on my wrist, keeping his attention on his hands. "Speaking of weddings …"

I withdraw my arm from his grasp, pulling his gaze up to meet mine. "Wedding? No. More like a pity marriage."

"Call it what you want. Doesn't change the fact that it would help you a lot." He scratches the back of his head, messing his slightly longer hair.

It's hard to wrap my heart around this idea, probably because my heart isn't supposed to have any part of it. My mind isn't supposed to recall my dreams of a big wedding with flowers in every shade of pink. Three different flavors of cake. A live band. A throng of family and friends. Of course, the family would not be mine … or most of the friends for that matter.

Zach is offering health insurance and a big bonus of cheap airfare by way of a little legal contract. Marriage. Not a wedding.

When I don't contribute any more to the conversation other than a frown, Zach stands and gathers the first aid supplies. Before he makes it three feet in the direction of the bathroom, I think of more questions—as if I'm seriously considering his ringless, loveless proposal.

"So … I'd still live here?"

He turns. "Only if you want to. I'd prefer you not live out of your car."

"And I'd date? Like … married to you but date other men?"

He offers a bemused smile. I don't like that smile,

and by *don't like* I mean I love that smile, but it's not good for me to love anything about Zach since love is not part of the proposal.

"Yes, Emersyn, you can date. It will be like we're not married, except when you need insurance, you'll have it."

"And when I need to fly, I'll get cheap tickets."

That bemused smile swells a little more. I don't care for pity or being the butt of a joke, however, I don't mind being the source of his amusement.

"If you're flexible with your schedule, yes, you'll get cheap tickets."

"And you?"

"And me what?"

Don't ask. Don't ask!

Ignoring the sound advice of my common sense, I ask anyway. "You'll date too. Right?"

That amusement vanishes from his handsome face. "I lost my wife recently. I have no desire to date. I have health insurance. I have the means to travel if I so choose. This isn't for me, Emersyn. This is for you."

Ouch.

The Young and Stupid virus strikes again. When will I try harder to see things through his eyes? Of course, he has no desire to date. Of course, this is all for me. Of course, my stubborn reluctancy is riding his last nerve. I see the endless possibilities in my future, and he can't stop gazing at the past like it's the last time he'll see the sun.

Again, he pivots to return the supplies to the bathroom. I inspect my arms and feel the stiffness in my neck from the healing cuts. This is my life at the moment. I'll no doubt go on to do great things, but right now ... I'm struggling.

I toss my pride onto the floor and squash it with my foot on my way out of the kitchen. "Yes. I'll marry you," I say just as he steps out of the bathroom.

Zach eyes me as if I ended my announcement with a comma instead of a period. He's waiting for the *but*.

No buts.

I'll marry him.

I'll dig myself out of debt.

I'll find a job.

Maybe even a new husband who loves me.

Pressing my lips together, so he knows I'm done speaking, I clasp my fingers in front of me.

"Okay. We'll apply for a marriage license next week, and we can be married the same day."

Oh my god. Oh my god. OH MY GOD!

My racing pulse radiates a deafening whoosh to my ears. I hope he's done speaking because I can't hear right now.

This is happening. I'm getting married next week.

————

ZACH GIVES me fifteen minutes because he has a dental appointment at four, so we need to get going.

Fifteen minutes to get ready for my wedding? Marriage? Nuptials? I don't know what to call it, nor do

I know what I'm supposed to wear. I go through five outfit changes.

"Emersyn, let's go!"

"Shit …" I mumble, not happy with the itchy fabric on my body. In less than ten seconds, I swap out the itchy dress for a knee-length skirt and pink, three-quarter-length sleeved sweater. It's not fair to ask someone like me—someone with such passion for clothes—to just throw on something to wear for my wedding.

"Emersyn—"

"Coming!" We're on the verge of our first fight, and we're not even married yet. I shove some makeup and my hair brush into my bag before running toward the backdoor with ballet flats in my other hand.

Zach's brows stretch toward his hairline.

"What?" I glance down at my outfit.

"Nothing."

I eye his jeans and pocket tee. It's basic, but unfaded and free of wrinkles, maybe something from J.Crew. "You think I'm overdressed? I wear skirts all the time. Don't read into this like I think today is special. I simply threw on the first thing I found that didn't need to be ironed." He's not a real husband. I'm not taking an oath to be honest. I don't think wedding vows address honesty. And lying is sometimes necessary.

The hint of a smile touches his lips. "You look nice."

After a quick pause to gage his sincerity, I mumble, "Thanks."

"You're welcome. Let's go."

On the way to the courthouse, I ignore his sideways glances while I apply a little makeup. Again, I wear makeup on days I don't get married. It's no big deal.

It's a huge fucking deal!

What I don't ignore is Zach singing to the radio, Imagine Dragons' "Next to Me." Suzanne wasn't lying; he has a great voice. I hum along since I don't know all the words. From the corner of my eye, I see him grin, but he doesn't stop singing. The words are poetic and oddly poignant for my life. Someone standing by you despite the messiness of life, believing in someone when they're at their worst, loving them unconditionally. Zach doesn't love me, but he's unquestionably a saint in my life right now.

A marriage license requires two forms of I.D. And in Zach's case, proof of death. I don't know if Zach feels my guilt and remorse when he has to hand over the certificate to prove that his previous wife died, but I turn to stone and hold my breath. Even my heart slows to act as invisible as possible.

With the license in hand, we head straight to the judge's chambers with a few minutes to spare before our scheduled appointment time.

"He'll use traditional, generic vows. It's not a requirement to exchange rings, so we won't."

I nod a half dozen times and swallow hard at least as many times. My nerves fire into overdrive as my gaze attaches to his left hand and ringless finger. He had it on earlier this morning.

"Is everything okay?" He brings me out of my racing thoughts.

"Um ... the kiss. Will he ask us to kiss?"

Zach shrugs like he's not sure and it doesn't matter. But it *does* matter.

"I think it's just permission," he says. "Not a requirement. Like you *may* kiss the bride. Doesn't mean we have to kiss."

"Okay. But won't it look suspicious if we don't kiss?" My voice won't stop shaking.

"If you're worried about it, then we'll just kiss."

We'll just kiss? Really? He's fine kissing me. Fine not kissing me. I'm a hot mess and anything but *fine.*

"Okay," I squeak out that one word.

"Okay to the kiss? Or it's okay if we don't?"

Before I get the chance to answer, the door opens, and we're beckoned into the judge's chambers.

I'm going to puke.

Don't puke!

The *he* judge is a *she* judge, and she greets us with a warm smile. I suppose she reserves her scowl for the days she sentences people to jail—like people who commit insurance fraud through a fake marriage. Zach stays cool. That's his gift. Flying hundreds of passengers through the skies and delivering them safely to their destinations is what he does best. A fake marriage must be an afterthought compared to that.

I excel at the nervous smile and occasional nod. After a little chit-chat that he handles, we get down to business. No coffee or last-minute counseling. Nope. She's reciting vows before I realize it's happening.

It's. Happening!

"Do you, Zachary, take Emersyn to be your lawfully wedded wife to have and to hold from this day forward ..."

I hear the words *faithful, love, honor, cherish, for as long as you both shall live.* My lungs crave oxygen, but I can't seem to get enough.

Breathe ... breathe ... breathe ...

Then, as if he reads my mind, Zach says, "I do," and leans forward next to my ear to whisper, "Breathe, Emersyn."

His words and his warm breath brand my skin.

"Do you, Emersyn ..." The judge continues like she has other things to do today. Maybe she has a dental appointment too.

Maybe I should have scheduled something today like a manicure or a psychiatric appointment. I could use some therapy.

There's the longest pause after the judge asks me that final question.

"...as long as you both shall live?"

It's times like these that I feel grateful for my experiences with Brady. I had anal sex in exchange for a shower. Is fraud really too big of a risk for health insurance and cheap airfare? I think not.

"I do," I say.

"I now declare you husband and wife."

I'm too busy being so proud of myself for coming to

terms with this and answering before things get too suspicious, that I totally forget the final—albeit optional—act.

"You may kiss your bride."

Oh shit ...

We didn't make a decision on this. He asked. I started to reply. The judge called us in here. And now ... we have to decide. I give a quick glance to the judge. She appears rather pleased and happy for us. We must look like an adorable, although fraudulent, couple. Forgoing the kiss will be a red flag. I feel it.

Inching forward a tiny step, I look up at Zach and rub my glossed lips together while gulping to keep my fear in check. He reads my silent acceptance and ducks his head until his lips are nearly touching mine. A breath of hesitation exists, even if the judge doesn't see it. I think, maybe I *hope,* he's taking this fraction of a second to get permission from Suzie or maybe to just remind himself it's only an act—a means to something greater. A humanitarian act if you will.

The kiss is short and soft, but long enough for everything in my head to spin until I forget what we're doing. My hand rests on his chest to keep me balanced, but he ends the kiss and grabs my hand, bringing it to my side and giving it a gentle, platonic squeeze.

It says we are friends. *I care about you as a friend. Here is your health insurance, but you don't need to know the outline of my chest.*

We get our marriage certificate and bounce before anyone has a chance to question us.

"I have time to run you home before my appointment," Zach says while retrieving his wedding band from his pocket and slipping it back onto his finger.

I ignore the little reminder that he's not mine and instead focus on the fact that he's spending our honeymoon with a dental hygienist. I might be slightly jealous that she's going to be in his mouth for forty-five minutes—up close and personal with my new husband. Good lord ... I hope Suzie can only read his mind and not mine. How do I break it to my best friend (or maybe admit it, since she already knew) that I have a massive crush on her husband? Oh ... and he's no longer her husband. He's mine.

I'm losing my mind! I'm not really crushing on Zach. I'm infatuated with the idea of Zach. The perfect man. And Suzie's voice is stuck in my head, making ridiculous accusations that Zach and I look at each other in some subconscious way that implies more than friendship. She was sick ... and, therefore delusional. Right?

"Okay. Or I can grab a cab." I shrug.

"No. I'll drive you." He opens my door. I try not to think the words *my husband is such a gentleman*, but I can't help it. As much as it feels wrong like I stole something invaluable from my best friend, it also feels a little amazing to be married to Zach. And now it bears repeating—I could use some therapy.

Chapter Eighteen

MARRIAGE HASN'T CHANGED Zach at all, not that I expected it to change him. I'm sure the only way he can make this right in his head, so quickly after Suzie's death, is to think of it as nothing more than a donation to a charity.

I'm the charity.

"Hey," he says, arriving home after being gone for four nights.

I glance up from the sofa with my computer on the arm of it and Harry Pawter on my lap. "Hey." It's hard to control my grin.

"Have you had dinner?"

"Yep. Pizza. There are leftovers in the fridge."

"Sounds perfect." He thumbs through the stack of mail on the credenza. "Look at this." He rips open an envelope and pulls out a card, holding it up for me to see.

I squint. "What am I looking at?"

"Your health insurance card. Let's get you scheduled with your doctor. Get your medication straight. And get you on the road to a normal life again."

"Driving. Get me driving again. My first hour's pay each day goes straight to paying for an Uber driver."

"Six months is six months ... well, five now. A doctor can't speed that up, but keeping you on track will hopefully prevent it from happening again. Wouldn't you like that?" He winks at me with a smirk on his face before he turns and saunters toward the bedroom to change his clothes.

A few minutes later, Zach retrieves the leftover pizza and a beer and comes back into the living room. "Happy birthday." He hands me a present wrapped in white paper and a pink ribbon.

I try to bite my lip to keep from grinning like a fool. Too late. "How did you know it's my birthday?"

"Birth certificate at the courthouse." He sits on the opposite end of the sofa. Just his nearness makes my day exponentially better. Just thinking that makes my guilt exponentially worse.

Carefully unwrapping the gift, I peel open the lid.

"For all your traveling," he says, a prideful smile stealing his lips.

It's a carry-on bag with lots of compartments for more camera parts than I own—yet. "It's perfect. I love it. But you shouldn't have. You've already done way too much." Before I realize what I'm doing, my body stretches across the sofa, giving him a hug while he holds out his plate of pizza in one hand and his beer in his other hand.

"Oof ... you're welcome."

Settling back into my spot, I wake up my computer and angle the screen. "I used to show these to Suzie, and she'd roll her eyes and tell me to delete them."

Zach sits up straighter, easing his head forward a fraction while squinting at the collage of photos, a half dozen candid shots of Suzie.

Her in the recliner, gazing out the window with a dreamy expression on her face.

One of her in the garden, perched on her garden cart, sniffing a handful of basil while the tails of her head scarf blow in the wind.

A crooked-angled one of her hands braiding my hair—she called me obsessed when I lifted my camera over my head to shoot it.

"That one." He points to the one of her ... and him. "Can you make it bigger?"

I forgot it was in this collage until after I angled my screen to show him. With a quick double click, it enlarges to take up the whole screen. In the photo, he's carrying her to the bedroom, the lights are dim, so it's almost a silhouette. I snapped it two days before he called hospice.

"I'm sorry," I whisper. "In hindsight, it feels like I shouldn't have taken it. Like the moment was private and not mine to record."

Zach's head inches side to side. "It's ... fine."

"The way you loved her ... well, it made me believe in love."

He leans back into the sofa, and I close my computer.

For the next several minutes he finishes his pizza, then he stands. "How do you feel about ice cream?"

"Uh ..." I laugh. "I think it sounds cold."

"But necessary? After all, it's your birthday." He eyes me like I didn't just shove painful memories into his face.

My laugh breaks free into a nervous chuckle. "Sure ..."

"Then let's go." He returns his dishes to the kitchen.

Ice cream?

I don't say another word. Zach's sudden change in subject and desire to celebrate my birthday has piqued my curiosity.

Fifteen minutes later, we climb out of his car and approach the ice cream shop. It opened a few weeks before Suzie died.

"I was going to bring her here, but ..."

I nod. There's no need to elaborate.

He orders chocolate mint, and I get salted caramel. With our waffle cones in hand, we stroll down the side-walk lined with stores, most of them closed for the night.

"Cute handbag," I say to a lady as she passes us with her tiny dog.

Her face lights up and her steps falter a bit. It's a

black purse. Nothing fancy. Nothing special. "Thank you," she says.

"It wasn't cute," Zach murmurs after she passes us.

"Doesn't matter." I shrug. "It's all about the bounce."

"The bounce?"

"Suzie always complimented my clothes, my hair, handbags, even my smile. And I don't think all of it was worthy of recognition. But after she'd compliment me in some way, I'd have an extra bounce in my step. It's so easy to give someone a little bounce. So why the heck don't we do it more often? It took two seconds and virtually no energy to compliment that lady's handbag, but she'll have that extra bounce in her step for ... well, potentially the rest of the night."

Zach licks his ice cream, and we continue our walk. I wonder how he feels about me talking about Suzie or showing him photos? Am I overstepping a boundary? Am I making it harder for him to move on?

"Cool shoes," he says to a guy passing us.

I rub my lips together to restrain my grin.

The guy with scuffed, ordinary shoes glances down at said shoes before giving Zach a half grin. "Thanks, man."

When the guy is out of earshot, I nudge Zach's arm. "You're a natural."

He grins, keeping his gaze in front of us.

"Were you really having a hankering for ice cream? Feeling like my birthday couldn't end with pizza and a great gift? Or is this spur of the moment outing for a different reason? If you're having second thoughts about ... what you did for me ..." I can't say marriage. It's still too weird.

Zachary Hays is my husband. Nope. It will never feel real, probably because *feelings* aren't supposed to be part of the deal.

He finds a bench by the bus stop and takes a seat just as we say goodbye to the last rays of daylight. I sit on the other side, facing the opposite direction.

"A few days before she died, Suzanne asked me for a favor," he says, keeping his gaze on the street while I focus on keeping up with my melting ice cream.

"What's that?"

"You're not going to like it, even though you should like it. But you're stubborn, so you'll fight it."

My head snaps to the side, eyes squinted. "I'm not stubborn."

A chuckle vibrates from his chest as he licks his ice cream. "You can't even say it without using a stubborn tone."

I clear my throat and frown, oblivious to whatever *tone* he thinks I used. "What am I not going to like?"

"Help. You don't like help, and that was Suzanne's request."

"Was it her idea for you to marry me?" My tone is one of shock and dismay ... in case he doesn't catch it.

"No. Well, not directly. She asked me to use some of her life insurance to pay off your bills."

"Bills? What bills?"

179

His tongue swipes along his upper lip as he glances in my direction. "All of them."

"All of them?" Parroting him is my weak attempt at making sense of this, buying time for my brain to process what he really means.

"Student loans. Medical bills. I don't know if you have credit card bills, but—"

"I don't," I mumble. "You're not using her life insurance money to pay my bills."

"She adored you. And there really isn't a dollar amount I can put on how much you enhanced her quality of life over the summer. So let me do this because it's what she wanted ... because it's what I want to do."

This is ridiculous. I didn't do anything that special. Suzie did more for me than I ever did for her. I should be paying *him* back for hiring me.

"I really think letting me live with you and ... the other part you've done ... is enough."

Again, he chuckles. "Other part? You mean the marriage?"

Holding my ice cream cone at my mouth, I return a tiny nod.

He sighs. "She really wanted this for you," he murmurs.

"Zach, it's ... it's close to a hundred thousand dollars. That's too much."

"It's not."

"Well, it is to me!" The regret is instant. Why did I snap at him? For being too generous?

His brows inche up his forehead as he eyes me.

I deflate, averting my gaze to the glitching neon *Closed* sign in the yarn store window. "For years ... I watched my mom give away pieces of herself for rent, for food, drugs, and alcohol. She wasn't a street-corner prostitute, but there was a bartering system. Some men stuck around for days ... maybe weeks. Most stayed less than twenty-four hours, but she always got something in return. Even the men who left bruises on her body, gave her something. One guy busted open her lip, then he handed me a hundred-dollar bill before leaving the apartment. He said, 'Go buy your mom some ice for her face and grab yourself dinner while you're at it, sweetheart.'"

Zach remains silent, allowing my focus to remain split between the past and that glitchy sign. "If I dig deep, beyond all the hideous things she's said and done, I suppose I have to give her credit for teaching me a few survival tricks."

"Like letting people help you when they offer?"

My head eases side to side. He has no idea that I've had very few people offer his kind of help. Well, nobody has ever offered his kind of help. "Like offering my ex-boyfriend anything in exchange for a shower at his apartment."

"Anything?" Zach murmurs before clearing his throat.

Answering with a slow nod, I exhale a long breath. "Mind games. I convinced myself it was a small price to pay for something I needed. He was my boyfriend. I'm not a prude. So I took it up the backside, showered, and managed to get to work only fifteen minutes late." Risking a quick glance at him, I shrug.

Zach's eyes narrow. "How did you take it up the backside?"

Pressing my lips together, my eyes widen. "Uh ... slowly."

It takes a few seconds before realization hits him. "Oh ... Jesus ... you mean you *literally* took it up ..."

My gaze falls to my lap. "Even then, I never thought I was like my mom. Nope. I first found a good boyfriend. Then I convinced myself that he would love me like no man had ever loved my mom. But..." I grunt a painful laugh "...the problem was I hadn't seen true love. Do you know how hard it is to find something you've never seen?"

"You've never felt love? Ever?"

Twisting my lips, my head inches side to side. "No. Well ... that's not true. Not anymore. I've experienced kindness. And I've *witnessed* love." Again, my attention returns to his face. "You and Suzie. Actually, before I met the two of you, I thought I knew what love was. Nope. Not even close."

"She loved you," he whispers.

Tears burn my eyes, so I blink several times and avert my gaze. "I know," I manage to say past the lump in my throat. "I loved her too."

"Then let me give you this."

"Give me what?"

"Financial freedom. She loved you. You loved her. *I* want to do this for her and for you. It's a no-brainer."

"It's too much. You need to save the money for retirement. Or buy something you've always wanted. Or—"

"Or do this for you. Technically, what's mine is yours. And what's yours is mine. I don't want to be in debt. So let's get the hell out of debt."

The confusion on my face only makes his grin swell. He shrugs one shoulder. "Georgia is a fifty-fifty state. You could divorce me and take half of my worth."

"Z-Zach ... I would ... never, like *ever* do that." The way I never *ever* considered a prenup before we got married. Was I naive? Was he? Was he completely irresponsible? What would his family think of his recklessness?

"I know," he says so matter-of-factly it makes my head spin.

Taking my crumpled cone sleeve to the trash by the yarn store door, I gnaw on the corner of my bottom lip and pivot just as he reaches around me to toss his napkin into the trash.

"I'll only agree to it if you acknowledge my need to repay you."

"Emer—"

"No." I shake my head. "It's nonnegotiable. I'm already the biggest charity case that ever lived. I can't take a nearly six-figure handout with nothing more than a thank-you and a smile in return."

"Fine. Repay me." His hands slide into his front pockets as he rocks back and forth on his feet.

Not expecting his quick, agreeable response, I struggle to find my next words. Finally, they come to me. "I could move out," I whisper. "With the insurance and no debt, I could afford a place of my own."

For a flash, not even a full second, something crosses his face—a shadow of doubt, maybe discomfort. He recovers from it in the next breath. "I suppose that's true."

"Or I could pack a bag and travel. Maybe see if I can make some money off my photography. Maybe start a travel blog. Build a bigger social media following."

"Or that." He shrugs before brushing past me, heading in the direction of his car.

"Maybe I'll wait until the first of the year and see how much money I can save, then I'll decide on travel plans. If ..."

"If what?" Zach's long strides make it hard to keep up with him.

"If it's alright that I stay."

"Why wouldn't it be alright?" He unlocks his car.

"Because I make okay money cleaning houses, and if I don't have debt, it's unnecessary for me to stay with you."

"Unless you're wanting to save money to travel."

I nod slowly, slipping into the passenger's seat. "I guess."

"Then stay."

Stay.

Stay and grow more attached to him.

Stay and risk falling for my husband.

Stay and realize it might already be happening.

Stay and get my heart broken.

Before he backs out of the parking space, I feel his gaze on me. "Who do you have?"

Picking at my fingernails, I shrug a shoulder. "What do you mean?" I know what he means. Answering his question will require me to voice my reality.

"If not me, then who? Family? Do you have any family to turn to? Someone willing to give you a bed or even just a sofa and a blanket?" He backs out of the parking space, and we head toward home.

"Nope." I let that one syllable echo between us for several seconds, but Zach doesn't budge. "I don't have family. No siblings. My dad has never been in the picture. Never met him. My mom had some drinking issues, then some drug issues, then some mean men issues. That's why I left. She didn't want my help, and I didn't want anything to do with that life anymore. She said I could accept her for who she was or get the fuck out. Her words."

I don't turn toward him, but I still catch his slight flinch. Even after all these years, it's hard to breathe when I think about my mother, the woman who is supposed to love me the most ... just letting me go. And it's a little embarrassing too. I clear my throat. "So the second I got my high school diploma, I left Athens with my mom's car because ... fuck her. She owed me.

Then I took out a gazillion loans to go to school. Had a half dozen different roommates. And slept out of my car as needed."

"So you're experienced at sleeping out of your car?" He gives me a quick sidelong glance.

"Sort of. Back then, it was for a few weeks in between apartments or roommates. Not months."

"I'm sorry to hear you had it so rough."

I shake my head. "I didn't. I had friends in school. I kept my chin up. My mom was so many awful things, but she never abused me—physically—and neither did her shitty boyfriends who felt it was okay to knock *her* around. I got a college degree, even if it's the most useless degree in the world. I followed my passion. I've always been a dreamer. Passion over practicality."

"And now you're cleaning houses."

His bluntness pulls a tiny laugh from my chest. "Yes. Yes, I am. I don't know." I shrug. "I saw it going differently, but I'm too young to give up. I'm going to continue to look for my place in this world."

Zach shakes his head. "You're like a battery-operated toy that gets tipped on its side, but it's still moving, even if it's not going anywhere. Suzanne was like that." When he glances at me, his grin falters. "Sorry. I'm sure you're tired of me comparing you to her, but it's in the best way possible."

"No. It ... it's not that I mind being compared to her. It's quite the compliment. It's just weird now."

"Because we're married?"

I nod, pressing my lips together as we pull into the

garage. "I mean, it's not like we're married in the traditional sense. I'm not sleeping with her husband." *Jesus* ... why does the filter between my brain and my mouth have such large holes?

Zach clears his throat, and I swear his cheeks turn a little red even if part of his face is covered with dark stubble. "Well ... technically I'm *your* husband now. So you're not sleeping with *your* husband. And just to get past this really uncomfortable unspoken ... *thing* between us, it's important to remember that she died. We lived. Tara died, and Suzanne lived. She moved on with her life. I'm moving on with my life too. I'm just doing it differently. Instead of finding love again, I'm doing a favor for a friend."

We climb out of the car.

With a nervous laugh, I feel my own cheeks fill with heat as I step inside the house. "And what a favor it is," I say through that nervous laugh. "I'm uh ... going to bed now. Thank you for the camera bag and the ice cream. It's been a great birthday." I risk a final glance at Zach.

He smiles, just staring at me for a few more seconds before returning an easy nod. "Night, Emersyn."

Chapter Nineteen

I TAKE the job with the wedding photographer, a second camera for a few local weddings and engagement photos. It's a part-time, temporary job, a fill-in position while his full-time assistant recovers from surgery.

Over the next few weeks, I experience an unusual kind of grief. Maybe it's that I just had a birthday, and twenty-four is a more hormonal age, but I doubt it. As crazy as it sounds, I'm a little lost. After feeling like a slave to my epilepsy diagnosis, my medical bills, and my student loan debt—oh, and getting married—I don't know how to handle this newfound freedom. My doctor adjusted my seizure medication. I'm physically feeling better. Exercising every day. I've been saving lots of money. And I'm getting paid to take photos without having to quit my cleaning jobs. So why am I scared out of my mind?

"I let you skip out on Thanksgiving, but you're not

sitting home alone on Christmas," Zach announces as he wraps presents on the living room floor. It's the week before Christmas.

I dust the end table and the lamp. "Skip out on Thanksgiving? You were working that day."

"But my family wanted you to have dinner with them."

His family is great. They've not once questioned his charitableness toward me. I think they know it's what Suzie would have wanted. Of course, they don't know the full extent of his charity. They only know he's been letting me stay here. "I'm not ready to attend holidays with them when you're not going to be there. I'd end up having one too many eggnogs and let it slip that we're married. Are you good with that?" I peer at him from behind the table lamp.

"Good point."

I smirk, feeling victorious with my reasoning.

"But I *am* going to be there on Christmas."

"Yes, but it's a gift giving holiday. That's just weird. Christmas feels like a more personal holiday. And this will be your first Christmas without Suzie. That feels a little ..." My nose wrinkles. "Sacred? And ... what are you doing?" I cringe as he wraps the gifts, if you can call what he's doing wrapping.

"What do you mean?"

"Have you ever wrapped a present before?" I toss the dusting rag over my shoulder and kneel on the floor next to him. "You need to cut off some of this excess paper so it rests flat against the side of the box.

You're wrapping a cube, and it looks like a clump of wadded paper. And don't even get me started on your ribbon-tying skills. I thought you had perfectionistic tendencies." I chuckle.

Zach holds his hands up. "By all means, Miss Art Degree Queen, feel free to wrap while I—"

"Finish dusting."

He belts out a hearty laugh as he stands. "No. While I read a book. Watch TV. Twiddle my thumbs. Play my guitar. The possibilities are endless."

Play his guitar. He's been doing it a lot at night. He likes to watch me edit photos, but I love listening to him play his guitar in his bedroom. Sometimes he hums and sings too. Those are my favorite nights. When I move out, I'll miss his fingers strumming those strings, my favorite lullaby.

"Endless possibilities ... I like the sound of that, Zachary. I think you are going to be okay in this life."

"This life?" He laughs from the kitchen.

I hear the crinkle of tinfoil. He's getting into the Christmas cookies I made.

"Yes. This life. I can't speak for any other life. You might be a hot mess in another life."

He pokes his head around the corner. Sure enough, he's eating one of the tree cookies I spent the afternoon decorating. "Can guys be a hot mess?"

"You can be a mess and ..." I bite my lips and angle my head away from him to hide my blush as I curl the ribbon with the edge of the scissor's blade.

"But not a *hot* mess?"

I shake my head in tiny increments at least a half dozen times. "I didn't say that. I mean ... yes. Some guys can be a *hot* mess."

"But not me?"

I shrug and sweat. God ... he makes me sweat way too much.

"I get it. You think of me like a big brother. You can't think your big brother is hot."

Big brother? No. I don't think of him as a big brother. That would be so inappropriate.

1. We're married.
2. I think about him *all* the time.
3. I mean ... ALL the time.

"No. I can't think of my big brother as hot. Maybe Aaron can be hot."

But you're not my big brother. You're my husband. And quite the snack.

Zach stops midbite, slowly chewing what's already in his mouth. "You like Aaron?"

I start working on (correcting) another present. "Sure. He's nice. He's funny. He's in his twenties. He's single. What's not to like?"

"He's my brother," Zach murmurs, licking the crumbs from his lips.

Grinning, I eye him over my shoulder. "I know. I didn't say I'm going to hook up with him or anything like that. I'm just making an observation since you asked."

"I asked because you brought up his name."

Zach is a little ... I don't know what. Agitated? I'm not sure why he would be agitated. Aaron isn't ugly. He's not Zach caliber (in my opinion), but he's worth a second look.

The pain or whatever he's harboring inside, that I've triggered, elicits a unique sadness in my chest. Legally, I'm his wife, but I'm not his source of happiness despite feeling invested in his happiness. Maybe not the source, but the angel watching over him, ensuring he's okay. That much I did promise Suzie.

"In other news..." I refocus on my wrapping "... my temporary job is coming to an end. His assistant will return from medical leave in two weeks. And I've found another job I'm considering. A photographer slash travel blogger. I follow her on social media, and she's looking for another photographer to travel with her next year. *So* many other people commented on her post. But ..." I grin. "She messaged me, and she loves the photos on my page. I'm going to meet her the day after Christmas in New York. That's where she lives, but she's rarely home. Zach, I think she's really interested in picking me!"

"So ... you'd travel with her and take photos?" Zach asks.

"Yes."

His lips twist to the side. "And she's going to pay you?"

"Yes. Well, I don't have all the specifics yet, but I'll

make a percent of what she makes on her social media pages."

Zach nods a few times. "An influencer?"

"Yes, but I don't think that's the bulk of her income, not yet anyway. She has her own photography business too, and she'll pay me a percent of those jobs if I'm with her to help shoot them."

"Huh. Interesting. So you'll get to travel."

I grin. "Yes. I think I'll be traveling most of next year. It would be an incredible opportunity to build my portfolio and my social media following."

"Sounds..." he studies me while pressing his lips together for a few beats "...perfect. You deserve all the best life has to offer. Suzanne thought so, and I do too." He lifts a single shoulder. "It's why I married you."

My gaze drops to focus on rewrapping his gifts. I know that's why he married me, even if my heart thrives on foolish dreams. It might be too early to tell him that Suzie wanted me to love him. And I think she wanted him to love me too. Can I fall in love with my husband *and* chase my dreams? Or are they mutually exclusive? "It would be ... a great opportunity. But I don't have the job yet. Still, I'm really optimistic. And I'd be out of your hair. That's good. Right?"

"When is your first trip?" He slides his hands into his pockets.

"Again, I don't have the job yet. But she's going to Hawaii in January." I can't hide my grin.

A sincere smile touches his lips the way it touches every inch of my skin. "I take it you've never been."

"Hawaii?" I laugh. "No. I've never been. You?" Before he can answer, I roll my eyes. "Duh. Of course you've been. There are probably very few places you haven't been."

He nods.

A slow smile slides up my face, and it feels so good. I don't need his approval to travel and experience my next chapter in life, but I want it. I want him to be happy for me. I want to know that he's going to be okay. "I'll spend Christmas with you."

He grunts, but it doesn't stop his face from relaxing into something resembling satisfaction.

"Besides..." I hold up a perfectly wrapped present "...I need to be there to take credit for these masterpieces."

"You think they're going to be more impressed with the wrapping than the gifts inside?"

"Yes. I overheard you last month talking to your mom. You guys exchanged gift lists. You might not know the exact item you're getting, but you know it's something on the list you shared. So the surprise will be lukewarm at best. But the wrapping..." I waggle my eyebrows "...is perfection."

"Oh, Em ..." He smirks before turning and disappearing down the hallway. "I'm not *that* predictable."

Em ...

He's never called me Em. Everyone calls me Em, except him. Until now. How did he make something ordinary and common *feel* extraordinary? How do two

194

letters and a sound so similar to a tiny hum make that beating thing behind my chest skip and flutter?

Butterflies ...

I could ... just maybe ... be on the verge of a new adventure starting in Hawaii—taking a risk and diving into the life I've always dreamed of having. But ... I also want this job because I need to run from these feelings. These feelings that I have for *my husband*.

Chapter Twenty

Christmas

Zach

"I'M NERVOUS," Emersyn says as we pull into my parents' circle drive nested in a neighborhood of older homes with spacious lots.

"Don't be."

"They live in a mansion."

I chuckle, killing the engine to my Mercedes sedan. "It's not a mansion, but it has been in our family for three generations."

Emersyn opens her door and makes a sloth's exit. Her jaw drags on the ground as she gawks at the white two-story with six garland-wrapped pillars framing the entry. An enormous chandelier hangs a few feet from the black-painted door adorned with a lush pine and winterberry wreath.

It's all just *home* to me. What must she be thinking after living out of her car? I'm so glad she's here. Suzanne would be too. But now, I think I'm glad for myself more than Suzanne.

Emersyn is no longer Suzanne's friend; she's my friend. And my wife. She's not a charity case. She's more. That definition of *more* still needs time to work itself out in my head.

"Are you going to help me carry the presents? Or are you too busy tinkling in your pants and chattering your teeth?" I ask Emersyn.

She shoots me her best scowl before loading her arms with presents.

"Breathe, Emersyn. You know them and they know you."

"As the maid. Maids don't attend the family Christmases of their clients." She follows me to the front door.

"You're my roommate. We're friends. That's what they think of you. I promise you won't have to do the dishes or any manual labor today."

"I'm going to do my part. That's just good manners."

I balance a pile of gifts on my lifted knee and give her a quick glance before opening the door. "Your part is being my guest. No dishes for you tonight."

"Merry Christmas!" My parents greet us in the foyer along with my brother.

They don't know we're married, but Emersyn is

freaking the fuck out on the inside. I can see it on her face.

"Merry Christmas. Thank you so much for having me," she says with a shaky and timid voice.

Aaron and my dad take the gifts from our arms.

"You have such a lovely home." Emersyn slips off her lightweight coat.

I take it from her before she even gets it all the way off.

"Thank you," she whispers, glancing back at me.

I wink, hoping it will ease her mind. A "just relax" wink. But her wide eyes don't convey my wink is doing anything to put her at ease.

She blushes.

The wink might have been the wrong move.

"We're so glad you're joining us," my mom says as she pulls Emersyn in for a hug.

Emersyn's fingers dig into my mom's back, like she's holding on for life ... like she needs a hug.

"You okay?" Mom asks as she pulls away from Emersyn and holds her at arm's length.

Emersyn nods and quickly wipes the corners of her eyes. "Yeah. Sorry, Cecilia. I get a little sappy on holidays. That's all. I love your earrings, by the way."

My mom touches said earrings and grins. "Thank you," she replies, almost with a bit of surprise. "Come in, honey. Let's get you a drink." Mom takes Emersyn's hand and guides her out of the parquet floor entry to a grand living room furnished with vintage sofas and chairs, wood tables with intricately carved legs, floral porcelain lamps, fringed area rugs—and a ginormous Christmas tree. From the size of Emersyn's bugged out eyes, I'd say it's the biggest tree she has ever seen.

Mom loves her tree adorned with hundreds of ornaments and lights weighting its beautiful pine branches. Aaron likes to give her crap about the room resembling a swanky department store at Christmastime.

As I grab drinks, I hear Emersyn complimenting my dad's ugly Christmas sweater and Aaron's nothing-special striped socks. She's giving everyone a little bounce in their step.

"Here you go." I hand her a glass mug. "It's my mom's famous slow cooker hot buttered rum."

Emersyn eyes me for a few seconds, probably because she's managed to put an unstoppable grin on my face in a matter of minutes since our arrival. She takes the drink from me and brings it close to her lips, inhaling the fragrant spices. "Mmm ..."

We sit together on the sofa, not at opposite ends like at home. She keeps a death grip on her mug while scraping her teeth along her lower lip over and over. The gloss is nearly gone.

"Zach told us you're going to Hawaii next month for a new job. Congratulations." My dad takes a seat next to my mom on the opposing sofa, and Aaron plunks into a high back chair adjacent to us.

"Zach." Emersyn's eyes narrow at me. "I don't have the job yet."

I smirk and shrug. "You will."

Her head inches side to side as she returns her attention to my parents. "*If* I get the job, then yes ... I'm going to Hawaii next month. But thank you, William. I hope congratulations are in order."

I'm happy for her. Suzanne would be too. I'm also a little sad. Emersyn's been a distraction.

A distraction from my grief.

A distraction from the silent void in my house.

A distraction from the crippling realization that my life is, in some ways, starting over again.

"To Emersyn, for finding a great new job." Dad holds up his glass mug in a toast before taking a drink.

"To Emersyn." Everyone else holds up their mugs.

"Thank you. I hope," she murmurs, her hand a little shaky as she raises her mug.

My parents shift the conversation to Aaron, questioning him about his recent change in jobs from an EMT to working with a horse trainer. "Aaron has half a medical degree and two years of an architecture degree ... and ADHD." Cecilia eyes Aaron playfully. "The way he talks sometimes ... I suspect he's looking into designing new humans."

Everyone laughs, even Aaron, who shrugs like she's not wrong.

After they exhaust all questions pointed at Aaron, Mom suggests we move to the dining room for dinner, letting me off the hook for now. It's possible they still think I'm doing nothing but mourning the loss of Suzanne when I'm not working, so who wants to bring up that subject?

Tonight ... sitting around a beautifully decorated dining room table, savoring good food, sipping home-made drinks, engaging in laughter and conversing about lighter topics like who knows the history of Georgia better ... I yearn for a sense of normalcy and peace again. I want to go a full day without feeling guilty about Suzanne.

Did I save her from more pain?

Did I cut her life short?

Do I need to tell someone so they can give me permission to truly let her go?

Will it ever stop eating me alive?

When our bellies are topped off with pecan and pumpkin pie, we return to the main room to open presents.

"Everything okay?" I lean closer to Emersyn and whisper in her ear.

She clears her throat and nods several times. "Just a lot of ... kindness."

"That's good, right?"

Again, she nods.

Kindness. She's doesn't have much experience with it, and that's its own tragedy because now she doesn't know what to do with it. Kindness is the hardest thing to accept because it requires true vulnerability to feel it. Emersyn is afraid to be vulnerable, to truly *feel*.

"My goodness ... someone had help wrapping presents. I was going to say something when you arrived." Mom picks up one of the gifts Emersyn rewrapped and hands it to Dad.

"I take offense." I attempt to feign outrage, but I can't keep a straight face. In fact, my cheesy grin, the one that shows all my teeth, seems to be my go-to when I'm with Emersyn.

While giving her a quick glance to admit she did a great job wrapping the gifts, I rest my hand on her knee and give it a gentle—playful—squeeze.

She stiffens under my grip, and her face turns red, matching the color of her off-the-shoulder sweater. Did I overstep again? She's my wife, but I'm not allowed to touch her leg, right?

My fucking brain, crippled with unsorted emotions, runs amuck. I don't know what to do with these feelings—the ones that include Suzanne, the ones that have been driving my generosity toward Emersyn, the ones that exist for the sole purpose of destroying my sanity.

I don't love Emersyn, but *like* feels inadequate. I'm doing this for Suzanne, and clearly for Emersyn, but I'm doing this for me too. Suzanne was right; it *does* feel good to do something selfless, to make someone's life better. But here's the crux: I don't want to just make *anyone's* life better; I want to make Emersyn's life better because it's making my life better. And that realization scares the hell out of me.

"Well, look at this." Dad unwraps the gift from me and holds it up. It's an umbrella with an animal head carved in wood on the handle.

"It's a James Smith & Sons," Mom says. "I bet *someone* was in London."

I grin and return an easy nod.

My family continues to exchange presents. Mom opens hers next. It's painted linens and a one-off porcelain pitcher in a unique glazed rose color from a shop I visited in Notting Hill. Aaron opens his two bottles of Jensen's Gin from Bermondsey and wastes no time twisting the lid to one, despite Mom's exaggerated eye roll.

As the present opening continues, I revel in the moment. I gobble up every glance Emersyn gives me. She assumed the gifts to my family were predictable—things they put on their lists—but I've surprised her.

She pinned *me* as predictable when I'm anything but.

The final gift of the night is for me. A reverent silence blankets the room as I open it. I don't like silence or people staring at me. And I definitely don't like my mom blotting a rogue tear from her cheek as I remove a black book from the box. My entire heart catapults from my chest to my throat when I open to the first page, the only one that seems to have anything on it. As I read it, Emersyn leans toward me to read it too.

> Zach,
> Make plans, my love. Life is too short.
> Yours,
> Suzie

"It's a little black book," Aaron says.

Cecilia nods. "She wanted us to wait until Christmas to give it to you." Again, she blots another tear and smiles as I glance up for a split second before thumbing through the blank pages of the planner.

The muscles in my jaw work overtime to keep my emotions in check. There's not a soul in this room who hasn't seen me cry over Suzanne. I'm better now, not awesome, but fully functional. I'm moving forward. Do I have to make actual plans?

Aaron jumps up and disappears for a few seconds before returning with a pen in his hand. He plucks the planner from me, flips to the first Wednesday in January, and writes: 7 pm - drinks with your favorite brother.

This brings a tiny smile to my face.

Then my mom takes the journal and pen and sets a date for *Brunch with Mom* on a Sunday in February. Dad adds *Golf with Dad* on a Friday in March. And when he stands to hand the planner back to me, Emersyn steals it and the pen then turns to a page in January.

Take Em to the airport.

After she hands the journal back to me, I stare at her words on that day. "Thank you," I whisper.

I'm not sure who I'm thanking.

My family?

Emersyn?

Suzanne?

By some miracle, this Christmas isn't awful. The

loss of Suzanne's presence is felt, but it hasn't robbed everyone of their Christmas spirit. As we gather our belongings and say our goodbyes, I take a minute to observe Emersyn interact with my family. They adore her.

I adore her.

When she moves on, when she follows her dreams, it will be bittersweet.

Chapter Twenty-One

Emersyn

LEAH RUE HIRES ME. We click like long-lost friends. Sisters. Like I did with Suzie.

"I got the job!" I yell, calling Zach from my hotel room in Manhattan after my meeting with Leah.

"That's great. When am I getting rid of you?"

I giggle. "Soon. January eighth. I put it in your planner on the tenth—just a guess. But I don't really expect you to take the day off for me. Oh my god ... I have to give all my clients notice. This. Is. Happening!"

"Stop. I *want* to take you to the airport."

"What are you doing?" I stare at the ceiling as I plop back onto the bed.

"I just fed Harry."

"Jesus ... HARRY!" I shoot to sitting. "Harry Pawter. Shit. I haven't even thought about him. I can't take him with me. Leah said last year she was at her apartment in Manhattan for less than ten days total. I ... I'm going to have to find a new home for him." The *male* cat I didn't want has me all choked up. Stupid Brady.

"Why? He has a home."

"No. He's not your cat. I won't dump that responsibility on to you. And you're gone a lot."

"If you could see him on my lap right now, you wouldn't say he's not my cat."

"Zach ..." I blink back my tears.

"It's fine. If I'm gone for an extended time, I'll ask a neighbor to feed him."

"I don't know ..."

"What? You're going to give him to some stranger? What happens when you're done traveling? Won't you want your cat?"

"Why are you so good to me?"

He chuckles. "Good question."

I grin and roll my eyes. "Will I see you in the morning? I'll be home early."

"Nope. I fly out early as well. I'll be gone overnight."

"Well, safe travels."

"You too, Em."

I disconnect and wince as my heart suffers in conflict. I got the job. It's a huge opportunity for me professionally and on a personal level. I can't wait to travel the world with Leah. But ... I'm going to miss my husband. So very much.

WE BLINK.

That's it.

One tiny blink and New Year's passes with Zach in flight and me watching the ball drop from the comfort of Zach's sofa with Harry Pawter next to me.

Some packing.

Several dinners together.

Good wine.

Many laughs. And a few tears when Suzie comes up in conversation—my tears. Zach is much stronger.

Then ... it's my day to leave for Hawaii *early* in the morning.

I remind Zach that I can get a cab or an Uber, but he's already taken the day off. On the way to the airport, Zach goes through a checklist of things for me, like: did I remember my medication, and do I have plenty of money?

When we get to the terminal drop-off, he sets my suitcase on the sidewalk and closes his trunk before turning to me.

My nerves are fried. It's the excitement and fear of what's to come for me; it's traveling to Hawaii, but mostly it's the goodbye that's just seconds away. The half bagel I forced down before we left home compounds the nausea from my nerves as it sits in my stomach like a brick.

"You have no idea when you'll be back?" he asks for the hundredth time.

I shake my head and shrug. "Leah lets life lead her.

We might be back in two weeks or two months ... or longer."

Ten days. Last year she was home ten days out of three hundred and sixty-five. That's three hundred and fifty-five days without Zach—*if* he's home when I come home.

Home. Is his home mine? Do I really have a home or do I simply have a cat and a man who gave me health insurance and a roof over my head?

"You have me as your emergency contact in your phone, right?"

I return another nod, rubbing my nervous lips together. I'll probably have a fucking seizure before he can pull away from the curb.

This is it. I'm going to lose it so hard, and there's nothing I can do to stop it.

Jesus ... here it comes.

"Hey ... no. What's this all about?" Zach palms my face with both hands and catches my tears with his thumbs like little windshield wipers. My lower lip quivers, and I fight like hell to keep from going into an all-out ugly cry.

"Happy tears." Again, I try to swallow that boulder in my throat. "They're happy tears." I do my best to reassure him, but it doesn't completely erase the concern in his eyes.

His beautiful brown eyes.

His handsome smile.

That sharp jaw covered in scratchy whiskers that he keeps at the perfect length—Zach is the most beautiful man inside and out. And I'm going to miss him like crazy.

"I ... I'm worried that I'm going to feel inadequate working with Leah. And ... there's you."

"Me?" Zach narrows his eyes.

"I know you're okay. I do. But what if you're not? What if you get a bad case of the blues? People do, ya know. It can be months, even years, after losing a spouse. I just need to know that if that happens, you'll call me to talk. Or your family."

Zach chuckles, still wiping my face with his thumbs. "Please don't worry about me. I'm good. I'll be fine. I'll hold my shit together. If for no one else, I'll do it for Harry Pawter."

"I know. Sorry." I pull away. "It's stupid. I'm stupid for acting this way. Maybe it's just the flight. It's a really long flight."

"Em?"

I glance up at him.

"You left the milk out last night, but I put it away."

It takes me a few seconds to realize what he's doing. It's the same thing I did to him behind the shed. A whiplash subject change to lighten the mood. To make me smile. So that's what I do. I smile. I can't help it. "Sorry," I say on a tiny laugh. "It won't happen again."

I didn't have milk last night. He just ... gets me.

Zach purses his lips and nods. "Good. I hope not."

That makes me giggle a little more.

"Now, get going."

"Yeah." As I reach for the handle of my suitcase, Zach grabs my other hand, turning me back to him.

My gaze goes right to my hand in his, then I find his eyes. They're contemplative, making me feel things I know I shouldn't feel. Not yet. Maybe not ever.

"Suzanne would be so proud of you. And she would tell you to get on that plane and not look back."

More tears sting my eyes as I nod. I know. I know she'd be proud of me. "And you? What do you say?"

He blows a quick breath out his nose and smiles. "I'd say listen to Suzanne. Have fun. This was the life you were born to live. But be smart."

I return another nod.

"Call if you need anything. If I'm flying, I'll get back to you as soon as I land. Okay?"

Again, I nod in lieu of speaking actual words that would choke me up. If he doesn't release my hand, I'm going to melt into a puddle at his feet, and it will be way more than the allotted ounces of liquid to be carried onto a plane.

I'm leaving my husband because I'm twenty-four and need to find my own life.

I'm leaving my husband because I owe it to my dreams to chase them until I catch them.

I'm leaving my husband because … he's not real.

Zach releases my hand and hugs me.

For a brief second, I stiffen, but the way I feel in his embrace feels too right not to relax into it, not to inhale him, not to miss him already.

"I'll work hard so this job leads to something

permanent. Insurance. Or a husband so you can be free of me for good."

Zach releases me as a few wrinkle lines form along his forehead. "Just ... follow your dreams. Make that your job and let the rest work its way out." He doesn't address the husband comment. Really, what do I expect him to say?

I love you, Emersyn. And you already have a husband.

He doesn't say that, so I take my suitcase handle again. "Okay." I smile, thinking of Suzie's final words to me. Goodbyes suck. I didn't say it to her, and I'm not saying it to Zach.

His smile barely moves his lips, but it's still there as he nods like that's his goodbye. No words, just a tiny acknowledgment.

Throwing my weight into it, I lug my stuff toward the door.

"Emersyn?"

My heart crashes into its cage with the velocity of my sudden turn. Then it completely stops beating for a few breaths to hear what he has to say. "Yeah?"

I wait for him to say something unforgettable, something romantic. I wait for him to say fuck it and rush toward me, taking me in his arms and kissing me with abandon. But my fairy-tale thoughts are just that —a fairy tale.

I wait.

And wait.

His gaze wanders to the side as if he's searching for

the words. The lines on his forehead deepen while he bites his lips between his teeth.

It's ... *killing me!*

When his gaze returns to mine, he offers a second helping of that barely detectable smile. "I love that hoodie on you. It brings out the blue in your eyes. And you have ... nice eyes."

Seriously ... my heart is on the verge of a prison break, but I gather my composure and cant my head to the side, feigning emotional confidence. "Mr. Hays, are you trying to give me a little bounce?"

Zach's smile doubles as he shrugs one shoulder. "Maybe."

"I like your ..." My lips twist for a second, then I shake my head slowly and head toward the automatic doors.

"You like my what?" he calls.

"It's too long," I say without glancing back at him. "The list is too long."

Chapter Twenty-Two

LEAH'S BEEN in Oahu a few days, so by the time I make it to the hostel, she's already settled into the dorm room, waiting for me in her bikini. "Hey, how was your flight?" She jumps down from the top bunk bed.

I survey the room.

"I know. It's small but affordable. We're not here to sit in a fancy rental or hotel room. It's all about the adventure and the landscape."

After a tiny shrug, I heave my suitcase onto the lower bunkbed. "Full disclosure?"

Leah pulls her straight black hair into a ponytail. The last time I saw her it was naturally curly. I know from her social media accounts that she never has the same look two days in a row; she might find me a tad boring.

"It's a little late for full disclosure. I already hired you, but sure ... what do you need to disclose?"

"I've lived out of my car more than once, so hostels will feel like five-star resorts."

"And they're cheap." Leah winks, sliding her arms into a pink and orange floral kimono cover-up. "Twenty-five dollars a night. Now get out of those boring jeans, put on your cutest bikini, and meet me out front. We have a car waiting for us and a full afternoon of work. You will never be homeless again, babe."

Work.

I grin while nodding. Is this really work?

Oahu has the most picturesque jungles and mountains, a volcano with deep craters down the side of it that look like claw marks, swirly textured rock formations at Lanai Lookout that are any photographer's dream, and the most vibrant blue and aqua water the Pacific has to offer.

How did this become my life? In less than a year, I've been homeless, stuck in a terrible relationship, buried in debt, hired by a couple who have changed my life forever, lost a dear friend, married, and now I'm traveling the world ... the freaking world ... taking photographs with a woman who is my spirit animal.

"So you never told me..." Leah clicks through the photos on her camera as we're driven back to the hostel just after sunset "...who are you leaving behind? I mean, when we met in New York, you casually said nobody, and I let it slide at the time. But everyone has someone they leave behind if they move, travel the world..." she glances over at me with a wrinkled nose, one nostril pierced with a small gold loop "...or die."

On a tiny laugh, I nod several times. "True. I suppose. I left behind a cat named Harry Pawter and ..." And what? Or *who*? Zach. My husband. Can I tell her that?

"And?"

I shake my head and stare out my window at the fading shoreline. "I have a mom who I haven't seen in years. No other family that I know of."

"Who's taking care of Harry Pawter?"

"A friend. Uh ... a roommate, I suppose."

"Whoa, whoa, whoa ..." Leah sets her camera on her lap and shifts her body, giving me her full attention. "A friend? A roommate *you suppose*? That's the story I want. Spill. I want every detail. I deserve every detail. We are spending the next *year* together. No secrets. When I hook up with someone, you'll know about it. When I'm having my period, you'll know about it. No personal boundaries. Sorry."

I give her a long look for several seconds, but she's right. A year is a long time in any relationship. "I've been staying with a couple who hired me to clean their house. They discovered I was living out of my car and insisted I stay with them. Suzie, the wife, died of cancer at the end of summer and..." I bite my lips together for a breath "...now I'm living with Zach, her husband. Ex. Whatever. He's taking care of Harry Pawter for me."

Leah's lips twist to the side for a second. "An older couple?"

"Older than me."

"You're twenty-four, so technically twenty-five—my age—is older than you."

"They're in their thirties. Well, were, I mean ... she was. She died. He's obviously still alive and watching my cat."

After a few slow blinks, her head cocks to the side. "You're living with a man in his thirties? His wife died, and you're still living in their house?" When she says it, it sounds weird.

It doesn't feel weird. Okay, maybe a little weird.

"Just temporarily. I became good friends with his wife. She wanted me to look after him."

With a slow raise of her eyebrows, she gives me several exaggerated blinks. "She found her replacement before she died."

"What?" I shake my head. "No. That's not it at all."

"Did they have children?"

I shake my head.

"Em ... wake up! Suzie chose you to replace her, to give her husband a new life and lots of babies. You are the healthy, fertile, young chosen one."

My face fills with heat as I avert my gaze to the rearview mirror, wondering if the driver is paying attention to our conversation. "No," I say in a soft voice. "Nice try."

"Is Zach sexy?"

This makes the driver shoot me a quick glance in his mirror.

I immediately slide my gaze back to Leah. "He's ...

217

fine. I guess. He was my friend's husband. I don't look at him like that."

"Liar." She grins.

I know ... deep down *I know* I'll end up telling her about the marriage, but not now. Not on our first day of a long adventure.

Chapter Twenty-Three

HAWAII.

Fiji.

New Zealand.

Tasmania.

Australia.

Five islands in twelve weeks. Twelve weeks of missing Zach and Harry Pawter ... but mostly Zach.

He's my number one fan on Instagram, always liking my posts and commenting with something like "nice tan" or a restaurant recommendation because he's traveled to so many of the same places.

We talk on the phone on those rare occasions that our schedules allow, like tonight. While it's night for me here in Australia, it's early morning for Zach. I bite my tongue every time we talk because the first words that want to sprint from my mouth are always "I miss you so much!"

"You're stamping your passport with a few places I

haven't been. Not gonna lie ... I'm getting a little envious of you," he says the second I answer his call.

"You haven't been to Australia? I find that hard to believe," I say instead of my desperate "I miss you so much!"

"I've been to Australia. But I haven't traveled to Fiji or Tasmania."

It thrills me to know that I've experienced places Zach has never visited. In a weird way, it makes me feel older than I am—experienced and mature. "It's a dream. I keep waiting for someone to wake me up and tell me I can't sleep in this parking lot."

Zach doesn't say anything. Is it too early for the homeless jokes? I *have* to laugh at my life to really appreciate where I am at the moment.

"You photographed a wedding last weekend," he says.

"Yes! Oh my god ... it was unplanned, like this whole trip seems to be. But the circumstances around the wedding gig are almost too crazy to be true... but it *is* true. Total luck on their part. We were minding our own business, sipping drinks on the beach while watching a wedding, maybe fifty yards down the way from us, and no joke ... the photographer just collapsed as the bride was making her way to her groom. Apparently, he was diabetic, and we were told he'd be fine, but it left the couple with no one to take photos.

"So leave it to Leah to traipse up to the couple, in her bikini, holding her drink in one hand and her camera slung across her body, and say, 'My friend and I can snap a few photos if you'd like.' So we did—in our bikinis! The couple insisted they pay us something, but Leah said they didn't have to pay us anything if they would sign a photo release and let us post the photos on her website and social media."

"Good timing," Zach says. His voice makes me miss him even more. "How have you been feeling? Are you taking your medication? Getting plenty of sleep? Staying hydrated?"

I roll my eyes. "Yes, Dad."

"Who are you talking to?" Leah asks as she opens the door to our tiny room after using the shared bathroom at the hostel here in Sydney.

I give her a *duh* look because she knows I only have one person to call, unlike her. Leah has a huge family spread all around the US, plus her unofficial extended family, aka friends, she's made around the world while traveling. I think she has lovers in at least a dozen countries as well. I didn't see her much in Fiji because of a sexy man named Nete that she calls Ned.

When my eye roll confirms who I'm talking to, Leah makes a few exaggerated hip thrusts, being her usual obnoxious self.

I love her.

"Leah just walked into the room," I tell Zach.

"But I can leave if you two want to have phone sex," she yells.

Dead. Right here. I'm in my grave. She had *way* too much wine with dinner.

"Oh my god ..." I shoot her an evil glare while flying off the single bed and straight out of the room. "She's drunk," I spew out in desperation while finding a private alcove in the garden area on the back side of the hostel.

Zach chuckles, but it sounds forced. Awkward.

"So how's your family? Have you been taking flowers to Suzie?" I rarely mention Suzie's name, but after the phone sex comment from Leah, I search for literally *any* change in subject.

"They're good. Aaron just got engaged."

"What? Are you serious?"

"Yup. I guess when you know, you know."

I nod to myself when another pregnant pause settles on the line between us. He doesn't elaborate or say anything about taking flowers to Suzie.

"Tell him congratulations and I can't wait to meet his fiancée."

"I will."

"So ... it's your birthday tomorrow, old man."

Zach laughs. "It is."

"Whatcha doing for your birthday?"

"Working."

I frown. "Figures. Will your crew be throwing you a party?"

"We actually went out tonight since we don't fly out until tomorrow night, and we can sleep in tomorrow morning."

"Okay." I giggle. "You're drunk. It's morning there. You mean you went out last night, not *tonight.* Or are you predicting the future?"

"No. We went out tonight. I'm a little buzzed, but not drunk. It's ..." He pauses for a second. "Just a little before eleven p.m."

I glance at my watch. It's ten fifty-five *p.m.*

"I told you I'm working. I'm a pilot. I fly around the world. Don't always assume I'm in Atlanta."

"You ... you're in my time zone."

"I am," he says so coolly, so matter-of-factly. "I love Sydney in April."

"Zachary Hays! Oh my god! Oh my GOD! You're in Sydney? Are you kidding me? This is not funny."

He chuckles some more as I pace three feet back and forth at least a dozen times.

"No joking. I was going to see if you were available for brunch tomorrow."

"Yes! Of course. Where? When?"

"My hotel has a good buffet. I'll text you the address and my room number. Ten sound okay?"

"Absolutely. I can't wait. I've ..."

Missed you.

"Um ..." I stutter with my words as they trip over my emotions scattered everywhere. I'm a mess.

And thrilled.

And excited.

And anxious beyond words.

I won't be able to sleep.

"I, uh ... I'm looking forward to seeing you."

"Emersyn?"

Em-er-syn

223

"Yeah?" I try to control my ragged breaths and the exhausting racing of my heart racking against my chest.

"I've missed you too."

I'm not sure why those four words send tears streaming down my face, but they do. It's kindness and friendly affection. Friendly ... we are friends. Married friends, but still friends. And friends can miss each other. Lately, the one thing I seem to do better than taking photographs is missing Zach. If missing him came with a paycheck and health insurance, I'd be set for life.

"I'll, uh ... see you in the morning."

"Goodnight," he says.

As soon as I return to the room, Leah sits up ramrod straight in bed. "I need the deets. All of them. And don't be coy like there's nothing to share because you left the room. You've never left the room while talking to him."

"You yelled the words *phone sex*. What was I supposed to do?"

Leah bats her wild, curly black hair out of her face. "He's the reason you're not hooking up with anyone. Isn't he?"

I grab my toothbrush and toothpaste and head toward the bathroom, ignoring her question. When I return, she's still eyeing me, so I don't look at her.

"When's the last time you got some?" Leah asks.

"Some what?"

She blows out a long breath "Dick. When's the last time you got some dick?"

I remove my jeans and bra and slip on a tank top. "Before we left for Hawaii."

"Zach?"

"What?" I force a quick glance in her direction.

"If it was right before we left for Hawaii, was it Zach or a random hookup?"

"It ... uh..." I shake my head and climb into bed, shutting off the light as quickly as possible "...wasn't Zach. We're just friends. And I didn't say I hooked up *right* before we left. It was with my ex-boyfriend."

"The gym guy?"

"Yeah."

"Emersyn! That was last summer. Are you saying you haven't had sex since last summer?"

"It's no big deal. I was busy helping take care of Suzie. Then the holidays ... then you hired me. Just so much life has happened."

"I'm not buying your excuse, but whatever. So what's new with Zach?"

My heart hasn't stopped its impossibly fast sprint since he told me his location. I'm shocked Leah can't hear me panting. "Zach is here."

"Here?"

"He's in Sydney. He flies out tomorrow night. Tomorrow's his birthday. So if you're good with it, I'm going to have brunch with him at his hotel."

The light turns on. A wide-eyed, tangled-haired Leah stands at the foot of my bed with her hands on her hips. "He's in Sydney? Are you fucking kidding me?"

Rolling my lips between my teeth, I attempt to stay calm and act unaffected as I nod several times.

"Why are you here?" she asks.

"Brunch isn't until ten."

"Why are you here?" She cocks her head to the side.

"It's after eleven at night."

"Why are you here?"

Sitting up, I slowly inch my head side to side.

Leah grins. "You fell in love with your friend's husband."

I continue to shake my head.

"I've listened to you talk about Zach for months. I'm not stupid. You can't convince me that you feel nothing more than friendship toward him. You can't convince me that you're not *dying* to grab a ride to his hotel right this minute and throw yourself into his arms."

My head continues to shake as I hold my breath and listen to Leah verbalize my every emotion.

"I bet he misses you too." She grins.

"He doesn't miss me the same way," I whisper, slowly showing her my feelings.

"Does he know how you miss him?"

"No."

"Then how can you possibly know how he misses you?"

"Because he lost his wife, and I don't think his

heart is capable of even coming close to having feelings for another woman or *missing* someone in that way."

"Well, how will you know if you don't get out of this bed right now and go see him?"

On a nervous laugh, I run my fingers through my hair. "And he opens his hotel room door and asks why I'm there? What do I say?"

"You say you couldn't wait until tomorrow to see him."

"By the time I get there, it will be midnight. So ... what then? I see him and he stares at me with tired eyes—which will make me feel bad because he a has a job in which he's responsible for hundreds of lives and he needs good sleep. So I say hi, turn around, and get a ride back here only to see him again in the morning?"

"Or you crash with him in his hotel room."

I shake my head. "That's crazy and weird."

Leah kneels on the end of the bed and reaches for my hands. "What are you afraid of?"

"Nothing."

She squeezes my hands. "How did you feel when he said he's here in Sydney?"

"I didn't feel—"

"Stop. Just stop." She yanks at my hands until I lift my gaze to hers. "Let me see it."

"See what?"

"Your heart. Your fears. The things you wouldn't dream of ever saying aloud. You *need* to set them free. I see it in your eyes; it's killing you."

After a few blinks, I avert my gaze. "I love him," I whisper. "But it's complicated."

"His wife dying isn't complicated. It's life."

"It's ... more than that."

"Cool." She readjusts so she's on her butt with her legs crossed, facing me. "I'm listening."

I glance at the alarm clock.

"Unless you have somewhere you need to go."

"This is one of the stupidest things I've ever done ..." I throw back the blanket and climb out of bed. "And I've done many stupid things," I say, pulling on a T-shirt and jeans.

"We have a tour at two tomorrow. Be back by one."

I tug on my brown leather ankle boots and glance up at her. "I'll probably be back in less than two hours when he sends me back here so he can sleep."

"I doubt it," she says just as I open the door.

I take my one-ton bundle of nerves and anxiety and drag it to the front of the hostel, where I order a ride to the hotel address he texted me.

Silent laughter at my own crazy assumption echoes in my head all the way to his hotel. All the way to his room, where I stand with a shaky fist held an inch from his door.

I'm so scared; oxygen feels in short supply at the moment.

Knock. Knock.

I tip my chin down, knowing he's going to look through the peephole to see me before he opens the door. Frightened out of my fucking mind isn't a good look, so I hide my face from sight until the door eases open.

Zach rubs his tired eyes while mine focus on his naked chest and black running shorts. "Emersyn ..." His voice holds as much exhaustion as the rest of his body.

This was a terrible decision even if my entire chest is ready to explode because it's been too long since I've seen him in person.

"I ... I couldn't sleep, and I thought with the huge time difference that maybe you couldn't either, but clearly you can. So I'll just come back at ten." I turn.

"Emersyn."

I stop with my back to him, my breath held hostage to the point of pain.

"It's so ... fucking ... good to see you," he says with such relief to his words.

All that relief rips the rawest emotions from me as I turn and throw my arms around him while I cry. Again.

"Those better be happy tears."

Keeping my face buried in his neck, I nod and sniffle.

"You've lost weight. I don't think you had weight to lose." He releases me, and I quickly wipe my face. I know his worry comes from genuine concern. He watched Suzie lose weight until she lost her last breath.

"Traipsing around the world, hiking, swimming, paddle boarding ... it's a little more exercise than cleaning houses and stopping at the gym for an hour several times a week," I say.

He closes the door behind us as I mosey into his room that's just a bed, a desk, and a single chair by the window.

"I'll eat several days' worth of food at brunch if it makes you feel better, but..." when I reach the window, I turn and slide my hands into my front pockets as he pulls on a T-shirt "...physically I've never felt better. Lots of vitamin D."

A small smile steals his lips. "You're quite tan. Makes your hair look white."

I frown. "It's been thoroughly bleached by the sun."

"It looks good on you. *You* look good."

That familiar blush blooms along my cheeks. "Thanks. So do you. Thirty-four looks good on you. Happy birthday, by the way."

Zach glances at the clock on his nightstand and nods. "What a great birthday present." He returns his attention to me.

"I told Leah it was a stupid idea to come here in the middle of the night." I shrug because I don't know what to say or do next. We're in a hotel room after midnight, and things start to feel awkward quickly.

"Want to see what's on TV?" He gestures toward the screen on the console.

"Sure."

Zach plunks down on the bed, leaning against the headboard and turns on the TV.

I lower into the chair.

He chuckles. "You can't see the TV from there. Sit next to me."

"It's fine. I'll just scoot it over a bit." I try to move the chair, but it doesn't scoot well along the carpet.

"I don't bite."

I glance up and shoot him a smile that matches my uneasiness. "I know." Giving up on the chair, I sit on the other side of the bed and toe off my boots before stretching my legs out and leaning against the head-board next to him.

"I want to hear all about your travels thus far." He turns on a twenty-four-hour news channel.

"I've told you everything on our calls and texts." I laugh.

"You tell me Leah has a new guy at every location, but you never share your ... social life." He flips through more channels, keeping his gaze on the TV.

"I fear I took the wrong job for finding a husband ... uh ... a real one ... or ... well, you know what I mean. It's hard to find more than random hookups when you're not in one place very long."

He says nothing for few seconds, then he exhales slowly. "You're young. I think traveling the world and finding random hookups *is* the point at your age. That's what I did."

I let his ... advice? Confession? Whatever it is, I let it settle for a minute before responding. "I'm not exactly hooking up with random guys. I haven't decided if that's my thing yet. Which is strange because that's all I knew from my mom while growing up. So if you were a man whore at my age ..." I shrug and grin. "That's on you, Zachary."

"Really?" He turns his head to give me his narrow-eyed gaze. "Man whore? That's what you're going with?"

I give him a quick side-eye before returning my gaze to the TV, crossing my arms over my chest. "If the shoe fits ..."

"It doesn't fit. A whore is a person who gets paid for sex. I've never been paid for sex. If you're not hooking up with anyone because you don't know what to charge, then I think we need to talk."

"Shut up." I grin. "That's not it." Climbing off the bed, I help myself to his minibar.

"That's not complimentary," he says.

I shrug. "It is if my name's not on the room." I twist off the top to a small bottle of red wine and down half of it as Zach's eyes widen a fraction with each gulp I take. "What can I get you?"

"I'm good. I drank too much earlier when I went out with my crew."

I nod and down more wine.

"Did you not have wine with Leah? You said she was drunk."

When I feel confident a new round of courage is close to reaching my veins, I set the bottle down on the desk and sit on the edge. "I had wine."

He nods toward the bottle. "But that's better?"

Grunting a laugh, I shake my head. "No. That's awful shit."

Zach chuckles and I feel it in my belly. "Then why drink it?"

"Because I should leave, but I haven't been here that long, so leaving now would make my whole middle-of-the-night trip here seem crazy." That shot of courage is making its way into my bloodstream at an unprecedented speed. I'm already saying the quiet part out loud.

"So you're biding your time by drinking shitty wine?"

"No. I'm hoping I pass out soon and don't have to make an uncomfortable exit. When that happens, just slip a pillow under my head. I'll be fine on the floor."

"Emersyn, if you leave now, I'll still be glad you came. It's not crazy that you came."

With a sharp nod, I slowly say, "Okay. But ... what if I don't leave? Would that be crazy?"

"I ..." He lifts one shoulder into a slow shrug. "I'm not sure crazy is the right word."

I yawn and drag my feet toward the bed. That was the perfect amount of wine for me to just ... lie down and not feel guilty for my trip here. "I'm tired, Zach," I mumble, closing my eyes. "And I've missed you," I say a little softer as the warmth from the wine spreads through my body. "I've missed..." I teeter on the edge of sleep, feeling barely coherent "...my husband."

Rolling to the side facing him, I force my eyes open halfway as he scoots down, facing me on his side. He doesn't say anything. Nothing really needs to be said. We're two friends wading through the stages of grief, finding comfort in each other's *friendship.* Just ... friend stuff.

Unfortunately, that partial bottle of wine overrules my silence. "Suzie wanted this ..." I whisper.

Zach remains silent, just an unreadable expression and his soulful eyes staring back at me.

"She wanted me to take care of you." My eyes blink heavily as I inch my face closer to his.

Zach doesn't blink. Not once. He doesn't move. I'm not sure he's breathing.

"I like taking care of you. But I hate ... I hate missing you." I barely register my own voice. I'm unsure if I'm thinking the words or saying them. "You're such a good man." The wine lets me lean in the final two inches, pressing my lips to his. It's not really a kiss because neither one of us move our mouths or any other parts of our bodies for that matter. I close my eyes and fall into a dream state.

In the morning, he's gone. His suitcase is here, but he's not here. No note. No text on my phone. Maybe he decided to eat breakfast without me. As I sit on the edge of the bed and rub my head, it comes back to me.

I kissed him. Sort of. What does that even mean? I pressed my lips to his. That's a kiss, right? It was less of a kiss than our wedding—our marriage ceremony— but more of a kiss than had I just kept my lips to myself.

Had I left the hotel instead of opening that bottle of wine from the minibar.

Had I stayed at the hostel.

Had I not fallen in love with my friend's husband.

Had I not fallen in love with *my* husband.

"Shit." I leap off the bed and shove my feet into my boots, grab my phone, and bolt toward the door before he comes back from … wherever.

I kissed him.

SHIT!

I kissed him, and it was a stupid thing to do.

Way to ruin your marriage by kissing your husband.

Throwing open the door, I'm stopped in my pursuit by a tall, sweaty Zachary Hays with his shirt draped over his bare torso, shorts riding extra low on his hips, running shoes just inches from the toes of my brown boots.

"In a hurry?" he asks.

"Um … I … I wasn't sure where you went, and I know you fly out tonight, and I probably kept you awake with my snoring. So …"

I have no idea if I snore or not, and I'm sure he knows I'm frantically talking out of my ass because I KISSED HIM!

"I guess what I'm saying is … we don't need to have brunch. I mean … we got to see each other, and I'm sure we'll run into each other again sometime. Right?"

He smirks. "I forgive you for kissing me. Now, can we do brunch at ten and forget about shitty minibar wine and meaningless mistakes?"

My lips part as my jaw makes a slow descent to the floor. I'm not sure how to respond.

Forgive me?

Meaningless mistake?

I need a new husband.

Who am I kidding? Zach isn't my husband. He's Suzie's husband. I'm like the child they adopted. Only they couldn't adopt a twenty-three-year-old, so Zach married me to give me health insurance, which is basically like illegal or fraudulent adoption of an adult.

And maybe I don't need a husband, real or otherwise. Maybe what I do need is a *meaningless mistake*, the kind that doesn't require an apology and doesn't have to feel like an actual mistake.

"Yeah," I whisper, wrapping a bandage around my delicate heart and tucking it away from Zach's reach. "We can do brunch. And I appreciate your forgiveness. I wasn't thinking at all. Stupid wine."

His smirk transforms into a full smile. I can't tell if it's genuine or not because I'm too focused on my own fake reaction to his words. I'm too focused on finding the quickest way to hook up with literally any decent, single guy so my delusional mind can recalibrate with reality again.

"You weren't making much sense. A lot of mumbling. You weren't yourself. See you back here soon?"

I nod slowly. "Sure. I'll uh ... just meet you downstairs at the buffet."

"Sounds good."

Chapter Twenty-Four

Zach

RULES.

Protocol.

Guidelines.

I need something.

Minimal thought was involved in my decision to request this flight to Sydney. After months of following Emersyn's posts on social media, I needed to see her. Really *see* her.

Why? Well, I'm still trying to figure that out.

Now I've seen her. Now I know how her lips feel against mine. That's not why I came here. I feel like I need to apologize to Suzanne. It's stupid, but feelings are exempt from any sort of reason or justification.

Emersyn had too much wine.

She said some crazy shit.

I was tired.

She was confused.

Period.

It doesn't have to be awkward. Maybe I requested this flight because being close to Emersyn makes me feel close to Suzanne. But I don't think that's it. I took this flight for the same reason Suzanne couldn't get enough of Emersyn—she doesn't look at me like a guy who lost his wife.

Emersyn didn't look at Suzanne like a woman dying from cancer.

I didn't fully understand the importance of that feeling until now.

So ... have I flown to the other side of the earth to feel alive again? It's looking like the most honest explanation.

After I get out of the shower, there's a text from Emersyn.

> I can't make it to brunch. Leah has a tour scheduled. Happy birthday. Safe flight home.

Reading it three times, I grapple with the disappointment I feel. We didn't say goodbye. With my next breath, I call her.

"Hi!" She answers as if she's excited, maybe even a little surprised to hear from me.

"Hey. Last minute tour?" I ask.

"Yeah. I'm so sorry. Leah is too."

"What time will you be done? We didn't get to say goodbye."

There's a long pause.

"Em?"

She clears her throat. "Unfortunately, not until later. And Leah and I have plans tonight. She's fixing me up with a friend of a friend. A date. That's good. Right?"

Another pause holds the line for several seconds.

"Sure. That's good. Be careful. Be smart."

"Yup," she says with a clipped voice.

"Em?"

"Hmm?"

"Are you happy?"

Her silence feels more honest than her next words. "Yes, Zach. I'm happy. I've never been happier in my life."

"I'm glad. I needed to hear that. Let me know when you decide where you're going next. Maybe we can meet up again."

"Sure."

"Bye, Em."

"Bye," she whispers.

I stare at my phone screen for several seconds before tossing it aside and pulling on a T-shirt. Plunking onto the edge of the bed, my head drops and my eyes close on a deep exhale. Marrying Emersyn wasn't supposed to be anything more than the gift of insurance and cheap flights.

Doing the right thing for the right reason.

Yet here I am ... sulking in a hotel room in Australia because I have a wife who is not Suzanne. A wife whose happiness is not my responsibility.

I really, *really* need to stop thinking the word "wife" when thinking about Emersyn.

Different kind of wife.

Different emotions.

Different mentality.

———

Emersyn

STANDING in the corner of the hostel lobby, sharing space with a tropical plant, I stare at my phone screen. Zach sounded overly concerned or something. God. I hate this. It's too late. I don't need a father. And he's not my husband, even if the state of Georgia thinks otherwise. Zach needs me to be happy. I hear it in his voice —a tightness, a hint of agony. Suzie asked me to watch out for him.

So that's what I'm doing.

He gave me a chance at a new life. I'll give him peace of mind in return.

It's not a lie, not completely. I am happy, but it also proves just how shitty my life has been for *this* agonizing time in said life to be the happiest I've ever been.

"Back before brunch?" Wearing a green facial mask, Leah glances up from her computer.

"It's not until ten. And I need to shower. But I'm not going to brunch."

"Why not? What happened? I mean ... you spent the night with him. That's good, right?"

"If by spent the night, you mean I drank too much wine from the minibar, said too much, pressed my lips to his in what was either not a real kiss or the worst kiss ever, before basically passing out from exhaustion and too much wine ... then yes. I spent the night with him. Was it good? No. It was awkward. And this morning, he completely dismissed it. Blamed the kiss, or whatever it was, on the wine and called it a meaningless mistake. But he 'forgives' me, so all is good."

I grab my toiletries and open the door to go shower. "I can't see him again. Maybe in another three months ... or three years. But the good news?" Glancing over my shoulder, I grin. "I agree with you ... I need dick that doesn't involve my dead best friend's husband. I need dick that has no strings attached. I need ..."

"Australian dick." Leah smirks.

I nod. "Yes. Australian dick. I'm thinking something rugged and confident, but not too clingy. Professional ... but free. I'm not paying for dick."

Leah giggles as I head to the shower. Sadly, no amount of water can wash off the embarrassment and overall cringe-worthiness of my actions last night— early this morning ... whatever.

I took it up the backside once for a shower. What's

241

a one-night stand to take my mind off Zach in comparison to that? I can do meaningless. Maybe I need to do way more meaninglessness after such a heavy experience with Suzie and Zach.

WE SPEND most of the day in Hunter Valley taking family photos at a vineyard for a couple and their two girls whom Leah met on social media over a year ago. After the family photos, we consume more than our fair share of wine, stuff ourselves with some of the best food I've ever tasted, observe kangaroos in the wild, and scrounge a ride back to Sydney.

"I'm so glad you decided to do this." Leah attempts to put a few curls in my limp hair with a wide-barreled curling iron.

"This?" I question.

"The perfect answer to unrequited love is reminding your body that a good orgasm doesn't require deep emotion."

"A photographer *and* a philosopher. And it's not love. It's just ... feelings."

Leah giggles. "*Feelings* ... whatever."

I slip into my version of a little black dress, which is actually a wide strapped, tangerine mini dress with a tie in the back.

One dress. That's all I allotted myself since I needed to keep my belongings to one suitcase. My love for fashion rejected the idea of one suitcase. Rewearing the same five outfits? Cringe.

Suzie would understand.

Leah's friends meet us at a bar not too far from the hostel. Noah and Mia let Leah sleep on their couch the last time she visited Sydney. She met them through social media and blindly trusted they weren't going to murder her. If I hadn't lived out of my car, blindly trusting that no one would murder me, I'd be more judgmental.

"Here they come," Leah whispers, adjusting her version of a little black dress—an off-the-shoulder midi with a hot pink floral fabric that's extremely sheer. Noah's best mates, Peter and Martin, partners at an architecture firm, saunter toward our table. They look like brothers with dirty blond hair and the sexiest smiles. "For the record, I hooked up with one of them."

My gaze rips from the hot guys headed toward us and sticks firmly to Leah's painted on smile. "What? Well, which one?" I ask frantically as they close the distance to our table.

"I'm not telling you because I want you to have first choice tonight. I'm fine with either one."

"What?" I whisper-yell at her. "No. You have to tell me."

Leah makes a turning-the-key gesture at her pursed lips. It's not a game. I don't want to hook up with the same guy she hooked up with on her last visit. As they near the table, I'm forced to smile like I'm not assuming sex is a forgone conclusion.

Are they?

Did Leah tell Noah and Mia I need to get laid?

As Noah stands to greet them with manly hugs, I search for any signs of either one of them eyeing Leah with the "hey, I remember you, we had sex" look.

A slightly bigger smile.

A tiny wink.

Wandering eyes.

Something!

I'm doomed. Both men greet Leah like they've met her, which they obviously have, and neither one gives me even the tiniest sign. Maybe she's lying. Maybe she hasn't had sex with either one of them, *or* maybe she's had sex with both of them.

At the same time.

No.

Well, maybe. I mean ... why not?

If I were Leah, I'd embrace every opportunity afforded me. Wait ...

I am Leah.

Single. *Figuratively.*

Young.

Free.

Adventurous.

And my husband is in love with memories. I can't compete with those memories.

"Hi." I smile, pulling myself from the train wreck of thoughts in my head.

Noah goes through the introductions. Peter and Martin give me the same level of attention as they give

Leah. Maybe it doesn't matter if she slept with one or both of them.

Over the next two hours, I let Zach fade from my thoughts with the help of a nice Zinfandel.

So much Zinfandel. Too much, really.

"Hey," Peter says as I bump into him after my second trip to the ladies' room.

I think it's Peter. Why do they have to look so alike? It might be the Zinfandel.

"Hey," I say as my gaze makes a sluggish trip to his face.

"I don't live too far from here." He rests his hands on my hips.

I lean into him out of physical necessity; it's not pretty. There's no disguising his intentions, no suggesting we take a walk (not that I could).

Or grab a coffee to sober up.

Or sip tea and share our life's goals.

My mind wants to return to Zach, but I catch it from slipping back into that self-destructive behavior.

"I need to tell Leah I'm leaving."

He nods, wearing a triumphant grin.

With nothing more than a quick goodbye to Leah and everyone else at the table, I let Peter ... or Martin ... take my hand and guide me to the door.

To his car.

To his apartment.

To his bedroom.

And I let the rest of the world fade away for a while.

"I could use some brekky before we give it another go. How about you?" His naked ass saunters out of the bedroom.

"Sure," I mumble just before falling asleep.

No "brekky" for me.

Chapter Twenty-Five

Malaysia. #adventure #LoveIt

I KNOW Zach will see my Instagram post, so I let that be my way of telling him I've arrived in a new location.

It's been three weeks since I've seen him. Three weeks since we've talked or texted. He comments on my social media posts, but nothing personal.

It's not that I'm hoping he's here in Kuala Lumpur, but I wouldn't complain. He isn't the easiest guy to erase from my mind—not that I want to forget him. I'd just like to go more than a few hours without thinking about him.

When Zach doesn't respond right away to my most recent post, I assume he's in flight or sleeping.

"Zach?" Leah asks as we lug our suitcases onto the subway.

"Yeah. No." I laugh. "Instagram. So indirectly Zach. Thought it might be kind of me to post that I'm no longer in Australia. He asked me to let him know where I was going."

"How nice of you."

"What's that supposed to mean?" I narrow my eyes as we find a spot to stand next to an older couple sharing kind smiles with us.

Leah shrugs. "It just means you're awfully nice to a guy who doesn't feel the same way about you."

"I don't know how he feels." I avert my gaze to the window. "And you don't know how I feel. I had no issue hooking up with Martin."

"Peter," she corrects me.

I wince. *Peter Martin*.

"My point is ... I'm being a kind friend. He cares about me in his own way, and when you care about people, you like to know they're safe. Sadly, Zach is the only person who gives a shit about my whereabouts. That's why I gave you his information as my emergency contact."

"*I* give a shit."

I roll my eyes. "Sorry. Present company excluded. And I simply posted a pic about my arrival in Malaysia." I hold up my phone so she can see the post. "I didn't hashtag MissingZach. I didn't send him a direct message saying I can't stop thinking about what it would be like to have his naked body all over mine."

The gentleman next to us clears his throat. He must speak English. I give him an apologetic smile.

Leah smirks and lowers her voice. "Oh ... my ... god." Her perfectly filled-in eyebrows slide up her forehead. "You didn't *say* those things, but you're thinking them."

"No."

"Yes," she insists.

I giggle. "No. And even if I were, it should be ..." My common sense gets ahold of my rambling tongue.

"It should be what?"

"Nothing." I shake my head.

"Something. It's something. But what?" Leah angles her head so she's in my face. There's nowhere to avert my gaze anymore.

Pressing my lips together, I engage in a silent game of who's going to blink first. I'm usually good at this game. It's how I managed to keep my homelessness a secret for so long. But I don't really want to keep my secret from Leah. I don't have any other friends— except Zach. This is the one thing I can't tell him, and I need to tell someone before I lose my ever-loving mind.

So I blink first.

"It should be okay for me to think whatever I want of Zach."

Leah's eyes narrow a fraction, curiosity drawing lines along her forehead.

"Because he's my husband."

Those lines on her forehead vanish, and a blank expression replaces all confusion like her heart stopped beating—like all emotion and coherent thoughts died on impact from my words. "Excuse me?" she whispers.

"Legally." I feel the need to put that out there.

"Is there any other kind?" The confusion returns as her head cants to the side.

I frown. "Sadly, yes."

"Em ... I'm lost."

We get to our stop, and I nod toward the exit. I'd rather not confess my legal indiscretions around English speaking people like the old couple. "He married me so I could have his health insurance."

Leah laughs. "That's crazy, Emersyn."

"It's not," I murmur. "I need it."

"Em, I went several years without insurance. If you're young and healthy, the chances of you needing it are slim, unless you get into some sort of accident. And if that's the case, you'll probably die anyway. So fuck the hospitals."

We merge into the sidewalk traffic and head toward our hostel.

"I have a little condition. It's not a big deal. I take medication for it."

"You said those were vitamins you take every day. What's your condition? I asked if you had any health issues that could interfere with traveling."

"It's under control, and it's clearly not interfering with anything."

Leah sighs. "Is it cancer?"

"No." I laugh. "I wouldn't call cancer a little condition."

"You'd be surprised at how many people who

wanted to check a bunch off shit of their bucket list would call cancer a little condition."

"It's epilepsy."

"Jesus ..."

"No." I laugh again. "Not Jesus. Jesus is the response to cancer. Bummer is the response to epilepsy."

"So at any moment, you could fall to the ground and start seizing?"

"I'm on medication. It shouldn't happen."

"But if it does ... what am I supposed to do?"

"Stay calm. I'll come out of it and be fine." Unless I injure myself like falling into the racks of an open dishwasher.

"Just don't. Please don't do that," she says.

"I won't." I laugh.

"And ... Zach married you so you'd have insurance. That's ..."

"Fraudulent?"

She chuckles. "Well, yes, but I was going to say incredibly generous."

"Agreed. He blew my mind when he suggested it. It took me a while to process it and agree to do it. After all, I was so close to Suzie, and he prefaced it with how it was basically a charity offer. A legal marriage but not a real marriage with emotions and ..."

"Sex?"

I grin. "Exactly. I mean, had he legit asked me to marry him like ... for real ... I would not have said yes. So I wasn't

251

disappointed that it wasn't a real marriage proposal from him. I was disappointed that it was my first marriage proposal. I was disappointed that my first marriage involved a trip to the courthouse. I was disappointed that five minutes after I said I do, my husband headed to the dentist for a routine appointment." I blow out a long breath. "It wasn't until after the wedding, after we'd been living together as husband and wife—only not really—that I realized I was, in fact, in love with my husband."

Leah points to the white two-story building to our right. "And ... you're allowed to hook up with whomever whenever?"

Following her to the main door of the hostel, I nod. "Yes. I'm in pursuit of a job with benefits or a husband with ... well..." I laugh "...benefits."

As soon as we step inside the hostel, she turns toward me, lowering her voice. "But you love Zach."

My smile fades as I give her the bad news. "I love Zach."

"Ouch." Her nose wrinkles.

I nod slowly. "Yeah. Ouch."

As she gets us checked in, my phone vibrates with a text.

> Zach: Malaysia is stunning. I'm a little envious. I've only been there once.

> Em: If you're in Kuala Lumpur, just tell me now.

Zach: Lol Sorry. I'm in Detroit waiting for storms to pass. Looks like things might clear by noon.

Em: Have you visited our girl recently?

Zach: Of course.

Em: Fuchsia tulips?

Zach: Of course.

Em: It's been almost a year since you hired me.

Zach: I know. Time flies.

Em: Unlike you today.

Zach: Touché

I stare at the screen. His quick responses make him feel so much closer than he is right now. Half a world away. And he could have liked my post or commented with something generic, but he texted me instead. Things feel a little more normal again.

Em: We just got checked in to the hostel. I have to go. Safe flight.

Zach: When do you plan to come home?

I grimace, wishing I could feel his words, the emotion, the context.

> Em: Harry Pawter missing me? I miss him.

> Zach: Yeah, him too. Lucky cat.

Him too. Does Zach miss me? Maybe the house needs cleaning. Maybe he misses my cooking. Maybe he misses watching me edit photos the way I miss listening to him play his guitar and sing the lyrics to songs while driving. Maybe it's more. I tamp that thought down before it runs amuck.

> Em: I don't know when Leah plans to go home. She's not much of a planner.

> Zach: All is good at home. Take your time. Be safe.

I hit the kiss emoji. Then I delete it. I type XO. Delete that too. I have a million unspoken feelings for Zach that I can't share—not even with an emoji. I feel like they would come across as more than a friendly sentiment. The kiss in the hotel room opened me up. I let him see something I wasn't supposed to let him see. Slipping my phone into my pocket, I opt to give him the final word for now.

Chapter Twenty-Six

LIFE WITH LEAH involves beach hopping and tours of breathtaking scenery, live videos on social media, editing photos, phenomenal food, and exquisite wine. Everything is great—mostly great.

"You okay?" Leah startles me as I comb my hair and contemplate asking her when she plans on making a return trip to the States. But we're a week into our time here, and I'm not ready to spoil anything.

"Uh ... yeah." I smile and toss my brush into my bag.

"Ready for dinner?" She checks her hair in the gold framed mirror by the pedestal sink as I grab my purse.

"Definitely."

"Leon and Andre are going to eat with us."

"They are?" I wasn't expecting this to be a night out with guys. I'm not sure I can be like Leah and have a Peter Martin in every destination.

"Yes." She eyes me in the mirror and grins. "You don't have to sleep with anyone. Now that I know you're married, I feel a little less enthusiastic about being your pimp."

"And now that I know you thought of yourself as my pimp, I'm feeling a little less enthusiastic about being your employee."

Leah giggles and turns toward me. "Live it up tonight. We might die tomorrow."

My eyes widen as I curl my lips inward and hum. "I didn't know death was on our itinerary."

"I've been told the descent into the Mulu airport is a little ... heart-thumping. It was that or the boat ride up the river through the snake-infested jungles. And just for the record ... if I were here by myself, I'd choose the boat. So don't say I never do anything for you." She winks.

I'm not sure if I should be insulted that she thinks I can't handle snakes or grateful because ... I can't handle snakes!

If I'm going to die abroad, what better place than Gunung Mulu National Park.

Caves.

Vertical cliffs.

Gorges.

And yes ... snakes.

Don't even bring me home. Find an ancient burial site and add me to the count.

"Did Leon and Andre invite us or did you invite them?"

Her glossed lips twist to the side. "I'm not sure, maybe a bit of both. It just came up in conversation while you were in the shower."

Leon and Andre are staying at the hostel as well. Cousins from France who speak fairly good English. Not that it matters because Leah manages to speak a little bit of every language we've encountered thus far.

"But *if* you decide to cheat on your husband again, just know that I'm a little partial to Andre."

"Funny. But you can have both. And for the record, my husband wants me to cheat on him. He wants me to find his replacement."

Leah's smile takes a dive into a pouty frown. "That's heartbreaking."

"It's not heartbreaking. It's life. Let's go."

We end up enjoying our night out with Andre and Leon. Their family owns a bakery in Bordeaux. Andre's area of expertise is cake decorating and Leon's is making sure the books balance every month.

"We should visit Bordeaux on our European leg," Leah suggests the second we drop our purses on the floor and collapse onto our beds after dinner.

"Think so?" I say with a little apprehension, wondering when that European leg will be? Before or after we make a return trip to the US?

"Definitely," she mumbles in a sleepy voice.

"Okay," I whisper.

———

Tuesday dinner turns into Friday dinner with Leon and Andre, where we tell them all about our exhilarating trip to Gunung Mulu National Park.

Saturday brunch.

Sunday breakfast.

And we've officially made new friends for life in Leon and Andre. It's the upside to staying at hostels. Less privacy equals more friendships. Sunday night we go out to celebrate Leon's birthday.

"No more." I shake my head when Andre orders another round of shots. I've had my limit.

"Last one, love. I promise." Andre gives me his irresistible wink, and I cave and take the shot.

While we close down the bar, my phone lights up with a call from Zach —his handsome face on my screen.

"Zach is calling." I stand to find a place less noisy.

"Who's Zach?" Leon asks.

Leah giggles. "Her husband."

I have just enough alcohol in me to not be upset with her. After all, who are Leon and Andre going to tell? Zach's family? The IRS? "We haven't consummated the marriage." I roll my eyes, leaving Andre and Leon with Leah and another round of shots while I weave my way through the crowd to the stairs of the swanky rooftop bar. "Hello?" It's hard to hear. "Just a sec ..."

On the main level, the music's loud and the lights are a technicolor of madness for my head. "Can you hear me?"

"Emersyn?"

"I'm at a bar," I yell. "I'm going to step outside," I say, shouldering past people in small groups, people dancing, couples groping each other.

My head.

"Emersyn?"

"Just a ..." I feel a little nauseous and dizzy—major vertigo.

Then ... nothing.

———

"Hey, Em." Leah comes into view.

"What happened?" I wince as I try to lift my head.

Something beeps behind me. I'm in the hospital.

"You had a seizure..." she squeezes my hand "...at the bar last night." She frowns and I know what she's thinking. This is the reason she shouldn't have hired me.

"My head." I reach for it.

"You needed a few stitches. Your head hit something when you went down. No concussion, thankfully. Don't worry, the nurse said your hair will grow back in that area. You might have to opt for a ponytail or a hat. You can totally pull it off."

"Great," I mumble. "Leah ... I'm ..."

She shakes her head. "It's too late. We're sisters now. I can be upset that you didn't tell me sooner, but then I might not have hired you, and that would have been tragic."

Tears fill my eyes.

"Listen ..." She cringes. "While I was freaking out after I realized the commotion below the rooftop bar was my friend having a seizure, Andre retrieved your phone from the floor and Zach was still on the line. So ..."

My eyes pinch shut. "Zach," I whisper.

"Yeah. He's on his way. He should be here shortly after they release you, which will hopefully be tomorrow if you're doing okay."

"How embarrassing ..." I open my eyes and sigh.

"I thought this wouldn't happen. You said you were on medication."

Guilt fills my chest; I feel terrible for *everything.* "I ..." I shake my head. "I messed up. I ran out of my pills, and the only way to get more would have been to see a doctor here. But I thought I was fine. I just ... always think it's fine until it's not. I guess the lack of sleep, the stress over running out of my medication, and too much alcohol were a perfect trifecta. I should have known better. I'm ... really sorry. I ruined Leon's birthday, and I humiliated everyone."

"*I'm* sorry. At least you're okay. And there's no reason to be embarrassed. I should have asked you about your medication after you told me about your condition. That's on me too."

Gazing out the window, the second wave of guilt hits me. "Zach is coming. I wish I could stop him."

Leah sits on the side of my bed. "Do you?" Her head tilts to the side.

I start to answer, reaffirming my original sentiment about him coming here, but the words die before they reach my lips.

Chapter Twenty-Seven

AFTER A FULL DAY and another night in the hospital, I'm discharged with new medication and instructions to rest for a few days. By dinner, I wake to a dim room at the hostel and a familiar figure.

"Hey." Zach gives me a reserved, tired smile from the foot of my bed.

I wet my dry lips. "You shouldn't have come. I'm fine," I whisper.

"I'm your husband and your emergency contact. I had to come."

I'm your husband.

Every time I see Zach or hear his voice after we've been apart, a truck crashes into my chest, crumbling the wall I've built around my heart to keep my emotions in check.

"Bet you want to divorce me now," I murmur, stretching to turn on the light by my bed.

Zach drags his gaze away from me, a tiny crease forming between his eyebrows. "I'd never say that."

"You don't have to."

"Why do you think you had a seizure?"

I lift a single shoulder, and now it's me who can't look at him. "I have epilepsy. Comes with the territory."

"But it shouldn't if you're taking your medication ... if you're taking care of yourself." He's too fatherly for me at the moment.

"Well ..." I swallow past the lump of anger and regret stuck in my throat. "I suppose I'm guilty of not taking care of myself. It's hard to be successful *and* practice self-care. And it's hard to be at a birthday party for a friend and not have a drink or two." I close my eyes and will away the tears.

"You should have seen a doctor here. I would have paid for it."

"I don't want you to pay for it!" That comes out a little harsher than I intend.

"Em ..." He rests his hand on my foot. "It's the whole reason I married you."

Dear Heart,

Don't listen to him. It will only make you break into tiny pieces.

The *whole* reason. I know this. I do. Always have. Always will. Still, it doesn't change my feelings no matter how much I want reality to dictate my emotions. Are emotions for unrealistic expectations any less real than all other emotions?

"Sorry," I whisper. "It's getting harder to accept your generosity when I'm not giving anything back to you. At least when I was living in Atlanta, I cleaned your house and helped make meals."

"I told you, having you on my insurance doesn't affect my life."

"Bullshit. You're in Malaysia. In case you don't know how far that is from Atlanta, let me help you out. It's on the other side of the globe. Don't say that being married to me, being my emergency contact, my healthcare sugar daddy, and paying off every ounce of my debt *doesn't* affect you. You're here, and you shouldn't be. Cleaning up my messes. Emersyn has a cat. No problem. Zach to the rescue. Emersyn is home-less. No problem. Zach to the rescue. Emersyn has fucking epilepsy. No problem. Zach to the rescue. Emersyn needs insurance. No—"

"I get it!" He stands and runs his hands through his hair while pacing the tiny room. "I just don't know what you expect me to do. Not care? Not come to your rescue? When you come back to Atlanta, I'll let you clean my whole house. Mow the lawn. Pull weeds. Wash my car. Whatever you need to do in order to not feel indebted to me."

"I had sex." If my goal is to silence him, mission accomplished. I don't know what my goal is, why I said that. Am I confessing my ... what? Infidelity?

"O-kay ..." He narrows his eyes, pausing his pacing. "You don't have to tell me that. We don't have that kind of marriage."

I laugh despite the pain tearing at my chest, making it ache more than my head. "I know we don't. But I'm attracted to you. And before you freak out, it's nothing."

It's *everything*. He's all I can think about. Lying is the most honest form of self-preservation. It sounds like an oxymoron. It's not. It might be the only form of self-preservation. The truth requires absolute risk. Truth preserves no one or anything *but* the truth.

I shrug. "For the record, I have a crush on Michael B. Jordan, K.J. Apa, and Charlie Puth too." My fingers lightly touch the bandage on my head. "So don't read into it."

Zach blinks several times. "And did you tell them you had sex?"

"Not yet. I'm sure I'll slide into their DMs later."

"I'm ..." Zach shakes his head slowly, brow wrinkled. "Flattered."

Grunting, I avert my gaze. "My intent isn't to flatter you."

Tucking his hands into the back pockets of his jeans, he silently demands my attention; the intensity of his gaze is palpable on my skin. When I inch mine back to his face, he asks, "Then what is your intention?"

Sitting up straighter, I pull my legs toward me, hugging them to my chest like a shield. "Want to know what makes a man really sexy?"

His cheeks turn a little pink, bleeding vulnerability. I love his vulnerable side. I fell in love with it first.

I stare at the end of the bed because I know every single feeling I have for Zach is in my eyes, impossible to hide from him or anyone else. "Kindness." Risking a glance up for less than a second, I peek at his reaction —clearly not what he expected me to say. Tucking my chin again, I blow out a slow breath. "Not kindness toward me, although you've been that times infinity. It was how you treated Suzie. Everything you did for her. The way you took care of her. The way you looked at her. The love. The *kindness*. It's like watching a movie where a character, whom you don't necessarily fall for right away, wins your heart because of their ... well, their character. Everything that's inside. Everything that's not a physical trait, social standing, or the balance of a bank account. It's just ... him. He's a good human being. *You're* a good human being, Zach. And I find that incredibly sexy. So some days it's hard to look at you, knowing you're my husband, but ... not *that* kind of husband, when I've spent so much of my life dreaming of the idea of you."

When he doesn't respond for so long it starts to get even more awkward, I glance up at him again. His unreadable expression.

"You think the idea of me is ... is..." he fumbles his words, eyes slightly narrowed like he's having trouble finding the right ones "...appealing. You hope that one day you'll find a man who loves you the way I loved Suzanne. Not really me. Just someone like me."

Is my heart ready to stop lying or am I still in self-preservation mode? It's *him*. I'm not confused. I love

Zach. I admired him. Sure, I envied Suzie because I wanted a Zach in my life. But I didn't fall in love with him, *Suzie's* Zach, until she died. I've felt his love, even if it isn't romantic. I still feel his love for me.

I don't say anything because I hate the lies, yet I'm so afraid of the truth. Instead, I nod slowly like I agree with him. I *don't* agree with him, but I understand what he's saying. And maybe he means it, or maybe he's lying to protect something he's not ready to share or admit.

The door to the room opens behind Zach.

"Hey." Leah steps inside.

"Hey." I smile like I mean it. "Have you two met?"

Leah gives Zach a grin and a nod. "Yes. I'm the one who let him in."

Of course. I didn't focus on that part when I woke to him in my room.

"What can I get you to eat?" she asks.

"I'm staying for a few days and taking her back to my hotel if that's okay with you?" Zach asks Leah.

"I'm fine. I have medication again. I'm ... fine."

Leah's gaze bounces between me and Zach. "Um ... you could definitely use a few days to recoup."

"I'm fine."

Her eyes widen as she rubs her lips together.

"It's nonnegotiable," Zach says.

"You're not my parent, Zach."

"I'm your husband."

Leah's lips part as she gawks at me.

Yeah, yeah ... I heard him.

267

I frown at her, then I share it with him. He doesn't know I told her. He said it anyway. "Think you can play that card whenever you want to make me do something against my will?"

"Yes." If the corners of his mouth didn't curl into a tiny smirk, it would be so much easier to give him a piece of my mind.

"I'll take one day off, but I'm staying here."

"Three days and you're staying with me." Zach crosses his arms over his chest.

"Or..." Leah interjects "...you can play it by ear. One day at a time. If you only need a day, then that's fine. If you need three, that's fine too. And given your head situation, it might be nice if you stayed in a hotel where you don't have to leave the room to use the bathroom. Maybe a place that has room service if you don't feel like leaving to get something to eat. A place with a television in your room instead of a shared space with other guests."

My frown turns into a full-on scowl at Leah.

"So it's settled. You're coming with me for one but most likely three days." Zach grins.

"Don't you have a job?"

"I do," he says. "I also have vacation time."

"Well, what a shitty vacation for you," I say.

"Kuala Lumpur is beautiful." He maintains his triumphant grin.

"So go see all the beautiful things. I'll be here recovering just fine by myself."

"I'm going to get your stuff packed for you," Leah says.

"Traitor," I mumble.

In less than five minutes, my suitcase is by the door and Leah's sliding my shoes onto my feet.

She hugs me and whispers in my ear, "Don't push him away. Dreams are meant to be chased."

Maybe. That probably means hearts are meant to be broken too.

On the way to his hotel, Zach reaches across the back seat and takes my hand, giving it a friendly squeeze. I ignore him, keeping my focus out my window, making sure he doesn't forget how manipulated I feel.

"Are you giving me the silent treatment?" he asks as we step onto the elevator. "Are we having our first official fight?"

I stare at the mirrored doors. He's staying at a fancy hotel, and it would normally warrant a comment from me, but I can't say anything because ... yeah, I'm giving him the silent treatment.

"What if I said I find you attractive too?" The door opens.

I whip my head in his direction. Zach smirks and steps off the elevator. "Are you seriously making fun of me? Did you fly halfway around the world to see if I'm okay or to make fun of me?"

"I'm not making fun of you." He wheels my suitcase down the long hallway and stops at the second to the last door on the right. After he opens it, he holds it for me and nods. "You're attractive. That's a compliment, right? Or did that stop being a compliment?"

I brush past him into the spacious room, a suite actually, with two separate bedrooms and a generous sitting area with two sofas, a modern glass coffee table, a television, and a full kitchen—not to mention the mesmerizing view of the city.

"Hungry?" Zach continues to make conversation while I continue to be mad at him.

"No," I murmur, hugging my arms to my body while gazing out the window at the illuminated picturesque view of the Petronas Twin Towers and the KL Tower. Sensing him close to me, I stiffen because it's hard to breathe when it's just the two of us. It didn't used to be this hard to breathe around Zach, but he does strange things to my heart, sending every breath out of my mouth with a little more force, every beat of it loud and vibrating against my chest.

"I'm glad you're ... taking advantage of your youth and meeting other people."

I cough a laugh, nearly choke on it. Is taking advantage of your youth code for sex? He's glad I had sex?

"What will happen when you stop making excuses?" I ask, slowly turning around, lifting my gaze to his since he's less than a foot from me.

"Making excuses?"

"Do you think I want to have feelings for you? Do you think it's convenient for me? Do you think I enjoy being married but not really married? Is playing dumb the easiest solution for you? Like ... lying is the easiest solution for me. I'll admit it. I downplay my feelings for you to keep you from feeling uncomfortable, to prevent our already weird arrangement from getting really weird ... really awkward. And you pretend that *being attracted* to someone and *finding them attractive* is the same thing, and a dictionary might agree with you, but we both know they're not the same thing. And I took advantage of my youth because it was a short reprieve from thinking about you. It made me feel normal and less delusional for one night. The next day I walked out his door, and I felt like a cheater."

Zach's eyebrows knit together. "You didn't cheat on me."

On a slow nod, I whisper, "Not in your mind."

"Emersyn..." he rubs his temples and closes his eyes for a few seconds "...I don't know what you want me to say."

I'm doing this all wrong. This isn't what Suzie wanted. I'm not supposed to add to his stress and confusion. And that's exactly what I am doing. After a few seconds of silence, I sigh and do the right thing. "I want you to say that you're going to clean the lint out of your navel before we go to the beach."

Zach opens his eyes and eases his fingers away from his temples. Several blinks later, realization hits, and he nods. "Only if you wax your unibrow."

I grin. "Low blow."

When the truth hurts, you change the subject to something so irrelevant that life feels balanced—normal—again, just long enough to catch your breath.

271

JEWEL E. ANN.

I'm letting Zach catch his breath, and maybe I'll take a minute to catch mine as well.

His expression says it all, the relief, maybe a little guilt too, but mostly relief.

"I'm going to lie down. I'm not hungry, but maybe we can get breakfast."

"Night, Em," he whispers.

I pad my way to the bedroom.

"Emersyn?"

"Yeah?" I keep my back to him.

"It's a line. Maybe a doorway. Maybe a fucking mountain ... I don't know. But I know there's no going back when I cross it. I know I can't take her with me. And there's been many days I've wondered about going with her ... going *to* her. It's never been something strong, anything more than a fleeting thought. For what it's worth, you've been the one person who's kept me looking forward. For what it's worth, you've been the reason I stand so close to the line, the threshold of that doorway, feet away from the summit. And maybe that's the real question ... What's it worth?"

When I know he's done, I slowly close the door behind me, crawl into the bed in my clothes, pull the covers over me, and fall asleep.

Chapter Twenty-Eight

"Rise and shine," Zach says, opening the blinds just enough to let me see him and the tray of food in his other hand.

"You need your medication, which means you need food. How's your head? Why did you sleep in your clothes?" He sits on the edge of my bed, holding the tray while I sit up and rub my eyes.

"Too tired to change my clothes," I say in a sleepy voice. "And my head is fine. I thought we were going out for breakfast. And I don't have to take my medication with food." I yawn.

He sets the tray on my lap and lifts the lid, revealing toast, eggs, and fruit. "We can go out for lunch if you're feeling okay."

I chuckle before taking a sip of coffee. "I'm feeling fine."

"You have stitches in your head."

"They don't hurt." I shrug, spreading jelly onto the

273

toast while glancing up at his handsome, freshly shaven face.

Zachary Hays is the unreachable pinnacle for all other men. That sucks for my next husband.

"I didn't figure you'd want to go out with that bandage on your head."

I finish chewing my bite and swallow. "That's what hats are for. Are you sure it's not something else ... like you're embarrassed to be seen with me and my broken head?"

"Of course I'm embarrassed, for both of us, really. But I can deal with it if you can."

My eyes narrow. "You're an ass." I teasingly flick my knife toward him and a glob of jelly flies onto his face just below his eye. "Oh my god!" I giggle and cover my mouth.

He flinches and wipes his thumb along his cheek, smearing the jelly.

"You..." I giggle more and reach for his face "...just made it worse."

"Says the woman who shot it at my face. It could have landed in my eye. I need my vision to do my job."

"Stop." I laugh, batting his hand away as he tries to the do same to mine. Then I gasp and stiffen, holding completely still as coffee soaks the bedding and my lap. Thankfully, the sheets and my jeans absorb most of the heat before it seeps through to my skin.

"Shit! Did it burn you?" Zach sets the tray on the nightstand as I peel back the sheets.

"It's fine. It didn't burn me." I ease out of bed. It

looks like I wet my pants. When I glance up, Zach grimaces, jelly still on his cheek. "I ruined breakfast in bed." I lick my thumb and wipe it along his cheek; this time he doesn't fight me.

He encircles my wrist with his hand, and I slide my gaze from the jelly to his eyes. With a slow, almost intoxicated blink, he rests his whole cheek in my hand. Turning his head ever so slightly, his lips brush along my palm. It's not a kiss. His lips don't move.

I don't move.

Is this the line? The doorway? The mountain?

Is my job to pull him to the other side? Is he straddling the line, wondering what's waiting for him on the other side?

Is that what he did for Suzie?

The words are heavy on the tip of my tongue. It feels right. I think. I … I don't know. Can I tell him?

I know what you did.

Would it change his state of mind? Make things better? Make them worse?

"After I lost my trailer, there was this one night …" I find something else to say. I always find something else to say. "A rough night for whatever reason, and I can't even remember why. I just remember the feeling because it wasn't me. I wasn't that person."

Zach opens his eyes, but he doesn't remove my hand from his face. I swear I see my own soul in the depths of his eyes, storms chasing the sunset.

"It felt like an out-of-body experience, like I didn't recognize myself, the thoughts in my head, the mess of

275

a woman in the rearview mirror. It felt like rock bottom, and I wasn't sure how I got there. I just knew that I lost my trailer because I needed medication. I hated the medication ... I hated why I had to take it. So..." I draw in a shaky breath "...I thought about taking the whole bottle. You know ... maybe there was something better on the other side."

He blinks, averting his gaze to the side for a quick second before meeting mine again. I give him a smile. It might look like a sad one, but it's not. It's a hopeful smile because I remember having this same smile when my phone vibrated with an email.

"That night, you emailed me and told me you got my name from the Mumfords. You asked me to come for an interview. So I didn't take all the pills, just the one I needed." I blink back a few tears. "We make decisions every day that don't just affect our lives, sometimes they affect others in ways we may never know. You didn't set out to save a life, you just needed a maid."

"Emersyn," he says it again, my name in three slow syllables.

When he doesn't release my hand, I pull away. "I need a shower. And I need to brush my teeth."

"You need to take your pill and eat something."

With a stiff smile, I grab a slice of toast and retrieve my medication from my purse. "Taking my pill ... eating something. Happy now?" I say on my way into the bathroom. Just as I reach the threshold, I glance over my shoulder. "I'm sorry."

"For what?" he asks.

"The pills. You used to remind and persuade Suzie to take her pills." I frown. "I don't want you to have to do that for me."

After several contemplative blinks, he returns a slow nod. "Yeah, well … it's what you do when you care for someone."

Oh, Zach …

Before I cry … before I let him see how much I've needed to feel cared for in this way, I shut the door and hop into the shower.

After I feel human again, managing to wash my hair fairly well without getting the stitches wet, I attempt to dry my hair.

Sundress.

Sandals.

My best smile.

"I could work with Leah today. I feel fine. But I know you're not going to accept that, so we need to go somewhere. Do something. I'm not a fan of staying in a hotel room all day, even if it's a nice one like this."

Zach shuts off the TV and stands from the sofa. "You're supposed to rest."

"I'm rested. We don't have to run a marathon, but I don't want to spend the day in a hotel room."

He twists his lips. "Have you been to the Cameron Highlands yet?"

I shake my head.

"Then let's go."

A grin slides up my face as I slip on my brown sun hat to cover my stitches.

Zach arranges a private tour for the day. By midafternoon, we're perched on a blanket overlooking the lush highlands and eating strawberries from the field we stopped at along the way. I slip off my sandals and my hat. Zach gives me a funny look as his gaze shifts to the stitches on the crown of my head.

"There's nobody around to see me. Don't freak out that I'm ruining your reputation here."

He chuckles, popping a strawberry into his mouth and chewing it despite his swelling grin.

"Can I take a picture of us and post it on Instagram? I won't show your face."

"What's wrong with my face?" he asks.

"Nothing." I roll my eyes and retrieve my phone from my bag. "I just don't want to have to put a name to your face."

"So you just want to start rumors?"

"Buzz. Not rumors."

"Buzz. Tell me more about this buzz."

I giggle. "Well, my following has grown exponentially since I've been traveling with Leah. I'm even making some money off my photos. So this bigger following is becoming interested in me and everything about my life. And photos that pique curiosity get more engagement." I clip my phone to the travel tripod and turn back to Zach. "Spread your legs."

He smirks and mutters, "Isn't that supposed to be my line."

My breath hitches, eyes unblinking. He just said that. It was a joke. I get it. But ...

On a nervous laugh, I manage one word. "Funny." I clear my throat and slip back on my hat. "Put your hands on my waist."

"If I put them on your ass, it would build more *buzz*. Right?"

Standing on my knees between his legs, with my camera catching the back of me and the scenery behind Zach, I glance down at him and frown. "If you put your hands on my hips, your wedding band won't be visible. If you put your hands on my ass, it will build buzz, but not the right kind. I don't need rumors that I'm married or having a strawberry picnic with a married man."

Zach's grin fades as he glances down at his left hand. "But you are married," he whispers.

"Yes," I say on a hushed breath.

His brow tenses into tight lines as he continues to inspect his ring. "And you *are* having a picnic with a married man," he says slowly, like he's not even saying it to me, rather to himself.

"Yes."

To my knowledge, Zach has only taken his wedding band off once, the day he married me. Until now.

With several twists, he removes it and holds it between his thumb and forefinger, staring. After slipping it into his jeans pocket, he glances up at me, rests his hands on my hips and then moves them to my ass.

I swallow hard.

"Are you going to take the picture?" he asks in a raspy voice.

"Um ..." I look at my watch." Yeah." Setting the timer on my phone's camera from my watch, I rest my hands on his shoulders and wait for it to capture the burst of photos. "It's done. Th-thanks." I can barely talk past the thick lust in my throat. His hands on my ass have paralyzed me.

"You're welcome," Zach whispers, but he doesn't ... remove his hands. "I have..." those immovable hands finally shift, slip ... ghost down the back of my legs "...a very..." his fingertips tease the back of my knees "... beautiful wife."

My chest aches from the violent pounding of my heart, from holding each breath impossibly long before releasing it with as much control as possible. His hands make a slow return to my butt, only this time they're underneath my dress.

"Zach ..." My fingers curl into his shoulders as his curl into my ass—a mix of flesh and pink cotton panties.

"Emersyn ..."

Em-er-syn

Those same three drawn-out syllables, but this time they're laced with need.

"Help me cross that line," he says.

Wetting my lips, I nod slowly before he kisses me. I think our driver is staying in the car until we're done here. *I think. I hope.*

We kiss for as long as we can, until it's not enough. Zach drags my panties down my legs as far as they'll go with me on my knees. He tastes like strawberries and smells like the shampoo from the hotel—a mix of citrus and leather. Sliding the strap of my sundress to the side, he frees my breast, squeezing it, kissing it, teasing my nipple with his teeth.

My brain misfires, thinking of things it shouldn't think about right now, like the morbid curiosity of wondering if he's missed the feel of a woman's breasts in his hands, in his mouth.

I don't want to think about that.

Claiming his hair with my hands, I force his face to mine, demanding he kiss my mouth again. It settles the chaos in my head—but only temporarily. He lays me down, discarding my panties and kneeling between my legs. His fingers work to unbutton his jeans, and I see it in his eyes. I see it because I'm thinking it too.

We're thinking about Suzie. What would she think? Would she approve? Is she somewhere watching us?

Zach pauses, and I feel it ... I'm losing him. He's not going to cross this line with me, and there's nothing I can do but lie here exposed, completely vulnerable with my chest wide open—no protection from his rejection of me. And I'm not even mad because I loved her too. She's unforgettable which makes him unattainable. At least ... his heart will never be mine.

As I roll my head to the side, to hide my emotions, he slides his hands along my inner thighs, bringing my attention back to him. "Do you want me to stop?"

He knows the answer. He *knows* I've completely lost myself in him.

Does he want an honest answer? Or is he asking me to save him?

"No," I whisper.

Gripping the top of his unbuttoned jeans, Zach pushes them down his hips just enough to free himself. He covers my body with his and kisses me with renewed vigor. My knees draw to my chest as he fills me, so warm, so mind-blowing because I never really thought this would happen.

Pause.

Breathe.

Hold on to my fucking heart because he's unknowingly attempting to destroy it.

We move with a manic desperation, like his whole body would crawl inside mine if it could. The slapping of skin, the sharp breaths and intoxicated moans ... the deafening pounding of my heart. I dig one heel into his glute and the other heel into the back of his leg as if I can hold him to me forever.

Mine.

My Zach.

My husband.

Instead of drowning in guilt when I lose control of my body, surrendering every last ounce of pleasure to him, I let my vision blur with slow, heavy blinks while melting into a bliss unlike anything I have ever felt.

Zach stills, cupping the back of my head like he's trying to protect it, protect the stitches. Then he rolls us, kissing me as my hair falls around his face. I feel his lips curl into a smile against mine. And I do the same.

Ghosting his hands up the back of my dress, he sits up, taking me with him, my legs straddling him as he stays deep inside of me. And once again, we move together.

We kiss.

My hands grip his shirt as his frame my jaw. Our kiss gains momentum and urgency. It's a pursuit of something. He's the predator, and I am the prey, willingly surrendering to the chase.

I want Zach to catch me ... I want him to devour me.

"Emersyn ..." His hands fall to my hips, gripping me hard while burying his face into my neck.

I grind into him several more times until my back arches, until he jerks his hips while repeating my name like he's praying, pleading, begging ...

Emersyn ... Emersyn ... Em-er-synn ...

We still.

There's no space between us for reality to slide in and ruin the moment. I won't regret this. I can't.

He kisses my neck while one hand returns to my breast, lightly cupping it, his thumb tracing my nipple.

It's gentle.

It's intimate.

It's a little heartbreaking.

Can he touch me *there* without thinking of her?

Zach lifts his head, his face hovering a breath from

mine—cheeks redden. The hint of a vulnerable smile bends his beautiful lips.

"I like how you feel ... right here ... inside of me," I whisper, heat flaming my own cheeks while my hand snakes between us. I hold my breath. And I think he holds his too. I don't know why I want to feel us *there*. Maybe it's still too unbelievable, and I need something more tangible.

"Yeah?" He sighs a tiny chuckle before dropping his forehead to my shoulder like he doesn't have the energy to hold his head up any longer. At the same time, his hand slips from my breast to my hip again.

"Yeah," I murmur, ghosting my lips along his ear.

"I like ... *this* too. So fucking much."

It's too much. I can't possibly construct a wall big enough to protect my heart.

"We should uh ... piece ourselves back together before the driver comes looking for us," I say.

Zach still doesn't lift his head, but he mumbles, "Uh-huh."

———

ON THE WAY back to the hotel, we sit in silence, fingers intertwined on the seat between us. I wonder what he's thinking? Does he regret it? Is he thinking of Suzie, or is he thinking that I should stay with him for the full three days? Maybe spend the rest of the time in bed? I didn't think I was a hotel person, but Zach could persuade me to stay naked in bed for eternity. My lips press together to hide my excitement over that possibility.

Zach shifts his body, and I glance over at him. His fingers fish for something in his pocket. Tension steals his face, trenching deep lines by his eyes and along his brow as he releases my hand and searches his other pocket.

"Zach?"

Unfastening his seat belt, he doesn't answer. He fishes in his back pockets and then both front pockets one more time. "Fuck. Turn around!" he barks.

Our graying, fifty-something driver eyes Zach through the rearview mirror. His eyes narrow above the glasses slid halfway down his prominent nose.

"Turn the fuck around! We have to go back!"

"Zach ..." I reach for his arm.

"I lost the ring. I lost my ring," he says like he can't breathe.

His wedding band.

"Are you sure? You put it in your pocket, right?"

"Sir, it's late. If you want to go back tomorrow—"

"Then let me out!" Zach tries to open his door, fumbling with the lock.

The driver swerves to the side of the road and stops.

I rest my hand on the driver's shoulder. "We'll pay you whatever it costs to go back before it gets dark." The sun is already starting to set. I'm not sure it will matter, but we have to try.

When we return to the spot where we ate our

strawberries—where we had sex—Zach flies out of the vehicle and sprints up the hill. I follow him, just not as quickly because I'm not sure I should be running with stitches in my head.

Dear God ...

It's hard to watch.

At the top of the hill, Zach crawls around on the ground, using the flashlight on his phone to see because the sun is nearly hidden beneath the horizon.

I bring up the light on my phone and crawl on my hands and knees to help him look too.

"Fuck. I shouldn't have ... stupid ... fuck. Fuck. Fuck." Zach groans and grumbles, anger and frustration rolling off his body in strong waves that bring tears to my eyes. Everything in my chest and the pit of my stomach tightens like a hard fist.

If I wouldn't have asked for the picture, he wouldn't have taken off his wedding band. If we wouldn't have had sex, it wouldn't have fallen out of his pocket.

I was wrong. Regret has a way of coming to the surface no matter how hard we try to drown it.

After crawling around for nearly forty-five minutes, the sky in the highlands reaches complete darkness. Zach sits back on his heels. Total defeat. He threads his hands through his hair as he looks to the heavens and closes his eyes. "I'm sorry," he whispers.

He's not apologizing to me. I know this. And it's okay. I don't want him to ever stop loving her, even if that means he can never truly love me. Suzie was my friend, and she deserves to be loved for eternity. Maybe

Zach and I are doomed to the hell that is unrequited love.

She has moved on, and he never will. And I ... well, I'm not sure where I stand. I have a roof over my head every night, but my heart remains homeless.

"Let's go," he says, barely a whisper as he lumbers to his feet and heads back down the hill.

Gathering the chipped and cracked pieces of my heart, I follow him.

When we return to the hotel after a long, silent ride, he heads straight to his room, pausing before shutting the door. "I need ... a minute."

From the other side of the room, I put on a brave face he can't see. "I understand."

The door clicks shut behind him.

Chapter Twenty-Nine

THE NEXT MORNING, I wake early and pack my suitcase. When I open the door, Zach is on the sofa, freshly showered, head bowed to his phone. He looks up and smiles. It's genuine, but reserved.

"Good morning." I return the smile and step into the main room, pulling my suitcase behind me.

His charming smile vanishes as he focuses on my luggage.

"I'm uh ... feeling fine. So I messaged Leah and told her I'd go with her today. She's taking engagement photos for a couple we met on our first day here."

He offers me a tiny nod, lips curled together like he's holding something back.

I clear my throat and infuse confidence into my posture and my voice. "Thank you for coming. It really was incredibly kind. And I feel bad that you wasted vacation time on me, but ... nonetheless I'm really grateful."

I feel terrible that you lost your wedding band.

"Of course," he says. Zach isn't himself at all. He *is* holding back.

As tempting as it is to push him to tell me whatever it is that's weighing so heavily on him, I think it's best to let it be. Let him go home without saying everything.

"I'll take you back to the hostel." He stands.

I shake my head. "I can grab a ride. No need to pay for a car back here."

He nods several times, being way too agreeable for the dad-mode Zach that arrived yesterday. "Do you have everything? Your medication? Plenty of money? Do you want me to get you breakfast?"

There he is, a little glimpse of the man from yesterday morning.

"Leah and I are going to grab breakfast when I get back to the hostel, but thank you."

I never *ever* dreamed that we'd be this amicable, this platonic, after what happened on that hill yesterday. It's utterly heartbreaking. Words fail me at every turn. My confidence is nonexistent.

"Have a safe flight home." I smile.

Zach makes his way to me, hands in his front pockets. I will never look at pockets again without thinking of him losing his wedding band and how devastated he was crawling around in the dark. With every step, it feels like I'm suffocating more and more, like I can either have oxygen or close proximity to Zach, but not both. I'm *barely* holding on right now.

"Where are you going next?" he asks.

"Sri Lanka in a week."

"Never been."

I find another forced grin. "I'll send you a postcard."

"That would be nice." Zach stops close to me, *so* close I can feel the heat of his body and smell the fake herbal scent of shampoo. "Yesterday—"

I shake my head a half dozen times. "No. You don't need to say a word about yesterday. I shouldn't have ... we ... it just ..." I can't stop shaking my head. "I'm *so* sorry." Everything from my chest to my scalp tingles with emotion as an ocean of unshed tears awaits like a tsunami for me to make it to the other side of the hotel room door. Turning, I reach for the handle, but Zach grabs my arm.

"Not like this," he says, forcing me to turn back toward him.

My gaze affixes to my feet.

"This isn't the goodbye we're going to have after yesterday." He lifts my chin with his finger. "I don't know what that meant yesterday. What *you* want it to mean ... what it *should* mean. But I don't want to regret it. And I don't want you to regret it."

What it should mean ...

I don't know. I can't be mad at him for not knowing because I honestly don't know either. For me, it meant everything in the moment, but what is *everything*? And can something that feels like everything really mean nothing in the bigger picture? The problem is, when I'm with Zach, I can't see past him.

Letting our gazes lock, I shrug. "I don't know what it meant, but I want it to mean *something*. Not a meaningless mistake."

"Okay," he whispers. "It meant something. But don't let it mean that you don't live your life to the fullest. Okay?"

My face wrinkles. "What's that supposed to mean?"

Zach blows a long breath out of his nose. "I want you to be twenty-four. Adventurous. Untethered."

Untethered.

I scoff. "You want me to sleep with other people?"

He grimaces, it's slight, but I don't miss it. "I want you to do whatever you want to do without worrying about me."

"Without worrying about my husband?" I cant my head to the side.

He rests his hand on his hip and bows his head. "Emersyn ... it's not that kind of marriage."

Fuck my life.

"It's not that kind of marriage," I echo while chuckling past the pain. If I don't laugh, I will cry so hard I'll crumble into dust. "Silly me." I turn and open the door.

When he tries to grab my arm for a second time, I yank it out of his grip. "No! Let me go." I get two feet out the door with my suitcase before he pins me to the wall, holding my arms to my sides. His fingers slowly lace with mine, his forehead pressed to mine, eyes pinched shut.

"I came to life yesterday. Inside of you ... I came to

life again. But I'm still figuring out who I am without her. And it's so fucking hard because I can't look at you and not see her. I *do not* want you to wait for me to figure this out because I don't know if I'll get there."

He opens his eyes to a stream of tears marking my face. "I thought I was there. I felt different. Then I lost my ring ... *and my mind*. And I have to figure out why. Why did I not think of her once when I was inside of you, then *all* I could think about was her? That ring. Her last breath. The hole she left in my chest. And how losing that ring felt like losing her again. But then I look at you, and she's there for a blink. Your pills are her pills. She was in the hospital. You were in the hospital. Letting her go was the right fucking thing to do. Is letting you go the right thing to do too?"

Not since the night Suzie died have I seen Zach this emotionally crippled. The thick ball of emotion in my throat won't let me speak; it's holding back an earth-quake of sobs. Tipping my chin up, I capture his lips, kissing him like I did yesterday.

No.

Kissing him harder than I did yesterday.

He releases my hands and grabs my face, giving me everything I'm giving him as I fist his shirt and hold him to me, not wanting to let go.

But eventually, I do.

I let go. Breaking our kiss and grabbing my suitcase handle, I take long, quick strides to the elevator without looking back.

———

"BABE ..." Leah frowns and hops out of bed as soon as I open the door.

I made it. That was the goal—to make it back here before completely losing it.

"Oh no ... what happened?" She hugs me as I go into a full ugly cry.

This is what I need. It's what I've needed for longer than I've realized. Suzie died and Zach became my friend; he filled the void she left. We bonded over our love for her. Then he became my husband. And when I fell in love with my husband, I no longer had a friend. I no longer had a home for my emotions.

Leah's given me a job, confidence, a boost in my pursuit of a career, but more than all of that, she's become my friend. In some ways, I needed a friend more than a job.

She listens.

I cry.

She gets emotional with me.

We talk through everything, yet we solve nothing. There is nothing to solve with Zach. I can't fix him because I think losing someone you love does irreparable damage.

However, I can travel the world with Leah. And that's what I do.

I build my portfolio and help her build hers.

I meet amazing people along the way and find

moments of solitude in what feels like uninhabited corners of the earth.

I drop postcards in the mail for Zach and text about nothing in particular, text like we didn't share something intimate—like friends, but not the kind of friends who share everything.

Zach keeps me up to date on Aaron and Danielle's wedding plans. I respond without showing my painful envy that his brother is marrying a woman for love and planning a real wedding.

This *friendly* exchange continues until the end of summer approaches and Leah gets a call while we're in the middle of recording a Top Ten Places to See in Israel video.

"Oh my god ..." She holds her phone with one hand while covering her mouth with her other hand. "Is he going to be okay? When's the surgery? Please give him a hug for me. Tell him that I love him, and that I'm on my way home."

"Leah?" I reach for her arm while her thumbs frantically work the phone screen.

"M-my dad had a heart attack. We ... we have to go home."

Chapter Thirty

I TEXT Zach before we fly out of Tel Aviv. When we arrive in London for a short layover, he still hasn't responded. Just as we board the flight to Atlanta, he texts me.

> Zach: Have a safe trip. I won't be
> home until Saturday. Tell Leah I'm
> sorry to hear about her dad.

That gives me two days at home without him. I might need the time to catch up on sleep, do laundry, spoil Harry Pawter, and get my head in the right space.

An Uber takes me home, and I drag my tired ass into the house. "Harry!" I don't even get the door shut before I pick him up and probably scare him to death with my intense enthusiasm.

He stays by my side over the next two days while I go to town with laundry and cleaning the house from top to bottom. I order groceries since I'm technically not supposed to drive for another month and a half to follow proper seizure protocol, which I know is important to Zach.

When I hear the back door open, I hold my breath and pause my photo editing from my favorite spot on the sofa. Why am I so nervous?

"Pawter," I hear Zach say, and it feels so good to hear his voice. Since Malaysia, there have been lots of messages, but we didn't call each other.

Not once.

Not a single video chat either.

The wedge between us has been silent but huge.

For me, I know it would have been too hard to hear his voice and not want to be with him. I'm not sure why *he* never called or wanted to see my face or hear my voice, but I've told myself it's the same reason for him too.

"Hi." Zach grins, peeking his head around the corner to the living room.

God ... I think he's even sexier than the last time I saw him.

"Hi." I let my grin have a big fat parade all over my face.

"Welcome home."

Home ...

Is this my home?

"Thanks. You too."

He chuckles, sauntering into the kitchen to get a

beer from the fridge. "I haven't been gone that long. I bet Pawter didn't even recognize you."

"*Harry* Pawter. And he absolutely recognized me."

Zach pops the top of his beer bottle and tosses it into the trash, pausing at the kitchen sink. "Did you … clean?"

"Yes. I cleaned everything. Thanks for noticing."

"Emersyn, you're not my maid anymore." He makes his way to his bedroom.

"You're letting me live here rent free. I have to earn my keep."

"You're never here," he calls from his bedroom or probably his closet, changing out of his uniform.

Closing my computer, I pad my bare feet along the hardwood floor to his bedroom and lean against the wide wood threshold. "I'm here now. And I'm not sure when Leah will be ready to leave again, so I'm going to do my part."

It's been almost five months since I've seen him. I wanted to come home for the anniversary of Suzie's death, but it wasn't convenient. Honestly, I wasn't sure he'd want me here for that. Five months feels like five years. My hands itch to touch him. Is he still mine to touch? I'm not sure he ever was mine for more than an hour one afternoon in Malaysia.

Zach emerges from his closet with a T-shirt in hand instead of covering his chest. My gaze takes liberty. It might be the two glasses of wine I had before he arrived.

"We'll split the cleaning while you're here." His suggestion drags my focus back to his face. He gives me a gotcha grin as he pulls on his shirt. Snatching his beer bottle from the nightstand, he takes a long swig before making his way to me.

I can't bring myself to move out of his way. When he stands in front of me, maybe waiting for passage, I slide the beer from his hand and take a small sip.

"Anything special you want for your anniversary?" he asks.

I eye him with a little surprise and curiosity. "My anniversary of what?"

He shrugs one shoulder, taking the beer back from me. "Ours."

I try to smile, try to keep the mood light, but it's hard with him standing so close to me. "That's next week."

He nods.

"I have it on good authority that we don't have that kind of marriage. And you're probably due for another appointment with your dental hygienist."

"Dental hygienist?"

I roll my eyes. "Yes. Clearly you don't remember much from our wedding day. Marriage day. Whatever. You said I do, dropped me off at home, and went to the dentist. So I threw the bouquet, took off my own garter, and ate all the cake without you."

Zach smirks. "Is that so?"

On another eye roll, I turn and head back to the living room. "Yes. That's so."

"What's the time limit?" he asks.

I glance over my shoulder just before reaching the sofa. He finishes his beer and sets the bottle on the counter then makes his way into the living room.

"Time limit on what?" I ask, plopping onto the cushion.

"How long do I have to wait before I can touch you?" He drags his teeth over his lower lip while eyeing me from head to toe. "Because I miss you."

"You miss me?" I whisper, and my skin tingles everywhere. Even my eyes burn with emotion. Holding my breath for five ... long ... months has been too long.

He nods.

I didn't know what to expect, but it wasn't this. After five months of nothing resembling anything more than friendship, not one single vibe of intimacy ... I had no reason to expect this.

"I'm right here," I say, just above a whisper.

Sliding his hands into his front pockets, Zach shrugs a shoulder. "Still missing you. Your big blue eyes tracking me while those full lips of yours press together as if smiling at me might expose your darkest secrets. Your delicate fingers threading through my hair, slowly, deliberately, like their sole purpose is to drive me mad with need."

I dare *any* woman not to fall in love with this man, and at the same time, I forbid myself from falling any deeper. I don't have my life figured out, and he's still dealing with the loss of Suzie. He doesn't have to say it.

I just know because *I'm* still dealing with the loss of her.

Dealing with discovering my true path in life.

Dealing with trying to do and be what Suzie would have wanted me to do and be.

Dealing with my feelings for Zach that make me want to align my path with his even if that means losing sight of my other dreams.

Still, I can't help it. I smile at Zach. "I miss you too. All the time. I miss the way you hum when you're cooking a meal or driving your car. I miss the lullaby of your guitar at night. I miss the way you refold the kitchen towels when you think I'm not looking. I miss sitting at opposite ends of the sofa with you, editing photos, knowing your eyes are on me. I miss the most mundane things like grocery shopping with you or pulling weeds while you mow the lawn. I miss your sly grins and carefully thought-out words. I miss watching you tie your hundred-year-old tennis shoes before you go for a run. And I miss..." I pull in a shaky breath, feeling a physical ache for his touch, the tingle of need along my skin growing more intense "...all the parts of you I've wanted, but I know are not mine to want."

"Still missing you," he whispers, taking a step toward me.

"I'm right here."

It's hard to not think about Suzie, to not feel a ghost of her presence in this house. It was easier in Malaysia. Is he thinking about her? Is he conflicted? Trying to claim the life he still has while keeping her alive, if only in his mind?

If he touches me, will he close his eyes and think of her? I'm messed up. I wasn't sure just how messed up until now. Zach losing his wedding band on the hilltop where we had sex and his reaction to it has left me brimming with self-doubt.

"Shut it off."

I lift my gaze as he kneels on the floor in front of me.

"Your mind." He grins. "Shut it off."

"How?"

"Fill it with other thoughts." He leans forward, resting his hands on my legs while kissing my neck.

My fingertips tease the nape of his neck. "You can't tell me you're not thinking about Suzie."

Zach sighs and sits back on his heels, head bowed. "I think about her. I don't think there will ever come a time where I don't think about her. I can't erase her from my mind. I don't want to erase her from my mind." He lifts his gaze to mine. "Remember when I told you that I went to the store and *didn't* think about her because I was thinking about groceries?"

I nod slowly.

"It's because she's gone. She's not here to be the object of my affection. She's not waiting for me at home. She will never climb into our bed. She will never walk through that backdoor with dirt smudged on her face and a basketful of vegetables. I'll never hear her laugh again. I'll never feel her touch. But I also know she will never be erased from your mind either. And that's why it's different with you. In a way ... we were three and now we're two."

I slide my feet between his spread knees, and he grabs my calves, shifting his gaze to my face. "I'm afraid of not knowing where we're going," I say. "I'm afraid that we can't stay on the same path and still be true to our other passions, and that eventually our paths will just stop crossing. So ... I guess I need to know where you see us going?"

After a few breaths, he shrugs. "I see us going to the bedroom."

My grin sneaks to the surface without permission. "What will we do in the bedroom?"

Zach stands on his knees again and unbuttons his jeans. Then he shrugs off his shirt.

My gaze makes the slow journey from his open jeans, along the taut terrain of his abs and chest, to his confident grin. When our gazes lock, he nods toward me.

My grin inflates because the man I never *ever* imagined would be with me is gesturing for me to take off my shirt so he can see me.

So he can touch me.

So *I* can be the object of his affection.

I slide my shirt over my head.

Another gesturing nod from him.

I remove my bra.

Zach wets his lips, letting his gaze linger on my

302

breasts for a few seconds before dragging it to my face. "Stand up."

It's pathetic how I'm a robot to his every command. I stand, but he doesn't.

Sucking my nipple into his mouth, he works the button and zipper to my jeans. He peels them down my legs along with my panties. Before I can step out of them, he stands and lifts me off the ground in a big bear hug.

"Zach!" I giggle as he waddles with his jeans at his knees. "Not yours," I say, stopping him from taking me to his bedroom—to *their* bedroom. "Just ... not yet."

He doesn't say a word. Instead, he carries me to my bedroom and sets me on my feet.

I kick off my jeans and panties.

"Do you even know how beautiful you are?" he whispers, pausing my motions, demanding I look at him and hear the sincerity in his words.

Those words wrap around my heart, one chamber at a time, an invisible vapor filling every empty space.

"Zach ..." I take a step into him, pressing my hands flat on his chest and touching my lips to his sternum over his heart.

He gathers my hair and pulls it off my shoulder, kissing along my collarbone, and it makes me shiver, awaking that kaleidoscope of butterflies in my tummy.

"Cold?" He brings his head up to look at me.

I shake my head.

"Your teeth are chattering."

I bite them together and swallow. "I'm nervous."

"It's not our first time." Zach brushes his knuckles along my cheek.

"It's our first time like this. The other side of the world felt like a cocoon."

"Then let's make a cocoon." He pulls back the covers. "Get in."

He removes the rest of his clothes and slides into bed on one side as I slowly do the same on the other side. My breath catches when he whips the sheet and comforter over our heads.

"Cocoon," he says before he kisses his way down my body.

I can't see much under the covers, but I can feel everything. His hands cupping my breasts as he settles his chest between my legs.

His exploring tongue all over my skin ... dipping between my legs ... In our little cocoon, I get to feel his flesh next to mine.

In our little cocoon, he moves inside of me, lacing our fingers together at my head, bringing our bodies as close as physically possible.

We fall asleep, sated and intertwined. It's ironically symbolic of our relationship. We've become this knot. And I don't know if it makes us stronger or if it simply complicates things ... keeping us from being free. I know he doesn't want to hold me back from my dreams, but I feel tethered to him, and it doesn't feel wrong.

Hours later, he wakes me by pulling my body on top of his torso and sliding into me with nothing but a slow groaning of my name. I'm so drunk on him, I can barely open my eyes, so I don't. I rock into him over and over, nothing but the mingling of our labored breaths and a slight rhythmic creak of the bed filling the air. His hands skate along my body, my back, my breasts, and between my spread legs where he moves inside of me until, once again, we release, collapse, and fall asleep.

Chapter Thirty-One

Zach

I NEED A FEW MINUTES.

As much as I want to stay in bed with Emersyn all day, especially after going so long without seeing her, I need a few minutes to sort through my thoughts.

Easing out of bed, I snatch my clothes from the floor, grab a shower, and brew a pot of coffee. It's been a year, and I thought the memories of Suzanne sitting at the kitchen table, gazing out at her garden with such pride, would have faded a little. They haven't.

The memories haven't faded. My love for her has not faded.

But I've miraculously managed to develop strong feelings for Emersyn. And these feelings for her don't feel wrong, but they feel like bad timing. We are in very different places in our lives, and while it sounds like the most cliché reason for a relationship not working, it's nonetheless a valid reason.

I'm settled into my life, into my job. Emersyn's just started a grand exploration, a search for her dreams, a passionate journey that should absolutely be the number one priority in her life.

I don't want to be a distraction. I don't want to be the reason she settles for anything less than her dreams.

The door to the bathroom closes, bringing me out of my deep thoughts, and a few minutes later, Emersyn peeks her head around the corner. I inspect her robe and wonder if she's wearing anything underneath it. Yeah, that's where my brain goes. If I could act like an animal reacting only on instinct, I'd lay her on this kitchen table and have my way with her before so much as a good morning.

I suppress the animal inside of me and opt for control.

"Morning," she says, giving me a shy grin that turns her cheeks pink as she pours a cup of coffee.

"Morning. How'd you sleep?" I sit up straight and nod to the chair. Suzie's chair.

Emersyn stares at it for a few seconds. She's thinking the same thing. It's not just me. She has her own set of issues with Suzie's things. Before I can say anything to ease her mind, she takes a seat, and it gives me a sense of relief that she's okay with it. "I slept well." She grins, digging her teeth into her lower lip. "You?"

I smirk, bringing my mug to my lips. "No complaints." After a sip, I set the mug on the table. "We have some catching up to do."

She nods, blowing at the steam from the coffee. "What have you been up to?"

I chuckle. "Working. You?"

She shrugs. "Same."

"You'll need to elaborate on that. I only get to see glimpses of you on social media, living it up. A free bird. I hope you've been happy."

Lines form along Emersyn's forehead as her lips twist. I'd give anything to know what she's thinking because I know it's not what she's going to let herself say to me.

"Are *you* happy?" she asks.

My eyes narrow as I study the half-empty coffee mug in front of me. "I'm good. Work is good. My family is good."

"Are you happy?" she repeats.

With a slight grunt and a smile to cover up any pain that prompted the grunt, I lift a shoulder. "Honestly?"

She nods.

"I'm hesitant to say."

"Why?"

"Because I don't want to hurt your feelings nor do I want to put pressure on you."

Taking in a shaky breath, Emersyn puts on a brave face. "Okay ... this is going to come out all jumbled, and I hope you don't take it the wrong way, but ... I don't expect to magically make you happy like Suzie didn't die. I think she wanted you to be *you* after she died. But she kind of made you who you were, her existence in your life. You were Zach: pilot, friend, brother, son ... and husband. And out of all those things, husband meant the most to you. How do you redefine yourself when what felt like the most important part of you no longer exists?"

After a few long moments, I whisper, "Maybe." It's like she reached into my fucking soul, grabbed every single emotion, and narrated them to me. I grab her hand and pull her toward me.

She surrenders, sitting on my lap so we're both looking out the window. I rest my chin on her shoulder and slide one hand to the inside of her robe where I discover she is, in fact, naked underneath it.

"Before you arrived home yesterday..." I release a long sigh "...I was struggling. I felt like the asshole who left you in Malaysia without anything concrete as to where we stood because I didn't know. I didn't expect those emotions to creep up on me and obliterate my sense of balance. Every day I've felt like something was missing. And the obvious answer seemed to be her. Maybe you're a little right. Maybe I miss the part of me she took with her. I've tried to figure it out. I just know that there have been days that I'm good, but not great. Content, but not necessarily happy. I'm grateful, but still a little resentful. Life is a new culinary concoction that I keep tasting, but it's always missing something. And no matter what I add, it's still not quite it."

"Zach …"

"No." I hug her tighter with my lips at her ear because I need her to really hear my words, feel my words. "When I saw you yesterday after so long—too long—I realized it wasn't Suzanne. She's not missing in my life. She's simply gone. You've been the one missing in my life. So if I tell you that, right now, I am deliriously happy, you'll feel responsible for my happiness. If I tell you I'm not happy, you'll feel responsible or even worse, hurt, by my lack of happiness after everything that's happened between us. So I can't win. It's an impossible question to answer."

"If you can't win, then just tell me the truth."

"I'm happy," I say without hesitation.

She releases a tiny sigh of relief.

"You're you," I continue. "I don't compare you to her. Not anymore. So don't ever think that. Don't ever think that you're living in her shadow or that you're not living up to who you think she was or my expectations. Just know that when I'm with you, happiness comes a lot easier. I'm just trying to figure out how to feel this way when you're not here because my therapist says I need to be my own source of happiness in order to share it with anyone else."

"Your *therapist*?" Emersyn turns ninety degrees to look at my face.

I smirk. "Don't say it. I've heard enough I-told-you-so's from my family."

Her head eases side to side. "I never told you to see

310

a therapist, so I can't say that. But I'm glad you're doing it."

I nod slowly. "Losing my wedding band was a wake-up call. I felt pretty messed up after I returned home from Malaysia."

"And now?"

"I'm better. Most days, I'm better."

"Does your therapist know you're screwing the maid?"

I laugh, tugging on the sash to her robe. "He knows about Malaysia."

"And?" She prompts me, greedy for more information.

"And he agrees that you're young and you need to live a little. And I need to work through my shit."

"Does he know we're married?" She narrows her eyes at me, but I'm too busy focusing on her naked body that I've just exposed.

"No," I reply.

"Does your family know about Malaysia?" She covers herself, tightening her sash and eliciting a frown from me.

I shoot her an are-you-kidding look. "They know you had a seizure and I went to Malaysia. But no, they don't know more than that. I'm not sure what I'd tell them. Aaron called me last week. He wants to fix me up with a friend of his. I said no, of course."

"Why did you say no?"

Did I hear her right?

"Why would you ask me that?"

She offers me a fake smile. "I think you should live your life. Enjoy your life. You're a man with ... *needs*. I'm the woman who's rarely here. You've given me more, so much more than I could ever repay. You owe me nothing, least of all any sort of loyalty."

"That's a terrible answer," I blurt before she finishes her last word. Does she really feel like a conquest of mine? Like just any other woman? Does she really think what happened in Malaysia meant nothing? I'm ... speechless. No, I'm gagged like a prisoner because I want to say all the words I'm thinking, but I refuse to be some needy fuck who holds her back in life.

Emersyn shrugs before taking her mug to the sink. "It's the best I have to give you. I'm sure Aaron has someone who is local, established in a career, and probably not epileptic. Bonus points for good health. Double bonus points if she's never lived out of her car."

"Just ... stop. I'm not ready to date."

Emersyn laughs, turning toward me and resting her backside against the counter, hands on the edge. "I was there last night ... in bed, in case you've already forgotten. I'd say you're plenty ready to date."

For the record, I *hate* this conversation.

"That's different."

"Why?" Her head cocks to the side. "Because you didn't buy me dinner first?"

"Because it's you." I scratch my chin.

"Me? What does that matter?"

"You're my wife." The words are out. There's no

reeling them back in. My biggest issue, one that I have not discussed with my therapist, is just how conflicted I am over having a wife. Do I love Emersyn like a wife? No. I mean ... I don't know. Do I love her at all? Jesus ... I hope so. But the connection between my heart and my head feels damaged. The signals are not clear. They haven't been clear since Suzanne was diagnosed with cancer. And when she died, I wasn't sure I'd ever feel again.

"No." Emersyn's head whips back and forth. "I'm the woman you gave an insurance card to because you were ridiculously generous. You can't use the wife excuse when it's convenient. You've told me too many times that we don't have that kind of marriage."

"You know what I mean. You're different. The exception."

"Why?"

I shrug and gaze at the floor, eyes narrowed a smidge. "Because I can be with you without pretending that I'm perfectly okay. Because you and Suzanne had something special. And it might not make sense to anyone else, but it makes sense to me, and I think it makes sense to you."

"Define sense? Because I'm trying to make sense of everything, and I'm struggling. I'm trying to figure out how to reconcile thinking about you all the time yet crawling into bed with some other guy because that's what you want me to do. Right? I'm trying to figure out what it means to have sex with my husband, but not think of us as really married."

I bite my tongue until I'm certain it's bleeding. What do I expect from her? How do I make a case for my true feelings and not hold her back? It's impossible.

"I think you need a better therapist," she mutters before sauntering to the bathroom to shower.

Chapter Thirty-Two

Emersyn

WE DO a great job of ignoring the unanswered questions. He flies. I work on photo editing and my social media pages. On our anniversary, he sends me a huge bouquet of roses. Again, I'm confused about this marriage right now. If it's not that kind of marriage, why send flowers?

Leah's dad dies, and I go to New York for the funeral. I'm not sure when she'll be ready to resume traveling, but I hope it's soon because it's painful to live with my husband and not really feel like his wife.

"Hey!" Zach grins as he pokes his head into the kitchen after being gone for two days. "Happy birthday."

I close my computer at the kitchen table and scoot back in my chair as he sets a pink box with a white ribbon on the table next to my computer before dropping a slow kiss on my lips.

"Thank you," I murmur and grin as he sits in the chair next to me, loosening his tie.

"You shouldn't have," I say while ripping the bow off the box. I don't really mean it. I haven't been given many presents in my life. I haven't had that many birthdays acknowledged either, so I selfishly enjoy this moment.

I lift the lid. There's a hardback photography book. *Diane Arbus: An Aperture Monograph.*

"Zach ..." I whisper when I see it's a 1972 first edition.

It's filled with portraits of unconventional poses of ordinary working-class people as well as those who lived on the fringes of society, like prostitutes and giants. He spent some money to buy this.

I hug the book to my chest. "It's too much, but perfect. You're so thoughtful. I ..." I stop before silly tears fill my eyes. "Thank you." Setting the book back in the box, I straddle his lap, wrap my arms around his neck, and *thoroughly* kiss him.

"What are you doing?" he says in a husky voice as I slide off his lap and kneel before him, my hands working the belt to his pants. "I didn't buy you that so that you'd ..." He pauses and draws in a long breath when my hand wraps around him. "I'm just..." he fumbles his words "...saying you don't have to ... fuuuck ..." He closes his eyes when my mouth replaces my hand.

. . .

TRUE INTIMACY IS hard to navigate. Feeling love toward another human in this way. Wanting to please Zach because I love him, not because I'm trying to pay him back or earn his love. Most days, I don't focus on how much my life has been impacted by not having a father. It's easy to pretend that I have a healthy grip on intimacy and relationships, but I don't. I'm still learning.

With nothing more than a satisfied and very appreciative grin, Zach saunters to the bathroom for a shower. "Get ready," he calls from halfway down the hallway. "I'm taking you to dinner."

I giggle, utterly giddy with excitement. He doesn't show signs of guilt, like I did it only because he gave me a present. He doesn't rush to reciprocate— although I have no doubt he'll show plenty of birthday gratitude later. It feels ... normal. In the least normal circumstances, I've found a little balance.

———

ZACH TAKES me to a Japanese restaurant where we remove our shoes at the door. I give him a curious look.

He winks. "First time?"

I nod.

"Good." His shoulders slide back, chin up, as a triumphant grin bends his lips. "I'm glad I'm giving you a *first* experience."

The hostess takes us to our table. I give him a second curious expression. He nods for me to be seated first, so I ease onto a pillow and slide my feet into the sunken space beneath the low table.

"It's zashiki seating," he says after we're handed our menus.

"And you know this because you come here often or you've been to Japan?"

Glancing at his menu, he shrugs. "Both. Oh ... Aaron and Danielle's wedding has been moved up to next week. So you'll be able to make it unless Leah's planning on leaving before then."

"Why is the wedding next week?"

"Danielle's grandma isn't doing well, and she wants to be at the wedding."

"I thought you were going to say she's pregnant."

Zach laughs, unfolding his napkin and laying it on his lap. "No. But that would make sense too."

"So I'll meet her for the first time at the wedding?"

"Probably."

"What's she like?" I ask.

We pause our conversation to order our drinks and meals, and as soon as we're alone again, Zach narrows his eyes at me. "Where were we? Oh, yeah. Danielle. She's a pharmacist. And she loves Aaron's bad jokes. They both want one child and a dog."

I smile, but it fades quickly as I nod slowly. "Can I ask you something?"

"Of course."

"Did you and Suzie plan on having kids?"

Zach's brow tenses like a sheet of lined paper. "Yes."

"Do you still want kids?"

He blows out a long breath, slowly shaking his head while rubbing a hand over his face. "I can't talk about this."

"I'm sorry," I whisper, tapping the side of my water glass with my fingernails.

"No." He drops his hand to his lap. "It's fine. I'm just not sure what I want, so it's hard to think along the lines of kids when I'm not even thinking about marriage again."

I frown.

Zach pinches the bridge of his nose. "Fuck ... I *am* married." He chuckles.

Following his lead, I snort a laugh. "I heard that rumor too. Are congratulations or condolences in order?"

"Emersyn ... I didn't mean it like that." He bites his lips together and shakes his head.

"It's okay. When the conversation starts with having kids and leads to the mother of your possible future children, I don't expect you to think of me as that woman."

Zach studies me with an unreadable expression before sliding his hand across the table and covering mine with a gentle squeeze. "Listen, I don't know where I'm going. I don't know where you're going. But I can say that right now I like where we're at."

I smile, and it's mostly genuine, but I don't feel like

I know where we are right now. It's an *uncomfortable* happiness.

———

A LITTLE BEFORE six the next morning, I head out for a jog, a weak attempt at clearing my mind. After pounding out just over five miles, I turn onto our street and see Zach in the driveway staring at his watch. He's breathing heavily and sweating. He, too, needed a good run this morning.

"How far did you go?" I ask.

He turns and a slow grin works its way up his face. "Good morning. Eight miles."

I roll my eyes as my spine deflates on a long exhale. "Of course you did."

"Go shower. I'll take you to breakfast."

"You took me to dinner."

"Well, now it's time for breakfast. And I want nothing more than to take you to breakfast." He steps closer to me and links his finger with mine, giving it a tiny shake that's just as playful as his expression.

"Yeah?" I say, feeling giddy.

His grin swells. "Yeah."

I duck my head to hide my ridiculous level of excitement as I speed walk to the front door and sprint to the shower. By the time I emerge from the bathroom with my hair doing its usual limp blond act, Zach is waiting by the back door.

He glances up from his phone and smiles. "Ready?"

"Ready." I slide my purse onto my shoulder as he holds open the door for me.

We don't say anything for a few blocks, and then Zach clears his throat.

"I know you supported Suzanne's Cap'n Crunch addiction."

I didn't see this coming. My gaze slides to him, but he keeps his attention on the road. *I know you gave her an overdose of morphine.* Again, I don't say that. Will I *ever* be able to say that? Will he ever confide in me?

"I don't know what you're talking about."

"Liar." Zach grins. "She hid it from me, just not very well." He chuckles. "Crumbs in the bed. Yep, I found crumbs after you two had been watching one of those trashy reality TV shows. So you knew."

I drum my fingers on my jean clad legs. "In my defense—"

"You don't need a defense. I fed her addiction too. It took her forever to go through a box, so it would go stale. I'd replace the box, eat a bowl or two of cereal when she wasn't looking, always leaving about the same amount that was in it when it went stale. Michelle knew. She'd pretend to buy it for Suzanne, but it was me. Always me."

Warmth floods my chest. Zachary Hays is a beautiful human. My love for him is fueled just as much by the kind husband he was to Suzie as the lover he is to me.

"I knew," he continues, "that she wasn't going to be in my life forever. I never let her see my weak moments of acceptance. So I played the obsessed husband on a mission to save his wife. And some days I let myself believe that I actually had that power. But most days ... I knew better. Those were the days I replaced cereal and painted her toenails with toxic polish. Those were the days I let her just ... be."

"Yeah. We've all been there. I told you that I dated Brady for as long as I did because I needed the free gym membership. And by free gym membership, I mean I needed the locker room showers. In hindsight ... who trades sexual favors for a shower?"

After a few seconds of silence, he coughs a laugh. "That's ... I can't ... Emersyn ..." Zach tries not to laugh, but he can't help it.

My story has nothing to do with his story, and we both know it. It's just another example of how we give each other a reprieve without asking for it. It's how we take the unbearable gravity from the moment. This is us. It's something that's uniquely us. I highly doubt he did this with Suzie.

Zach pulls into a café and turns off the car. When he unfastens his seat belt and glances at me, I return a goofy tight-lipped grin. We get out of his car without saying a word, and then he steps in front of me before we make it two feet past his car. "I don't regret a single second with you, in case you think that."

My gaze cuts to his.

Before I can say a word, he continues, "I'm trying so hard not to live in the past, to stay grounded in each moment. There have been many moments lately where your touch has saved me. I realize things happen in the moment without thinking too much about the ramifications for the future. My expectations are low. The lowest."

Rolling my lips between my teeth, I nod slowly. "That's a little sad. You should raise your expectations."

"Maybe." He nods his head toward the café. "Let's eat."

After the waitress hands us menus, I eye Zach over the top of mine as he scans his for a few seconds before glancing up at me.

"What?" He grins.

Tracing my fingernail along the edge of the menu, a mix of bacon and maple syrup waft past me as the waitress delivers food to the booth behind us. "If we're never more than a fake marriage and mind-blowing sex, do you think you'll ever tell anyone about us? Would you ever tell your family that you married me to give me insurance? If you marry again, will you tell your next wife?"

When enough time passes and he doesn't answer me, I shift my attention from the menu to his contemplative expression.

"Mind-blowing, huh?" He doesn't look at me, but he smirks. "Have you been asked if you're married? When traveling, has anyone ever asked you that?"

"Yes," I answer him honestly.

"And what do you say?"

"I say no."

"Why?"

I laugh a little. "You know why."

Zach returns a slow nod. "Do you ever think of saying yes?"

I shrug. "Sometimes."

"Why?"

Another shrug. "You said it yourself; I like the idea of you."

"The idea of me ..." He echoes with a partial grin.

"A husband. A home. Family. A man unlike any man I have ever known." My lips twist. "Granted, I've never met my father, and my mother didn't exactly parade the greatest men through our apartment. So the bar has been set incredibly low, but I have a feeling you surpass even the highest bar. And I think I knew it from the day we met and I saw you with Suzie. The day I witnessed true love."

A hue of pink fills his face as his gaze averts to the right. Sliding my water and the wrapped silverware toward him, I move to his side of the table. "Scooch over."

He eyes me suspiciously but obliges.

I sit next to him and rest my elbow on the table, cheek in my hand, as I gaze at him and smile. "My first year in college, I went on a date, and this couple ... maybe in their thirties ... were sitting in a booth, on the same side. They must have ordered one of everything on the menu because their table was filled with food when we were seated, and they were still there when we left the restaurant. I watched them more than I paid attention to my date. They laughed. Ate. Playfully nudged each other. And sometimes he leaned into her and whispered something in her ear. She grinned. He kissed her cheek. They seemed to take turns resting a hand on each other's leg. It was like they had all the time in the world. And they certainly didn't care what anyone else in the restaurant thought of them because they were so engrossed in each other." My other hand rests on Zach's leg.

He smiles and it's a little reminiscent of the smile he used to give Suzie.

"So," I continue, "I remember thinking that one day I would find a guy worthy of sharing the same side of a booth with me."

Zach's grin intensifies, warm like the sun hitting its highest point in the afternoon sky. His fingers curl my hair behind one ear while he leans into me and whispers, "I'm going to order the Belgium waffle with a side of eggs." Then his lips brush along my cheek, dropping a kiss on it.

I giggle.

We spend the next hour and a half eating, flirting, touching, and simply being totally engrossed with each other. It's butterfly season in my belly. Did Suzie know Zach would be the one to give me them? Was it more than just a casual hope, a wink of approval?

Chapter Thirty-Three

THREE DAYS BEFORE THE WEDDING, I slide out of bed and hit the pavement for a long jog. Sometimes exercise gives me clarity, but not this morning. By the time I arrive home, Zach is dressed and watering the plants in the jungle. "You snuck out early," he says as I inspect a few of the plants and pinch off the dead leaves like Suzie taught me to do. "You should have woken me; I would have gone with you."

"I needed some headspace," I say.

"O-kay ..." Zach sets the watering can aside and rests his hands on my hips, inspecting me for a few seconds. "Are you better now?"

"I think so."

He kisses me, and I can't help but surrender to him. I don't like feeling so out of sorts about our situation.

"Do you have a dress for the wedding?"

I take a step back and laugh. "I'm a fashion loving woman ... you're not actually asking me that, are you?"

Zach chuckles. "You're right. But fashion loving women can never have too many dresses."

"Zach, Zach, Zach ... you speak my language. I might never let you go."

Something in his expression changes. He looks ... fearful? Surprised? I can't tell.

"Do you have a tux rented?"

He shakes his head. "It's a small gathering, immediate family and a few friends. Aaron said I can wear a suit."

"I need to see your suits."

"Why? There's nothing wrong with my suits."

I shoulder past him toward the bedroom. "I'll be the judge of that."

"So now you're judging my wardrobe?" He follows me.

"Yes. I am absolutely judging your wardrobe. I've silently judged it since the day we met." I sift through all two of his suits that aren't for his job.

"The gray one. Suzanne liked it best," he says.

I glance over my shoulder, one eyebrow raised. "Agreed. You look very handsome in this gray suit. But ... you wore it to her funeral. You are *done* wearing it."

"No one will remember that I wore it to her funeral. It's a plain gray suit. Nobody pays attention to stuff like that."

I set his black suit on the bed and return to the closet to inspect his shirts and ties. "And by nobody, you mean men—men don't pay attention to stuff like that. But I guarantee your mom will remember you wore this suit. I'm sure the image of her oldest son standing in his gray suit next to his wife's casket is branded into her memory forever."

"Suzanne loved this suit," he murmurs, a fixed gaze on it.

"She loved *you*." I pull several shirts from their hangers. "Those are threads woven into a suit. Now it's a memory of a very sad day."

"So is my bed."

I fold the shirts over my arm and glance up at him. "Then get a new bed."

"Do *you* want me to get a new bed?"

I shake my head and return to said bed, layering the shirt beneath the suit jacket. My knee-jerk reply is to tell him that at some point I'm leaving again. If this bed brings him comfort, I would never deny him that when I'm halfway around the world.

I don't tell him that. For the moment, I'm going to pretend that I'm not leaving.

"Do you like the bed? Is it comfortable for you? If so, then keep it. You can flip the mattress. Get new bedding. Change out the headboard. Rearrange the room. Paint the walls. Hell, you could move to a different house. You should do what you need to do. And if you need everything to stay the same, then leave everything as is. The heart has little control over what it needs. And I have no opinion here. Other than the suit. I cannot, in good conscience, let you wear it to the wedding."

Zach sits on the edge of the bed, hands folded

between his spread legs. "It doesn't bother you? The bed. The house. The chair and quilt. She's everywhere and you're okay with that?"

With a slight chuckle, I return to the closet, snatching ties and shoes. He only has two pairs of dress shoes as well. And one is a black pair he wears for work. We need to go shopping. "Sometimes I think you forget that I loved her too. She was my best friend even if I wasn't truly hers. I liked her *way* more than I like you."

I lie.

"That's harsh." He gives me a funny look as I emerge from the closet with ties and shoes.

"No. Harsh is your tie and shoe selection. Zach, this is not okay. I'm not going to lie, I'm a little disappointed in Suzie for allowing you to have such a boring wardrobe. I mean ..." I stand back and inspect every-thing laid out on the bed. It's cringe-worthy. "This isn't going to work."

"I'm not buying a new suit for this wedding. I rarely wear a suit that's not my uniform. It's a waste of money."

"Then a new shirt, tie, and shoes."

"There's nothing wrong with my shirts."

"Zach ..." I frown. "You're killing my fashion-loving heart right now. *Killing* it."

He rolls his eyes. "Fine. A new shirt."

"Tie and shoes."

"Nobody will be looking at my shoes."

"I will!" I rest my fists on my hips and glance up at the ceiling, blowing out a breath of frustration.

"Then just keep your eyes on my face."

"Zach ..."

"Emersyn ..." he mocks me. "New shirt and tie. Final offer."

"Fine." I huff and march down the hall to my bathroom. "I'll take a quick shower. Pack up my breakfast. I'll eat it on the way."

"I could join you in the shower."

"No, Zachary. Fashion is foreplay. That's why women wear lingerie. You've ruined the moment."

As I close the door behind me, I hear him chuckling. It makes me grin. I'm proud of myself for being brave (courageous) enough to show maturity when he asked me about the bed, about Suzie's presence that will linger in this house forever.

———

"THAT'S A FEMININE TIE," Zach says as I hold up several ties.

"I'm going to request that you not speak. If we got on a plane, I would not tell you how to fly it. M-kay, pumpkin?" I say in my sweetest voice.

"I don't like this. I'm not a mannequin you can dress up. I just want that to be on record."

"Noted. But overruled."

His eyes bulge at the price tag. "It's a hundred-dollar tie."

"I know. They're all cheap ties, but we don't have a big choice with so little time."

"Cheap? A hundred dollars is *cheap* for a tie?"

"In the fashion world, yes."

"Jesus Christ."

"This will work. Shirt and tie for under three hundred dollars. My treat." I saunter to the checkout.

He tosses his credit card on the counter. "You're not buying my clothes."

"I am." I give the sales lady a wink while handing her my credit card.

She smirks, shooting Zach a quick glance.

"Hey, Zach ..."

I turn as a couple approaches us. They look close to Zach's age.

"Oh, hey!" He grins.

"How's it going?" the guy asks.

I sign for the tie and shirt and take the bag.

As I sidle up to Zach, the couple eye me and then him.

He seems at a loss for words, so I extend my hand. "Hi. I'm Emersyn."

"Rob. And this is my wife, Jill."

I smile. "Nice to meet you."

"Yeah ... um ..." Zach fumbles his words. "Emersyn was just helping me pick out a new shirt and tie for Aaron's wedding."

"Aaron's getting married?" Rob asks.

"Yes. Just a small wedding at our parents' house."

"Tell him congratulations."

Zach nods. "I will." He gives me a quick glance, and I return a tight smile. "Rob used to work with me. Now he works for a private jet company."

I nod. "Ah, I see."

"And ..." Zach shifts his attention to Rob and Jill. "Emersyn used to clean our house. She and Suzanne became close. Now she travels the world taking amazing photos and videos with another photographer."

"Wow! That's pretty exciting," Jill says.

It is exciting. Though not as exciting as this really awkward conversation where Zach has no idea how to explain who I am in his life. Yes, I was Suzanne's friend, but she's dead now. Yes, I cleaned his house, but it's no longer my job. I can see the unanswered questions on their faces.

"Well, you owe me lunch now." I gaze up at Zach while slipping my hand into his back pocket—something a friend or ex-maid would not do. Then I prepare myself for the backlash ... for his body to go rigid or some other subtle rejection.

He doesn't. There might be a two second pause, but that's all it takes for him to hook his arm around my waist and pull me closer. "Yes, let's get lunch," he says.

I don't expect this, and it makes me feel guilty for doubting him. Maybe all he needed was for me to show him that not everything needs a verbal explanation. Rob and Jill see that we are more than friends, and we didn't have to say one word about it.

"Well, enjoy your lunch," Rob says before we stroll toward the exit.

As we make our way to the car, Zach says, "Thank you."

"For what?"

He leans to the side and kisses my head. "You know what for."

I grin. Yes, I do.

Chapter Thirty-Four

"It's still a feminine *pink* tie," Zach grumbles as I tie his *cranberry* tie.

"Fashion foreplay, remember?"

"Is that code for I'm getting laid later?"

I stay focused on his tie, making the perfect Windsor knot. "Untie my sash if you want to know what you're getting later." My lips purse into a tiny smirk.

"Untie this, huh?" He tugs the tie to my satin robe.

My hair is curled in loose waves. Makeup applied, including *cranberry* lips. I just need to slip into my dress and heels before we leave.

My robe falls open when he unties it.

"Well ... fuck ... me ..."

My smirk breaks into a bigger grin, eating up every ounce of his reaction to my black lace push up bra and matching thong. The lace bra does nothing to hide my nipples. It's really just a tease.

"Oh, trust me ... I'm going to insist you leave on the tie, but everything else can go later when we do *fuck*."

"The wedding doesn't start for two hours ..." The pad of his thumb circles the lace over my nipple.

"Don't even think about it. I'm not messing up my hair and makeup."

"Em ..." His fingertips ghost along my stomach, his thumb sliding into my lace panties. "I can enjoy *my wife* without messing with your hair and makeup."

My breath hitches, and my hands grip his arms. *My wife.*

The couple at the mall. And now making claim to me as his wife. I like this shift. This shift plants so many possibilities into my head ... and my heart. Acceptance. I feel accepted and acknowledged for who I am.

Not a charity case.

Not a checked-off box on a list of good deeds.

Not a dirty little secret.

"Zach ... no ..." I attempt a weak protest as I notice, for the first time, that the jar of rocks is gone. I wouldn't have cared if he kept them, but their absence is one more thing that affirms there is an *us* and we are real.

"You wanted me to see this ..." he says with a low and seductive voice that brings a rush of adrenaline to my veins, pumping my heart faster. "As a preview. So I want to give you a preview of what you can expect from me later."

"Zach ..." I swallow hard as he backs me into the

vanity. My hands grip the edge while he kneels in front of me, sliding my panties down my legs.

"When you leave with Leah again..." he sets my panties on the vanity stool and gives me a wicked grin while easing my legs apart with his hands on my knees "...I'm going to miss many things about you." He slowly wets his lips, and I instantly feel drunk with need. "But this ..." His gaze shifts to my spread legs. "The look in your eyes when I do *this* ... I can't begin to describe how much I'm going to fucking miss it."

The first swipe of his tongue rips a harsh gasp from my chest, but within seconds of his warm mouth covering me *there* ... I draw my knees up, close my eyes, and come completely undone.

One hand fisting his hair.

My other hand clenching the edge of the vanity.

It's more than love. It's more than physical gratification.

Zach makes me feel sensual. He sparks passion inside of me. Our intimacy builds my confidence as a woman. I don't know if I can trust him with my heart, but I trust him with my body. I trust him with my physical vulnerability.

Life is a series of moments, and we deem some moments more important than other moments. I won't remember standing in line for coffee, but I'll remember the first time Leah complimented one of my photos while we sipped coffee at the interview. I won't remember the shirt I picked out for Zach to wear to this wedding, but I'll remember the cranberry tie and what he did to me after I tied it around his neck for the first time.

People devote their lives to God and sacrifice their human desires, so it would seem ridiculous for any human to put sexual gratification high on a list of important moments in life. Yet, here I am, adding this moment to a rare list of moments that I will never forget, and one that I'm not sure I can live without. It's the words he says and the way he says them.

Every subtle grin, like he'd rather not, but he can't help himself.

Every kiss to the top of my head, where he inhales deeply just before his lips make contact.

Every time he pulls me into his body, on a sofa or just standing next to him like he can't get close enough to me.

Every. Single. Moment.

I'm going to miss them, and I'm going to compare every new moment to them.

———

ZACH CAN'T STOP STARING at my black lace overlay gown with a slightly off-the-shoulder neckline and a generous slit up the leg. I think it's the *cranberry* sash around the waist that has his attention. Also noteworthy, everyone— even Zach's dad—compliments him on his tie.

"Do I get to say I told you so now ..." In one hand I

hold a glass of champagne and my other hand strokes Zach's tie. "Or do you want me to wait until later?"

He sips his champagne. "You didn't tell me the tie thingy to your dress was pink."

I chuckle. "Because it's not pink. It's cranberry."

"Red."

I shake my head. "Cranberry."

"Cranberry ..." he mouths seductively, and I can't help my snort and giggle.

"What a lovely dress." Danielle's mother stops on her way to the newlyweds to give me a quick once-over.

"Thank you." I smile.

Zach makes the formal introduction like the gentleman he is. "Vicky, this is Emersyn. Em, this is Danielle's mom, Vicky."

"Will the next wedding here be yours, Zach?" She winks. "Or ..." She twists her lips and squints as if trying to recall something. "Are you already married? I feel like I heard you were married."

Before my heart has a chance to form a solid opinion about the appropriate response to Vicky's questions, Zach speaks up, taking a step away from me.

A.

Step.

Away.

From.

Me!

"No. I'm not married. I *was* married, but my wife died."

I step closer to him and reach for his hand, but he slips it into his pocket.

The world stops turning. Life as I know it comes to a screeching halt. Reality rears its ugly head, and I feel the wrath of my own stupidity cut right down the center of my heart.

Today is the day ... or it was supposed to be the day. Today his family was going to find out about us. We didn't discuss it. It was implied. Wasn't it? Just hours ago, he lovingly called me his wife and did something incredibly intimate to said wife.

Wife. I am his wife!

Or ... I'm fucking delusional.

"I'm very sorry to hear that." Vicky continues toward the cake table.

My brain trips over the flood of thoughts and potential explanations for what he just said.

Did he legitimately *forget* we're married? He's relaxed, sipping champagne like that interaction, the *lie*, did not just happen. And I know ... I really do know that spilling the truth to Danielle's mom before anyone else would not be the best idea. At least my brain knows it. My heart is too busy bleeding to process actual thoughts. The rational kind.

Why are we hiding now? We weren't real, but ... we're real now. Right? We don't have to tell anyone, just let them see it.

Us holding hands.

Him whispering in my ear and brushing his lips along my cheek while grinning.

Until this exact moment, I didn't fully understand how much that elephant in the room mattered to me, my feelings toward Zach, and my decisions about my future.

"Want some cake?" Zach asks.

I shake my head slowly. I don't want cake. I want to know why today is *not* the day to just put it out there.

"Gather around, single ladies!" Vicky calls. "It's time for Danni to toss her bouquet."

It's a small wedding, maybe thirty people. So there are only two single ladies here: Danielle's best friend and her younger sister.

"Miss Emersyn ..." Vicky crooks her finger at me. "Bring your pretty, single self over here."

Three. Apparently, there are three single ladies here.

Zach gives me a little nudge with his hand on my lower back. I shake him off, shooting him a scowl over my shoulder. I want to kill him. I'm certain I *will* kill him. It's only a matter of time.

Still, I keep a semblance of composure, even if it's only a thread.

"Get going, single lady," he says, and it's fire to my fuse.

The thread breaks.

Everything inside my body feels ... tight and warm. Feverishly warm. An unnerving, prickly sensation spreads along my skin. I stand way back, giving the other two single women ample room to catch the bouquet.

"One, two, THREE!"

Danielle tosses it over her head, and holy fucking Tom Brady arm ... she surpasses the other two girls as the cannonball of flowers nearly takes off my head. I catch it, earning me disappointed frowns from her sister and BFF. Flipping it back into the air like a game of hot potato, it lands in the arms of her sister.

"No. You caught it." She hands it back to me.

The small gathering claps. And that sparked flame? It hits the other end of the fuse. I'd say I'm seeing red ... but it's really *cranberry*. I see nothing but cranberry. Feel nothing but pure rage. Hear nothing but the *whoosh* of blood in my ears as I turn and stomp my heeled feet toward Zach. I guess everything in life is fine ... until it's not. *Not fine* rarely comes with any warning.

He's grinning, but that grin begins to fade with each enraged step I take on my way to him. His gaze follows my hand clenching the bouquet like an ax. With my final two steps, I lift the bouquet over my head.

"I AM NOT SINGLE!"

WHACK! WHACK! WHACK!

"YOUR WIFE IS NOT DEAD!"

WHACK! WHACK! WHACK!

"I AM YOUR FUCKING WIFE!"

WHACK! WHACK! WHACK!

"YOU INSENSITIVE ASSHOLE!"

All that's left in my hand is a wad of flowerless stems tied with a ribbon. I drop the stems as Zach

341

slowly lowers his arms that shielded his head while I clobbered him with the bouquet because he said his wife was dead.

Because he stepped away from me.

Because he called me his wife before he put his face between my legs.

Because he stuck his hand in his pocket when I went to hold it.

It's so quiet I not only hear my own pounding heart, I think I can hear his too.

What have I done?

Did Zach ask himself that same question after he gave Suzie an overdose of morphine? Were his actions well-thought-out? Or was he acting on impulse, letting his fragile heart make the decision?

"Y-you're married?" Cecilia's voice breaks through the air as she appears at Zach's side.

The lifeless expression on his face mirrors mine. He knew about the elephant in the room. He chose to ignore it. Now it's come out of the corner and destroyed everything with its raging stampede.

"Yes," he whispers.

"W-when?" Cecilia asks.

Zach blinks several more times, the only part of his face that moves. "Last year."

Cecilia's hand shoots to her chest. She knows that means we got married not long after Suzie died. She just doesn't know why. And maybe it's none of her business. And maybe I should have held my shit together—there's no *maybe* about it. I channeled my inner three-year-old, and I can't undo what I just did. But love makes people do crazy things. *It* won't sit idle in a corner. Love demands recognition or ... it explodes.

"Were you ..." Cecilia gets a little choked up. "Having an aff—"

"No," Zach cuts her off.

"Then why?"

I can't take my eyes off Zach, and he can't take his off me.

"Do you want to tell everyone why we got married?" Zach asks me. His tone holds no anger. It's the epitome of surrender. Defeat.

Be mad, Zach. Please be mad. Be human!

I blink, releasing my tears, feeling toxic with regret. "No," my voice cracks. "I ..." My head inches side to side. "I just wanted to be acknowledged as your wife." I sniffle while snot works its way down my nose. A lovely accessory to my fancy dress.

"Well ... now everyone knows you're my wife. Happy?" Zach pivots and worms his way through the small gathering. A few seconds later, the front door slams shut.

I chase after him, but he's already pulling out of their driveway. Lifting the skirt of my dress, I run to catch him, but my heels can't keep up. When I reach the end of their long drive, I wipe my tears through my labored breaths.

"I'm sorry," I whisper to his taillights.

By the time I return to the porch, everyone's gathered at the front of the house, gawking out the windows. I open the door and the crowd scatters— everyone except Cecilia.

"I am ... *so* sorry," I say to her. It hurts to look at her, so I don't. I retrieve my purse and wrap from the library and order a ride.

"I'll take you home or wherever you want to go if you please tell me what just happened," she says.

"Your son is a good Samaritan. That's what happened. He's given me more than I deserve. And it wasn't enough. That's on me. And I've ruined a wedding and ruined my relationship with him. I am incredibly sorry." I wipe a stray tear as I make my way to the front door again.

"I still don't understand."

As I open the door, I glance over my shoulder and offer her a painful smile and slight shrug. "It's no longer my story to tell. It never really was. Please give my sincerest apologies to Aaron and Danni."

When my ride arrives, I have no choice but to return to Zach's house. My stuff is there. My passport. My cat.

A haunting silence greets me when I open the door and slip off my heels. I swallow my fear and deflated pride while dragging my feet to his bedroom. My shaky hand wraps around the handle to push it down, but it won't budge.

He's locked me out.

Making a fist, I lift it to knock, but I stop short. My

fingers uncurl, and I rest my palm on the door, closing my eyes. What have I done?

"I'm sorry," I whisper again before retreating to my bedroom. I don't have the energy to remove my makeup or put on a nightshirt. I manage to get out of my dress and crawl into bed in my bra and panties. My arms hug a pillow to my body, and my tears eventually dry.

My mind settles.

And I fall asleep.

———

THE NEXT MORNING, the high-pitch churning of the coffee grinder brings me out of my coma of regret. Before I can make the walk of shame, I shower and slip into jeans and a tee. Hair wet. Eyes still a little red and swollen. As much as I wish I could teleport myself to literally anywhere else in the world, I can't. So I pad my way to the kitchen.

Zach doesn't look up from his plate or his phone next to it. He keeps one hand curled around his coffee mug, slowly bringing it to his lips like I'm not in the room. I pour myself a cup of coffee and ease into the seat next to him. Still, he acts like I'm not here.

"I think ..." I press my lips together and carefully weigh my words. "I think I wanted to be your real wife. And yesterday you made me feel like a nobody after you made me feel ... well, like *somebody* to you. You actually took a step away from me to announce your widower status. And when I tried to hold your hand, you shoved it into your pocket."

I ease my head back and forth. "I can't be intimate with you *and* be a nobody. Maybe I thought I could, but I can't." I cup my coffee mug with both hands and stare at the black water instead of waiting for him to look at me. "My mother never married. She never demanded someone be accountable to her for more than one night. She never dared to dream big, to feel like she deserved a place in this world where she truly belonged, where she felt security and unconditional love.

"My whole life I've dreamed of love, even when I didn't know what that meant. I think I've wanted it more than absolutely anything else. I've dreamed about beautiful weddings, first houses, and the pitter patter of tiny feet. The dream. I've dreamed about ... the dream.

"Instead, I got a courthouse marriage, a loveless marriage, cheap airfare, health insurance, and a Get Out of Debt Free card. And if I sound ungrateful, I'm not. I'm really, *really* not. I'm truly sorry for the mess I've caused with your family and for acting so impulsive at Aaron and Danielle's wedding. I'm not proud of what happened, and I would take it all back if I could. But I'm not upset that the truth is out. Even if I don't really know anymore what the truth is between us."

Still, nothing from him.

"I'm sure you're silently counting down the minutes until I'm gone." I quickly wipe away a tear.

This is a whole new level of ghosting. I've never had someone do it to me in person ... while we're in the same room.

The muscles in his jaw flex, hard and unforgiving. There's an earthquake of tension rolling off his body, leaving a mark on my heart with aftershocks I will feel for a long time. He takes his plate and coffee mug to the sink, letting them drop in the basin with a crash as he drops his chin to his chest.

"I don't know when you think you fell in love with me, but I didn't suggest the marriage for any other reason than helping you. We crossed a line, and I thought I was in control. I thought I was prepared to deal with the ramifications of crossing that line, but I wasn't. I'm not. I'm ..." He rubs his temples. "Fuck, I ... I don't even know right now. This is on me, not you. I will deal with the mess. I didn't think our marriage would be anything more than a benefit to you."

Zach lifts his head and cuts his gaze to mine, his face marred with so much agony. "The marriage ..." He pauses, closing his eyes for a brief second. "It..." he shakes his head "...it was all so backward. You have been a true lifeline for me, and I think about you *all* the time. I also can't reconcile the marriage and the intimacy. You are so much more than a friend, and, by law, you are my wife. But in my head, and maybe even in my heart, you are not my wife. And I'm sorry if that hurts you. I fucked up. I've called you my wife more than once because I've been trying to make sense of what we have become. I've tried to see where we truly fit into each other's lives. And until I figure that out, I can't explain it to myself, least of all my family and friends. So if you needed me to be publicly accountable for our marital status, a heads-up would have been nice."

There are so many things I want to say to Zach. I think I've always had so many things I've wanted to say to him. The timing is never right. My heart doesn't know how to be that brave. So I hold everything inside and let it fester until the pain is too much to bear. Maybe the words I'm getting ready to say are not the right ones; it's highly likely they're not, but they are the most honest ones.

"Labels shouldn't matter. Deep down, I know this. But sometimes a label feels like validation. Validation of one's feelings. Validation of one's intentions. I don't know how to love you *and* be married to you yet not be your wife. And that's just my truth right now."

Zach takes his time, proving to be the patient man I met the day he hired me. "Well ..." He turns, crossing his arms over his chest. "I have a lot to figure out. We are on completely different paths in life, which makes it overwhelming to feel responsible for your future as well as mine. So after yesterday's events, I realize the *only* way I can be with you right now, is if I don't think of myself as your husband."

Ouch ...

I will feel those words for a long time, maybe forever.

Much like last night, we have another stare down. I

can't help but wonder if he's struggling to find words or if he's like me and struggling to find the *right* ones in a mess of a million desperate thoughts swirling in his head.

He seems to rest his case with an idle tongue.

And while I have so much fight left in me, the words my conscience keeps whispering are, *"You don't know how to love him without losing a piece of yourself."* That's my reality at this time in my life.

It's also hard not to think about Brady and how he seemed to love me (I use that word lightly) for the person he knew I could be instead of the person I was at the time. If Zach really does love me, what version does he love? Who I am or who I could be?

Love is not good at chasing expectations. It thrives on acceptance.

With a silent nod, I show my love for him, my *acceptance* of him and his feelings about me. And I rest my case too with an idle tongue.

"I'm going to pack."

"Where are you going?" I see the anguish in his eyes. It says everything. Why couldn't we have found each other at a different time, maybe in a different life?

"To New York. I booked the flight when I woke in the middle of the night. Leah could use a friend right now."

He nods slowly, and I head to my room.

I pack.

I sit in Suzanne's chair with her quilt hugged to my chest.

I'm not sure where Zach is right now. Maybe he left. I can't blame him. Goodbyes suck.

A little after one o'clock, I roll my suitcase to the door and get Harry Pawter in his carrier. Just as I bring up the app to order a ride, Zach comes through the front door, pausing when he sees me and my stuff ready to go.

I offer him all I have which is a nervous, heart-breaking smile. "I was just ordering a ride."

"I'll take you."

"You don't have to."

He brushes past me to the kitchen, getting a glass of water. "I know I don't have to, but I want to."

I nod and swallow the building emotion in my throat as he gulps down the glass of water. When he sets the empty glass on the counter, his sad eyes meet my gaze.

An intense ache settles into my heart, a yearning for him to say something to make this okay—to make *us* okay. When he comes up empty, I let my gaze fall to the floor the way my heart sinks into the pit of my stomach with a slow, throbbing beat. Zach grabs my suitcase and my carry-on bag and lugs them to his car.

"Let's go, Harry," I whisper as we follow Zach.

When the silence hurts too much, I lean my head against the window and close my eyes. The hour drive to the terminal feels like ten hours. It's killing me to go. It would kill me to stay. There is no escaping the pain. I can only hope distance will be a salve. Work will be a distraction. And time will grant perspective.

Right now, I can't see anything through my blinding emotions.

When his car stops at the curb, neither one of us reaches for our door handle. I'm not ready to let go, but if I'm honest, I'll never be ready. Life doesn't care if we're ready. It marches on, demanding we keep pace or fall behind in a cloud of dust, suffocating in the past.

"I love you, Emersyn."

Here they come … all the tears.

"I just…" he blows a breath out his nose "…love you."

I wipe my eyes and climb out of the car, frantically retrieving Harry from the back seat while Zach takes his time unloading my suitcase and carry-on.

My chest feels completely crushed, stifled by … *life*.

Of course, he knows I'm crying, choking, clawing at my bags in a desperate attempt to get out of here, to find a breath again.

He is not my oxygen.

My heart will beat without him.

I let these words—this truth—loop in my head over and over again. It has to be my new mantra.

Maybe it's because I'm twenty-five.

Maybe it's because I'm a girl.

Maybe it's because I'm a romantic.

Whatever it is … it feels like he's a little hurt, maybe a little disappointed, and yes … a little in love with me. But it also feels like it's too easy for him to say goodbye.

I'm not dying (at least I hope today is not my day), so I don't expect him to mourn me leaving like he

351

mourned losing Suzie. However, a tear, a little red emotion in his eyes, a word or two breaking under the weight of that emotion—something, *anything*—would make me feel loved so much more than simply saying the words.

Stupid me. I really did think all I needed was to hear him say it. I was wrong. My heart can't hear. It can only feel.

"Text or call me when you land."

I nod, but I can't look at him.

He hugs me, but I can't hug him back. I'm afraid I would never let go.

He kisses me, but I can't kiss him back. I won't take what no longer feels like mine.

"Em ..." He holds my face and keeps us so close our noses touch.

There's a slight agony to his voice, and I inhale it, feeding it to my heart, recording it in my soul where we keep all the tiny moments in life from when we truly feel loved.

"Touch me." He grabs my hands and brings them to his face.

"I can't," I say through a strangled sob.

"Kiss me." He presses his lips to mine again. They're desperate and demanding. They're everything I need. Still ... if I give in, I will never leave.

"I can't." I pull away.

His shoulders sag inward. I hate that my need for self-preservation feels like rejection to him, but the cruelest thing we can give each other is false hope. It is a mirage, nothing but a slow death.

"I'll let you know when I land." I gather my things again and head toward the entrance without looking back.

Chapter Thirty-Five

"OH ... YOU BROUGHT YOUR CAT." Leah wrinkles her nose when she meets me at the back of her car to load up my suitcase ... and Harry Pawter.

"Hope it's okay. I couldn't leave him this time."

"Well, we won't tell my landlord." She winks, closing the hatchback. "But why couldn't you leave him?"

We get into the car and fasten our seat belts. "Because I don't know if I'm going back."

Shooting me a wide-eyed glance, she parts her lips into an O.

I frown. "It's not good."

"Sorry to hear that. When do you want the bad news from me?" She pulls away from the curb into the bumper-to-bumper traffic.

"Might as well lay it on me now."

"My mom's struggling emotionally. I don't know how quickly she's going to move through the bereavement phase, but I don't want to be too far away if she needs me. So I want to stay in the US for now ... well, excluding Hawaii and Alaska."

"That's understandable."

"So ... are you going back for Thanksgiving?"

I shake my head. "I don't have anyone to go back to. I'm definitely not going to be welcomed at Zach's family gathering. And you know the situation with my mom. It's no big deal. I'm good on my own."

"You'll spend the holidays with me and my family. They're dying to meet you."

"Leah, I don't want to intrude. I'm really grateful for your sofa. That's plenty."

"Don't say that until you feel my sofa. It wasn't purchased for comfort. It's a beautiful prop. If you promise to behave, I'll let you sleep with me."

I manage a grin. "I'll see what I can do."

"So ... things are really messy with Zach? Or did you manage a clean break?"

"We're legally married. I'm not sure there's such a thing as a clean break. What felt like *one*, but now is *two*, will always leave remnants—little crumbs everywhere. I didn't leave Zach behind; I took little pieces of him with me, even if not by choice."

"You're breaking my heart, babe."

I nod. "Mine too," I whisper as I pull out my phone and message him as promised.

Em: Landed safely.

355

He messages me right back with a thumbs-up emoji.

I SPEND my time working hard on social media, slowly building a highly engaged following. People just want to connect. They want to be heard. They want to feel validated like their existence and their opinions matter. I'm getting so close to a hundred thousand followers, which means I will go ahead and monetize my page. If I can make enough money on my own, I can get an okay health insurance plan. Then I don't need to be Zach's wife anymore. And that's both liberating and soul robbing.

Right before Thanksgiving, Leah and I take the train to Boston to shoot boudoir photos for a group of wealthy women who just turned forty. One of the women has followed Leah since she first started her Instagram page.

"What are you reading?" Leah glances over my shoulder as we wait for the clients to arrive. It's a rented studio on the second floor of an old brownstone with spectacular natural light, various textured walls, an old bathtub, and a wrought iron bed with white sheets and fluffy pillows.

Two different velvet sofas and lots of old hardwood flooring.

"Tips for Better Boudoir Shoot?" She reads the article title on my phone.

I shrug. "I haven't done this before. I don't want to mess up."

She laughs. "Just be yourself. We'll ask them about their strengths and insecurities while sharing our own to form a connection with them. The most important part is to talk to them. Silence only invites awkwardness. Shower them with praise. They are not professional models. They'll need encouragement. Use the mirror to create more space. Use the windows for reflections, just make sure your reflection isn't in the photo. Encourage them to think of special people or special moments in their lives so you don't have a bunch of shots with meaningless expressions."

I nod. "Okay."

"And if we have time left after they leave, I'll take some photos of you."

My gaze shoots to hers. "What? Why? Like headshots?"

Leah chuckles. "Sure. Your head can be in the shot too." She winks.

"I don't need boudoir photos." I shake my head.

"Well, I need them for my page and my website. I don't do a lot of these sessions, and only a handful of clients sign release forms for me to share photos."

"What makes you think I'll sign a release?"

She rolls her eyes before turning on her camera and checking the settings. "You already signed a photo release when I hired you."

"That's ..."

"Clever?"

JEWEL E. ANN

I scoff. "No. It's ... I don't know. But I'll think of it."

Over the next three hours, I find myself drawn to this kind of photography. It's intimate and revealing, but not just in a physical sense. It's emotionally intimate as well. It's an honor to be invited to share in such vulnerability. Leah says the same thing about shooting birth photos.

"You're up," she announces, checking her watch after the women leave.

"We only have twenty minutes. It's going to take us that long to pack up everything."

"I only need ten minutes to pack and five minutes to get some shots of you."

"I don't have anything to wear. Maybe some other time." I slip my camera into its bag.

"Take off your clothes. I promise these will be the most tasteful images you've ever seen. I promise you'll want to share them on your own page."

I continue to shake my head.

"Do it or you're fired."

I giggle. "Stop."

She goes straight into desperation mode. "Come on! Just do it."

"Fine! But so help me ... if you make me look like some hussy on a trashy website ..."

"It's like you don't even know me. I'm truly offended."

I don't buy into her feigned offense, but I go ahead and remove my clothes. After sharing a room in

358

hostels for nearly a year, and now sharing her studio apartment, we've seen each other naked too many times to count. No modesty is necessary at this point.

"A little music to get you in the mood." She winks at me as I stand in front of her, totally naked with my hands on my hips.

Lana Del Rey sings about her "White Dress" as Leah guides me through a series of poses around the room. As promised, it only takes five minutes. I throw on my clothes, and we load up the equipment, exceeding the allotted rental time by only two minutes.

As soon as we get back to the hotel for the night, Leah brings up her photos of me on her computer.

"Whoa ..." I gawk at them. "They're ...."

She smirks. "Gorgeous. You look like a work of art. Every curve. The shadowing. You're showing everything yet oddly nothing all at the same time."

I nod slowly.

"Can I put a few on my page?" she asks.

"Oh, I do get a choice?"

"Yes," she says with theatrical exasperation, "you get a choice."

"You can put any of these on your page." I point to the ones that are the least revealing. Granted, I'm naked in all of them.

"Cool." She doesn't waste a single second before grabbing her phone and airdropping the photos from her computer.

After dinner, we hang out at the hotel bar so Leah

can flirt with the bartender and I can stare at my phone. The photos she posted of me already have over two hundred thousand likes and nearly twenty thousand comments, most of them fire or hot pepper emojis.

A message from Zach pops up at the top of my screen, and I quickly click on it. I haven't talked to him in over a month. It's not like us. And I've missed him, but I've also felt like we've needed this space. So why am I giddy over a text?

> Zach: Um … where are your clothes?

"Oh my god …" I cover my grin, eyes wide as I hold my phone up so Leah can see his message.

"Yeah, baby! Eat it, Zach. The world is looking at your naked wife."

"Shh …" I laugh. "I'm cutting you off." I waggle a finger at the bartender, and he just smirks.

"Seriously, like … what do I say?"

She grabs my phone and types: ???

He responds right away.

> Zach: I'm not blind or stupid.
> WTF????

"I think he's legit mad."

"Let him be mad," she says. "He had his chance with you." Merlot and a few too many shots have made her bold.

Maybe I need a few more drinks before I respond.

"Don't you dare reply to him."

My thumbs move over my screen. "I can't exactly ignore him forever. And I don't think he really did have his chance with me. He's still in the past, and I'm racing toward my future. Living in the present is too hard right now, maybe impossible."

"You *can* ignore him. Those are just excuses. If you were meant to be together, you would be. Period. But you're not together, and that's it. That's your answer."

> Em: They're called boudoir photos. Leah needed a model. I'm glad you like them.

Nope. I delete the last line. I don't want him thinking I care what he thinks.

> Zach: I have a beautiful wife.

His stupid reply robs me of all excitement. "Fuck you, Zach," I whisper.

Leah glances at my screen. "Oh ... that's so sweet." She flip-flops with one text.

"It's not sweet. It's manipulative. *Wife* ... he likes to claim me as his wife when it suits him."

My thumbs go to work, saying as much.

> Em: Your wife died. You don't have a wife.

Harsh? Yes. But sometimes harsh is necessary.

He doesn't respond.

I wait.

And wait.

"Welp, you told him."

I nod, feeling terrible. Truly terrible. "Yeah," I whisper. "I told him."

Chapter Thirty-Six

THE PROBLEM with saying things out of spite? It's impossible to take them back. There are not enough "I'm sorry's" or "I didn't mean it's" to erase memories. Forgiveness, at best, is a bandage to cover wounds. Words leave emotional scars. My mom left a lot on me, and I fear I've inflicted some on Zach.

Knowing these very basic facts is the reason I haven't jumped on a plane and headed back to Atlanta, groveling and begging for forgiveness. The collapse of whatever we are or were is far from one-sided. What more can be expected from two people years apart in age, married out of convenience, and emotionally bound to unrealistic expectations and the haunting memories of a woman who unknowingly (or maybe not so unknowingly) brought us together?

Thanksgiving passes and no word from Zach.

Christmas passes and no word from Zach.

Granted, I could make the effort to contact him, but I don't know if there's anything left to say.

The new year brings a long list of goals and a new sense of independence. Feeling completely resigned to … fate, I balance my checking account and text Zach.

> Send me the divorce papers.

It hurts everywhere. I'm angry, but I don't know who's to blame.

Zach?

Me?

Suzie?

I settle on Suzie because she planted the seed in my head. I've felt like my being with Zach was, in some small way, her dying wish. In theory, we belong together. But we messed up. We had all the right ingredients but mixed in wrong order—solving a mathematical expression without using the order of operations.

Wrong time.

Wrong place.

Wrong order of events.

Wrong … lifetime.

Just after everyone cheers and finds literally anyone to kiss when the clock strikes midnight, I get an unexpected call. Shouldering my way through the crowd of people in Leah's favorite Manhattan bar, I look for a tiny corner where I can hear and see the screen of my phone better. I desperately want it to be Zach, but it's not.

I squint at my screen, not recognizing the number. "Hello?"

"Is this Emersyn?" a man's voice asks.

"It is."

"I ... um ... my name is Brad. I am ... *was* ... a friend of your mom's."

Friend? My mom never had male friends. She had guys who used her, abused her, and hung her out to dry.

"Okay ..." I say slowly. "I don't know why you're calling, but I haven't seen or spoken to my mom in years."

"Yeah ... um ... I know. You see ..." He clears his throat. "I don't know how to say this but ..."

"Just say it. I'm a little busy at the moment."

"Your mom passed away yesterday."

Silence fills the line. Even the noise in the bar disappears, and I realize I'm only hearing the slow beat of my heart.

I don't move.

I haven't cried for my mom since the day I left home. And even then, I think the tears were more for me—the feeling of complete rejection. The feeling that she abandoned me long before I stole her car and never looked back.

All this time ... she never called me. Not once. She had my number and never called.

Maybe that's why now, amidst the news of her death, I have no tears. Not for her. Not for me.

"Since you are her next of kin, we need you to come take care of things."

I shake my head and open my mouth to speak, but I can't find the right words. There's nothing to take care of. I'm only her daughter in name, and I have half of her genes. That's it.

"I don't know how you got my number, but I'm not the person you're looking for. Maybe you should contact her boyfriend. I'm sure she had one. Unless ... that's you?"

"No, ma'am. I was in her AA group. I've been sober for two years now, and she just celebrated one year. And to my knowledge, she lived alone. I got your number from her landlord. I was supposed to pick her up and drive her to the meeting. Her door was cracked open, and that's when I found her unresponsive in bed. She ..." He clears his throat again. "There was an empty bottle of fentanyl and several empty bottles of vodka. I ... I just had no idea. I'm so sorry. The last time I saw her she seemed to be doing really well. Ya know?"

I rub my forehead and close my eyes. "No. Sorry ... I don't actually know."

"Listen, I didn't know who else to call. I don't know what your relationship was with your mom. She talked about you with great pride. I just ... I'm really sorry."

I nod slowly before dropping the phone to my side and closing my eyes.

———

ATHENS, Georgia, isn't Los Angeles—that's where Leah is while I deal with next of kin stuff. Making arrangements for my mother's cremation isn't a day at the beach. I envy Leah right now.

The landlord lets me into my mom's apartment. It reeks of alcohol, cigarette smoke, and other things I don't want to think about. The lone, green sofa looks like something from the seventies. It's the only sofa she's ever had since before I can remember. Dirty dishes overflow in the sink, and flies fighting over the rotten food congregate on the mismatched bowls and plates.

"There's vomit in the bedroom, and cigarette burns on the countertops. I'm afraid I won't be able to refund her deposit to you," the landlord says.

I grunt a laugh but don't say anything before he leaves me alone in the two-bedroom hellhole. There's nothing to save here. He wants me to empty this place, but I'm not going to touch a damn thing. There's a reason I walked away from her. Hell, I sped away—in her car.

There are a few pictures in dusty frames with cracked glass. I take out the one of us and slip it into my purse without giving it much thought. I'll walk down memory lane later because right now I'm ready to lose my breakfast from the stench. Making a quick stroll through each room, peeking in a few drawers, and trying hard to ignore the empty vodka bottles still on the floor next to her bed, I search for anything else worth taking. There's nothing.

No heirlooms.

Nothing that belonged to me.

No hidden cash or jewelry.

Not a shred of sentimentality in this apartment.

I know that Brad guy said she had been sober for a year. He said she had talked about me with some sort of pride. I don't believe it. I think he walked into a bad situation and simply told me whatever he thought might lure me back here to deal with the dead body.

The fact that the words dead body come to mind before *Mom*, or anything more personal or endearing, just shows how much she destroyed us long before she died.

With nothing more than a photo in my purse and a predictably painted canvas in my mind of how her miserable life ended, I bypass the landlord's apartment, jump into my rental car, and put as much distance between me and the entire city of Athens as possible.

Am I a terrible daughter? A terrible person?

I paid to have her cremated, but I didn't stay to collect the remains.

I visited her apartment, but I took nothing more than a photo.

It's been three days since I received the call about her death, but I've not shed a single tear.

Yes. I'm definitely a terrible person.

When I reach Atlanta, I have no idea what to do

next. My ticket was one-way because I didn't know how long it would take to get my mom's things in order—clearly not that long since her life was void of order before she died.

After driving around for another hour, I find a hotel and get a room for the night. I'm so numb at the moment. Collapsing onto the bed, I stare at the ceiling, eventually counting the drips from the faucet in the bathroom.

One.

Two.

Three.

Is this how my mom felt? Alone? Counting drips from a leaky faucet? Wondering how she got to that point in her life and where she was going?

Did she ever miss my dad or any of the truly hideous men that rotated in and out of her life for years?

Did she miss me?

Will I miss her?

I stop counting drips at two hundred and fifty, grab my phone, and call Leah. She doesn't answer. So I text her.

Em: Call me when you get a chance.

She's on Los Angeles time, so I know she's not asleep. And I have no one else. Leah. That's where my list ends. It's crazy to think about the number of people I've met while traveling the world, yet only one makes the list of people I would call after my mom dies.

I sit up and run my hands through my hair before retrieving the photo from my purse. I don't know who took the photo, but it portrays a false picture of a happy mother and daughter on the beach, lower bodies buried in the sand, and squiggly lines making the sand mounded over us look like mermaid tails. I shove the photo back into my purse and sigh. "Fuck it."

I have a husband here in Atlanta. A husband who has made no effort to contact me recently.

No divorce papers.

No surprise visits.

Nothing.

With my emotions all over the place, I grab my bag and ride this tiny wave of courage all the way to his house. I spend the next ten minutes convincing myself that this is not a good idea, but it's a necessary one.

With three knocks on his front door, I wring my hands together in front of me and hold my breath. After I'm confident he's not home, I pivot and head back down the driveway—equally relieved and disappointed.

"Hello?"

I turn back toward the voice.

A woman holds her hand up to her forehead, squinting against the setting sun. "Are you looking for Zach?"

I was. Now, I'm not so sure.

"He'll be home in a few hours, if you want to check back."

I'm rarely speechless, in fact, nervous rambling is my specialty. I have no idea what to say to this woman. My thoughts won't give me a good response; they're too busy imagining who she might be. Why she's at Zach's house when he's not here ... and an onslaught of other destructive emotions and images.

He's not mine.

He never was mine.

I know this. And I hate that I have to repeat this in my head so many times. I hate that it doesn't sink in and *feel* like the truth.

"Is everything okay?" she asks. And why wouldn't she?

I don't move.

I don't speak.

I must look crazy.

"Everything is fine." I manage three words—one big lie. In the next breath, my legs take me back to my rental car in quick strides.

At the hotel, I order room service and raid the minibar. My mom died. I should be allowed a night of overeating and drinking myself into a comfortable state of numbness. Surely there's at least a day-pass from reality when you lose a parent.

Once I've consumed three tiny bottles of whisky— which I hate—and stuffed myself with greasy fries and a cheeseburger that tastes *amazing* because it's been so long since I've eaten this much salt and grease, I flip on

371

the TV and melt into the pillows piled against the headboard. I'll return to the minibar in a bit.

Midway through my mindless cable channel surfing, my phone rings. Probably Leah finally calling me back.

"Shit." I frown at the screen. It's not Leah. "Ciao," I answer with a manufactured enthusiasm only three tiny bottles of whisky could offer.

"Hi. Where are you?" Zach asks.

Mystery woman must have been a little too descriptive in telling him about the barely coherent woman who stopped by earlier this evening.

"Um ..." I close my eyes, feeling oddly at peace with the day's events. I must say, whisky tastes like horse piss (not speaking from experience), but it makes life seem a little less shitty. Tonight, I give it five stars and a glowing recommendation. "In a hotel room with a leaky faucet but a well-stocked minibar. Where are you?"

"What brings you to Atlanta?"

Why does he get to ask all the questions?

"Oh, you know ... the ush ... vacation ... and my dead mother ..."

"Emersyn ..." he says with *so* much pity in his voice.

Doesn't he know by now that I despise pity? For Christ's sake, I lived out of my car because I refused to let anyone take pity on me. I would rather choke to death on my pride than feel weak.

"Anyway ... I'll be heading to LA in a day or two. I gather that you're calling me because your girlfriend..."

that word tastes worse than the whisky in my mouth "...must have mentioned I stopped by. I was just in the area. No big deal."

"Where are you?"

I laugh. "I told you, in a hotel room with a—"

"Emersyn, that's not what I mean. What hotel? What is your room number?"

"Can't say. You know ... stranger danger and all that. And I haven't seen or heard from you in a while, so you're pretty much a stranger to me by this point."

"Jesus, Emersyn ... just tell me where you are."

Emotion strangles me. Just the sound of his voice manages to rip open the parts of my heart that I've been trying to heal for months. I'm not sure there are enough bottles of alcohol in the minibar to numb this kind of pain.

"You know ..." I wipe my tears. "You need to send me those papers. Did you get my text? I'm ... I'm good. I don't need your insurance anymore. I'll manage on my own. If you have them, I could sign them before I go home. And then you would be free."

"Emersyn ..."

"Just ... think about it. Okay?" I end the call before he can respond.

I stare at the TV for another hour, not really registering what I'm watching. Baseball, I think. The whisky starts to wear off, and I contemplate moving on to vodka. Instead, I text Zach the hotel address and my room number.

Zach

SINCE THE WEDDING INCIDENT, I've let Emersyn have time to herself and space for clarity. I needed it too.

I did it because I love her.

Does that make me gallant, selfless, stubborn, or just plain stupid? The jury is still out on that.

I've thought about calling her a million times.

A text.

A message on her phone at two in the morning.

Even snail mail—anything to appease my need to feel close to her again.

The naked photos were a wake-up call. Her replying with a not-so-subtle reminder that my wife died only solidified what I already knew—I'm the asshole who let things get out of hand. She evokes a storm of emotions inside of me.

Love.

Lust.

Fear.

Hope.

I've tried to let her go, but I haven't. I've held on with a piece of paper that says she's my wife and I am her husband. But it's just that ... a piece of paper.

I am not her husband. She is not my wife.

Every ounce of hope that I have given her, every ounce of hope that I have allowed myself to feel, is nothing more than a subconscious attempt at derailing her future.

She's too young to lose focus of her dreams, and I'm too old to be selfish by asking her to choose me.

But dear god ... oh, how I've wanted to be selfish.

Emersyn opens the hotel room door. Her wrinkled shirt, old jeans, and makeup-less face complement the defeated slump of her shoulders.

"Hey," I say.

It takes me a minute to move, speak, or even breathe, for that matter. "Em ..." I step inside and the door clicks shut behind me. Taking two more steps toward her, my arms reach for her waist. "I'm so sorry to hear about your mom."

Emersyn jumps back, bumping into the TV console like my touch might burn her. Holding up her hands, she shakes her head. "Nope. I'm good. I don't need a shoulder to cry on or a hug or whatever you think I need. Just the papers. Did you bring the papers?" She escapes to the other side of the room, putting as much distance between us as possible.

"I haven't had time. Are you in a rush?" I slip my hands into my back pockets. It's a lie. I've had plenty of time.

"It just ..." She shakes her head. "It needs to end. Whatever good deed you promised to Suzie or God or whomever ... you've more than fulfilled it. And it has to be a little awkward to date other people when you're technically married."

"I'm not dating other people," I say with little

emotion. It's taking all I have not to let her see me bleed.

"Well ..." She shakes her head and waves a hand. "Dating. Hooking up. Whatever. I'm just saying ... your charity saved me. It got me to where I am today. I will forever feel indebted to you. But ... your generosity is no longer needed."

"Charity. Generosity." I nod slowly. "I see," I whisper, rubbing my lips together. "And where you're at today is in a hotel room eating overpriced room service by yourself and raiding the minibar. If this is where my charity and generosity got you, then I'm not overly proud of myself."

"Zach, stop."

"And for the record, the woman you saw at my house is a friend, a fellow pilot. She ended up in Atlanta with a longer layover than originally planned, so I offered to let her stay with me instead of at a hotel."

She gives me a tight smile. "As you would because you're generous to a fault. Maybe she needs good insurance too. And I'm hoarding your wife status at the moment, so all the more reason to have me sign the papers."

"Em ..." I drop my head and sigh. "I don't know what you want from me." *I don't know how to love you ... fairly.*

"I just told you."

I lift my head again. "You want a divorce?"

"I want you to be free," she says.

BEFORE US

"Who says I'm not?"

"Not *one* call. Not *one* text. If not the woman at your house, is there someone else?"

"No." I shake my head.

"Have you dated?"

"No."

Emersyn grits her teeth for a second before taking a hard swallow. "Are you waiting around for me?"

"No." My voice shakes, a little on edge. I'm waiting on myself. I'm waiting for ... fuck, I don't know.

Time.

I'm waiting for time. Isn't that the most simplistic answer to the question?

In time, she'll find someone else, someone who's on the same path.

In time, I'll feel like she truly doesn't need me, instead of her telling me that when I know it's not yet true.

"Then what are you doing?" She raises her voice and immediately flinches with regret.

"I work. I spend time with family and friends. I take care of my house and yard. I get haircuts. Go to the dentist. Shop for groceries. Watch TV. I'm living. That's what I'm doing."

And missing her. God ... I've missed her every single day. It's no longer tomato paste and peanut butter that distracts me from thinking about Suzanne. It's Emersyn. *My wife.*

"Well..." she shrugs "...there you go. You've just made my point."

377

"Which is?"

"That you have a life. A job. Family and friends. And if on rare occasions you have time alone to miss your wife, I'm not the wife you're missing."

I wince. I can't help it. That fucking hurt. "Why would you say that?"

"Uh ..." She crosses her arms over her chest. "Maybe because you haven't made contact with me in months!"

Another wince. "If you needed me, you could have called me. I would have come to you, talked on the phone, whatever you wanted."

"So ... you make time for your family and friends. Does that mean they call you when they're in need?"

"Not necessarily."

Emersyn gives me a careful nod. "You see them because you want to see them?"

Inching my head side to side, I narrow my eyes. "It's different."

"Of course it's different. You obviously care about them. You *want* to talk to them. You want to know how they're doing."

"I care about you."

"Obviously," she scoffs.

"Em ... I'm giving you space and time. I've told you this. Your dreams matter the most to me. It's *because* I care—" I pinch the bridge of my nose. "It's because I *love* you that I'm not demanding your time. Let's just be really clear about this, okay?"

She draws in a shaky breath, tears in her eyes, jaw set.

I continue. "I. Love. You. I knew it in Malaysia; I just had no clue what to do with this love. I miss all the moments we've shared together and all the moments we may never share. But loving you means not letting you get sidetracked with *us* when you're so young with such a bright future ahead of you. And when you left, I knew that my presence in your life and our unconventional relationship was a distraction. I refuse to be a hurdle or an excuse for you to give up pursuing your passion. To what? Be a wife? Is that your life's goal? I may have given you encouragement and the means to follow your dreams, but I'm no longer that person in your life. I'm nothing more than your weakest link, a rusty old anchor that will keep you from experiencing passion ... the passion you have within yourself. Don't let anyone keep you from that."

Emersyn closes her eyes and bites her lips together.

I hold my hands out to my sides. "I'm here. Living. I've pursued my dreams. Nobody stood in my way. Nobody kept me from staying focused. I didn't force anything in my life. When I met Suzanne, I took an instant interest in her. Then I found out she was with Tara. So I kept doing my thing. I worked. I dated other women. I *lived*. And I had no clue that fate would bring us together, but it did. Life is *all* about timing."

She slowly blinks open her eyes. "It's not our time," she whispers.

"It's not our time," I echo.

"It was the photos."

I shake my head, eyes narrowed. "It wasn't the fucking photos. I couldn't care less about the photos." That's not entirely true, but it's not my point.

"Was it what I said at the wedding? Does your family hate me?"

"They don't hate you. They understand why I married you."

Emersyn nods several times. "Not one call ..." she says, getting choked up again.

I feel her. I feel all the things she's afraid to say because I'm afraid to say them too. It sucks to have irrational and impulsive emotions when it comes to love.

"What would I have said?" I whisper.

She sniffles and blots the corners of her eyes. "That you miss me."

I grunt. "Seems a little cruel to say that. Sounds like a guilt trip when you're working so hard to pursue your dreams. If you called to tell me that you miss me, I'd be on the next flight to you. I'd wait by your door for you to come home. And I'd never want to leave you again. How dysfunctional is that? How would I do my own job? Long-distance relationships work because of all the things that *aren't* said."

"Bullshit!" She balls her fists. "It's been *months*. That's not a long-distance relationship; it's abandonment. Fine ... don't call me to say you miss me. Call me to say you love me. Call me to wish me a merry Christmas or a happy fucking new year. Call me and tell me about your day. Or what your plans are for the weekend. Send me pictures of the garden or pictures of your smiling face. You follow me on Instagram. I know you're seeing pictures of me. You know what's happening in my life. But you *never* post anything. You never share your life."

If I surrender, if I let myself fall, I will crush her.

Her dreams.

Her future.

Her independence.

"Then why didn't *you* call me? Why didn't *you* ask me about my day? Why didn't *you* request I send you pictures? You're all pissed off that I didn't call you, but you didn't call me!" Instant regret. Every. Single. Word.

She draws in a shaky breath that makes her whole body shiver. "How was your day?" she asks in a soft voice.

"Shitty. The woman I love won't let me touch her. And it's really fucking killing me." I take a step toward her.

And another.

Then another.

"I should have called," I whisper because pretending like I'm the strong one no longer makes sense. *We* have survived too much.

When her gaze meets mine again, the floodgates open into uncontrolled sobs. "My m-mom d-died ..."

I obliterate the last few inches between us, wrapping her in my arms. If I could wring every bit of pain and grief from her and absorb it into my own heart, I would do it. Resting my lips on the top of her head while stroking her hair, I whisper, "I know, Em. And I'm so very sorry."

Easing onto the bed, I bring her whole body onto my lap, cradling her in my arms. There are no right words. They all feel inadequate.

Does she know this? Does she feel my love for her?

The love she didn't get from her parents.

The love she never had from siblings.

The love that fell short in all of her relationships before me.

This love, whatever it may be, is bittersweet. It's everything, yet never enough.

Wrong fucking time.

When her well of tears runs dry, and her tired eyes refuse to open, her body refuses to move from this spot in my arms. We lie back, and sleep claims us.

"Em." I press my lips to her forehead before the sun rises.

I've missed this feeling so much. Her touch.

"I have to go. I have work today," I say, breaking our bubble.

"Why is one of us always leaving?" she whispers without moving an inch. "Why can't we hide in a cocoon forever, forgetting goals, redefining dreams, living in the moment and only for each other? Why is that so hard? So complicated?" She nuzzles her nose into my shirt and inhales. Then she works her face into the crook of my neck and does it again.

It keeps awakening that hope for a few breaths before leaving my heart stranded again. And it never gets easier.

Seeing her.

Leaving her.

Missing her.

Loving her.

"I hate that I have to leave." I kiss her forehead again.

Emersyn's fingers claim my shirt as her lips brush the skin along my neck. They don't taste. They don't playfully nip. They just *feel*.

I'm speechless. Everything has been said over and over again.

I love you, *but* ...

I want you, *but* ...

Over and over again, we grapple with a reality we just don't want to accept.

My hands thread through her hair, tipping her head back. She's captive in my hold, in my eyes. My lips tease hers, and those unavoidable feelings ignite. The kiss grows more intense.

I want to live in the moment, but my heart knows it will suffer a long hangover and destroy her in its path.

"Zach ..." She turns her head, proving to be the stronger one this morning.

I bury my face in the bed just above her shoulder. "I know."

She's here. She's *everywhere.*

Emersyn. Not Suzanne.

The beat of her heart, chest-to-chest with mine.

Her parted legs nestling my pelvis as I try to hold back the urge to move against her.

Those demanding hands in my hair.

The lingering warmth of her lips.

The floral scent along her skin.

"I like this bubble." She sighs, ghosting her fingers along my back. "I like it too much. It's blinding and all-consuming. But it *always* pops, and I'm left feeling so deflated and empty inside it's debilitating."

I slowly climb off the bed.

Pop!

The bubble breaks with one look. Our time has once again expired. We're going our separate ways again with an uncertain future.

"Do you need help booking a flight home?" I ask.

Emersyn sits up slowly and straightens her shirt. "No. I've got it."

"Do you need a ride anywhere?"

"I have a rental car."

I scratch my jaw. "Do you need *anything*?"

Pressing her lips together, she averts her gaze for a few seconds. "Time," she whispers.

After a few slow blinks, I nod.

Turning away from her, I slide open the curtains several more inches, letting in the first rays of the sunrise. "Ask me to stay. Skip my flights. Crawl into bed with you and forget about the world."

It's so impulsive. And stupid. But Emersyn makes me feel young and alive again. She dominates my thoughts from half a world away.

And I know ... I *know* the answer to my ridiculous request, but I say it anyway. I say it because when I walk out that door, I don't want her to ever question my heart.

When she doesn't respond, I turn back toward her. What do I really expect her to say? I feel like an old man with tired eyes and sad lips. A little grayer in my whiskers. A little less strength in my posture. She can do better.

"Ask *me* to stay," she whispers. "Quit my job. Crawl into bed with you and forget about the world."

It's not funny. It's sad ... so heartbreaking, but my lips curl into a tiny grin. She's testing the waters. Hell, she might be chasing more than one dream. I don't know. What I do know? I'm not a destination. Not for her. I'm the obstacle. The distraction. A fucking pair of training wheels when she needs to ride on her own. She's ready, even if I'm not.

After a minute or so of silence, each of us weighing our next words, idly watching our future together slip further and further away, I cup one side of her face.

As she leans into my touch, I give her one last smile. My very best one. "Have a safe trip home, my love."

Chapter Thirty-Seven

Emersyn

HOME.

It's official. He's acknowledging that Atlanta is not my home, that *he* is not my home.

I close my eyes and fight the ache in my chest, the tightness in my throat. His touch fades. His entire presence fades. And I'm left with the tiny echo of the door clicking shut.

When I feel too much time has passed for him to turn around and come back to me, I text him.

> Em: Send me the papers.

Everything he said to me repeats in my head, a haunting echo eating away at my emotions.

If I needed him?

How was I supposed to respond to that? If I need

him, does that make me weak? I've survived without him. Does that mean I don't need him?

Need …

The list of things I need is pretty short. Food. Water. Oxygen. And Zach?

At the airport, I take a photo of my grande coffee along with my feet propped up on my carry-on bag. **California bound. #deathisoverrated**

As I scroll through my Instagram feed, I come to an abrupt stop, slowly inching back up said feed. I smile, stopping on Zach's first official post. It's miles of sky above the clouds. **The second most beautiful sight I've seen today. #PilotLife**

The joy I feel at this moment trumps how I felt in his arms. Everything we're not, everything we can't have, seems to suffocate who we *are* and what we *do* have when we're together.

I double tap his picture, giving it a heart, and contemplate commenting on it, but I don't. We've said enough for now. Maybe our destiny isn't anything more than friends.

First.

Last.

And always.

When I land in LA, I text Zach even though this is the first time he didn't ask me to do it.

> Em: Home.

It's not really home. I don't actually have a home

right now. It's nothing new.

Within seconds, he heart emojis my text. He's making an effort at something. I'm not sure what yet. And it's most unexpected since my parting text to him was: Send me the papers.

The next morning, Leah drags my emotionally drained ass to breakfast at her favorite juice bar. She thinks a shot of wheatgrass will cure me of *all the things*. The smile on my face makes up for the lack of bounce in my step because ... I woke up to another Instagram post from Zach. It's a photo of him from behind, walking through an airport with his bag slung over his shoulder. It's quite candid and sexy. I'm not sure if he asked someone to take it (which oddly thrills me if he did) or if it happened to him unknowingly until said person showed it to him. **Good morning, Honolulu. #PilotLife**

The fucker's in Hawaii. I smirk at the vulgar, jealous thoughts running through my head. What I wouldn't give to be on a beach in Hawaii with Zach. After a quick double tap on his photo, I snap a pic of my new white sneakers that Leah gave me, an overflow of free products that companies send her. The shoes retail for just over three hundred dollars. **Work perks. #ShoeWhore**

———

I'M NOT sure what prompted Zach to start posting on Instagram (I hope it was me), but he continues to do it.

One post a day over the next couple of months. Every post is a glimpse into his life as a pilot, and he uses one hashtag: PilotLife. Until ... he posts a picture of a woman's pregnant belly with a henna tattoo on it. For a second, my heart falters, skipping more than one beat.

Can't wait to meet my niece. #ProudUncle

I break my no-comment rule after liking the post. It makes me a little emotional. Is it bittersweet? Is he thinking of the baby he never got the chance to have with Suzie?

Congrats to Danni and Aaron ... and Uncle Zach. <3

An hour later, Zach likes my comment. No reply, just a one-heart acknowledgment. That's enough.

I waste no time sending five new outfits to Zach's house for him to give to Aaron and Danni, along with a card for them (again apologizing profusely for disrupting their wedding with my outburst), and a congratulatory card for his parents as well. On the note for Zach, I write:

Please give these to your family. I'm so happy for all of you. Much love, Em.
P.S. I hope you're happy.

For whatever reason that I don't care to acknowledge, I find myself posting more often. I want Zach to see that I'm fine, whether I really am or not. And maybe ... that's the same reason he's posting. I'm fine. He's fine. Life didn't end when we did.

So many posts:

Leah hunched down on the beach, taking a picture of a newly constructed sandcastle in the sunset with a young child blurred in the distance. **#MalibuSunset #Bloggerlife #photography**

Santa Monica Pier. **#Westcoast #Bloggerlife #Photography**

Me having coffee early in the morning while working on photo edits. **#Bloggerlife #photography #LoveMyJob**

I share my life with Zach in a public way, and he does the same with me. No phone calls. No texts. I think we're moving on without saying the words.

Except ... he's never sent me divorce papers.

I'm making enough money to get my own insurance as long as I don't end up with some huge hospital bill.

In April, I post a photo of a wedding we shot in Utah.

Have you found your happily ever after? **#Forever #Weddingphoto #IDo #Lovers**

Zach has given a heart to everything I've posted, and I've done the same to his posts. Until today. He posts eerie-looking clouds from the cockpit. I post about a wedding dress. And he doesn't acknowledge my post at all?

"Why the sad face, babe?" Leah asks, plopping down on the bed beside me.

"Nothing. I'm just reading into ... nothing."

She plucks my phone from my hands. "It's a great picture. If I got married tomorrow, I'd legit pick out a dress just like hers."

"It's beautiful." I nod several times and roll my lips between my teeth.

Leah hands my phone back to me and narrows her eyes. "What?"

"Nothing. I mean ..." I groan and flop back onto my pillow. "He didn't like it."

"Who didn't like what?"

"Zach. He didn't like the photo. He likes all of my posts ... without fail."

She chuckles. "Maybe he hasn't been on to see it."

"Yes, he has. It shows that he was on just over an hour ago. I posted it three hours ago. And he's following less than a hundred people. There's no way my photo didn't show up in his feed."

"So ... why do you think he didn't like it?"

"Because it's a wedding. And we're still married because he hasn't sent me divorce papers. And ... I don't know. I'm going crazy. Why ... why do I care if he likes my photos. I'm so stupid." I close my eyes and blow out a long breath.

"You know ... there's nothing saying that you can't send him divorce papers."

It's nice of Leah to state the obvious. I know this. Just like I knew I could have texted or called him last winter when I was going crazy.

I know. I really do know.

It's possible I'm not moving forward as much as I thought. It's possible our keeping in touch via Instagram isn't the best mode of communication. The only thing that's worse than the inability to contextualize messages is the complete ambiguity of emojis and the timing of liking one's social media posts.

"I keep thinking..." I roll toward Leah, propping my head onto my bent arm "...that I'll figure my shit out if I just take enough pictures, if I can just make sense of the world, piece it together like a puzzle."

She scoots down and mirrors my pose while exhaling and offering a warm smile. "Mmm ... I like that sentiment. I've never thought about it like that. You're wise for a young, orphaned adult."

I roll my eyes. "Funny. My mom had very little to do with molding me into the woman I've become, but the one thing she said in defense of her own actions— during a rare moment of sobriety and clarity—has become quite relevant in my own life. She said, 'The most complicated relationship you will ever have is the one with yourself. We are our own greatest mystery, our own biggest challenge. Life isn't a quest to find ourselves; it's a quest to define ourselves.'"

Leah hums again, eating up every word I speak. And right now, I have so many words because my mind won't stop racing with a million thoughts. In a world filled with all kinds of definitions and labels—child, friend, daughter, woman, photographer, lover—how do I put them in order of importance? Or does it depend on the day or time in my life?

Chapter Thirty-Eight

Zach

"Happy birthday, bro." Aaron hugs me right before we're seated at my favorite steak house. Danielle has been put on bed rest, and our parents are in Seattle visiting friends.

"Thanks. How's Danni?"

"Bored." He rolls his eyes. "But good." His smile is gold. I've never seen him so happy. "How'd you get your birthday off?"

I shrug as we take a seat and open our menus. "Just luck, I guess. I have an early flight tomorrow, though."

"Did you ever call Sadie?"

I nod. "I did."

"And ..." He glances up at me from his menu. "Did you go out with her?"

I nod slowly.

"And?"

"She's nice."

"Nice," Aaron repeats.

"No one will be Suzanne. You know that, right? I mean, surely your therapist has worked that shit out with you."

"I'm not seeing a therapist anymore."

Aaron eyes me.

"Don't give me that look." I roll my eyes. "I'm fine."

"Fine, huh? Okay, so are you seeing Sadie again?"

"I don't know. And it's not because I'm expecting her or anyone to be Suzanne. I'm just not sure what I'm looking for in a relationship at the moment."

"Would it have anything to do with the fact that you're married to a woman you never see? If Emersyn's working, making decent money, I don't understand why you're still married."

"I've been busy," I murmur, acting overly interested in the menu when I know exactly what I'm going to order because I always order the same thing here.

"Busy? It's a phone call to your attorney. That's it. Where is she anyway? When's the last time you talked to her?"

I set my menu on the table and take a sip of my water. "It's been a while. I follow her Instagram posts. This morning she departed for London. Leah's mom is doing better, so they've decided to spend the summer in Europe. I pieced that much together from both Leah's and Emersyn's posts. She texted me happy birthday." I look around the restaurant, feeling Aaron's gaze on me, inspecting me, judging me.

"Do you have feelings for her like she clearly has or had feelings for you at my wedding?"

"Feelings," I scoff like it's a crazy question. "What does that even mean? We're friends. We're good. We've been through a lot. Of course, I care about her."

"Yeah, I get that. Obviously. You married her to give her insurance. But have you had feelings for her that go beyond friendship? Mom thinks she's in love with you. Danni does too. They agree that Emersyn wouldn't have acted so crazy had it not been love."

I shrug as if I don't know.

No. All I have to tell Aaron is no. I don't have feelings for her beyond friendship. Then I should call my attorney and make a clean break. No more questions asked. As these thoughts play in my mind, it leaves a pregnant pause in the conversation, which answers Aaron's question before I utter a single word.

"Jesus ..." He shakes his head. "You *do* have feelings for her."

"It's complicated ... or it was complicated. I don't think it's all that complicated anymore."

"Dude ... no." Aaron slaps his menu down on top of mine. "There's nothing complicated about my question. Either she thinks she's your fake wife getting free health insurance, or she knows your feelings for her aren't fake like the marriage."

Rubbing my fingers over my lips, I nod several times. "She knows she is ... or was ... more than a fake wife."

"When? How?"

I glance away from him and mumble, "I had sex with her in Malaysia." He only needs a small percentage of the truth to get the gist.

Truth ... I'm not sure I know the truth at this point.

"What?" He leans forward, turning his head to bring his ear closer to me. "You ransacked her metaplasia?"

"No." I can't help but grin as I shake my head and clear my throat. "I had *sex* with her in Malaysia."

Aaron presses his lips together to hide his smirk. "You had sex with the maid?"

I wince and trace my finger along the beer glass, smearing the condensation. "Technically, I had sex with my wife."

"And how do you think Suzanne would feel about it?"

Grunting, I shake my head. "Well, I think if she were here to think anything about it, there would be nothing to think about because I'd still be married to her. I wouldn't be married to Emersyn or even thinking about her in any sort of romantic way. So really, that's a stupid question, and you know it."

"Do you love her?"

I let his question hang in the air between us, echoing in my head, and sinking into that place deep in my chest—the place that knows the answer is a big, fat yes.

"I never planned on falling in love with Emersyn. When I fell in love with Suzanne, it felt fated, intentional. Tara died. Suzanne grieved. Our friendship grew. And one day it felt right to move beyond friends. With Emersyn, it happened before I even realized what was happening. Suzanne's dying wish was for me to make a difference in the life of someone else. I now think that request had less to do with someone else and more to do with me. I think she knew it would force me to dig my heart out of my dead chest and allow it to beat again."

"Fuck ..." Aaron grins and shakes his head. "You love her. That's ..."

"The end," I say, tossing him a sad smile. "It's the end. I'm going to end the marriage. It's served its purpose. I'm going to let her find her life. Nobody stopped me from finding mine. And her feelings for me stem from not having a father in her life, never having a truly kind man in her life. She fell in love with the idea of me. I think she fell in love with Suzanne's husband. And one day, she'll wake up and realize she fell for the first guy who treated her well, not necessarily the *right* guy."

After a few slow, thoughtful nods, Aaron takes a sip of his water and then blows out a slow breath. "What if you're wrong? What if it's not the mere idea of you? What if it's actually you?"

"It's not. She asked for the divorce months ago."

As the waitress approaches us, Aaron gives me a slight smile and shrugs. "Then you divorce her. End of story."

"End of story ..." I echo.

"Bro ..." Aaron runs his hands through his hair and

laughs. "What are you doing? Seriously. If you love her, go get her."

"I ..." I shake my head. "I don't want to go get her. That's just it. I'm here. I have a job. I have my life. She's nurturing her passion and chasing her dreams. And I love that about her. I won't take it away. I won't even ask her to choose me. It's not even a choice. This is her *life*. Suzanne spent an entire summer living vicariously through Emersyn. She ... *we* ... became invested in Emersyn's life. So even if I let my brain imagine a world where Suzanne wanted me with Emersyn, it's no longer relevant. I'm not living my life for Suzanne. I'm living it for me, and my conscience won't let me clip Emersyn's wings. That's not love."

The anguish on Aaron's face is a reflection of my own. He takes a long pause to stare out the window before returning his attention to me. Leaning forward, he holds out his hands. "Come here."

I hesitate for a few seconds before leaning toward him.

Aaron's big mitts frame my face. "I'm so proud of you, Bro. You cracked open that mummified chest of yours and let someone into it. So maybe she's not the right woman, or maybe it's just crap timing, but you did it. And I'm just ... so fucking proud of you."

Chapter Thirty-Nine

Emersyn

"MAIL." Leah tosses a large envelope in my direction as she walks into the flat we've rented for the summer. "I'm going to talk my mom into moving to London." She opens a bottle of wine as I sit cross-legged on the sofa and open the envelope. "I want to call this my home. You should too."

Eyeing her with suspicion, I pull out the contents of the envelope as Harry Pawter hops off my lap. "You've said that about so many places we've visited."

"Yes..." she pours a glass of wine "...but I've never suggested relocating my mom. I've never suggested you move with me. This is my fourth time here, and I love it just as much as the first time. Really, I love it more every time I visit. Tell me you don't love it here too."

I shrug a shoulder. "You know I do." My eyes trace the words on the papers in my hands.

"Then we do it. Nothing is holding us back. Right?"

My heart breaks a little. Correction: it breaks a lot.

"Em, what is it?" Leah shuffles her bare feet in my direction, peering over my shoulder at the divorce papers from Zach with little sticky tabbed arrows where I need to sign.

"Oh ... that's ..." She takes a seat at the opposite end of the sofa, drawing her long legs underneath her. "Good. Right? You asked him to send you the divorce papers months ago."

I can't speak, so I just nod ever so slightly.

"It's a sign. At the very moment that I suggest we move here, you open an envelope with divorce papers —that last thing tying you to America."

"Yeah," I manage the hint of a whisper.

"So why do you look so miserable?"

"I ... I just ... I don't know. He didn't call or text me, giving me a heads-up that he had finally done it. And he's been his normal self, posting on Instagram, commenting and liking my posts. He posts photos of Aaron and Danielle and his new niece, Nila. Just ... the usual."

"Just because you're getting a divorce doesn't mean you still can't be friends. It means you've come a long way. You're making a good living doing exactly what you love, and he's taking back the piece of himself that he loaned you because you no longer need it." She sets her wine glass on the coffee table and scoots closer to me, resting her hands on my knees. "We love. We let go. We move on. And ... eventually, we love again."

With the closest thing to an actual smile that I can muster, I nod once.

"Maybe he met someone."

Squeezing my knees, she forces me to look at her instead of the papers in my hands. "That's a good thing. It means he's stopped grieving Suzie. And I think you helped him do that. I bet he's so grateful for that, and Suzie would be too."

Clenching my jaw, I hold my breath and tell myself not to blink, not to move one inch because I'm one straw away from collapsing.

"But..." Leah frowns "...it wouldn't be wrong for you to have a good cry about it right now."

I nod at least a dozen times, shaking the tears from my eyes just as my whole face contorts into an ugly cry.

"Oh, bae ..." Leah leans into me as my arms wrap around her neck. I have a good, *long* cry because I married the man of my dreams without a bended-knee proposal, without a diamond ring, without all the excited butterflies.

No dress.

No family.

No friends.

We barely kissed.

And then he went to the dentist.

Still ... I loved (love) Zachary Hays, and I can't imagine any man even coming close to him.

———

ZACH TOOK his time sending me the papers, so I take my time signing them. Two weeks after they arrive, he sends me a text.

> Zach: Did you get the papers?

> Em: I did. Thanks.

That's been it.

I let them reside in my nightstand drawer for the rest of the summer while Leah and I photograph five weddings, a slew of family pictures, boudoir photos, and sport all the free stuff we're sent for being influencers.

It doesn't take long for Leah to talk me into moving to London with her and her mom. At the end of the summer, we return home to pack *all* of our stuff. I have nothing to pack, but I have some loose ends to tie up, so I fly to Atlanta while Leah goes to New York to get the last of her belongings and her mom.

As the driver pulls into Zach's driveway, unannounced, I notice an unfamiliar car. It takes me a few breaths to deal with the possibilities that unfamiliar car might represent. I hope life has been kind to him, and that he's found a woman who makes him laugh. It might be the closure I need before opening the next chapter of my life.

The lights are on, and that brings a whole new rush of emotion that I thought I had under control. Taking several deep breaths, I get out of the Uber and force my heels to click their way to his front door, suitcase in tow. My shaky finger rings the doorbell. After a few seconds, an unfamiliar man answers the door.

"Hi." He smiles. "Can I help you?"

"Is Zach home?"

His forehead narrows. "No. Sorry. He no longer lives here."

"Oh ..." I clear my throat, trying to process this information. "Do you happen to know where he lives?"

I'm an idiot. Why do I insist on these surprise visits? I have his phone number. It's hard to explain, but I just want it to be a surprise.

"Sorry. I don't."

"Okay. Um ... thanks." I return a quick smile and order another ride as I make my way back down the driveway.

So much for the element of surprise. I'm the one who is surprised. Why did he sell the house? Too many memories. Another woman?

On the way to the nearest hotel, I make the call. It rings four times, and I consider hanging up instead of leaving a message, but then he answers. "Hi."

I start to speak, but his voice still does things to me. "Hi." My voice wobbles.

"How are you?" he asks with way more confidence than I can muster at the moment.

"I'm uh ... good. Actually, I'm in Atlanta. You moved."

"I did. What brings you to Atlanta?"

Jesus ... he resurrects all the butterflies in my stomach. "Um ..." I can't believe he's asking me this. He has to know why I'm here. "Tying up some loose ends."

"I see. Well, I happen to be in Atlanta as well."

"Good timing," I say before a long pause of silence hovers between us. "I've loved your Instagram photos. Nila is precious. Aaron and Danni look so happy. You look happy too."

"Ha. Yeah, so many pictures. Megan. She's the reason for the posting. We've flown together quite a bit. She's all about Instagram."

Okay ... I made the assumption I was the reason. Keeping us connected. "Flight attendant?"

"Pilot," he says.

I have *no* right to be jealous. All the usual suspects line up in my mind's reoccurring self-lecture on reasons I'm letting go of Zach. However, my mind seems to do a great job at multitasking. I can give myself the lecture *and* be irrationally jealous of this Megan chick taking pictures of my husband's ass. Soon to be ex-husband.

"Is she married?"

"Single. Why?"

"No reason."

"Oh! Megan has a cat named Professor Dumbledore. I told her about Harry Pawter. She thought that was awesome." Is it Professor Dumbledore giving him such joy, or is it single Megan?

"You told her about my cat?"

"Of course."

"So you told her about me?"

"I told her I have a friend with a cat named Harry Pawter."

Jesus ... what are we? Fine. I get it. He doesn't want to tell the world he's married, but have I not earned ...

I don't even know where that thought is going.

Girlfriend?

I'm not his girlfriend. We ended without saying the words. I can't ask him to wait for me while I find my place in this world. And he can't ask me to be with him as if he is that place.

He's not ... right? My *place* in life can't be a person. Can it?

My entire psyche twists into a big knot. We're over. I have the divorce papers in my carry-on to prove it.

He interrupts my thoughts. "Where are you? Have you had dinner?"

"I'm getting out of an Uber at a Marriott. I'll probably order room service."

"I'll pick you up and take you to dinner. Which Marriott?"

"Um ..." I smile at the Uber driver and mouth, "Thank you," as he sets my suitcase on the curb. "No. I haven't had dinner. Peachtree Center Ave."

"Meet you out front in twenty?"

"Sounds um ..."

Painful.

"Fine."

After I get a room and quickly fix my hair, I head down to the lobby. As soon as I make it through the front door, I see Zach leaning against the side of his car, a huge grin on his face.

Be cool.

I can't. There is not an ounce of coolness left inside of me as my feet race toward him, as I throw myself into his arms. How many couples end their marriage with this much enthusiasm?

"Miss me?" He chuckles.

I try so hard to keep from crying. And I succeed, but just barely. "No," I say as he sets me back onto my feet. I quickly wipe the corners of my eyes and laugh a little. "You really looked like you needed a hug."

Zach scratches his scruffy face. I love him clean-shaven or growing a beard. I love him all ways—I love him *always*.

"I think I did." He winks.

My face hurts from this grin he brings to it.

"Greasy burgers and fries?" Zach opens the passenger door for me. "Or has London ruined you for shitty American fare?"

I laugh. "Not even close."

As he pulls away from the curb, I find my gaze glued to him. Superglued. "Why did you sell the house?"

He keeps his eyes on the road and shrugs. "It was time."

"I thought you loved that house."

"I loved the life I had in that house, but I'm gone a lot now. It became nothing more than empty rooms that reminded me of what I'd lost. So I sold it in less than a day. And I bought a tiny home."

I snort. "I'm sure it's not *tiny*."

"No. It's an actual tiny home. It's on my parents' property. When I'm working, my mom uses it as a She Shed to get away from my dad."

"You bought a tiny home?"

He grins.

"Funny ... I thought ..." I shift my attention to the street.

"You thought what?"

"I thought you met someone. I thought maybe it was weird for them to be in the same house where Suzie lived with you."

"My dating life is pathetic on a good day. It's why I didn't find a serious relationship until I met Suzanne. She traveled with her job just as much as I did."

"Your Professor Dumbledore friend would have a similar schedule. What's her name?"

"Megan."

"Megan ..." I echo.

"What about you? Seeing anyone? A British bloke?" He pulls into the parking lot of the restaurant.

"Not really. Lots of great friends, but that's about it. I have a male friend taking care of Harry Pawter while I'm here. But he's gay, so I don't see that going anywhere." I open my door and follow Zach into the restaurant with my handbag and the signed divorce papers inside it.

Once we're seated and place our orders, Zach shifts

his drink and silverware to my side of the booth. For a second, I squint at him. "Scooch." He slides in next to me, resting his hand on my leg.

Leaning over, he whispers in my ear, "I heard all the cool couples sit on the same side of the booth."

Then he kisses my cheek as I laugh through tears.

So.

Many.

Tears.

My lips quiver as I say, "I signed the papers." I love him *so* much. And this hurts *so* much. It's just not our time. Not our lifetime.

Leaving his lips hovering between my cheek and my ear, he whispers, "I figured." His hand gently cups the back of my head, and he pulls me into his chest, letting me sob on his shoulder.

How is it possible to be so happy and so broken-hearted at the same time?

Zach doesn't ask why I'm crying; he just holds me. After my silent sobs subside, I lean back and wipe my messy face.

"It's been an honor..." Zach gives me a smile that conveys complete truth and *love* "...being your husband."

"Liar." I sniffle while my salty lips bend into a half smile.

He doesn't respond; he doesn't have to. I see it in his eyes. He means it. "So what's next?"

I finish wiping my eyes and sniffle, fighting to regain a little composure. "Funny you should ask

... I'm moving to London with Leah and her mom."

With wide eyes, Zach's jaw goes slack. I'm not sure I've ever seen real shock on his face. "You're serious?"

I find a real smile because I *am* excited about the idea of living in London. "Serious. Leah got us both jobs with a magazine. We'll still be able to travel and keep our blogs going. They're encouraging it because they're a travel magazine. So instead of jumping into another fake marriage just to live in London, I've officially been hired and sponsored by a UK company."

Zach frowns. "I hate the term fake marriage."

I roll my eyes to lighten the mood. "You know what I mean."

"I do," he says as the waiter sets our food in front of us. "But it wasn't entirely fake ... not for me anyway."

I place my napkin on my lap. "Well, it was ... something. Crazy? Impulsive? Overly generous? Life-saving? I'm not sure what to call it, but we can't call it a real marriage."

"No?"

Taking a bite of my cheeseburger, I shake my head while chewing it. "I won't call a marriage real..." I wipe my mouth "...unless there's a ring involved, words so romantic I want to cry, and a long engagement while my fiancé and I decide if our wedding will be in a gothic cathedral or on an island we rent and invite only a handful of friends and family. Either way, a beautiful white dress will be involved." I pop a fry into my mouth. "Nothing about my life has been normal or conventional. I'd never slept in a house with a Christmas tree until I met you and Suzie."

Zach's eyebrows slide together, offering pity I no longer need—not that I ever did. "Growing up, you never had a Christmas tree? Not once?"

I shake my head. "My mom decorated a doorway or two with red and silver tinsel garland, but don't feel bad for me. She made up for it on Easter Sunday ... that's when she'd hide eggs. But I had to be very careful not to break them because they were our breakfast for that week."

Zach's frown deepens. "No candy? Chocolate bunnies? Marshmallow Peeps?"

I shake my head.

"Just hardboiled eggs?"

"Oh, no. They weren't hardboiled. I'd wake up on Easter morning and eventually rouse my mom out of her drunken stupor. It usually involved an 'Oh shit, baby ... I'm sorry. Give me five minutes.' I'd wait in the bathroom for closer to thirty minutes while she ran to the store, bought a dozen eggs, then hid them—uncooked. So yeah ... when I get married *for real*, the wedding will be its own fairy tale, Christmases will involve a big, *real* tree, heart-shaped boxes of chocolates on Valentine's Day, and the most spectacular Easter egg hunt ever. You know ... the kind that's a treasure hunt leading to a monstrous basket of jellybeans, chocolate bunnies, and yes ... those Peeps. And don't even get me started on Halloween ..." I laugh.

Finally, Zach lets go of his pitiful expression and

offers a little chuckle. "I guess I've lived a charmed life. I feel a little guilty for that."

"Don't." I shake my head. "I've never buried the love of my life, and if I never have to ... at least not for another sixty-plus years ... then I will confidently be able to say that it was I, not you, who lived a charmed life. No amount of perfect holidays can erase the kind of pain you experienced with Suzie."

There it is. The look I've been waiting for. If there were ever a time to tell him, it's now. He needs to know I saw him the night that Suzie died. I know what he did. And it's okay.

"Zac—"

"I'm—"

We start to speak at the same time.

"You first," I say.

He nods several times. "I'm okay. I've married the two greatest women (not counting my mom) who I have ever met. I love my job and my family. I don't have an ounce of debt. And a tiny house. I ... have a tiny house." Bringing his fist to his mouth, he chuckles.

I can't help but giggle at his take on life. "Suzie would be proud of this glass-half-full attitude. And thank you ..." A little sobriety for the moment settles between us as I wait for him to look at me. "It's been an honor being your wife ... your friend ... even your maid."

For a second, I swear I see a little emotion in his eyes, but then he clears his throat and focuses on the world's most interesting hamburger again. "Yeah, well ... you were a shit maid."

I snort. "I was not."

"You were. When you weren't letting Suzanne braid your hair, you were half-naked chasing your cat around my backyard."

Opening my mouth, I nearly respond to his craziness, but I just as quickly clamp my jaw shut. Resting my hand on his leg, I lean toward him and whisper in his ear, "I'm going to miss you, Zachary Hays." As my lips brush his cheek, giving it a soft peck, he swallows hard. I'm not sure he could speak right now if he wanted to. So I rest my forehead on his arm and just breathe a few slow breaths.

He brings his hand to mine on his leg and interlaces our fingers.

On our way back to my hotel, I break the silence just as he attempts to do the same thing.

"Zach —"

"Suzanne was—"

I grin. "You go first."

"Suzanne wasn't *the* love of my life. She was *a* love in my life. Her and her ridiculous theory about soulmates, not S O L E mates, well ... it wasn't ridiculous after all. I don't want you to ever think back on us and feel like you were ... less." Zach shrugs a shoulder. "Anyway ... I just didn't want anything left unsaid between us." He smiles. It's not as sad as I remember it being in the past when he talked about her.

I'm not sure what to say. Did I deep down know? Or

have I let myself feel like I was a little less? Like I had to earn space in his heart?

Zach stops his car at the entrance to my hotel, and I reach into my bag and pause. "I posted a photo of a bride on Instagram a while back, and you didn't like it or comment. I know it sounds stupid, but it bothered me for a while because you've commented on or liked all of my posts. Did you not see it?" I glance up from my bag.

Zach confesses his truest love for me, and I can't let go of a stupid missing like on social media.

A long pause lands between us before he nods several times. "It's when I realized that while I gave you something important, I also took something too."

I mirror his slow nod. I think I understand, but I don't know what to say so I pull out the divorce papers and hand them to him. For a few seconds he stares at them, like if he touches them it will make things *real*. I know the feeling. It's the same one I had when I signed them.

Every day since Suzie died, we've been searching for something real when it's been real all along. And now it's too late. We are over, and that's our new reality.

After he takes the papers, I unfasten my seat belt and open the door. "If you're ever in London ..."

He does that hard swallow again. "Absolutely."

I climb out of his car and duck my head back inside, giving him my very best smile. "Zach, you're still the greatest human I have ever known. And I don't think you give yourself enough credit. That's ... that's what I started to say earlier. I just thought you should know. That's why I'm surprised someone hasn't grabbed ahold of you. I know I never wanted to let go."

He's not lost his ability to keep me captive with a look, and after a long, silent pause, he gives me what I know has to be his very best smile too. "Thank you, Emersyn."

I catch the door at the last second, gripping the handle until I can't feel my fingers, and I close my eyes.

I don't want anything left unsaid between us.

I ease back into the passenger's seat, keeping my eyes straight ahead, my heart hammering until I feel my whole body vibrate.

"Em?"

Drawing in a long breath, I swallow hard. "I ... know." Again, I swallow past the emotion. "The night she died, I heard the commotion. I tiptoed to your room and just ... watched. I *know* what you did."

I can't look at him. He doesn't seem to move or even breathe. Then all at once, a painful sob breaks from his chest, and his whole body trembles. As I blink a river of tears, I close my eyes, reach my hand over and rest it on his leg. His hand covers mine, squeezing unbearably hard.

He no longer bears this secret alone. I love him too much to walk away without taking some of his burden, the way he's unconditionally carried so much of mine.

"I've n-never seen s-such..." I can barely speak past the ache in my chest "...a selfless, beautiful act of love."

I climb out and shut the door.

Chapter Forty

Zach

THREE KNOCKS at the door to my tiny house. It's Mom. Always three knocks.

"Come in." I close my book and stand from my chair.

"Hey, look who wanted to see you."

I grin at Nila asleep in the carrier attached to my mom. "She can't see me while she's sleeping, and we both know you're not going to let me hold her."

"You are so wrong, my dear boy." Mom unfastens Nila and hands her to me. We manage to make the exchange without waking her. "I need to pee before I wet myself."

I softly chuckle as she bolts toward my toilet.

Easing back into my chair, my nose goes straight to Nila's head. The addictiveness of baby smell is real, minus poop and spit-up.

"Tell me you still want a family someday," Mom says when she exits the bathroom and takes a seat in the chair adjacent to mine.

Keeping my chin tipped to my chest, I stare at Nila. "Want ..." I whisper. "I'm not sure life cares about what I want. I'm pretty much at its mercy. Taking whatever it gives me and trying to accept it."

"You know ... she didn't die."

My gaze lifts to hers as I narrow my eyes.

"Emersyn. She didn't die. You willingly let her go."

I shake my head. "Willingly is not the right word."

"No?" Mom's head cants to the side. "Then what is the right word?"

"I stepped aside."

She frowns. "Willingly."

Again, I shake my head.

"Yes, Zachary. You let her go; she didn't leave you."

"Same difference."

"It's not."

I grunt. "What was I supposed to do? Ask her to give up on her dreams to clean houses and pop out my babies?"

"Zachary Kendrick Hays." Mom's frown deepens. "Just ... stop."

"Stop what?" I ask, feeling a little annoyed with this conversation.

"Stop making excuses. Stop pretending you've moved on. Stop pretending that you're a martyr, only looking out for everyone around you. I'm not buying it. And I'd let it slide if I weren't watching you do the same darn thing every day. Work. Eat. Sleep. Longingly admire what your brother has. Wash. Rinse. Repeat."

"We're on different paths. We're at different places in our lives. It was just ... bad timing. And I've accepted that. Sorry if I haven't jumped into another relationship. I was lucky enough to find two great women to love in my life, maybe that's it for me."

The door opens behind us.

Mom looks over her shoulder at Dad. "Oh good. I need you to take Nila into the house. If she wakes, change her diaper." She plucks Nila from my chest, waking her in the process, and hands her to Dad.

He takes her while giving me a wide-eyed expression.

"Go," Mom says. "I need a few minutes with Zach, and it could get loud, so I don't want to startle Nila."

It's going to get loud?

Dad gives me a "you poor bastard" look before closing the door behind him and Nila.

"Do you love her?" Mom parks her fisted hands on her hips.

It takes me a second. I feel ten again, on the verge of being sent to my room or having my Nintendo taken away for a week. "Of course. But—"

"No buts! Pack a bag and go to her. Get on one knee and say everything that you've been too afraid to say since the day you first realized you're in love with her. Spoiler alert: she'll say yes. That young woman loves you. And you ..." She points a finger at me. "You, my precious boy, are worthy. You are worthy of love. You are worthy of every dream. You are worthy of happiness. Emersyn left because you didn't give her what she needed. You pushed her away."

"I didn't want her to stay. You're not listening to me!" I stand, pacing a few feet in each direction while lacing my fingers behind my neck.

"Zach?"

I continue to pace. Life is good as long as I can keep my emotions separated, rationalized, and ten feet away from my heart at all times.

"Zach?"

I stop pacing when I notice my mom's voice has lost its edge.

"She *had* to leave?" she asks.

I nod several times.

Mom gives me her sad smile, her you-stupid-boy smile. "Okay, but you don't have to stay."

I start to speak, but I can't. Her words are too heavy in the air, crushing my chest with their truth.

"I know you think Emersyn needed your insurance, needed you to pay off her debt, needed a place to stay … but I don't believe that. I think she needed you. And you just couldn't see that. Maybe it was because your relationship with her has lived in the shadows of Suzanne—her memories, her lingering presence here. And Emersyn was too afraid to dream big. She was too afraid to dream of having everything. I'm sure the young woman who had nothing for so long must have felt greedy for asking for *everything*.

"She is worthy, Zach. You are worthy. Get on a

plane and go to her. Love has no boundaries. You can fly planes anywhere. Hell, you can afford to retire early and ... bag groceries at the store in your free time if you wanted to. Or you could just spend the rest of your life watching her do all the amazing things you know she's going to do. A family ... you could have a family, sweetheart. You don't have to hold her back; you can walk beside her. That's love, my dear. And you ... are worthy."

Chapter Forty-One

Emersyn

I MOVE TO LONDON.

Get settled into our new place.

Get settled into my new job.

Then Zach sends me a copy of the divorce decree. We are officially divorced.

I fold it into a million little pieces, a pathetic attempt at origami, and shove it into a drawer.

Since I left Atlanta, he's been posting more on Instagram. I like to think it's for me and not Megan. It's no longer just photos of #pilotlife. He shares photos of his family, especially his adorable niece. Photos of his tiny house, which is adorable in its own right. Last week he was in France, and he posted a photo of Amiens Cathedral—a gothic cathedral.

The week before that, he posted a Halloween photo

of him dressed as Iron Man. When he's not posting about his life, he's liking and commenting on mine. In some ways, I feel closer to him now than I did when we lived together—when we were married. But I know ... *I know* one day I'm going to see him post a selfie with a woman who is not his mom, his sister-in-law, or his niece, and it's going to break my heart again. I think hearts are the one thing in life that work better broken. All those cracks and holes let the love inside. Love is fluid, filling every space, moving with time, a solvent for all other emotions. Until it breaks, I'm not sure we really feel true love.

A week before Thanksgiving, Zach texts me that he'll be in London tomorrow, but just for the day.

> Em: I don't think I'll be wrapped up until four. Would love to see you though.

> Zach: Let's grab an early dinner.

> Em: Okay. I'll let you know when I'm done.

He replies with a thumbs-up emoji.

Leah and I spend the day in Oxford at a photoshoot for the magazine.

By the time we get back to London, it's a little after four-thirty.

"Dinner with Zach isn't going to make you relapse, is it?" Leah asks, stopping in front of my place.

"He's my friend, not a drug." I laugh, opening the door.

She rolls her eyes. "Just great. You're already lying to yourself."

"It's a simple dinner. I've never been at a better place in my life. And I think he'd say the same thing. Be proud of me. Bye, babe." I blow her a kiss and shut the door, quickly sending off a text to Zach as I climb the stairs to my flat.

An hour later, I arrive at the restaurant he chose. After a quick glance around, I take a seat at the bar and order a drink. The bartender pours my glass of wine while I text Zach.

Em: You almost here?

Zach: I'm here. Just watching you.

I swivel on the barstool, unable to hide my grin as I scan the restaurant again. It's crowded, and I can't see him.

Em: Stop. Lol Where are you?

Zach: I've missed you.

I look like a fool laughing to myself as I search in every direction.

Em: Then stop hiding.

> Zach: Before Suzanne died, she said, "Em is a good soul. A survivor. A giver. A nurturer. Any guy would be lucky to have her."

He's drunk. That's the only explanation. I call him.

"You look stunning tonight," he says.

Holding my phone to my ear with one hand and my wine glass in my other hand, I start to navigate the restaurant. "How much have you had to drink?"

"Too bad your shirt is on inside out."

I glance down at my blouse. I'm not sure why because there's no way to put a button-down on inside out and actually button it. "Ha. Ha. What are you doing? Seriously, how much have you had to drink?"

"Did you know you don't actually have to be British to work for a British airliner?"

My nose wrinkles. "What are you talking about?"

"Since you have no family, I went to Suzanne's grave and got permission."

"So drunk, Captain Hays. You are so drunk with your gibberish. Where are you?" As I continue to weave my way through the restaurant, patrons begin to stare. I'm sure they're wondering what I'm doing. Until ... they stop.

Stop eating.

Stop talking.

Stop moving, like someone pressed pause on all life.

Silence.

So I stop because something is wrong.

"Zach," I whisper, feeling uneasy. "Where are you?"

"I'm here," he says, but his voice isn't coming from my phone, it's coming from behind me. I quickly turn, *so* freaked out by what's happening around me.

"One knee?" he asks.

I can't breathe when I see him, when I see *Leah* ten feet away with her camera held to her face, barely hiding her huge grin and the tears on her cheeks.

"I think your next proposal was supposed to involve one knee. Correct?" He gets on one knee and pulls a ring from the pocket of his best suit—cranberry tie. "Emersyn ..."

Em-er-syn

"You should get the lamb tonight. I hear it's phenomenal," he says as if he can help ward off my tears.

A nervous laugh rattles my chest, eyes burning with indescribable emotion. Swallowing past the lump in my throat, I nod and try to hold back the inevitable. "Your mom should have told you to get a haircut before you came here."

His grin swells as he nods. "I'll get a haircut."

"I'll order the lamb," I whisper.

"But the real question is ... will you marry me? Because it's all I think about ... all day ... every day. I dream of a long engagement. Getting measured for the perfect tux with a tie in some shade of pink. I dream of gothic cathedrals and private islands. I try not to imagine you in a white wedding dress because just the thought takes my breath away—but not as much as imagining you having my babies." He places his free hand over his heart. "Can you just imagine? Can you imagine traveling the world together? Making love on grassy hilltops? Picking out Christmas trees? Hiding chocolate eggs for our kids?"

He lets all the *just imagines* linger in the air around us as I spell out my answer in tears.

"I love you," he says. "I love you as much as one human can possibly love another human. I have never loved anyone more than I love you. So just ... marry me, Emersyn."

"Zach," I glance around the restaurant. He planned this. I don't know how he did it, but he has exceeded my dreams times a million. "We just got ..." I lower my voice. "Divorced."

"Is that a yes or a no?"

"Zachary ..." I shake my head, wiping my cheeks. This is insane.

He gets up and cups my face, kissing my tears, whispering over my cheek so that only I can hear him, "Be my wife, Em ..."

With a shaky lower lip and several tiny nods, I whisper back, "Yes. I'll be your wife ... again."

He grins just as he kisses me.

Just as the restaurant erupts into applause and whistling.

Just as Leah snaps a slew of shots of this moment to capture the exact one where I hand him the rest of my heart.

At this moment, I hear Suzie so clearly. "*You are courageous. You found your soulmate. Humans are inter-changeable puzzle pieces. We fit into more than one space. You fit with Zach. I always knew you would. Be happy, my dear friend.*"

Epilogue

SOME PEOPLE AREN'T MEANT to live traditional lives. As much as I thought I longed for the simplicity of tradition, it's not in my blood.

"You may kiss the bride."

As Zach leans down to kiss me, I say, "I think it's just permission. Not a requirement. Like you *may* kiss the bride. Doesn't mean we have to kiss."

He grins and shrugs. "Have it your way."

My jaw drops in disbelief as he takes my hand and starts to lead me back down the aisle—the narrow path of sand dividing the small gathering of family and close friends. Leah catches everything with her camera and her new assistant captures it on video.

"Zachary Kendrick Hays." I tug his hand to stop him.

He turns, wearing a victorious grin. "Emersyn Jane Hays."

"Kiss Mommy!" Clara Suzanne Hays yells. Yeah, we

427

may have conceived her the same night he proposed to me. Life hasn't followed the dreams of all the things I thought I was missing in my life. Turns out ... I wasn't missing anything. We've made our own traditions. Our own rules. We've forged our own path. The unexpected has felt *real*. The unpredictable has given greater meaning to each day. Every day with Zach is the life I never dared to dream.

It's taken us three years to squeeze a wedding into our busy lives. Once I had his love, his arms, his declaration to the world that he loved me, and his baby ... the marriage seemed a little less important.

We chose lazy mornings with just the three of us in bed.

We chose trips to Italy and quick hops across the pond to visit Zach's family.

We've made London our home base, and the world has been a playground, a canvas on which we've drawn the most beautiful adventures of our life thus far.

I grin at Clara in her light pink flower girl dress before returning my attention to Zach.

"Are you and our daughter done bossing me around?" he asks.

The small gathering laughs.

I nod, biting my lower lip as he slides his hand behind my neck and pulls me to him for the kiss of all kisses while his other hand rests against the side of my six-month-pregnant belly. Barefoot and pregnant with our second child on our wedding day. Nothing traditional about us.

"I love you, my beautiful *wife*."

I thought he was the right person at the wrong time in my life. I was wrong. Zach taught me patience. Patience with my life, with him, and with myself.

There's rarely a day that I don't think about Suzanne. She's the reason I have Zach and our precious family. I know she's watching us, and she's smiling. She knows Zach doesn't love me more, just differently.

Different. I think every part of life is fluid, ever-changing. Suzie taught me that. Love is inclusive and something humans share in many ways. It doesn't define us, it refines us—makes us better for having taken a chance on it. We are different people at different times in our lives. Today, I'm basking in that sweet spot—artist, friend, mother, and *wife*.

Acknowledgments

Max, thank you for going on this journey with me.

Jenn, I can't believe I made you cry! Thanks for making this book release possible in record time. You are truly The World's Best Assistant.

To Joan, aka Nina, thank you for all the hours of Zoom calls and for letting me vent about things that have nothing to do with books.

Emily, thank you for this beautiful cover. You nailed it!

Thank you to the rest of my team for polishing this story. Leslie, Sarah, Bethany, and Becca, your generosity with your time over the holidays was appreciated beyond words.

Thank you to Charlie for letting me pick your brain on all things pilot life.

Missy, I'm so glad we met through the book world. Thank you for helping me with my research for this story. You are a true gem.

Thank you to every blogger, bookstagrammer, booktoker, and ARC team member for sharing this story and your creativity. I feel like I can't thank you enough.

Finally, thank you to my husband for listening to all the ups and downs this story has taken on its journey to my readers.

Also by Jewel E. Ann

Standalone Novels

Idle Bloom

Undeniably You

Naked Love

Only Trick

Perfectly Adequate

Look The Part

When Life Happened

A Place Without You

Jersey Six

Scarlet Stone

Not What I Expected

For Lucy

What Lovers Do

Before Us

If This Is Love

About The Author

Jewel is a free-spirited romance junkie with a quirky sense of humor.

With 10 years of flossing lectures under her belt, she took early retirement from her dental hygiene career to stay home with her three awesome boys and manage the family business.

After her best friend of nearly 30 years suggested a few books from the Contemporary Romance genre, Jewel was hooked. Devouring two and three books a week but still craving more, she decided to practice sustainable reading, AKA writing.

When she's not donning her cape and saving the planet one tree at a time, she enjoys yoga with friends, good food with family, rock climbing with her kids, watching How I Met Your Mother reruns, and of course...heart-wrenching, tear-jerking, panty-scorching novels.

www.jeweleann.com

Printed in Great Britain
by Amazon

17749144R00254